Clay was smiling down at her, his face close to hers as he held her against him. He cradled her in his arms. He bent his head and she felt his lips, warm on her cheeks.

Her arms reached out and she clung to him, her fingers pressing into the hard muscles of his back. Then his mouth claimed hers in a long, hard kiss. He forced her lips apart, so that he was kissing her in a way she had never been kissed before.

She started to tremble as she felt the heat of desire stirring in her for the first time. There was a soft roaring in her ears, like the sound of the sea and she moaned deep in her throat.

She knew then she would be Clay's forever...

Fawcett Gold Medal Books
by Diana Haviland

DEFY THE STORM

LOVE'S PROMISED LAND

Proud Surrender

DIANA HAVILAND

FAWCETT GOLD MEDAL • NEW YORK

Chapter One

MEGAN RAFFERTY moved briskly behind the long counter, dusting the oak surface, stopping to arrange several lengths of brightly colored ribbons in the showcase. The late-afternoon sunlight, slanting through the window of her uncle's shop, touched her tawny-blonde hair, and she narrowed her eyes against the glare. Soon it would be closing time, but first she would arrange the stock in the ladies' department so that it would be neat and orderly for the next day's customers.

She had come over from Ireland only a few months before, and she was grateful to her uncle, Jim Rafferty, for taking her in and giving her a chance to earn her keep, but she could not help wishing that her uncle's business was located in a less unsavory part of Natchez.

She tried not to think about the walk home to her uncle's house, which was located in an alley in the district called Natchez-under-the-Hill. She told herself that she had been fortunate in finding a home with Uncle Jim in this strange new country, that she was making a place for herself and paying her own way by helping out in her uncle's store. Her uncle,

1

his wife, Kathleen, and their daughter, Belle, were all the family Megan had left in the world.

She was lucky, too, that Uncle Jim ran a respectable business, for Natchez-under had little claim to respectability. At the base of the bluffs that lined the Mississippi River, a collection of alleys straggled down the shore line. Cheap taverns, gambling houses, and brothels were clustered along the alleys and up the length of Silver Street. Sailors from the river boats came down to Natchez-under looking for a good time after the long trip down river; and now, in the late spring of 1865, with the war just ended, there were Yankee soldiers down here, too, seeking relaxation, and carpetbaggers from up North.

Megan's heart sank, for in a few minutes she would have to make her way home to dinner through the crowd that swarmed through the alleys. Even though she had learned to keep her eyes straight ahead, to ignore the lewd remarks from the men who shouldered their way along the rough boardwalks, she dreaded the few minutes it would take her to get home.

If only Uncle Jim lived up there on the bluffs, in Natchez proper. He could have afforded a small place up there, but he chose to remain in a shabby house across the alley from the livery stable and warehouses that, like this store, were a part of his business holdings.

Often, during the past few weeks since her arrival here, Megan had longed desperately for Ireland, for the village of Kilcurran where she had grown up. But there was no going back—she knew that—for even at seventeen, Megan Rafferty had a hard streak of realism in her.

Both her parents had died years ago, and Terence, her brother, had been killed only a few months before in a raid on a British garrison. Handsome nineteen-year-old Terence had joined the Fenians, a secret society, pledged to drive the hated English out of Ireland by force of arms. She had come home one evening from her work as a maid in the home of Lord Trevanion, the landlord of the village, to find her brother dying on the floor of their cottage, his body torn with bullets, his blood soaking into her dress as she held him. . . .

She pushed the memory away and bent to smooth a length of pink satin ribbon, then straightened as she heard the *ting* of the shop bell.

The girl who entered the shop walked with sinuous grace, her head held high so that in spite of her shabby calico dress, she was a striking figure. Her black hair curled about her face, and there was a glowing warmth in her skin, her dark-brown eyes.

"Ah need a shawl, please," she said.

Uncle Jim did not stock expensive shawls, for there was little demand for them down here. "We have some pretty shawls from Cuba," Megan said, taking down a cardboard box with the help of a ladder and displaying the cheap but colorful fringed squares.

"This one's beautiful," the girl said, her slim fingers stroking the sleazy silk.

The shop bell sounded again, and this time it was a tall young man who came in. He was prosperous looking, although his clothes were not like the flashy garments of the carpetbaggers who swarmed along Silver Street, with their brocaded vests and brilliantly colored satin cravats, their diamond stickpins and stovepipe hats. No, Megan was sure that this man was not one of the Yankee newcomers who were descending on the conquered South with all their possessions crammed into a carpetbag, avid for quick money.

Megan looked at the young man, whose dark-gray broadcloth coat was obviously not brand-new. She saw that it strained a little across his wide shoulders and chest. The garment had been made by a good tailor—Megan could see that—and although it was not cut to the latest fashion, he wore it with easy assurance. He reminded her of the fine gentlemen who used to come to stay with Lord Trevanion and Lady Anne back in Kilcurran during the hunting season.

"Opal! What the devil are you doing here?"

Although the man spoke with the soft drawl Megan had come to recognize as that of the native Southerner, she caught the anger just under the surface. His dark-blue eyes narrowed. He strode across the store to confront the black-haired girl, who shrank back against the counter.

"Mr. Drummond, suh. Ah'm buyin' this here shawl—"

"I can see that." He towered over her, his tanned, hard features set in an impatient frown. "Don't you know that your mother needs every pair of hands to get ready for this ball?

You'll have some fancy explaining to do when you get back to Montrose."

"Ain't goin' back, suh." The girl's fingers plucked nervously at the fringe of the shawl. "Ain't goin' back t' Montrose at all." But her voice lacked confidence, and she did not look up. Megan had seen tenants who looked like that when they were caught in a confrontation with Lord Trevanion or his estate agent. "Ah'm leavin' Natchez for good, Mr. Drummond."

"And where do you think you are going?" he demanded.

"New Orleans," the girl said.

"Without a word to your mother—to any of us?"

"Mama, she wouldn't understand," the girl said. "She'd only try to get me to change my mind."

"Because she's got good sense," the man said. "I have my carriage outside, Opal. You go get into it and wait there for me, and when I've finished my business here, I'll drive you back to Montrose."

The girl hesitated. "You heard me," the man told her. Then, as if aware of Megan for the first time, he removed his wide-brimmed Panama hat. Why, Megan wondered, had he not removed his hat for Opal?

"Ah tol' you, Mr. Drummond, sir—Ah—" Opal reached into her pocket and carefully removed a folded bill. "How much is the shawl, please?"

"A dollar," Megan said. "Shall I wrap it or—"

"Ah'll wear it," Opal said. Then, turning back to the man, she said half defiantly, "Ah earned the money. Miz Abigail paid me for makin' her that new dress for the ball—and Miz Samantha paid me, too."

"And how much will you have left when you've finished paying for the shawl?" Mr. Drummond demanded impatiently.

"Enough to get me to New Orleans," Opal said.

"And when you get there, what then?"

"Ah'm goin' to find Noah—him and me, we're gettin' married. He's a good carpenter—y' know that, Mistuh Drummond, suh. He'll be able t' take care o' me, and he—"

"How long since you heard from Noah?"

"Nearly a year, but Ah'll find him."

The man put a hand on her arm. "I've had enough of your

nonsense. You put away that money and march yourself back to my carriage."

Opal did not move, but she looked uneasy.

"Ah got a right t' go, suh. Ah got a right. Maybe mama don't understand that the Drummonds don't own us no more, but Ah—" Under the man's hard, unwavering gaze, her voice trailed off, and her dark eyes filled with tears. "Y' been good t' us, suh. Ah ain' sayin' y' hasn't. But Ah got t' go."

Megan's eyes widened with swift comprehension. Opal was the daughter of a former slave, and she herself must have been a slave until less than a year ago. And this arrogant young man had owned her as if she had been a dog or a horse.

As the full realization of the circumstances came to Megan, she felt a fierce anger welling up inside her, for she believed that it was horrible, obscene, for one human being to own another. Why even back home in Kilcurran, Lord Trevanion, the English landlord, had not *owned* the Raffertys and their neighbors, although he had controlled many aspects of their lives. But English tyranny had had its limits.

"The ball is less than a week off," Drummond said tightly. "You will stay at Montrose at least that long. Afterward— we'll see. Now get outside and wait for me."

He took the shawl from Opal and handed it to Megan.

"You may put this away, miss," he told Megan.

Megan let the shawl drop back into the box, and her hands clenched tightly. She wanted to cry out to Opal, *Why don't you stand up to him?*

But before she could speak, Opal said, "Yes, suh. Ah'm goin'—But after Ah've helped out at the ball, Ah—"

Her voice trailed away. Slowly, she left the store, and Megan watched as she climbed into a carriage that stood outside.

"The fool! The silly little—" The man stopped short, then turned to Megan. "Forgive me, miss," he said. "I wish to see Jim Rafferty. Please tell him that Clay Drummond is here."

Once again, Megan was conscious of the change in the man's manner when he spoke to her.

She snapped. ' My uncle is not here."

"I'll wait," Clay Drummond said politely.

Megan did not reply. She glared at him, then turned her back on him and went to place the cardboard box of shawls on one of the shelves. She could not reach the shelf from where she stood, and she rolled the ladder over.

Her mind was not on her task, for she was still seething over the scene she had just witnessed. How dare Clay Drummond impose his will on the girl, Opal, now that she and her kind had been freed? And what might he do to her once he had her back at his plantation—Montrose, he had called it?

Would he lock her up? Have her beaten? Megan shuddered, her mind recoiling at the thought. She reached up over her head to put back the box, balancing precariously.

Clay Drummond came around to the back of the counter.

"If you'll permit me," he began.

"I can do it myself."

She shoved the box back into place; then, as he put out a hand to help her descend the ladder, she jerked away. The ladder rolled slightly on its wheels, and she lost her balance.

Clay caught her in his arms. For one moment, she was startlingly aware of him, of the warmth of his body, the hardness of his chest.

"Let go of me."

He released her at once, his blue eyes glinting with mixed amusement and exasperation. "You might thank me for saving you from a tumble," he said.

"I'd rather have broken my neck than to have you put your hands on me," she told him.

"You scarcely know me," he said. "Don't you think we should become better acquainted before you decide that you dislike me?"

"I know what you did to that poor girl, Opal." Megan's voice trembled with anger. "What you and your kind did to your slaves before the war. And Opal—why she isn't even black. She looks—"

"Opal is an octoroon," Clay said, the amusement fading from his eyes. "She is one-eighth black, to be exact. Her mother, Rachel, has been our cook at Montrose for many years. I could not permit Opal to run off to New Orleans on a whim. Montrose is her home, too."

"Home? Our cottage back in Kilcurran was more of a home to us even though the landlord owned it. At least I was not driven to work in the fields by an overseer's whip or—or—"

"How long have you been here in Natchez?" Clay demanded.

"Nearly three weeks, and I—"

"As long as that?" He did not bother to disguise the irony in his voice. "Nearly three weeks and you are passing judgment on the South. And on me, Miss—"

"I'm Megan Rafferty. And I've read all about the plantations. Lady Anne, up at the manor house, used to subscribe to the newspapers from London, and I read them, too. And I know—"

"You know nothing." He looked past Megan at the street outside. "Come here."

He put a hand on her arm and led her over to the shop window. "Look out there. That's right. Look at that hotel across the street."

She obeyed and saw a dark-skinned girl, darker than Opal, leaving the hotel with a Yankee soldier.

"I've no doubt that girl's run off like Opal, seeking a taste of her new freedom."

"And suppose she has? What's wrong with that?"

"Miss Rafferty, that Yankee soldier will teach her about freedom. He'll turn her silly head with a lot of fine promises, and what do you think will become of her when he's finished with her?"

Megan felt her cheeks grown warm as she realized the implication behind Clay Drummond's question.

"I don't know," she said, avoiding his eyes.

"Then let me tell you." Clay's hand was still on Megan's arm, and when she tried to draw away, his fingers tightened. His palm was hard and calloused, like that of a day laborer; it was at variance with his appearance, his soft, cultured voice and aristocratic manner. "When her Yankee protector gets tired of her or is ordered to another post, she'll be left to starve in some filthy shanty settlement. Or to die of disease. Oh, yes, Miss Rafferty, such things have been happening all over the South since the end of the war."

"But Opal said that she was going to be married—"

"To Noah. He used to be one of our people at Montrose. Hard working and an expert carpenter. But suppose she can't find him? Opal's like a child. No knowledge of the world outside of our plantation. Young and pretty, too. Maybe she won't end up in a shanty town. Maybe she'll land in one of the fancy houses in New Orleans—"

Megan drew in her breath sharply, shocked by the bluntness of Clay's last speech. His hand dropped away from her arm, and she saw that he was controlling himself with difficulty. "I beg your pardon, Miss Rafferty. I forgot myself. I did not mean to speak so plainly to a young lady. Not even a young lady as opinionated and muddleheaded as you."

An angry retort sprang to her lips, but before she was able to reply, the door opened, and her uncle, Jim Rafferty, a big, hulking man with a thatch of red hair, came into the store.

"Drummond," he said. "Sorry I'm late. My teamsters are loading up a big shipment for Vicksburg, and I decided to pitch in. I can still load a wagon with the best of 'em, I can." He nodded to Megan, then took Clay's arm. "Let's go into the office here and we'll talk business." Then, over his shoulder, he added, "You wait for me, Megan, and I'll walk you back home."

Ordinarily, she would have been relieved at the prospect of having her huge, powerfully built uncle at her side during the homeward walk, but now she was preoccupied. What business would a fine gentleman like Clay Drummond have with Jim Rafferty, she wondered?

The office door closed behind the two men, and she busied herself arranging the stock, then polishing the glass on the front of the showcases. Her years as a maid in the landlord's manor house had made her automatically tidy, for Lady Anne had been a stickler for neatness. Megan had been only ten when she had started working at the manor house, first as a kitchen maid, then parlor maid, and at last, as personal maid to Lady Anne herself.

How bitter her brother, Terence, had been about that.

"Fetchin' and carryin' for the damned English," he had said, his eyes burning with resentment.

Megan had refused to be drawn into a quarrel, reminding herself that she was learning the ways of the gentry. She had even learned to read, to write, to do sums, and, with careful practice, to speak without a brogue. She would not marry a village lad and bear a brood of children, only to watch them die of starvation and plague during the next famine. She would save her wages, and one day she would open a little shop in Cork or even, perhaps, in London. Terence would help her run the shop and forget all his dangerous foolishness about the Fenians.

But her plans had been shattered that night when Terence had come stumbling home to the cottage they shared, his body torn by English bullets. Alone, Megan had dug the shallow grave and said the words over him. Alone, she had fled from Kilcurran, hidden in the back of a tinker's wagon, had made the miserable voyage as a steerage passenger to New Orleans, and had made her way from there to Natchez. But she had not given up hope of bettering herself. She did not belong in Natchez-under. . . .

The office door at the rear of the shop opened, and her uncle emerged. He shook Clay's hand.

"Ye've me word on it. If ye can get Senator Aldrich to back yer plans fer rebuildin' that railroad spur, I'll have all the teamsters ye'll be needin'. And later, a fine, hard-workin' crew of lads to lay yer ties and hammer yer spikes."

"I'll get Aldrich's backing," Clay said. "He and his Yankee friends will give us the support we need. We'll settle the business at the ball at Montrose next week."

"There's more t' rebuildin' a railroad than gettin' the backin' of the politicians," Uncle Jim said.

"I know." Megan saw Clay's face harden and his blue eyes turn cold and bleak. "I can lay rails myself, Mr. Rafferty, and I know how to swing a pick and a sledgehammer."

"Do ye now? And where did ye learn all that?"

Clay went on as if he had not heard the question.

"I don't plan to do that part of the job myself. Get me the right crew, the best men you can find. Men who can lay two to five miles of track a day through the fever swamp. Men who can put down four rails a minute, working in teams. Get me the horses and wagons to carry the rails, the spikes, the bolts, and the fishplates. I want wagon beds with rollers so the men can get the rails out fast."

Megan was startled by Clay Drummond's obvious familiarity with railroad building, and she guessed that her uncle was, too. How had a plantation owner come to know about

such details? Then she remembered the feel of his hand against
her skin, his hard, calloused palm.

And she remembered something else. Although it was not
easy for Megan, with her stiff-necked pride, to apologize to
anyone, she hurried to Clay, stopping him before he could
leave the shop.

"Mr. Drummond—about Opal. I shouldn't have said what
I did. I had no way of knowing—"

"I imagine there is much you don't know about Southerners.
You should get to know us better."

She looked at him blankly, bewildered by his words.

"Will you do me the honor of accompanying me to the ball
at Montrose next week—with your uncle's permission, of
course."

"Why I—"

"Or perhaps you'd prefer to cling to your ideas about us
without putting them to the test," he challenged her.

He was mistaken, but she could not tell him the real reason
for her hesitation. She shrank from the prospect of having Clay
Drummond call at the shabby cottage across the alley. Then
their eyes met, and she could not look away.

She was not ashamed of her family, she told herself firmly.
Uncle Jim had made a place for himself in this new land; his
business was honest and respectable. Still, she would have to
mingle with Clay's guests and his family. What of it? Hadn't
she learned the ways of the gentry back in Lord Trevanion's
manor house?

Abruptly, she turned away from those searching blue eyes,
for she sensed that she felt something stronger than her fear or
her pride. It was a need to see Clay Drummond again. "I will
come to Montrose, Mr. Drummond," she heard herself saying.
He smiled.

"Thank you, Miss Rafferty." She felt a curious emotion stir
to life within her.

For the hardships of her life, although they had forced her
to be practical, had not quite destroyed the deep strain of Irish
mysticism that was so much a part of her character. And when
she said, "I will come to Montrose," she had felt a sense of
commitment, a sharp certainty that she had set her foot on a
new path and that there would be no turning back.

Chapter Two

∽

MEGAN SAT in the shiny gig, with its high yellow wheels, beside Clay Drummond, who maneuvered the smart little vehicle skillfully through the milling crowd on Silver Street. She smoothed the amber silk skirt of her new ball gown with nervous fingers; it was the first silk gown she had ever owned, and she had worked on it every evening since Clay had invited her to Montrose.

Uncle Jim had provided the money for the silk, the lace trimming, and the velvet ribbons that ornamented the bustle. "Yer a Rafferty, and ye'll look as fine as any of them ladies up on the bluff if I have anything to say about it," he told her. Then, with a warm smile, he had added, "Ye'll be prettier 'n any of them, that's fer sure."

But Megan's cousin, Belle, although she had helped with the making of the gown, had been openly spiteful. "Probably Mr. Drummond's only invited ye because of his business dealings with Pa," Belle had said.

Ever since Megan's arrival at Uncle Jim's home, Belle's

intended, Gavin O'Donnell, had been too attentive to Megan, and Belle, a plump girl with pale-blue eyes and ginger-colored hair, had been resentful of the newcomer.

Megan tried to disregard Belle's words, but she could not help remembering them now, even as Clay drove the gig up Silver Street, out of the stench and squalor of Natchez-under. Surely, Megan thought, a man as good-looking and well connected as Clay Drummond might have had his choice of the prettiest daughters of plantation owners to take to the ball tonight.

She forced her doubts to the back of her mind, telling herself that she was the one Clay had chosen. If only she had met him in respectable surroundings. She did not know Clay well enough to explain how miserable, how out of place she felt, down here in Natchez-under. Indeed, she scarcely knew him at all.

Megan flinched and drew closer to Clay as a pair of drunken Yankee soldiers, bearded and disheveled, their blue uniforms spotted with food and liquor, staggered in front of the gig so that the horse reared and the gig rocked dangerously. Clay got the animal under control with practiced skill, but not before Megan heard one of the soldiers arguing loudly: "We're goin' to Maggie's place," he said. "Maggie's got the best girls— and a fancy new piano and mirrors with gold frames—"

"I ain't goin' to pay no two dollars for piano music and mirrors," the other solider said. "What I want right now—"

Clay slapped the reins across the horse's back, but although the startled beast broke into a trot, Megan could not help hearing the soldier's hoarse voice, describing in shocking detail exactly what he did want. She felt her cheeks go hot with shame, and she cringed inwardly, but when she gave Clay a swift, sideward glance, she saw that he looked composed. His voice was casual as he said, "It'll be cooler up on the bluffs, Miss Rafferty. And Montrose is set on a hill overlooking the river to catch the breeze. Grandfather Drummond planned it that way—like the houses he'd seen in the West Indies. There's a gallery running all around the second story. . . ."

Megan guessed that Clay was speaking of the house to distract her from her embarrassment over the ugly talk they had just overheard, and she was grateful for his instinctive courtesy.

"Did your grandfather come from the West Indies?" she asked.

"The Drummonds came from Scotland originally, but my grandfather lived on the island of Barbados for a time," Clay replied. "He worked closely with the architect who designed Montrose. He wanted the house to be as cool and airy as possible." He smiled faintly. "I hope that our Yankee guests won't find the heat too oppressive tonight."

They had reached the top of the bluff now, and Clay turned the gig onto the esplanade. Megan gratefully breathed in the mingled scent of jasmine and wisteria. Up here, the houses, although spacious and once handsome, bore the marks of the war: fences and gates sagged; lawns were straggling and un-cared for; shutters, gray for lack of paint, creaked on broken hinges.

"I don't understand how you could have invited a Yankee delegation to your home after—" Megan broke off, fearing that she had said too much. She must learn how to guard her tongue, to restrain her forthright Irish way of expressing her feelings.

"I'd have invited General Sherman himself to Montrose if I thought it would have furthered my plans," Clay said, and his eyes were hard.

"But you—you fought against the Yankees. Uncle Jim said that you were in the cavalry and that you—"

"Go on." His voice was expressionless, controlled.

"He said that you were captured and sent to one of the worst of the Yankee prison camps—somewhere in Ohio—"

"Johnson's Island. Out in Lake Erie."

Looking at Clay in the last rays of the setting sun, Megan saw an expression on his face that she was sure she had seen before. But when? Oh, yes, during their first meeting, when Uncle Jim had remarked on Clay's knowledge of the details of railroad construction. That look of icy self-control, with leashed anger just below the surface. She stumbled on. "It—must have been a terrible place—"

"No worse than our own Confederate prison camp at An-dersonville," Clay replied grimly.

"And yet you've invited a delegation of Yankees to your home—"

"The war's over now, Miss Rafferty. And I need the co-operation of Senator Horace Aldrich and his fellow politicians. I'll have to get government land grants, government funds, to go ahead with the work of rebuilding the railroad spur. After that, I plan to extend the line through Louisiana and Texas."

"The railroad means a great deal to you," Megan said softly.

"It means everything to me—and to the South. Our lack of industrial power cost us the victory in this war. We can never have such power without the kind of system of railroads they have up North."

"But you're a cotton planter," Megan said. "Surely now that the war is over, the English cotton mills will be paying top prices for your crops."

"I wouldn't have expected you to know about such matters," Clay began, but Megan interrupted him.

"I come from County Cork, Mr. Drummond, not the wilds of Africa."

"Ah, yes," Clay said with a faint undertone of mockery in his voice. "And you did say that the London newspapers came to the manor house back in—Kilcurran, was it? You must have been a frequent guest of the landlord and his wife."

Megan forgot for the moment her determination to keep up her fine lady's façade. Hard, honest work was nothing to be ashamed of. "I worked in the manor-house kitchen; then I was a parlor maid, and after that, personal maid to Lady Anne, the landlord's wife."

"And you still found time to learn to read?"

"And to write and do sums." And it had been no easy matter, Megan thought, picking up scraps of knowledge from old Mr. Simmons, Lady Anne's English butler. "You look surprised, Mr. Drummond," she said, challenging him.

"I am, a little," he admitted, but he was smiling now, and there was warmth in his blue eyes as he looked down at her. "My sister Lianne, you see, never reads anything except the descriptions that appear with the fashion plates in the ladies' journals. She used to drive her governess to despair. Her dancing master, on the other hand, found her an apt pupil."

Megan's heart sank as she realized the width of the gulf that stretched between her and Clay and his family. Governesses and dancing masters. How could she hope to make a good impression on the Drummonds?

Then she heard Clay speaking quietly. "My sister Jessica is quite different. She has read most of the books in father's library. And as for Samantha—"

"How many sisters do you have?" Megan asked.

"Samantha's not my sister. She is my sister-in-law. She married my half brother, Reed."

Clay lapsed into silence abruptly and turned the gig off the esplanade and onto a road shaded with live oak trees. The last rays of the setting sun gilded the long veils of lacy Spanish moss that hung from the branches and turned the loop of the Mississippi River, down below the bluffs, to pale gold. A deep hush lay over the countryside, and Megan was reluctant to speak. She clasped her hands in her lap and tried to convince herself that she would be a credit to the Raffertys tonight, and Clay would not regret having invited her to Montrose.

In the master bedroom, in the west wing of the plantation house at Montrose, Samantha Drummond stood before her mirror pinning on a garnet brooch. Fastened at the center of the low-cut neckline, the brooch emphasized the deep cleft between her full, firm breasts. She fingered the brooch thoughtfully, possessively, for it was one of the few treasures she had been able to keep after the Tollivers had lost their money and their own plantation up river from Montrose.

Samantha's full red lips closed in a tight line as she thought of papa, dead of fever, of mama, bewildered and shaken, living with Aunt Emma and Aunt Clara up in Jackson in the kind of genteel poverty that had become so common all over the conquered South. Three women without a man to protect them and mama afraid of the blue-coated Yankees who roamed the streets and even more terrified of the former slaves who were everywhere in the state capital, enjoying their new-found freedom like children, untaught, unprepared.

If Clay's plans for his railroad prospered, Samantha told herself, surely he would contribute to the support of mama and Samantha's maiden aunts. He could scarcely begrudge money to keep his sister-in-law's family in comfort.

His sister-in-law. Bitterness and frustration stirred within Samantha. All those years when everyone had taken it for granted that Samantha Tolliver would marry Clay Drummond, and now . . . Oh, God, if only Clay had not been reported dead on Johnson's Island. If only she had waited before marrying Reed.

For a moment, she longed to throw herself down across the broad canopied bed, to pound her fists against the pillow, to sob out her despair. But she drew comfort from her image in the mirror. Opal had done a fine piece of work in making the wine-red-taffeta ball gown. It was cut in the latest fashion, for now the Southern women were receiving paper patterns from up North again. Samantha fingered the garnet brooch, then moved back gracefully, watching as the candles on either side of the mirror struck sparks from the glittering stones and gave a rich luster to her dark-brown hair, accenting the auburn highlights in the soft curls that framed her face.

A sound at the door made her turn quickly. It was Rachel, Opal's mother, who carried in the tray Samantha had ordered, with its silver coffeepot, its single cup and saucer of Spode china.

"I'll take the coffee to my husband," Samantha said, dismissing Rachel with a gesture. Rachel, who now served as both cook and housekeeper, would have more than enough to do tonight. How lucky that Clay had intercepted Opal as she was preparing to leave and had brought her back to Montrose. The foolish girl, planning to run off to New Orleans to find Noah, as if that black buck would remember that he had promised to marry her! He was probably living with some yellow slut in one of the shanty-town settlements that were growing like mushrooms all over the region, cadging food from the Freedmen's Bureau and whiskey from the carpetbaggers.

Then she dismissed Noah and Opal from her mind, for she had more pressing concerns. She moved quickly through the half-open door between the bedroom and the adjoining dressing room. Seeing Reed sprawled in his chair sipping brandy, she had all she could do to keep from lashing out at him in anger; but in spite of all the changes caused by the war, a lady was still a lady, and she did not raise her voice when she spoke to a gentleman—not if she wanted to get her own way, surely.

"Reed, darling," Samantha said softly, cajolingly, "here's your coffee, nice and strong, the way you like it."

"I prefer brandy, thank you," Reed said, ignoring the dark, steaming brew she poured for him. He was still in his dressing gown.

"We have to go downstairs," she said, an edge to her voice now. "It's getting late."

"I'm quite comfortable right here," Reed told her. Was there a trace of sardonic humor in his gray eyes?

"But the ball—our guests—"

"Senator Aldrich and his Yankee friends are not my guests. Clay invited them."

"Yes, I know. But Senator Aldrich is the chairman of the senate railroad committee. He's an important man."

"Not to me." Reed did not raise his voice, but there was bitterness beneath the soft drawl. "Or did Clay promise to give us shares of stock in this railroad line of his?"

"I don't understand about shares and—"

Samantha broke off. When Reed got into one of his moods, there was no way to reach him. His fair-skinned face was already flushed, his speech slightly slurred. He had been drinking brandy since noon, and if he was not yet drunk, he soon would be.

"There may be no shares for anyone, my love," he was saying. "Clay may not get what he wants from the senator."

"He has that loan from the bank in New Orleans," Samantha pointed out.

"Oh, yes—against a mortgage on Montrose. He's mortgaged the place to put up a fine front for these Yankees tonight. But he doesn't have nearly enough to rebuild the railroad spur, and as for his plans to extend the line to the West—"

Reed set down his glass and rose to his feet with an easy, graceful movement. He was good-looking, Samantha thought with a kind of surprise. Maybe even better looking than Clay, in a conventional way, for although he was only a little over middle height, he was lean and wiry, with blond hair so light it looked like silver gilt, like Abigail's. Abigail Drummond had been Vance Drummond's second wife, and it was she who had held Montrose together after Vance's death during the first year of the war. Too bad that Reed had not inherited at least a little of his mother's ruthlessness, her shrewd opportunism, Samantha thought bitterly.

"Clay will get his railroad," she told Reed. "He gets whatever he wants."

"Not quite, my dear," Reed said. "You married *me*, Samantha." He put his arms around her and tried to draw her to him. "You belong to me." If there was mockery in his voice, it was directed against himself now. "You do belong to me, don't you? And our marriage is a great success?"

"It could be," Samantha said, twisting free of his embrace, "if you would not drink so much and if you would stop going down to Natchez-under—"

"A man has to take his comfort where he can find it, my love," Reed said. "Clay goes down there, too."

"On business," Samantha retorted.

"Business? The girl Clay is escorting to the ball here tonight comes from Natchez-under."

"I don't believe you—You're lying—you're trying to—"

"Oh, it's true enough. Megan Rafferty's her name. A lovely little thing, Clay told me."

Samantha looked away quickly. Reed must not see the pain that she knew was there in her face. Lifting her taffeta skirt, she moved swiftly back into the bedroom. She tried to close the door, but Reed was too fast for her.

He stood confronting her, resting a hand on one of the intricately carved posts of the wide mahogany bed. How many months had it been since she had last shared the bed with Reed?

The mockery left his face, and Samantha saw that he looked once again like the adoring young man who had proposed to her after they had received the news of Clay's death.

"Samantha, I need you," he pleaded. "I'll try to be what you want me to be if only you'll—"

He tried to embrace her. "Reed, no! My dress—you're crushing it. We can't—the guests will be arriving—"

He released her. "Ah, yes. The guests." The tenderness had gone from his face. "I might just come down, after all," he said. "I'd like to get a look at the lovely Miss Rafferty." His eyes moved over Samantha. "I've always admired Clay's taste in women."

Chapter Three

WHEN CLAY led Megan into the entrance hall, only a few of the other guests had arrived. They stood talking in small groups. The ladies, although lively and animated, were not fashionably dressed. Their gowns had been carefully refurbished, but the wide crinolines were out-of-date; once-expensive taffetas and satins showed unmistakable signs of wear. Even so, there was a self-assurance about these plantation ladies and their husbands, and Megan felt her heart sink. Only she was an outsider here.

The air was heavy with the scent of roses and lilacs, which filled the tall vases set in the wall niches. From the ballroom at the right, she heard the orchestra tuning up; through a half-opened door opposite, she caught a glimpse of a long table, draped in spotless white linen, where some black servants were setting out trays of food.

But her attention was caught and held by the small group at the foot of the stairway. The plump woman in her late forties was tightly corseted, and her elaborately coiffed blonde hair was a shade too bright. With her were two younger women: one was small and dainty, with soft, dark curls framing her face; her gown of pale-blue organza, obviously new, was trimmed with flounces of creamy lace. The sound of her high, tinkling laughter came to Megan over the conversation of the guests.

The other young woman was tall and slender and bore a striking facial resemblance to Clay; but the strong jawline, the high, jutting cheekbones, and the thick, dark brows that gave Clay his look of strength and determination were not at all becoming to a female. And her dress, though fashionable, was a dull brown that did nothing to emphasize her large blue eyes.

The stocky, florid man who stood beside the blonde woman wore the uniform of the Union army. Surely, Megan thought in bewilderment, none of Clay's family had fought for the North.

Clay led Megan forward and performed the introductions. The blonde woman was Mrs. Abigail Drummond, Clay's step-mother; the man beside her was Major Taggart. "And these are my sisters, Lianne and Jessica," Clay said. Jessica, the plain one, gave Megan a warm smile, but Lianne only nodded politely as Clay said, "Miss Megan Rafferty."

Major Taggart's eyes lingered appreciatively on Megan's high, rounded bosom. "A pleasure, Miss Rafferty," he said, his voice loud and a little hoarse. "Perhaps you'll save a dance for me, my dear."

"Why I—" Megan began uncertainly.

"Now I won't take no for an answer," the major persisted. "You needn't worry, Miss Rafferty. I won't step on the hem of that pretty dress. I can dance as well as any of these young bucks, can't I, Abigail?"

"Indeed you can," Abigail Drummond agreed. "And I'm sure Clay will spare Miss Rafferty for one dance, won't you, Clay?"

But Clay did not reply, for he was looking past Abigail and the major. A regal young beauty was descending the free-standing, curved stairway, with its ironwork railing, her head held high, her full skirt swaying gracefully. She was dazzling in her wine-red taffeta, a garnet brooch glittering on her bosom.

Her dark-brown hair was arranged in a chignon, the simplicity of the style accenting the perfection of her features.

"Samantha," Clay said, and there was something in his voice that Megan, with her heightened attention to all he said, found disturbing. "And where's my brother?"

"Reed will be down shortly," Samantha said.

"I hope so," Clay said. Then, remembering his duties as host, he said, "Megan, allow me to present my brother's wife, Samantha. Miss Rafferty is a newcomer to Natchez. I know you'll make her welcome."

"Yes, indeed," Samantha said with a frosty smile. "Are you visiting with friends in Natchez?"

"I'm living with my uncle, Jim Rafferty, and my Aunt Kathleen," Megan said.

"Rafferty? Jim Rafferty?" Samantha sounded genuinely puzzled. "I don't believe I know the name. There is a family up near Jackson—"

"My uncle and his wife live in Natchez." Megan spoke carefully, trying to ignore her mounting uneasiness.

"There is a Jim Rafferty who owns a livery stable and warehouses down in Natchez-under," Major Taggart began. "Made a tidy pile for himself hauling Confederate cotton down to Galveston to be shipped out through Mexico. That was before we tightened our blockade—"

"Oh, really, major," Samantha said. "You surely can't mean to imply that Miss Rafferty is related to anyone like that. The major has a peculiar sense of humor, Miss Rafferty. I hope you're not offended."

"Major Taggart is quite right," Megan said, her legs feeling unsteady now. Her skin prickled, and she had to press her hands together to keep them from shaking. "My family does live in Natchez-under. I work in my uncle's general store down there."

But even as she spoke, her head high, she longed to turn and flee. For she felt again like the barefooted, ragged ten-year-old who had come to the manor-house scullery to plead for work, any sort of work....

A terrible time that had been, with her father dead of the fever that had been ravaging Ireland after the worst of the famine had passed, her mother dying in childbirth, and only Megan and Terence left in the cottage that had once housed eight Raffertys.

Terence had said that it would be better to be driven out of their cottage, to see it torn down, to die of hunger and exposure in a ditch, as had so many of their neighbors when they had been unable to pay their rent.

"Anything's better'n beggin' from the damned English," Terence had said, his thin, hollow-eyed face hard with hate, even at twelve.

"I'll not go t' beg," Megan had told him fiercely. "I'll get work at the manor—"

"Fetchin' and carryin' for the landlord and his lady? Scrubbin' chamber pots—"

"If I must. But I'll not lay down t' die."

"Miss Rafferty, are you all right?" Megan was brought back to the present, and she realized that Jessica Drummond had spoken to her with concern.

"Perhaps Miss Rafferty is fatigued after that long drive all the way up from Natchez-under," said Samantha. "One of the maids will show you upstairs to the ladies' dressing room," she added to Megan.

"I'll show Miss Rafferty upstairs myself," said Jessica. Gratefully, Megan followed Jessica up the long, graceful curve of the staircase. The upstairs hall was impressive, with its French, hand-blocked wallpaper, its crystal sconces reflecting the light of the candles, mirrors in gold-leaf frames, and portraits, presumably of departed Drummonds, who seemed to look down on Megan with icy disdain.

So many Drummonds, Megan thought. It was as if they, like Samantha, knew her for the interloper she was, as if they wanted her out of here.

She stopped for a moment, trying to shake off the foolish notion.

"Is the heat troubling you?" Jessica asked with genuine concern. "Newcomers often find it quite overpowering, and we are having an unusually warm spring."

She led Megan into the guest bedroom that had been set aside this evening for lady visitors. "Come out onto the gallery," she urged. "Right through these doors."

Megan allowed the tall, angular young woman to lead her across the dressing room and outside, through a pair of French doors, onto the rear gallery. "You see, there is a breeze from the river. And down there is the garden."

Megan momentarily forgot her inner turmoil. "Oh it is lovely," she said. She breathed as deeply as her tightly laced stays would allow. Looking out over the gallery railing, she drank in the beauty of the view below.

The moonlight sent a track of silver across the river and touched the white roses, the camellias and magnolias, with a frosty light; Japanese lanterns, blue, green, and yellow, had been strung between the trees. As Megan watched, a large, old-fashioned carriage drove up from the river landing to discharge a group of visitors who had come to Montrose by boat.

"But I mustn't keep you from your other guests, Miss Drummond." Megan said.

"Do call me Jessica, won't you?"

What a pity that Jessica was so plain, Megan thought. Would any man ever want her for her warmth, her kind disposition? Not likely. Why she must be twenty-five, at least. A woman stood little chance of escaping spinsterhood at that age.

"I'm quite all right now," Megan assured Jessica. "Please don't be concerned about me."

"Very well, if you're sure. Why not stay out here a little longer. The dancing won't begin for a while yet."

Jessica started to leave, then turned back briefly.

"You must not mind Samantha," she said. "She and Clay—well, no matter. You are most welcome here at Montrose."

Then she was gone, leaving Megan to stare down at the garden.

Clay and Samantha.

Was Clay in love with his half brother's wife? Oh, no, Megan told herself. She must not let her imagination overpower her common sense. She was startled, even a little frightened, by the tide of jealousy that surged up in her. She had no right to be jealous, she told herself firmly, for she was Clay's guest here tonight, nothing more.

"It's true, Violet."

Megan heard a woman's voice close by. Two of the guests had entered the dressing room with a rustle of taffeta skirts.

"Her name's Megan Rafferty, and she comes from Natchez-under-the-Hill. I heard Samantha ask her, and she admitted it, brazen as you please."

Megan stood transfixed, the night breeze ruffling her hair.

"But surely you misunderstood. There's nothing down there except saloons and gambling dens and—and—"

"Sporting houses," said the other woman.

Megan edged closer to the French doors where she could see the speakers.

"Winona Hunter!" said the small, thin woman with mousy brown hair. "What a thing to say!"

"Oh, really, Violet." Winona, a stout bosomy woman, smoothed the skirt of her plum-colored gown. "We've both been married long enough to know that men have these—these needs. Thank goodness there are places like Natchez-under where they can go to satisfy them, I say."

Violet's sallow face flushed. "I'm sure that Jeff has never— Anyway, you were telling me about that girl. What can Clay be thinking of to bring such a person to Montrose?"

"If you want my opinion, he did it to show Samantha that he's gotten over caring about her. Can you imagine what he must have felt, coming home and finding her married to Reed, living right here at Montrose—"

"Now you can't blame Samantha for that. Clay was reported dead, shot while trying to escape from Johnson's Island. And I suppose Samantha figured that she was better off married to Reed than becoming an old maid like poor Jessica," said Violet.

"I'm not blaming her," said Winona. "But after all those years when everyone took it for granted that Clay and Samantha would be married— And Reed's not half the man that Clay is." She sighed. "I suppose Samantha will have to make the best of it, though."

Violet nodded. "She's made her bed, and now she must lie in it—"

"There are a number of beds at Montrose," said Winona acidly. "Let's hope Samantha doesn't forget that it is Reed Drummond whose bed she—"

"Winona, hush! I won't hear another word. Samantha is high-spirited, but she is a lady. Which is more than you can say for that girl from Natchez-under." She sighed. "I'm really a little sorry for—What did you say her name is?"

Megan's body went rigid, and she felt a rage within her such as she had seldom known. How dare these women presume to judge her?

Somehow she was back inside the dressing room, her face white with fury, her eyes burning amber gold, like those of an angry cat. But when she spoke, her voice was clear and steady. "My name is Megan Rafferty," she said.

Violet made a small, squeaking sound that reminded Megan of a trapped ferret; Winona's mouth opened, and she took a step backward.

"You need not feel sorry for me," Megan went on. "I don't need your pity—or anyone else's."

Megan looked from Violet to Winona; then, lifting her skirt, she swept past them, her head held high, and moved out into the long hallway, past the portraits of the Drummonds, down the long curve of the stairs.

But when she reached the open doors of the ballroom, where the first waltz had begun, she felt the anger begin to subside, leaving her trembling. How could she possibly go inside? How could she spend the rest of the evening here among these cruel strangers who would turn on her in scorn as soon as they learned where she had come from?

And they would find out, she told herself grimly. Trust those two fishwives, Violet and Winona, for that. *I must get away,* she thought. *Quickly, before . . .*

"Megan, here you are."

Clay, who had been standing close to the entrance to the ballroom, came to her side, and before she could protest, he had taken her in his arms. He whirled her into the crowd of dancers.

She tried to think of some excuse for leaving, but all at once she heard him saying softly, "I'd almost forgotten."

Something in his voice made her ignore her own inner turmoil. She looked up at him and found that she could not look away.

"Forgotten?"

"What it feels like to dance with a beautiful girl. It's been four years since I've had the chance." His eyes were shadowed briefly, and she was sure that he was remembering the war.

The fighting, the killing, and then that dreadful prison camp. She put aside her own uncertainties, her fears about the impression she might make on people like those two women upstairs. She longed with an instinct she did not yet quite understand to help him forget those memories.

Without a trace of coquetry, she said, "I'm glad I'm the first girl you've danced with since—since you've come home."

His blue eyes warmed as he looked down at her, and his arm tightened around her waist.

"So am I," he told her.

Chapter Four

M EGAN LONGED to go on dancing with Clay all evening, but the waltz came to an end, and Major Taggart claimed her for the next dance, a polka. After that, she danced with another Yankee, the major's adjutant, a boyish young lieutenant. As they moved across the floor, Megan became aware of a flurry of interest at the opposite side of the ballroom, where a party of latecomers, all of them men, had just entered. She saw Clay go to welcome them.

"That's Senator Aldrich," the lieutenant told her. "The stout man with the fancy waistcoat. He was one of the leaders of the Abolition movement. He—" The lieutenant's face reddened. "I beg your pardon, Miss Rafferty. That was, perhaps, tactless of me—"

"Oh, but I'm not a Southerner. That is, I only arrived here in America a few weeks ago. From Ireland."

The lieutenant, much relieved, asked her if she was homesick.

"Not any longer," Megan said. The words came unbidden

but with a calm certainty; since the moment when Clay had led her out onto the ballroom floor, had taken her in his arms, she had felt that this proud house was the one place she wanted to be. Reason, common sense, had nothing to do with it. She knew that she belonged here, because Clay was here.

And although she could not help but be impressed by her surroundings, by the beauty and dignity of Montrose, she knew, too, that she would have felt the same if Clay's home had been a farmhouse with a sagging roof and weathered shingles, like those she'd seen on her river boat trip from New Orleans a few weeks before.

She had to force herself to listen to the lieutenant, who was explaining that two of the others in the senator's party were Northern businessmen: one, a New York financier, the other, the owner of one of the largest textile mills in Massachusetts. The remaining member of the party, a tall, dashing-looking young man who sported a large black moustache, was a journalist who had come along to report to the readers of his Cincinnati newspaper on conditions in the South. Megan nodded and made appropriate comments, but it was Clay who held her eyes as he moved through the crowd with easy assurance, pausing here and there to introduce his Yankee guests to his planter neighbors.

"Almost time for supper, isn't it, Abby?" asked Major Taggart as they moved to the beat of the waltz.

"In a little while, Preston," Abigail Drummond assured him. The major appreciated good food and plenty of it, she thought; and his enjoyment of other sensual pleasures was equally keen, as she had good reason to know.

Abigail had always instinctively understood how to satisfy a man's needs, and that knowledge had served her well. Her father had owned a small, respectable hotel near Asheville in the mountains of western North Carolina, a pleasant place but too isolated for Abigail's tastes. While her three sisters had been content to marry farmers in the vicinity, Abigail had held out for something better. After her father's death, she had taken over the running of the hotel and had made a good job of it, for she had always been a shrewd businesswoman.

She had worked night and day until her meeting with Vance

Drummond. He had lost his wife the year before and had come to spend the summer at the hotel with his three small children. Lianne's slow recovery from the typhoid fever that had killed her mother had made Vance fearful. He must not lose Lianne, too. The healthful climate of the mountains was known to be beneficial in such convalescent cases, his doctor had assured him.

His stay at the hotel had certainly been beneficial to Abigail, who had gone out of her way to pamper all three of the Drummond children, particularly the frail Lianne. With her own hands, Abigail had concocted special delicacies to tempt the little girl's appetite. At the same time, she had been warm and responsive to Vance Drummond, still shaken by the loss of his beloved Emily.

The Drummonds' planter neighbors—the Shepleys, the Hunters, the Surgets—had been surprised and somewhat critical when Vance had returned from North Carolina with a second wife; true, she was a Southerner, but the ladies observed that Vance would have done better to have chosen from one of the eligible local belles. And, they asked each other, was it quite respectable for a woman to have been running a hotel all by herself?

Abigail had gone her own way, holding her head high, secure in the knowledge that she was mistress of Montrose, and if her interest in the welfare of Emily Drummond's three children had lessened, no one could say that she showed any marked preference for her own son, Reed, born two years later. She was received by her neighbors for Vance's sake, and she made a place for herself in the plantation society of Natchez, although she had few close women friends.

Tonight, she told herself smugly, she was far better off than most of her neighbors. While they were hard put to feed their families, she was able to give a ball as lavish as any that had been held during the days before the war. Montrose had remained intact, thanks to her friendship with Major Taggart.

But the major's money had not paid for the ball, for the impressive supper even now being spread on the long mahogany table in the next room, for the hired orchestra from New Orleans, or for her fine new taffeta gown. Clay had paid for the ball out of a bank loan. He agreed that it was fair enough since

the ball was being held to further his plans for rebuilding the
railroad spur.

Under other conditions, she might have protested the mortgaging of Montrose, for she was by no means sure that Clay's
plans would come to fruition. But since Vance had seen fit to
leave the plantation to his eldest son, Abigail had decided that
her future lay elsewhere. She would marry the infatuated Major
Taggart and go back to Boston with him. Reed would be furious; he had already made his resentment of Taggart obvious.
But that, Abigail told herself, was Reed's problem. She had
her own future to think about.

It was close to midnight, and the guests had nearly finished
supper. There were still endless platters on the table: ham baked
in wine, braised pheasant, soft-shell crabs in a sauce of champagne, rich with butter and cream, as only Rachel could make
it, sherbets and meringues and nougats, punch for the ladies
and whiskey and brandy for the gentlemen, who were properly
appreciative, for good liquor had been in short supply during
the last years of the war.

Perhaps, Abigail thought, Reed had been partaking a little
too freely of the brandy, for she saw that his face was flushed,
and although she could not hear what he was saying to Senator
Aldrich, there was a tension in his stance. He made a wide,
sweeping motion with one hand that threatened to upset a flower-
filled epergne. And Megan Rafferty, standing beside the senator, looked distinctly uneasy.

Megan had been delighted and a little overwhelmed when
the senator had singled her out for his attentions during supper.
He was a tall, heavy-set man with a mane of white hair and a
deep, resonant voice, and Megan guessed that he was used to
being deferred to. A little pompous, perhaps, but then—he
was a member of the U. S. Senate, and over here he had the
same importance as a member of Parliament back home, Megan
thought. Imagine, only a few weeks in this new country and
here she was, talking with a senator.

Then Reed had joined them, and Megan's pleasure gave
way to anxiety, for Reed had responded to the senator's attempts at polite conversation with barely concealed hostility.

When the senator had praised the beauty of Montrose, Reed had retorted, "I suppose we can consider ourselves fortunate that Montrose is still standing. Some of our neighbors were not so lucky. Take the Surgets—Frank and Charlotte. Your army destroyed their home. It was dynamited by the order of the chief federal engineer. The Surgets were given three days to get all their possessions out of their home. Priceless works of art, paintings and statuary from Europe, rosewood and satin furniture. But then I suppose the Yankees have little appreciation of such things."

The senator stiffened. "We were fighting a war, sir. Such losses are regrettable but inevitable."

"Perhaps now the Surgets' house can be rebuilt," Megan began. She must do what she could to placate the senator, she thought, for his backing was essential to Clay's plans for rebuilding the railroad spur north of Natchez. "Now that the war is over, perhaps—"

"Homes like Clifton can never be rebuilt, Miss Rafferty," said Reed. Although his voice was strained, he spoke with the politeness due a lady. "And even if the interior of the house could be restored, there are no longer the people to tend the gardens, the conservatory. Frank Surget had one of the finest gardeners in this part of the country. A mulatto he bought in Jamaica—"

"Then perhaps it is as well the gardens remain as they are," said the senator. "Beauty built on the forced labor of the helpless bondsman—"

"This isn't a political rally," Reed interrupted. "I think we all know your views, senator. May I remind you that this house was built by blacks—and they were better off working for my grandfather than they are likely to be now, with your Freedmen's Bureau filling their heads with a lot of damned nonsense. Your pardon, Miss Rafferty."

Megan looked about the room anxiously. Where on earth was Clay? If only he would come and stop this before it was too late. But she caught no glimpse of him in the crowd, and after a moment's hesitation, she forced herself to intervene.

"Clay Drummond believes that the future of the South lies in the development of industry," she began carefully. "He told me so."

"He is a man of foresight," the senator said. "The South had a wealth of untapped natural resources. Lumber, mineral wealth. But factories are needed, and mills—"

"Needed by whom?" Reed asked, his voice too loud. "Your Carpetbagger friends, perhaps. Not our neighbors, our guests here tonight. We're planters. We don't want the countryside ruined by smoking chimneys. We don't want our cities filled with hordes of unwashed immigrants, like those who are crowded into the slums of New York and Boston."

Megan flinched. So many of those immigrants to whom Reed was referring were Irish. Had he meant to hurt her, or had his anger against the senator made him oblivious of the feelings of anyone else present?

Megan swallowed her resentment. "But surely when the railroad spur is rebuilt, it will benefit the planters, too," she said. "If you don't want the mills down here, then you'll need the railroad to ship the cotton up North, won't you?"

"I don't think you understand the difficulties of rebuilding the spur. Oh yes, I know all about my brother's schemes, but they aren't likely to work."

"And why not?" Megan asked, struggling to keep her temper under control.

"I would not expect a young lady to understand such matters," Reed said. "And when she is as charming as you are, Miss Rafferty, there's no need for her to trouble her mind with—"

"Perhaps you'd like to explain to me why the railroad spur can't be rebuilt," the senator said. "Your brother seems to think—"

"My brother returned from your prison camp with many peculiar ideas. I've no doubt that the treatment he received there has left him a changed man," Reed shot back.

The senator's face reddened under his mane of white hair. "You still haven't given me any concrete reasons why it would be impossible to rebuild that spur," he said, his voice ringing as he challenged Reed to explain himself. Some of the guests standing nearby stopped talking and turned to listen. Megan caught a glimpse of Violet Shepley's ferret face, her eyes avid, and of Winona Hunter, her full lips pursed disapprovingly.

"I'll give you reasons," Reed said belligerently. "No self-respecting white man in these parts is going to take a job swinging a pick on a railroad. And as for the blacks, you won't get a lick of work out of them. They're too set on enjoying their freedom—the freedom you and your kind gave them. Without a work crew, Clay won't stand a chance of rebuilding that spur. So you see, senator—"

"My uncle will provide the work crew," Megan heard herself saying. "Irishmen who'll be glad for a day's pay and enough to fill their bellies—" She broke off, horrified by her words. She had learned at the manor house to speak in genteel words, but now her hard-won training had for the moment deserted her.

She heard Violet Shepley titter and saw her raise her fan, lean toward Winona Hunter, and whisper something.

"Your uncle?" The senator looked surprised.

"Jim Rafferty," Megan said. Carried away by her need to help Clay with his plans, she went on recklessly. "Uncle Jim worked on the canals down in New Orleans right after he came over here from County Cork. He and hundreds like him. They aren't afraid of swamp fever, and they aren't ashamed to swing a pick or lay ties. Uncle Jim says he can get men from the Irish Channel in New Orleans who'll lay two to five miles of track a day—and—and put down—"

The room was quiet now, and Megan, finding that she was the center of derisive or hostile looks from the planters and their ladies, began to flounder. Ordinarily, she had a good memory for figures, but now confusion and embarrassment were surging up in her. Oh, why hadn't she maintained a ladylike silence?

She had shamed herself and Clay, who had invited her here as his guest. Tears pricked at her eyelids, but she blinked them back.

"Jim Rafferty's crew will be able to put down four rails a minute, senator."

She turned and saw that Clay was standing beside her. "And his teams will haul the rails out to the end-of-track," Clay went on. He was not looking at Megan but directly at Senator Aldrich. "I have the figures down in black and white, sir. If you will join me in the library, I can show them to you."

"Yes, indeed," said the senator. "Miss Rafferty, if you'll

excuse us—" He made a bow in her direction, and then, pointedly ignoring Reed, he walked through the crowd with Clay at his side. Near the doors of the dining room, they were joined by the other men of the senator's party.

After they had disappeared, Megan stood still, trying to collect her thoughts. She had done what she could to help Clay, but she had made a spectacle of herself. She didn't belong here. She had to get away.

She heard the orchestra in the ballroom start the first measures of a polka. Samantha came to Reed's side, moving gracefully, a set smile on her face.

She took her husband's arm. "It's so warm in here," she said. "Shall we take a stroll in the gardens?"

Reed hesitated, glancing at Megan. "I'm sure Miss Rafferty will excuse us," Samantha said sweetly, her dark eyes mocking Megan.

After they had gone, Megan felt alone and painfully conspicuous. Her palms, inside her new kid gloves, grew damp. The gentlemen were leading their ladies away from the supper table now, back to the ballroom.

How long would Clay remain in the library with the senator and the other Yankee visitors? For hours, perhaps. And what was she to do in the meantime?

She looked at the table with its half-empty platters. She could scarcely remain in the dining room, when all the others had obviously finished their supper.

"Megan, my dear." She turned to see Jessica, who approached her, followed by a middle-aged gentleman. "This is Judge Garnett, down from Selma," she said. "He hopes that since Clay is otherwise occupied, you will give him the pleasure of a dance."

The judge bowed courteously, and although Megan suspected that the judge had been maneuvered into asking her to dance, he made her a gallant bow and said, "If you'll do me the honor, Miss Rafferty."

Filled with gratitude toward Jessica, who, for the second time that evening, had helped her out of an embarrassing situation, Megan took Judge Garnett's arm and let him lead her into the ballroom. Her spirits began to rise. Let the ladies ignore her or whisper about her. She was not sorry for what she had done, for without her intervention, Senator Aldrich might have been drawn into an open quarrel with Reed. And that certainly would not have aided Clay's plans for winning the senator's backing for the railroad.

But by two o'clock, when Megan was still seated in a corner of the now-deserted ballroom, she felt her elation fading, for she had hoped for so much from this evening, and she had had only one dance with Clay. And now he still had not reappeared. The members of the orchestra had departed, and from outside she could hear the last of the guests saying their good-bys; and still Clay had not come.

"Why, Miss Rafferty, you're still here." She flinched at the sound of Samantha's silvery-sweet voice, at the barely concealed triumph in her dark-brown eyes. "Oh, but of course— you're waiting for Clay. I should have arranged for some of the other guests to take you home, but—well—none of them will be going down to the waterfront."

"I'll wait for Clay," Megan said stubbornly.

"Oh, but that would hardly be practical. Your family would be concerned if you did not return before morning, wouldn't they?"

"Megan will get home before morning."

Clay stood in the wide entrance to the ballroom. His lean, tanned face was composed, unreadable, but Megan saw that there was a curious kind of barely restrained excitement in his eyes. "Come along, Megan," he said.

She hurried to him, only vaguely aware of the cold anger in Samantha's face. What did it matter how Samantha or any of those other women at the ball felt about her? Clay was here. He hadn't forgotten; he would drive her home through the warm, flower-scented darkness, along the road that followed the curve of the river. Even though she had had only one dance with him, even though she had been snubbed and whispered about, she and Clay would be together during the drive home.

He led her out into the long, high-ceilinged hallway, deserted now, but he stopped before a pair of massive doors and gestured. "The talk's still going on in the library there," he said. "We may be at it until dawn. I won't be able to drive you home myself, but I've ordered the gig hitched up and brought around. Silas will drive you. He's one of the few stable hands who didn't go off. He's old, but he can handle the gig well enough."

Megan tried not to show her disappointment. She could hardly have expected Clay to leave the senator and those other men who were so important to his plans, but the disappointment was a bitter one, all the same. Then, remembering Clay's plans, she asked, "What about the railroad spur? Are you going to get what you want, Clay?"

His full-lipped mouth curved in a smile that made his face look almost boyish. The excitement she had sensed in him a few moments before was even more plain now.

"I already have it," he said, and his voice was vibrant with triumph. "Oh, there are details to be worked out—those Yankees are practical men—and I have to go over all the facts and figures. But I have it, Megan. I have my railroad."

Then, before she sensed what he was going to do, his arms went around her, and he drew her against him so tightly that she found it difficult to breathe. She felt the length of his tall, heavily muscled body pressed against hers so that the buttons of his coat cut into her, even through the silk and lace that covered her breasts.

A moment later, he picked her up and swung her around so that her amber silk skirt and ruffled petticoats billowed around her legs.

"I've got it. And you—you helped make it possible."

He was smiling down at her, his face close to hers as he held her against him. He cradled her in his arms.

"Why when I heard you talking to the senator, smoothing things over—Megan, you're wonderful."

He bent his head, and she felt his lips, warm on her cheeks. Her arms reached out, and she clung to him, her fingers pressing into the hard muscles of his back. Then his mouth moved to hers, and his lips claimed hers in a long, hard kiss. He forced her lips apart so that he was kissing her in a way that she had never been kissed before.

She started to tremble as she felt the heat of desire stirring within her for the first time. The pupils of his eyes had widened so that the blue was nearly gone, so that she was looking into blackness. There was a soft roaring in her ears, like the sound of the sea. She moaned deep in her throat.

"Silas got de gig waitin' like yuh said, Mistuh Clay, suh."

Clay straightened and set Megan on her feet so swiftly that she had to clutch at his arm to steady herself.

Megan blinked at the sight of a tall, thin woman with coffee-colored skin who wore a spotless starched white apron and a neat turban.

Megan's fingers shook as she smoothed her skirt and tried to pat her hair back into place. She heard Clay saying, "Thanks, Rachel."

Then, turning to Megan, he said, "You'd better go now. You'll have a long drive home." He glanced at the closed library doors, and it was plain that his attention had already returned to the men inside. "Good night, my dear."

Later, as the gig began its slow descent down the bluffs, Megan still remembered Clay's kiss. Why had he kissed her that way? Only out of gratitude or in the elation of the moment? She could not forget how his arms had tightened around her, how his mouth had covered hers, hot and seeking.

Oh, if only he could have taken her home, if only he was beside her now on the seat of the gig.

But no, better that he had not been able to drive her back, for if they had been alone now, this moment, and if he had wanted her, she was not sure that she would have been able to hold him off. Or that she would have wanted to.

Chapter Five

⌒

THE HOUSE was silent and dark when Opal, carrying a small, carefully wrapped bundle, moved quickly down the long, curving stairway and into the downstairs hall. She was not tired, although she ought to be, she thought, after all the work of getting ready for the ball, cleaning up afterward, then helping the Drummond ladies to get ready for bed. Only a few years ago, each of the ladies had had her own maid, but now, with so many of the house servants gone, Opal had been pressed into service as a maid as well as a seamstress for all of them.

Only a little while before, she had helped Old Missus, then Miss Lianne and Miss Jessica, unbuttoning their gowns, brushing their hair for the night. But when she had gone to Miss Samantha's bedroom, she had found it empty, the coverlet smooth and unwrinkled, the pillows undisturbed, and Miss Samantha gone. And Mr. Reed had been sleeping in the dressing room beyond, on the camp bed, as he had been doing for the past several months; Opal had heard him muttering in his sleep. She shook her head. There he was, with a beautiful young wife like Miss Samantha, and sleeping alone. . . .

And where was Miss Samantha? Opal shrugged slightly. None of her business, not anymore. The Drummonds didn't matter, for tonight she was leaving Montrose for good. Going to New Orleans. Going to Noah. She'd be on the same river boat that would be stopping at the Montrose dock to pick up that Yankee senator and his friends.

The night air was cool on her face as she left the house. She hesitated. Mama would be asleep now in the lean-to that had been built on to the separate kitchen quarters. As in most of the big plantation houses in this part of the state, the kitchen quarters were located a short distance from the main house so that the heat from the stove and the ovens would not bother the white folks.

Opal had wanted to tell mama good-by, but there was no sense to it. How many times she and mama had quarreled when she had tried to explain about going to Noah in New Orleans.

"Noah's a good man—I ain' sayin' no different. But I ain' fergettin' what Mistuh Vance done fo' me—and fo' you, Opal."

Yes, mama had reason to be grateful to Vance Drummond, dead and gone now. He had first seen mama, a handsome woman then, light skinned and erect, on the auction block down in New Orleans, on Royal Street, near the St. Louis Hotel. Opal, a terrified ten-year-old, had clung to mama's skirts while a big, loud-voiced man had run his hands over Opal's body and fingered her thick black ringlets. "Dat dealer—he wanted to sell us apart—said y' wouldn' be no use to a man yet, but he could get a good price for y' for one 'o dem fancy sportin' houses—said they'd train y' der—"

But when Mr. Vance Drummond had bought mama, a fine cook who knew how to make the fanciest French dishes, she had pleaded with him to buy Opal, too, and although he had said that he didn't need another little black wench on the place, he had finally given in. Mama had told Opal the story thousands of times, always adding that they both owed Mr. Vance and his family everything. And nothing Opal could say would change mama's mind, so now she had to leave Montrose without saying good-by. It hurt real bad, but she had to be with Noah. She had to.

* * *

The sky was getting gray, and the dawn wind was stirring in the pecan trees when Samantha, in the summerhouse near the river, heard the sound of hoofs on the path. She left the summerhouse, a small white structure built like a miniature Greek temple and covered with wisteria vines. She stepped out into the road so quickly that Clay's horse, a black and white stallion, reared and whinnied. Clay got him quieted down, then said, "Samantha, for God sake, what are you doing out here?"

She tried to answer, but the words would not come. He dismounted. "What's wrong?" he demanded.

"Clay—in here—I have to talk to you—"

He stared at her for a moment, then tied his horse to the limb of one of the pecan trees and followed her inside. The gray light filtered dimly through the latticed roof with its tangle of vines and leaves. "Here," Samantha said. "Sit next to me here." She sank down on one of the wide wicker settees. The cushions were a little damp from the moist night air.

After a brief hesitation, Clay sat down beside her. Was he remembering, as she was, their meetings here before the war? Those times when she had allowed him to kiss her, and even, once, to cup her breast. His fingers had trembled a little.

Oh, he had wanted her then, but she had been far too well trained to respond. Men had these needs, but it was up to a young lady to hold herself aloof until after marriage. Even then, she would take no pleasure in sharing the marriage bed; so her mother had said. Children were a woman's only compensation for bearing with the animal desires of her husband. As to exactly how a man might express those animal desires Samantha had formed only the vaguest idea.

Now, of course, she knew. But it would have been different with Clay than it had been with Reed.

"Samantha, it's nearly morning. If you'll tell me what you—"

"I've been waiting for you," she said quickly. "I knew that you'd have to come back this way after you took your—your Yankee friends down to the dock. Oh, Clay, how awful for you, having to be nice to people like that." She put a small hand lightly over his. "I don't know how you stood it."

"I managed," he said dryly. "And I got what I wanted, the

promise of Senator Aldrich's support in rebuilding that railroad spur. I couldn't get an outright promise of land grants farther west—not yet—but I will once I've proved myself here in Mississippi."

"I don't want to hear about the railroad, not here, not now. Clay, Montrose belongs to you. Your father left it to you. Why can't you put your mind to planting a new crop—"

"I'll leave that to Reed," Clay said. He moved restively. "Right now, I think we should both be getting back to the house. I want to get a few hours' sleep before I leave."

"Leave?"

"I'm going out to the railroad site, but first I want to stop and talk to Jim Rafferty, to tell him to start getting together a work crew—"

"Oh, but why must you do that? I mean, can't you get an overseer or a—a foreman to take care of all that? It's bad enough you have to associate with the senator and his friends. Why must you have anything to do with Jim Rafferty?"

"I like Jim Rafferty," Clay said quietly.

"And his niece? Wasn't it going pretty far, inviting her to Montrose? All the ladies were scandalized, and Violet Shepley said—"

"I'm afraid I don't really care what Violet Shepley said. Come along, Samantha. We can ride double back to the house."

Was it possible, Samantha thought, that it meant nothing to Clay that they were alone here together? Could he have forgotten those other times they had spent here, when he had pleaded for her favors and she had either teased him or pretended to be deeply offended when he had tried to take liberties? She longed to ask him outright how he felt about the Rafferty girl, whether he had only invited her here to cement his business relationship with her uncle or whether he cared anything for her. But no lady would ask such a thing, not directly.

Instead, she forced a smile and said, "Really, Clay, it wasn't kind of you to ask the poor little thing to Montrose. She was completely out of place, and I felt so sorry for her when she made that scene—"

"What scene?"

"Why with the senator and—and Reed—"

"It seems to me that it was Reed who made the scene. If it

had not been for Megan's quick thinking, Senator Aldrich and his party might have left before I had a chance to speak with them. Megan—"

"Oh, Clay, I don't want to talk about Megan Rafferty. Not here. Surely you can understand that. I know that you haven't forgotten. . . ."

"That was a long time ago," Clay said. And Samantha was aware, as she had been so many times since his return to Montrose, of how different he sounded. He was not a boy any longer. He was harder, more reserved.

She told herself it was because she was married to Reed that he could not allow himself to express his real feelings for his brother's wife. But now she was becoming afraid that it was more than that.

Clay was attracted to Megan Rafferty. She had sensed that at the ball this evening. And the little slut would take full advantage of his feelings, would use all the wiles that girls like her must know. She couldn't be a virgin, not living down there in Natchez-under. There would be no need for Megan to hold Clay at arm's length. Maybe she had already given herself to Clay.

But none of that mattered. Clay belonged to her, and her marriage to Reed had changed nothing. For Reed had never once been able to arouse her. But it would be different with Clay. In what way, she could not know, for she had never yet experienced sexual fulfillment. But she and Clay belonged together, and with Clay she would know complete joy.

Then the memory of Megan came into her mind to torment her. How pretty the girl had been—in a common, vulgar way, of course, but undeniably pretty, with that tawny-gold hair, those strangely colored eyes. And she had carried herself with assurance, had danced gracefully. And had spoken with only the slightest trace of a brogue, just enough to give a soft, musical lilt to her voice.

Samantha fought back the anger that threatened to engulf her. It would never do to show that side of herself to Clay. Instead, she turned a little away from Clay and covered her face with her hands.

A moment later, she felt his hand on her arm.

"Samantha?"

She did not answer.

"Samantha—my dear— Don't. You are Reed's wife, and nothing can change that."

"But you changed that," she said. "You came back." She turned and looked at him in the growing light of dawn, and her words were wrenched from a place deep inside her.

"If I'd thought there was the slightest chance that you were still alive, do you suppose I'd have married Reed? I never loved him, and I never pretended to. Why even on our wedding night he—I—"

"That's enough," Clay said harshly. "What's between you and Reed is none of my business. I don't want to hear—"

He *was* jealous, then, she thought, and her heart lifted in triumph.

"I know how difficult it's been for you since I came back to Montrose," he was saying. "The three of us living under one roof. Don't you think that I—" He stopped, drew a deep breath, then went on quickly. "But things will be better once I've gone away again. I'll be out at the railroad site most of the time until the spur's been rebuilt. And after that, I'm going to get the senator's support to extend the road on into Louisiana and Texas—then northwest to—"

"I don't care about the railroad," Samantha cried. "I don't care about anything except— Oh, Clay, I'm not Reed's wife, not really. It's been months since we've shared the same bed— I can't stand to have him touch me."

"And Reed? How does he feel about you?"

"What does that matter?" she demanded. "I don't care how he feels. I only want you. I want—"

She reached out and tried to embrace him, but he wrenched himself away.

"You're a child, Samantha," he said. "A spoiled, selfish child."

"That's not true— I'm a woman now."

"Oh, no. Marriage hasn't made you a woman. You think only of what you want. You don't even see other people and their needs. My brother needs you, Samantha. He needs your loyalty, your respect, if nothing else. You're his wife."

There was no need for Samantha to pretend to be crying now. Tears of rage and frustration ran down her cheeks. "Because of a mistake," she said, sobbing. "Because of a crazy mistake. Because of a report—from the War Department—telling us that you were shot trying to escape from Johnson's Island—" Her voice rose, hysterical, out of control.

Clay grasped her by the shoulders, his fingers hard, biting into her flesh. "Stop that! Now!"

Somehow she managed to speak more quietly. "I won't give you up because of a mistake. We belong to each other. We do, and you know it, too. You know it. . . ."

For a moment, there was a charged silence between them. A few faint streaks of pale golden light struck through the river mist, touching her face, her hair.

"Samantha," he said, and then he was holding her, drawing her down on the dusty cushions of the wicker settee. He pushed up her skirts, and his hands moved swiftly, baring the softness of her belly and thighs.

She gave an outraged cry when she realized that he was going to take her without preliminaries, without the gentleness that he had shown her in the past. But the cry changed to one of triumph when he penetrated her, deeply, hungrily. . . .

Opal, hurrying along the path leading down to the dock, stopped short, frozen by the sound of a woman's voice. A cry of pain? No, not that. Her lips parted in surprise as she stood, unmoving, close to the summerhouse. The sky was growing lighter, and she saw the tall shape of the stallion that had been tethered to the pecan tree, next to the small, latticed building. Mr. Clay's black stallion with the white star-shaped patch on its forehead and the white dappled legs. The animal pawed the damp earth restlessly as if it, too, had been startled by the sound of the cry.

The first golden light was pouring through the trees, coming from out there across the river. Opal knew that she must hurry if she was going to get aboard the river boat that had stopped to pick up Mr. Clay's Yankee guests, the boat bound for New Orleans. But still she could not bring herself to move on.

Her mind moved swiftly, however. Miss Samantha's bed, empty, the covers smooth, the pillow untouched, and Miss Samantha not there. And Mr. Reed asleep in the dressing room.

Opal, like all the other house servants at Montrose, knew how it used to be with Mr. Clay and Miss Samantha before the war. She knew, too, that Miss Samantha and Mr. Reed had not shared the big canopied bed for months now. And Mr. Clay was home again, back from that awful prison up North.

Opal shook her head and reminded herself that none of the Drummonds were any of her concern, not anymore. That river boat down at the landing—she had to be on that boat.

She hefted her bundle and hurried on, ignoring the sounds from the summerhouse. Mr. Clay's voice and Miss Samantha's. She couldn't make out the words. None of her business. She was on her way down to New Orleans. To freedom. To Noah. . . .

"I'll go back to the house first," Samantha said shakily. "It wouldn't do for both of us to get there at the same time. Someone might be awake already."

"I suppose so." Clay sounded remote, abstracted, and Samantha felt the beginnings of uncertainty. For a few moments, Clay had belonged to her, completely. Now, incredibly, she felt alone. But how could she ever feel alone again after what they had shared?

In the dappled early-morning light that came through the latticed roof, his face looked hard, composed. He did not try to touch her. His hands were jammed into the pockets of his trousers.

Was it possible that he had not felt as she had about what had happened here? She wanted reassurance, but she could not bring herself to ask for it.

Until now, she had been unawakened physically, for those few nights she had shared with Reed in the big canopied bed had stirred no feelings in her except embarrassment and a slight revulsion. Reed's very worship of her, his desperate eagerness to please her, had filled her with contempt for him.

But Clay was different. And, she thought miserably, what had happened a few moments ago could not have meant to him what it had to her. For she had no illusions about Clay. He had known many women. There had been rumors about his carryings-on in Natchez-under even before the war.

She had always been cool and remote, but now that she had

yielded, had she lessened her value in his eyes? She shivered.

"Yes," he said slowly, "you'd better go back to the house alone. I'll follow in a few minutes."

His voice hardened. "I'm going to pack my things. I'll be gone before you come down to breakfast."

"But you can't go—not now—"

"I can't stay. Not even for a few hours. Surely you must see that." His voice was harsh.

"Where will you go?"

"Why to the railroad site, of course," he told her with a finality that left no room for further discussion.

Chapter Six

"I THOUGHT ye liked workin' in yer uncle's store," said Kathleen Rafferty, looking at Megan with surprise. "It's more genteel than the warehouse, that's sure."

"But I'd be more useful in the warehouse right now," Megan said. She tried to sound crisp and businesslike.

It was early September, but the damp, stifling heat still blanketed the streets and alleys of Natchez-under. Megan's aunt, a short, stout woman with a fringe of ginger-colored hair, had opened the top buttons of her wrapper and was fanning her ample breasts. Belle, a younger edition of her mother, although so far she could only be called plump, looked equally hot and untidy.

From the livery stable across the alley came the shouts of the teamsters as they unloaded their wagons. Megan winced as she heard a crate come crashing to the ground and a string of oaths from one of her uncle's men. In the weeks since the ball at Montrose, the Raffertys' cottage had become more distasteful than ever to her.

"If yer thinkin' that ye'll be seein' more of Gavin O'Donnell at the warehouse," Belle began, her round, sallow face reddening, "let me tell ye here and now—"

"I wasn't thinking of Gavin," Megan said sharply. "It's a matter of complete indifference to me whether I see your precious Gavin—"

"Now, girls, that's enough," Kathleen interrupted irritably.

"It isn't fair," Belle whined. "Gavin and me, we had an understandin' before Megan came here. Puttin' on them fancy airs, flouncin' around like she was somethin' special, and smilin' at him—"

"I've done nothing to encourage Gavin," Megan said, trying to keep a rein on her temper. That was true enough. She liked Gavin, but as for trying to take him away from Belle— Why, the notion was ridiculous. Ever since that evening at Montrose, there was only one man that Megan wanted. She took a deep breath, then spoke quietly. "I can't help it if Gavin talks to me," she said. "But I give you my word, I've not been flirting with him. I wish he'd ask for your hand and leave me alone, for I'd never consider marrying him."

Although Belle should have been placated, she was not. She put her hands on her ample hips and demanded, "And just what makes ye think yer too good for Gavin?"

"I didn't say—it's only that—" Megan was fast beginning to lose patience. Although she managed to look crisp and tidy even on this sultry morning, she was suffering from the heat as much as the others, and she was sickened by the damp stench that rose from the green-scummed puddles in the alley, the odor of decay that hung over the waterfront neighborhood. "Aunt Kathleen, will you talk to Uncle Jim about my working at the warehouse?"

"If it ain't Gavin, then why do ye want to work there?" Belle persisted. "It wouldn't be because of Clay Drummond, would it now? Ye wouldn't be thinkin' of gettin' around him that way?" She gave Megan a spiteful little smile. "Oh, I'm not sayin' that Mr. Drummond wouldn't like a bit of sport with ye. But if it's marriage yer thinkin' of, forget it."

"You don't know anything about Clay Drummond," Megan snapped.

"I know he didn't even take the trouble t' bring ye home

from the ball at Montrose," Belle said. "Sent ye home alone that night, didn't he?"

"I've explained that. He was discussing railroad business with the senator—"

"That railroad is all he thinks about," Kathleen put in. "He ain't been back to Natchez, not once, since the day after the ball. Ain't even gone up to visit his own folks at Montrose."

"But he will come back," Megan said, half to herself. She turned away from her aunt and started for her room, a small cubicle at the back of the cottage. She was remembering the night of the ball, Clay's mouth on hers, the strength of his arms around her. He had been grateful to her then for helping to avoid a scene between Reed and Senator Aldrich, for helping to further his plans for the railroad. And when he returned, he would find her here, doing what she could to keep the accounts of the supplies for the railroad. Even Uncle Jim had said she had a head for figures.

She went into her room, closed the door, and went to stand by the window. Why had Clay remained away so long? Both Uncle Jim and Gavin O'Donnell had made frequent trips between Natchez-under and end-of-track, some twenty miles to the north of the city. Shipments had been delayed or had gone astray, and Uncle Jim had complained about the disruption caused by the war and its aftermath. Jim had asked Megan to write letters to some of their Northern suppliers and had praised her neat hand and her skill at composing these business letters. But Clay had not once come back to Natchez.

He would come back, though, and when he did, what would be more likely than a trip down here to the warehouse to check on supplies? Megan knew that she was being forward, planning to put herself in a position where Clay would be bound to see her again, but she also knew that she would have to fight for what she wanted, that, for her, there was no other way and never had been.

She reached up to the small, splintery shelf and took down the Waterford goblet, her fingers moving over its glittering surface, turning it to catch the light. Sunlight and firelight and a rainbow of colors, all caught in the hand-cut crystal. Lady Anne had given Megan the goblet after one of Lord Trevanion's guests at a hunting party had set it down with too much force,

being flown with wine and deep in an argument over the relative
merits of his own favorite hunter and that of his host.

"What do you want it for, Megan?" Lady Anne had asked.

"I want it—just to keep. To look at."

"But it is damaged."

"It's still beautiful, my lady," Megan had said. "Please,
may I keep it?"

And it was beautiful, Megan knew—a part of the more
elegant world in which she was determined to make a place
for herself. As Lady Anne's maid, she had taken pains to learn
the ways of the gentry.

She could never go back to Ireland, but from the moment
she had entered Montrose, she had felt the same gracious elegance, the way of life she longed for. Montrose drew her like
a magnet, possessed her thoughts, and not because the Drummonds were wealthy; for Uncle Jim had said that Clay's family
had lost their money during the war. What Clay had, he had
raised by mortgaging the plantation, and except for the money
he had spent on the ball, everything was going into the railroad.
It wasn't enough, of course. He had the invested capital from
Senator Aldrich and his Yankee associates as well as the right-
of-way that the senator had gotten for him. If he could complete
the spur in the time allotted by the railway committee, he would
be given land grants farther to the west and additional capital.
If not, he would lose not only the railroad but Montrose as
well.

But that could not happen. Clay would not let it happen.
Montrose would remain his; she was sure of it. And his wife
would have a secure, gracious life. His children would grow
up strong and proud.

His children. Something stirred inside her so strongly that
she caught her breath. His children and hers?

Oh, maybe Cousin Belle was right. Maybe a man like Clay
Drummond would never consider marriage to an Irish immigrant girl from Natchez-under. She flinched, remembering
Belle's other remark about how Clay would not mind taking a
bit of sport with her. But that was not what Megan wanted.

She desired Clay as a man, although her feelings were still
unformed. Living in the manor house all those years, she had
no more than a vague notion of what it would mean to be

married to Clay—or any other man, for that matter. For Lady Anne had been as prim and reserved as Queen Victoria herself, and Megan had ignored the gossip in the servants' hall.

One thing she did know. She wanted marriage, solid, respectable, lasting. She wanted her children to be able to hold their heads up, to take their place among the gentry in this new land.

Once more, she ran her fingers over the goblet. She thought of her mother, who had died shortly after giving birth to her fifth child. The neighbor women, who had labored in vain to save the infant and the mother, had called to Megan at last, and the skinny ten-year-old girl had gone into the cottage.

Pa had died the year before, and only Megan and Terence, of all the Rafferty children, had survived the bitter hunger of these past years. The cottage was damp, and the peat fire had not been sufficient to warm even that small single room where Deirdre Rafferty lay dying.

Megan had bent close to the bed, fighting down the grief and terror that threatened to engulf her. She could scarcely catch her mother's words. "It won't always be like this," her mother had said. "Not for you. You must not let it be. For you, there must be somethin' more. . . ."

The words had stayed with Megan all these years, had become a kind of litany. When she should have been praying for her mother's soul, the prayers would not come. Instead, she would find herself whispering over and over again: "There must be something more. . . ."

The words had continued to sustain her during those years when she had worked at the manor house. They had been with her the terrible night she had fled from Kilcurran, her dress still soaked with the blood of her dying brother, Terence. And they had given her courage to endure the misery of the steerage passage from Cork to New Orleans.

Now they had a new meaning. Something more. Montrose. And Clay Drummond.

"Won't be long now, Mr. Drummond," said Gavin O'Donnell. He drove the wagon, while Clay sat on the seat beside him, staring at the desolate landscape on the eastern side of the Mississippi River. Houses where he had visited as a boy, where he had gone to dances as a young man, now had fallen into decay; the swampland growth encroached on the once-fertile cotton fields; the gardens were sun scorched and neglected. "Guess ye'll be glad t' see yer family again after all this time."

Clay forced a faint smile. "Yes—of course," he told Gavin. "But I'm not staying overnight at Montrose. I'm heading down to Natchez-under tonight. We've got to have those rails, and if some damn clerk has mixed up the orders, I'll—"

Gavin laughed. "Better not say what ye'll do, Mr. Drummond. The clerk's Miss Megan Rafferty. Saw her there on my last trip down to Natchez-under." He glanced at Clay curiously. "Didn't ye know about it, Mr. Drummond? But I'm fergettin'—this'll be yer first trip back here since we started work on the railroad spur, won't it?"

Clay nodded.

"Been workin' as hard as any of the men, ye have," Gavin went on. "Guess ye want t' be sure t' finish in time to satisfy that senator and his Yankee friends."

"We'll finish in time," Clay said grimly. "We'll need more men, though."

"Don't worry about that," Gavin told him. "I'll round up the best bunch t' be had in New Orleans. But first, I'll be makin' a little stop in Natchez-under— I'll have to go down there t' get the river boat in any case." He grinned. "I'm goin' t' pay a call on Megan."

Clay stiffened slightly but made no reply, and Gavin, who had not noticed, went on: "I got plans for Megan and me, Mr. Drummond. She's been kind o' standoffish so far—got a lot of notions, she has. But I'll get her t' change her mind." A self-satisfied smile spread across his broad, sunburned face. "I mean t' make Megan Rafferty my wife."

Clay was startled by his own feeling of instant resentment. "I didn't know," he said evenly.

Gavin laughed. "Neither does Megan, not yet. Truth is, I've never thought much about marryin' before. But since Megan came t' live with her aunt 'n uncle I can't get 'er off my mind. She's pretty. Smart, too. She can tote up a column of figures faster'n most men. And she writes a fine hand. Course, once we're married, she'll not have time fer all that. With a houseful o' little ones to care for, she'll have enough to do."

Clay wanted to answer, but the words would not come, for he felt repelled by the other man's words and all that they implied. He remembered how he had held Megan in his arms when they had waltzed together on the night of the ball. She was slender and delicate, a lady to her fingertips. Megan, married to Gavin O'Donnell. Bearing his children in some stifling shanty in Natchez-under. Oh, Gavin was a decent enough sort, hard working and shrewd. But no husband for Megan.

"You can let me off here," Clay said, his tone abrupt, harsh.

"No trouble drivin' ye right up to the door of Montrose," Gavin said.

"I'll walk." Then, realizing that Gavin was looking at him in surprise, he added, "I can use the exercise."

Gavin shook his head, then grinned. "I'd have thought ye'd had plenty o' exercise up there at the railroad camp," he said. "Let me tell ye, Mr. Drummond, the crew couldn't stop talkin' about it, the way ye pitched in that day we were crossin' that bad patch o' swamp—the way ye helped them, shorin' up them timbers, swingin' a hammer like ye'd been doin' it fer years."

He paused, obviously waiting for Clay to say something, but there was no reply. Clay looked away, staring out over the fields of Montrose toward the house with unseeing eyes. Yes, he knew how to shore up timbers, how to handle a hammer, to lay ties. He'd never worked in steaming swamp country, though. It had been bone-chilling cold up there in northern Ohio, with the wind from Canada coming in across Lake Erie. His face had been flayed raw by the unfamiliar cold. His hands had blistered from hammer and pick, and the blisters had broken before his palms had grown as calloused as those of the rest of the crew. . . .

"Somethin' wrong, Mr. Drummond?"

Clay shook his head, forcing back the memories. "Not a thing, O'Donnell," he said. "Just make sure you get down to New Orleans as quickly as you can—get me those men. And get them back to the site. Jim Rafferty can take over from there."

Gavin nodded. "He knows how t' handle men, Jim does," he said. "Don't you worry, sir. We'll get that railroad spur finished on time."

Gavin brought the wagon to a halt long enough for Clay to swing himself down, then went on along the river road. Clay turned off and took the path to Montrose. It should be close to dinner time now, he thought. He would have a meal with his family, find out how the plantation was faring, and then go on down to the warehouse to check on a shipment of rails that had been delayed. He'd see that an order was put through for salt, too. The supply at the railroad camp was running low.

The Irish were good workers and had proved that they could do a day's work on potatoes and tea, but they needed salt, particularly in the heat of the swamps, where every man was drenched in sweat. A few of them had already doubled over with heat cramps from lack of salt.

They kept going, though. They liked and respected him; they'd made that plain. But their first loyalty was to Jim Rafferty, for he was one of their own.

Clay reached the kitchen quarters and saw Jessica emerging from the neat brick building adjacent to the main house. She looked tired, a little haggard, but when she caught sight of him, a smile lit her dark-blue eyes, and she hurried to embrace him. "Oh, Clay—we all wondered when you'd be back. You're in time for dinner."

He held her away and looked down at her. She was wearing a plain white apron over her calico dress, and he asked, "Have you been cooking?"

"No—not really," she said quickly. "But Rachel has far too much to do, especially since Opal left—"

Clay put an arm around his sister, and they started for the house together. "Opal—gone?"

"The night of the ball. She didn't say a word to Rachel. You don't seem surprised."

"I'm not," Clay said. He was remembering that day at the general store, the day he had met Megan for the first time. "Opal's gone off to join Noah. If she finds him, maybe she'll be all right. Otherwise—" He shook his head. "And you—I suppose you've taken over some of the chores."

"I like to cook," Jessica said quickly.

"That's beside the point. I don't imagine that Lianne has offered to lend a hand. Or Samantha." He did not give Jessica time to answer. "Never mind. When I get this railroad spur finished and start building a line to the West, things will change for all of us. You'll have all the hired help you need." He looked at the railing of the veranda at the back of the house. Paint was flaking off, and there were weeds growing tall. "There'll be a lot of changes as soon as I can afford them. All the same," he added, "it seems to me that Reed could do more. Why hasn't the north field been planted? It'll go right back to being swampland unless Reed takes a hand. I'll talk to him about it."

"Oh, please—not at dinner," Jessica begged.

"And why not?" Clay demanded.

"Reed's terrible angry. Abigail announced only this morning that she and Major Taggart have set a date for their wedding, and Reed—"

"Surely Reed's not surprised. High time the major made an honest woman of Abigail." Clay's laugh was brief and harsh.

He felt Jessica flinch and asked, "What's wrong, Jess?"

"You don't sound like yourself." She hesitated, then went on. "Ever since you came back from the war, you've been so different. Hard and— You're like a stranger."

"War changes people."

"I can understand that," Jessica said as she and Clay climbed the steps of the back veranda. "You've never talked about Johnson's Island—never even explained why you were reported killed there. Maybe if you did talk about it, to me—"

"No, Jess." It was impossible to think of discussing such things with his shy, gentle, bookish sister. "It's over now, and I don't want to be reminded of it."

The atmosphere in the dining room was strained. Reed greeted Clay with a nod, but he asked no questions about the progress of the railroad spur, and he volunteered no information about the plantation and the prospects for this year's cotton crop. When Rachel served dinner, Reed ignored the platters of golden-brown chicken, the steaming bowls of okra, rice, and peas; he refilled his wine glass from the decanter that stood near his elbow. Samantha, Clay saw, was paler than usual, and there were violet smudges under her dark-brown eyes. She, too, had little appetite. Only Lianne chattered lightly about the gossip of the county. As for Abigail, she looked smug and self-satisfied when she began to outline her plans for the future.

"The major and I will be going up to Boston right after the wedding," she said. "It's going to be a small affair, but once we're up North, his family will have no end of festivities for us. A reception first, and then I'll give a series of musicales." She sighed. "I'd hoped that Opal would make my trousseau. I'd even have taken her along to Boston with me to work as my personal maid and seamstress. Preston's family is quite wealthy— But that ungrateful girl went running off without a word. There's your emancipation. Filling the heads of silly young girls with nonsense." She shrugged her plump shoulders. "Downright ungrateful of Opal—"

"Abigail, please," Jessica interrupted softly, glancing at Rachel, who had just come in with the dessert: her own special nut cake with sherry icing.

"Rachel knows perfectly well how I feel about Opal's disloyalty," Abigail said. "Oh, well, I'm sure there are many fine seamstresses in Boston. And Preston has said he will take me to New York to buy a wardrobe. We'll spend our summers in Saratoga, or perhaps Newport. Preston says—"

"We've all heard enough about Preston Taggart." Reed spoke loudly, his words slurred. Only three in the afternoon and he was already drunk, Clay thought with disgust. But he felt sorry for Reed, too, for he had always had a strong, protective feeling toward his younger brother.

I'm not the only one who's changed since the war, Clay thought. Vance Drummond had taught both his sons to drink like gentlemen.

Reed stood up, pushing his chair back with such violence that it tipped over and crashed to the floor. "Shall we have a toast for the bride-to-be? Would you like that, mother?"

"Reed, please," Samantha began, but he ignored her.

"Too bad the major isn't here," Reed went on, his eyes narrow with unconcealed anger. "I suppose he's down in town with his bluecoats. Have you heard, Clay? Up in Jackson, there's black Union soldiers occupying the city. Under the command of men like your Major Taggart—"

"Reed, that has nothing to do with Abigail," Jessica began,

and it was plain to Clay that in addition to taking over the running of the household, Jessica had also become the family peacemaker. No wonder she looked drawn and tired.

Clay felt a rising resentment against Reed. While he had been working day and night out at the railroad site, living on potatoes and driving spikes with the Irish crew, Reed had stayed here at Montrose, too self-absorbed to run the place properly.

Maybe Reed had a right to be angry with Abigail. After all, she was his mother, not Clay's. But although Clay had never been particularly fond of the woman, he could not condemn Abigail too harshly. She was an opportunist, but her liaison with Major Taggart had preserved Montrose from the depredations of the Yankee troops. Its priceless furnishings had not been destroyed or stolen by the invaders, and its crops had not been carried off. At least Jessica and Lianne and Samantha, too, had had enough to eat during the last years of the war, when other Southern ladies went hungry.

"I won't have you speaking disrespectfully of the major," Abigail was saying to Reed. "One more word against him and you may leave the table."

"I'll leave," Reed said. He turned and started for the hall, his steps unsteady, but when Clay put out a hand to help him, he said, "I'll be all right." He managed a bow. "Excuse me, ladies."

A moment later, they heard him stumbling upstairs. Abigail's plump face was scarlet with annoyance, and Samantha's full lips were set in a hard line. Jessica looked close to tears. Only Lianne tried to keep up the pretense of a pleasant family meal.

"Reed's thinking of hiring Jeff Shepley to oversee our field hands," she said.

"Jeff? What about his own place?" Clay asked. "I'd think Jeff would have his hands full, making Holly Ridge productive again."

"The Shepleys have lost Holly Ridge," Jessica said. "It's being sold for taxes. Reed says that since we don't have an overseer and that cottage is standing empty—"

"I don't know that we can afford an overseer right now," Clay said. "I should think that Reed could manage without one."

"Not with these free field hands," Abigail said. "Jeff's a

hard man—he'll get the work out of them."

"I don't doubt it," Clay said. Jeff Shepley had always been known for his unusual harshness with his own slaves before the war. But such methods no longer worked now that the blacks were free. They certainly had not helped Jeff to keep Holly Ridge. But perhaps there had been other problems; perhaps Jeff had been refused credit at the bank, or perhaps his taxes had gone up too high. Clay dismissed the matter of Jeff Shepley, reminding himself that his concern at the moment was the railroad.

Unless the spur was completed in the allotted time, the bank would foreclose, and the Drummonds would lose Montrose. But he was not about to let that happen no matter how hard he had to drive himself and his work crew.

"That was a fine dinner, Rachel," he told the housekeeper. "I haven't had a meal like it since I went out to the railroad. Potatoes and tea, that's our daily fare."

"Ah'll bring yuh anothuh pot of coffee, Mistuh Clay. It's nice an' cool out on the veranda, an' Ah'll bring it out t' yuh."

"Thanks, Rachel," Clay said, shaking his head. "But I have to leave at once."

"Oh, but, Clay, you don't have to go so soon, surely," Jessica said.

"I have business in Natchez-under, at Rafferty's warehouses." He said good-by and left the dining room, knowing that it would be useless to try to have a serious talk with Reed right now about the running of Montrose; perhaps an overseer might be necessary at that, he thought grimly. But the delayed rail shipment came first.

He left the house and started off for the stables, but before he had gone more than a few yards, he heard the rustle of skirts, and then Samantha called to him softly.

"Clay—wait."

He stopped and turned to face her. He had hoped to avoid seeing her alone like this.

"You can't go off this way," she said, her voice a little breathless. "At least spend the night. Your room's all ready for you—I saw to it myself."

She moved close to him, so close that he could smell the delicate perfume she wore. There was no mistaking the look she gave him or the inflections of her voice. Another clandestine meeting, this time in his room, on the same floor as the room she shared with Reed. The momentary desire that welled up in him turned to a kind of revulsion. What had happened between them that night must not be allowed to happen again. His anger against Reed was tempered with the old loyalty that had been a part of their growing-up years.

"I'm sorry, Samantha," he began.

"Sorry—is that all you can say? That night, after the ball—you wanted me then. You still want me, Clay, and I want you. Nothing else matters—"

"You're wrong," he said, his voice hard and remote. "Reed matters. And this house."

"The house?" It was plain that Samantha hadn't the slightest idea what he was talking about.

"Montrose stands for something to me. My grandfather created it out of a wilderness. My father made it thrive. And I—"

"You weren't thinking about Montrose or the Drummond honor that night in the summerhouse."

Clay took a step backward. It was as if he were looking at a shrill-voiced stranger.

"As I recall, you didn't try to fight me off," he heard himself saying. Then he turned his back on her and went down the path to the stables.

Samantha stood watching him go. But she could not let him go, not like this. She took a few steps after him, then stopped. Damn Clay Drummond. He'd taken his pleasure, and now he could talk of her duty to Reed, of Montrose and the honor of the family. He could shame her by making it seem that she had thrown herself at him. For one brief moment, she was forced into the realization that there was some truth in his words. She had given herself to him willingly, freely. She pushed the thought away, unable to cope with it.

He'd be coming back, and then everything would be different between them. She would make him plead for her favors, humble himself before she gave in. They would run away together. It didn't matter where. Clay belonged to her now more than ever.

Because she was carrying his child.

For a while, she had been in doubt, but these past few weeks she had been certain. And as she stood staring out at the river below the bluffs, at the shore line beyond, bathed in the golden light of late afternoon, all her other emotions gave way to the one overwhelming feeling of fear. She tried to push away reality, as she so often did, but it was useless.

Clay was going back to his railroad, and she would be left here at Montrose. It would not be long before Reed would have to know the truth. And she realized, with a start, that she was afraid of her husband. Reed might love her, he might give in to her over most things, but he was a Drummond. He would not accept the fact that she had betrayed him with Clay, that she was going to bear Clay's baby.

He would seek Clay and challenge him; she was sure of it. And one of them would die. If it were Reed . . . But she had no way of knowing that it would be Reed. Her husband had been an officer in the Confederate army; he was as expert with a pistol as Clay. And the scandal that would follow. She could not face that kind of scandal. She went cold at the thought. Few would blame Clay, but she would stand condemned in the eyes of her neighbors, people she had known all her life.

If she could stop Clay before he left Montrose, tell him about the baby, plead with him to run away with her . . . Hadn't Jeff Shepley said something about the need for ex-Confederate officers in the Mexican army?

Then sanity returned. Clay had set his mind on building a railroad, and nothing, no one, would turn him aside; she knew him well enough to be sure of that. There had to be another way.

She thought of Reed lying upstairs in a drunken stupor. How long had it been since she had shared her bed with him? At least six months. And he wanted her. He had never stopped wanting her. It wouldn't be difficult for her to get him into her bed tonight, when he had sobered up. She would play the dutiful wife. She would be beside him when he awoke, her hair loose about her shoulders, her body warm against his. She shrank from the thought. But there was no other way. . . .

Chapter Seven

MEGAN RAISED her eyes from the ledger on the desk before her when she heard a man's footsteps coming up the outside staircase to the warehouse office. Oh, surely, she thought, it could not be Gavin O'Donnell coming back again. Gavin, unwilling to take no for an answer to his proposal.

Then her heart lifted, and the weariness she had been feeling disappeared; although it was late, after ten, she felt fresh and renewed, a warm current of excitement moving through her, for it was Clay Drummond who stood on the threshold.

"Megan. I didn't expect to find you still here at this hour. And no one downstairs in the warehouse. Surely it isn't safe."

"I wanted to finish checking this list of orders to your suppliers," Megan said, trying to keep her voice impersonal, businesslike, in spite of her inner turmoil. Looking up at Clay, she felt anything but businesslike.

In the wavering light of the oil lamp overhead, she could see that Clay had lost weight, although he was as fit looking as ever; his face was thinner, the deeply tanned skin drawn tightly over his high, jutting cheekbones and prominent jaw line.

"Gavin said you would be coming to the warehouse," she began.

"He's been here already?"

"Oh, yes," Megan said. "He must be on his way to New Orleans by now, though."

"And did he—" Clay broke off, and Megan thought that he looked a little uneasy.

"Did he what?" she asked.

"No matter," Clay said briskly. "I'm here about the shipment of rails from Farley and Sons up in Pennsylvania. They were supposed to have arrived two weeks ago."

Megan ran her finger down the page of the ledger.

"Oh, yes," she said. "I've written to them twice—I know how important the rail shipment is. They keep promising to deliver, but—" Her eyes were anxious. "Clay, you won't have to stop work on the railroad spur because of the late shipment, will you?"

"Not yet. But I can't wait much longer. We can't delay because of a late shipment of rails—or anything else."

"I have the names of three other manufacturers," Megan said. "Uncle Jim gave them to me. If you wish, I'll write at once, tonight, and inquire about prices and shipping schedules. There's a boat that will be stopping here tomorrow afternoon before going on up river. I can have the letters ready and take them down to the landing myself."

Clay smiled down at her. "I shouldn't think you'd be asking for extra work," he said, glancing at the stack of ledgers, the bills of lading pushed down on a metal spike in one corner of the big oak desk, the compartments stuffed with additional papers.

"I don't mind," Megan told him quickly. "I like my work here, and besides..."

She saw no need to tell him about the uproar in the Rafferty cottage across the alley a few hours before when Belle had questioned Megan and had needled her into admitting that Gavin had gone to the warehouse to propose. Megan flinched, remembering the fury in her cousin's voice. Finally, Belle had collapsed in a fit of angry weeping. "He didn't even come to see me at all," Belle had sobbed. "Oh, I wish ye'd stayed over in County Cork—I do—"

Even Aunt Kathleen had given Megan a grim, disapproving look, and Megan had understood: she was only a niece, after all, but Belle was Kathleen's own daughter.

Yes, the warehouse office had served as a refuge tonight. Even now, Megan caught the smell of the coffee she had put up to boil on the small iron stove.

Rising, she poured a cup for herself and one for Clay, then led the way to the sofa in the corner, a once-fine piece made of rosewood and upholstered in velvet, now shabby. Uncle Jim had bought it, along with the desk, from an impoverished planter up river.

"Sit down," she urged, and Clay settled himself on the sofa. He made no objection when she added a stiff shot of her uncle's whiskey to his cup.

"You really like working in the warehouse?" he asked. "I'd have thought you'd have preferred the general store. Selling frippery to ladies."

"We don't get many ladies down here," Megan said. "Most of my customers at the store were girls from the gambling houses and the—"

She did not have to say anymore, for Clay surely must have understood what she meant.

Tactfully, he changed the subject. "We'll have to get a new supplier for the rails," he said. "And we'll be needing extra salt right away."

"I wrote up an order for the salt already—Gavin's taking it to New Orleans." Her eyes were troubled as they rested on Clay. "Gavin said you've been working in the worst stretch of swamp with the crew. You shouldn't have done that."

"Why not?"

She sought for the right words. "You shouldn't be working with your hands, driving spikes and laying rails. You're a gentleman. Like—like Lord Trevanion back in Kilcurran."

"And did his lordship lead a life of complete idleness?"

"He and his guests went out hunting. And trout fishing. And sometimes he went around with Mr. O'Dowd—the estate manager—to make sure that the fields were being worked properly. But he didn't mend the roofs of the tenants' cottages himself. Or drive the pigs to market."

Clay gave a short, mirthless laugh. "Maybe he didn't have to. But the war's changed everything for us here in the South. Although many of my neighbors have not yet learned to accept the changes—even my own brother."

He fell silent and sipped his coffee.

"But you—you've already learned to accept them," Megan said.

Clay's blue eyes were hard and remote. "Yes, I learned." He set down his cup. "Maybe I learned too well," he added.

Megan looked at him in bewilderment. She sensed the anger, the bitterness in him, and something more, something she could not name.

"Reed was in the war, too," she began a little timidly. "But he wants life to go on exactly as it was before. Those things he said to Senator Aldrich at the ball about not wanting factories and mills in the South—or new railroad lines, either."

"Reed never got any farther north than Vicksburg," Clay said. "I had the privilege of seeing the North firsthand."

"As a prisoner of war?" He nodded, and there was a bleak, withdrawn look on his face that stirred her, that made her want to reach out to comfort him. "That must have been terrible for you," she said.

"Johnson's Island wasn't too bad at first except for the climate. We Southerners aren't used to the winters up there, and the island was out in Lake Erie. But our treatment was fairly decent—until the end of '73."

"What happened then?"

"The Yankee guards started hearing about one of our Confederate camps, a place in Georgia. Andersonville. Reports of how Yankees were being brutalized down there. I suppose it was natural for some of our guards to seek revenge. And then, too—" He broke off for a moment, his eyes haunted. "There are men who take a twisted pleasure in inflicting suffering."

"I know," Megan said.

"You—how could you know?"

"There was a British garrison near Kilcurran," Megan said. "Some of the troopers stationed there—"

"Megan, I didn't know. Forgive me—such things are better forgotten."

"Are they? I can't forget how my brother, Terence, and some of the others from the village were killed in a raid on the garrison. I'll never forget. Before he died in our cottage, he told me to leave Kilcurran. He said that if the British picked me up for questioning, they'd not spare me because I'm a woman...."

Clay put his hand over hers. "You might understand, then. One of the men who'd been under my command was mistreated by a guard. I complained to the commandant. The guard was reprimanded, but I was singled out after that. I tried to escape twice. Each time, I was brought back, beaten, and thrown into solitary confinement. But the third time I made it."

"You were reported killed while trying to escape—"

Megan remembered the conversation she had overheard between Violet Shepley and Winona Hunter.

"I was wounded, but I managed to escape all the same. There was a boat that took our dead to the mainland for burial— I hid myself among the bodies. The Yankees didn't bother to examine their—cargo—too closely. So many of the dead had been victims of typhoid, smallpox—"

Megan felt her throat tighten painfully, and a new emotion stirred to life within her. Until now, she had seen Clay as poised, invulnerable. Now, with her quick sympathy, she saw him ragged, bleeding, lying among the bodies of his dead comrades.

His hand still rested on hers, and her fingers closed around it. He seemed unaware of the gesture.

"After we landed at Sandusky, the Yankee guards went off to get drunk before tackling the job of digging a trench for a mass grave. I managed to get away. I kept going until I stumbled into a railroad camp a little way from Sandusky. I must have been out of my head when the foreman of the crew found me and carried me to the bunkhouse. He didn't ask questions. He was short of able-bodied men to work on the railroad."

"You weren't able-bodied," Megan pointed out.

"He dug the bullet out and cauterized the wound with a white-hot bolt from one of the supply wagons. I came around all right, and he gave me work with his crew."

Megan nodded, understanding now why Clay was able to work along with her uncle's men. "It wasn't as bad as Johnson's Island," she said quietly.

"It was a lot better. But I was building a railroad for the Yankees—" She saw the anger in his face, anger against himself.

"You did what you had to do," Megan said. "You survived. You came home."

"Yes, I came home. Maybe it would have been better if I hadn't—"

"You don't believe that," Megan cried. "You mustn't believe that. You're here now. You're doing what you wanted to do. Oh, you'll finish the railroad spur on time. I know you will. And that will be only the beginning because you'll go on. You'll build a railroad through the South, into Louisiana and Texas. You'll give the people down here the trains they need, just as you said you would—"

"Megan," he said, and she knew that she had brought him back from the gray fog of the past, of bitter memories and regrets. She felt a swift surge of triumphant tenderness and pride that she had been able to do this for the man she loved. For she did love him; she knew that now beyond any doubt.

He moved closer, and she felt the hard length of his lean body pressing against hers, felt the swift tensing of the muscles in his chest and arms as he drew her against him.

He was forcing her down against the worn, dusty velvet of the sofa, and now a new emotion stirred within her. She felt the beginning of fear.

They were alone here in the warehouse, and for the first time she realized that, for Clay, words would not be enough; not tonight when he had shared his feelings with her, when she had reached out to him in swift understanding.

There was a hunger in him, a kind of violence, that part of a man's nature that she had never dealt with before.

And in spite of her lack of experience, she knew instinctively that his hunger could only be released, satisfied, in the act of love. Kisses, caresses would not be enough—not now. Sensing her resistance, he said softly, hoarsely, "Megan, I need you." His voice was muffled, for his mouth was pressed against her hair. His hands moved over her body, and she felt their hard, commanding strength.

She cried out wordlessly, and he lifted himself from her, one hand still cupping the swell of her breast.

"What's wrong?" His eyes searched hers. "Is it because of Gavin—"

"Gavin?"

"He said—did he get you to promise you'd marry him?"

"No! Oh, Clay, no. I could never marry Gavin O'Donnell."

"Why not?"

"Because I don't love him. I could never love him, because I—"

She did not go on, and she tried to look away, for she was sure that if her eyes met Clay's, she would never be able to conceal her feelings for him. But he caught her chin in a strong grip, forcing her head back, searching her face, and his voice was harsh with the urgency of his need.

"I want you, Megan. Here. Now. If you don't feel the same way, tell me so. If you want me to leave, to go back to the railroad site, say so. Now, Megan."

The command in his tone frightened her even while it stirred her, and although she tried to speak the words that would send him away, she could make no sound. All her dreams of remaining aloof and controlled until he asked her to marry him, all her fantasies of being mistress of Montrose, of presiding in dignity and pride over the lofty, white-pillared house, the broad acres, all those pictures she had created in her mind were vague and far away now, curiously unimportant. For Clay was here in her arms, and she could give him what he needed: she could feed the hunger and blot out the memories that tormented him.

She made no answer, and he drew her close again.

Then, in the flickering light of the oil lamp overhead, he was stripping off her dress, her undergarments. He released her and began to unbutton his shirt, and she closed her eyes quickly, turning her face away so that the velvet back of the sofa was warm against her face. A pulse in her throat began to hammer, and she felt the warm tide of her blood coursing through her. All of her senses were more alive than they had ever been before. She listened to Clay as he moved about briefly. Then she started as she felt the heat of his naked body molded against the length of hers.

His work-hardened hands were moving with swift assurance over her shrinking flesh, and she stiffened in instinctive resistance, fearing what lay ahead. But his voice was soft, caressing, reassuring, and he said, "Megan—love. It's all right. You're not afraid of me, surely?"

"Not you—it's only that—I've never—"

"I know that," he said quietly. "I know, love."

He held her against him, his body unmoving, and she knew that he was giving her time to get used to this new and frightening sensation, leashing his own passion. He slid the pins from her thick, tawny-gold hair and drew the soft, waving cascade down around her shoulders.

Then his lips touched her face lightly, and when she did not resist, they began to trace a fiery trail down the soft skin of her throat, her shoulder, the curve of her breast. He touched one nipple with his tongue, and she caught her breath, feeling the shock, half pleasurable, half frightening. He drew the nipple into his mouth and she felt waves of sensation moving downward until every nerve in her body began to tingle.

She did not know how to deal with these strange new sensations, and she put a hand on his chest as if to delay him. When she touched the skin of his shoulder, she felt the hard, raised scar. Until now, she had not looked at his body, and when she did so, she saw the dark, jagged mark against the tan of his skin, the brand mark left by the white-hot bolt with which the foreman, up there in Ohio, had cauterized the bullet wound Clay had suffered during his escape from the prison camp.

In that instant, it was as if she shared the pain he must have felt, as if that pain were a part of her. She forgot her fears as she moved to touch her lips to the scar. She heard Clay's swift intake of breath, and she drew back, but he was saying, "Don't stop now, love."

Her shyness slipped away, and she trailed kisses down the hardness of his chest. Her arms encircled him, her hands caressing the muscles of his broad back, lightly, hesitantly, at first, then with a growing assurance. For she knew that the closeness between them made modesty false and meaningless.

She longed for even greater closeness, although she still feared it. But his body spoke to hers in an ancient, primitive language, as simple and strong as the earth, the rain, the fire, and her own flesh answered.

He parted her thighs, and his fingers moved upward, stroking her softness until she cried out in mingled fear and pleasure. But she lay still, making no attempt to draw back.

It was only when he shifted and moved to kneel above her, when she felt the first quick, hard thrust, that she cried out in reproach against the harsh, burning pain of his entry. He remained still for a timeless moment, whispering reassurances, soothing her, giving her time to accept their joining.

Then she felt him moving inside her with long, slow thrusts. A new sensation sprang to life deep within her. She clutched at him, her fingers pressing into his back, drawing him closer, deeper, accepting the hurt until slowly it lessened, giving way to a tremulous hunger that grew and grew until it filled her. Her hips lifted, and she was matching her rhythm to his. Her whole body arched upward, demanding release and then finding it in the shattering, explosive moment of fulfillment.

She awoke to see the first gray light of dawn at the window, and she felt Clay moving away from her. She made a small, wordless sound of protest, and he raised himself on one arm to look down at her. Then he brushed her hair back from her face and kissed her lightly.

"Are you all right, love?" he asked, and when she smiled up at him, he raised himself from the sofa and began to dress.

"Where are you going?" she asked a little uneasily.

"Back to the railroad site, of course," he said, and she could sense him moving away, his mind already on the work that lay ahead. She wanted to call him back, but she knew that she must not cling to him. She had given herself willingly, and he had made her no promises about the future.

He accompanied her out of the office and back to her uncle's cottage across the alley, and when they stood on the porch in the growing light of dawn, she could not help asking, "Will you be coming back to Natchez soon?"

His blue eyes were remote. "I don't think so. There's still so much to be done. As soon as I get that new shipment of rails, the crew can start moving ahead full speed again."

She hesitated, then forced herself to smile as she said, "I'll write those letters and get them on the boat this afternoon."

He smiled down at her then. "I know I can count on you." But although his voice was warm, there was no longer any passion in it. She longed for him to hold her, to kiss her, to reassure her that their lovemaking had meant as much to him as it had to her. But her pride would not permit her to ask for such reassurance, and so, instead, she kept her voice even, putting a light hand on his arm, saying, "Don't drive yourself too hard, Clay. You'll have your railroad, and on time."

"Megan," he said, looking down at her. He brushed a lock of hair back from her face. "I've never known a girl like you. I only wish—" Then his lips covered hers in a long, searching kiss, filled with tenderness and passion, a kiss that caused her spirits to rise, that made their parting bearable for her. Now she could watch him cross the alley, mount his horse, and ride off into the early-morning river mist. Slowly, lost in a pleasant trance, she entered the cottage and started down the narrow hall to her room.

She needed to be alone, to relive each moment of the night before, to try to understand the completeness of the change in her. For she was changed; she was a woman now, and nothing would ever be the same for her. She touched her fingers to her lips, where Clay had kissed her, and as she walked, she could feel the slight trace of pain deep within her, reminding her of that moment when Clay's body had joined with hers.

"And where have you been, my girl?"

Aunt Kathleen's voice startled Megan even as the older woman's short, stocky body, encased in a faded cotton wrapper, blocked her way. Whether Uncle Jim was here or out at the railroad site, her aunt kept to her habit of rising at dawn to light the big coal stove and prepare the oatmeal, a thick, coarse mixture that took a full two hours to cook.

"I was working in the warehouse office—" Megan began. "I fell asleep and—"

"None of that, Megan." Her aunt's pale-green eyes raked over her, and she felt as though she were being stripped naked. She realized that she was wearing the same cotton dress she had had on when she had gone to the office the previous night, and her hand went to the bodice to find that two of the buttons had been ripped off in the violence of Clay's first embrace, before he had forced himself to be patient, gentle. . . . Her hair was loose about her shoulders, not pinned up in her customary neat chignon. But more than this, she was sure that her face had changed, that her eyes, her mouth, were somehow different, that her secret was plain to her aunt.

"Ye were with a man. No, don't bother to deny it. I heard your voices outside. What man was it?" Her aunt's lips thinned; her eyes narrowed. "Was it Gavin O'Donnell? Did he come back t' see ye?"

"Gavin must be halfway to New Orleans by now," Megan said, "and I've told you—and Belle, too—that I care nothing for the man."

"Then maybe ye found yerself a stranger. A Yankee soldier, maybe. Plenty o' them out on the streets here lookin' for a bit o' pleasure."

"How can you even think such a thing?" Megan went taut with anger.

"What am I to think, then? Stayin' out all night. Comin' in lookin' like an alley cat that's got what she needed. I'll not have ye carryin' on that way while ye're livin' under my roof. Goin' out after strange men—"

"He wasn't a stranger!" The words came out before Megan could stop them. "Clay Drummond came to the office to check on a shipment of rails—"

To her surprise, Megan saw the anger fade from her aunt's flushed face. "Clay Drummond, was it," Kathleen said slowly. A faint smile touched the corners of her lips. "Well, now . . ."

"Oh, Aunt Kathleen, I know that I shouldn't have—but I love him, and he loves me."

"He told ye that?"

"Why he—" He had spoken to her tenderly, had called her "love," but had he said that he loved her? Had he? Oh, but he must love her. He had been so gentle with her, so patient, as a man would be with his bride on their wedding night.

"Clay's a fine man, a real gentleman," Kathleen was saying. "And you'll be a credit to him. You'll make him a good wife, Megan."

"Wife?"

"He did say he'd marry ye, didn't he?"

"We didn't speak of marriage. Clay has to finish this stretch of railroad. It's important to him."

"And so it should be," Kathleen said. "But he has a duty to you, and he must be made to see that." She patted Megan's arm. "Ah, but ye've been without a mother all these years. No one t' raise ye proper." She smiled. "No matter. I'll speak t' Clay Drummond. And I'll not be losin' any time about it."

"Oh, no—you mustn't do that!"

"Mustn't?" Kathleen looked hurt. "I'm yer aunt—and yer dear mother, rest her soul, would want me t' see that ye were safely married after what's happened."

Megan felt a mounting confusion, but she managed to speak calmly, evenly. "This concerns no one but Clay and me. When the time comes—"

"Don't be foolish. Suppose ye find yerself in the family way. What then?"

For a moment, the full meaning did not dawn on Megan, and when it did, she felt stunned. Her aunt, taking advantage of her shock, said, "You don't want him t' think ye're just another cheap trollop—we have plenty of those down here. Oh, I've no doubt he'd give ye money, but that's not what ye want, is it?"

Megan put out a hand to steady herself against the frame of the kitchen door. "I don't know—I never thought—"

"No, ye didn't. And neither did he, I suppose. Now don't look so scared, Megan. Back in Ireland, when these things happened, the girl's family saw to it that she was treated right and proper. Better if ye'd waited fer the weddin', but there now, I was young once myself, and yer Uncle Jim was a hot-blooded young man, that he was. A man needs a bit of a push when it comes t' marryin'—don't know what's good for him. Ye'll make Clay Drummond a fine wife."

"I won't force him—"

"Now who said anythin' about forcin'? He'll be lucky t' get ye, and that's the truth. Ye're prettier than any one o' them plantation ladies up there on the bluff—and ye've got sweet, ladylike ways. Ye'll be a help t' him in his work, too. What more could a man ask?"

It all sounded so right, so sensible, the way her aunt put it, and yet— Megan remembered that back in Kilcurran, all marriages were arranged by the parents of the bride and groom. And she would make Clay a good wife. She would bear him fine sons and help him in his work. She would be a comfort to him, a source of strength.

She thought briefly of his family, of the hostility they would probably feel toward her. But she could win Jessica over; she was sure of that. As for the others, surely they would see that she was the right wife for Clay. Not immediately, perhaps, but after a while. . . .

"Now ye go off to yer room and let me take care of everything. Clay Drummond's a decent, honorable man, like his father was. He'll want t' do what's right. And ye'll thank me for my help when ye're married and mistress of Montrose. . . ."

Chapter Eight

$\approx$

IN THE humid dimness of the boxcar that served as both his living quarters and office, Clay Drummond, his sweat-soaked shirt open to the waist, slapped at a mosquito, swore, then looked up, annoyed at being interrupted. His makeshift desk was piled with papers and surveyors' charts, and his eyes felt gritty from lack of sleep.

"Ted—what do you want?"

The boy who helped the cook and carried water to the work crews said, "There's a—a lady t' see ye, sir."

For a moment, Clay did not recognize Kathleen Rafferty, for he had met her only once, briefly, when he had come to take Megan to the ball. Now her stout figure was impressively encased in black bombazine trimmed with white braiding; a black bonnet framed her round, flushed face.

"Mrs. Rafferty. What the— Why have you come out here?"

The only other females at end-of-track were four somewhat bedraggled prostitutes who followed the railroad and who had been installed in a tent by their enterprising madam.

"If you've come to see your husband, he's a few miles from here," Clay began. "He and his crew—"

"It ain't Jim I've come to see," Kathleen Rafferty said, and Clay heard something in her tone that made him immediately alert to trouble. He buttoned his shirt, then drew out a chair for her. There were only two in the boxcar. But she remained standing.

"This ain't a social call, Mr. Drummond. I came here out of my sense of duty, to do what's right and proper, Megan bein' my niece, the daughter of Jim's brother, Connor, God rest his soul."

"Mrs. Rafferty, I hardly see—"

"Megan's a good girl, she is," Kathleen Rafferty went on, "but a bit flighty in her ideas, and yer askin' her t' Montrose t' that ball, well, it was only natural she'd think that yer intentions were serious since ye had her meet yer family and neighbors."

Clay understood now. Since returning to camp, he had been far too absorbed in work to give much thought to Megan during the days. But at night, when he lay in his bunk in the corner of the boxcar, he felt stirred, remembering the way her slender body had felt, molded against his, the way she had reached out for him, clung to him, afraid yet willing; he remembered the sweetness of her and the warmth. Megan was no trollop even though she lived in Natchez-under, but she was not the sort of young lady with whom he had danced and flirted and gone riding in those days before the war—no carefully raised plantation owner's daughter trained to guard her virtue until the marriage vows had been spoken. What kind of a girl was Megan Rafferty? Where did she fit into his life, his plans for the future?

He needed time to think, to try to understand what had happened between them and what it would mean to both of them. But here was Kathleen Rafferty, her small, plump features set and implacable.

"Mrs. Rafferty, I understand your concern for your niece. But you must see that this is not the time nor place for a discussion about—about my relationship with Megan. I have a railroad spur to complete, and we are behind schedule. Every moment counts."

"Ye had time enough fer Megan the other night in the warehouse. Oh, yes, I know all about it. No use tryin' t' deny it—"

"I have no intention of denying—anything." Clay felt a mounting anger. "When the railroad is finished, when I return to Natchez, I'll speak to Megan."

"Ye'll do more than speak t' her—ye'll marry the child. That's all she is, a poor, innocent child. And there was no one before ye, I can tell ye that. Ye were the first—"

"Keep your voice down," Clay said. "There's no need to let the whole camp hear what you have to say. Megan and I will deal with this when I return."

"'Tis me ye'll be dealin' with, and now," Kathleen said. Clay heard the hard, unshakable certainty in her voice, and he caught the steady look in her faded green eyes. This was no hysterical fluttering female, but a force to be reckoned with. All the same, he was damned if he would be ordered about by her.

"If you don't wish to see your husband, I think you should start back for Natchez," he said. "It's far from healthy down here—several of my crew are laid low with malaria. I can spare a man to drive you back."

"One o' Jim's teamsters drove me out here in a wagon, and he'll get me back. After we've settled our business."

"I have no business with you. As I've already told you—"

Clay looked past Kathleen and caught sight of young Ted, who hesitated in the doorway of the boxcar.

"Beggin' your pardon, Mr. Drummond, but we're runnin' awful low on water, and ye said that the men who are in the fever shed were to have all they needed, but Pete, he says he can't cook supper for the crew without water, and he—"

"I'll talk to him. Right now."

The boy nodded and hurried off. "Look here, Mrs. Rafferty," Clay said, "you see how things are. When I come back to Natchez, I'll have a talk with Megan—"

"Ye'll have yer talk with me—and ye'll not leave here until ye do."

Clay's face flushed, and he wanted nothing more than to take this stout old harridan by the arm and march her back to the wagon and send her on her way. But there was something in her eyes that held him back.

"Ye'll come t' Natchez by the end of the week, and ye'll ask Megan t' marry ye—or there'll be no railroad at all."

Clay began to rise from his chair.

"Stay where ye are," she said. And Clay sat back, for he had glimpsed on her face the same look he had often seen across a poker table. Kathleen held a winning hand—or thought she did. She smiled now. "We'll finish our little talk," she said. "Then I'll be on my way."

In the small, stuffy parlor of the Rafferty cottage, Clay took Megan's hand in his and slid the betrothal ring on her finger, and it was only when she looked at the ring that the events of the past few minutes became real. "This belonged to my mother," Clay said. His voice was curiously empty of feeling, Megan thought, and he did not even try to hold her hand after he had placed the small circlet of pearls on her finger.

"It's beautiful," Megan began. But Clay silenced her, his eyes cold.

"I'm glad you find it satisfactory."

Megan stared up at him. She could not have been more bewildered if he had struck her. Could this be the same Clay who had held her in his arms that night in the warehouse office, who had made love to her with tenderness and passion? Where was the closeness she had felt that night, a closeness not only of the body but of the spirit?

She studied his face, seeking reassurance, but his eyes did not meet hers. She waited, her body aching for his embrace, but he did not draw her to him.

Confused, hurt, she tried to find some words to fill the lengthening silence between them. Hearing the clink of china and cutlery from the dining room across the hall, she said, "Aunt Kathleen has prepared a fine dinner. After you've eaten and rested awhile, perhaps we might go out for a drive along the bluffs."

"I can't stay for dinner," Clay said. "I'm sorry. I thought you understood. I have to get back to end-of-track as quickly as possible."

"Oh, but surely tonight you can spare the time to—"

"I'll be back when the railroad spur is finished. That will be before the end of the year. We'll be married on New Year's Day."

"Oh, Clay, I—"

"Is there a problem?" he asked.

"I'll have to speak to Father Donovan. And the children— our children—"

"You want them raised in the Catholic faith?" Clay shrugged. "You can bring them up according to any religion you choose— it's of no concern to me."

Megan was relieved but confused. "Surely, you must care. Your own family—"

"My father was a Methodist," he said. "As for me, I haven't given the matter much thought for years now." He looked at her sharply. "You have no reason to believe that you're pregnant already, do you?"

For a moment, the icy reserve that she had felt in him changed, and she heard the concern in his voice. That night in the warehouse office, she had not given any thought to the possibility that she might become pregnant; Clay had reached out to her in his need, and she had given herself without fear of the consequences. "Answer me, Megan," he demanded.

"No—I'm sure I'm not." She might be going to marry Clay Drummond, but she could not possibly bring herself to tell him plainly why she was sure that she was not carrying his child as a result of that night they had spent together. Evidently, he understood.

"So you didn't even have that for an excuse," he said softly. He turned and started for the door.

She was completely confused now and afraid. She put a hand on his arm. "Clay, don't go yet."

"Is there something more?"

"Why, I— Oh, Clay, I love you—" She clung to him. "Kiss me," she pleaded, knowing how shameless she sounded but driven by her need for reassurance. "I won't see you again for months—"

She looked up at him, baffled by his coldness, and saw that his blue eyes under their straight, heavy, dark brows were remote, that his face was taut, without a trace of tenderness, his mouth set in a hard, thin line. Bending, he touched his lips to hers, his hands resting lightly on her shoulders. Then he drew away, turned, and left the parlor, while she stood alone, filled with misgivings, and listened to his footsteps going down the hall. A moment later, she heard the front door closing, and she hurried to the window to see him mount his horse and ride off without a backward glance.

She looked down then at the circlet of pearls on her finger and told herself firmly that she was being foolish. He had asked her to marry him, had given her his mother's ring. Later, when the railroad spur was finished, when he had been able to pay back the loan on Montrose, there would be time for tenderness. When they were lying side by side in one of the high-ceilinged bedrooms at Montrose, he would once again show her that he loved her.

"Oh, Megan, ain't it grand? You and me, both gettin' married. And only a week apart."

Ever since Christmas, when Gavin O'Donnell had come to Natchez-under and had proposed to Belle, her attitude toward Megan had changed completely; she forgot her hostility, her resentment. And–why not, Megan thought? Gavin, in his matter-of-fact way, had transferred his affections back to Belle once he had learned of Megan's engagement to Clay Drummond.

"Of course, Gavin and me won't be havin' a grand reception like you and Clay. But pa's promised us a fine spread right here in the house. All the teamsters and the men from the railroad crew." Even as she spoke, Belle, seated in the parlor, was stitching away at a length of muslin that was to be a nightdress. Belle looked up. Her eyes narrowed with curiosity. Megan, who was threading a length of blue-satin ribbon through the lace that edged the camisole she had just finished making, felt her fingers become unsteady.

"Sure now ye don't act like a bride-to-be. Haven't changed yer mind about Clay Drummond, have ye?"

"Certainly not," Megan said quickly. She rose, laying the camisole aside. "I need more ribbon," she told Belle, and hurried out of the parlor and down the hall to her room.

Once she had closed the door behind her, she went to the shelf and automatically took down the chipped Waterford goblet. Her hand closed lightly around the surface, and she held it as she would have held a talisman.

She called up her mother's words and told herself that they had proved true. For her, there would be something better. In only a few days, her future would begin, with Clay Drummond as her husband and Montrose as her home.

Chapter Nine

IN THE large bedroom in the west wing of Montrose, overlooking the gardens, Megan prepared for bed, relieved that the wedding supper was over but dreading the moment when she would be alone with Clay for the first time, as his wife. In spite of the fire in the marble fireplace, she shivered. Her thin cambric nightdress, one of the half a dozen she had sewn and embroidered, was too thin for this damp, chilly night: the first night of the new year, 1866.

Megan's fears had been growing since early that day when she and Clay, accompanied by Uncle Jim and Aunt Kathleen, had left the small church in Natchez under heavy, low-lying clouds and had entered the Drummond family carriage that was to take them to Montrose. They had gone only a short distance from the city when a fine rain had begun falling. It grew heavier in the course of the ride, pelting the carriage windows.

Uncle Jim had said that he would be pleased to hold the reception in his own home, as he had done for Belle and Gavin when they had been married only a week ago, but Clay had refused quickly, explaining that his brother's wife, Samantha, was getting close to her time and that it would be unwise for her to attempt the journey from Montrose down to Natchez-under in a jouncing carriage over the war-devastated roads.

The real reason for Clay's refusal of her uncle's offer, Megan knew, was that he would not have wanted Lianne or Jessica to attend any sort of social gathering in Natchez-under; better to invite Jim and Kathleen to Montrose even though they would be out of place there.

The wedding supper, in the large, stately dining room, had been an uneasy affair, however, with Clay a cold-eyed stranger who went through the motions of acting the bridegroom without showing one trace of affection to Megan. Instead, he had turned his attention to the other men present—Reed, Jeff Shepley, and Jim Rafferty—and had drawn them into a discussion about the Natchez–Fort Worth Line, which, thus far, existed only on the maps made by the young surveyor Clay had hired a few days before. Even now, Gavin, accompanied by Belle, was in New York City, where he had been sent by Clay to arrange with a labor contractor, a distant O'Donnell cousin, to bring over a boatload of Irish laborers for the new railroad line.

"You'd do better to hire blacks," said Jeff Shepley, a short, barrel-chested man. "Plenty of those black bas— plenty of them running around loose, not knowing how to take care of themselves, now they've got their freedom."

Reed shrugged slightly. "That's the whole trouble, Jeff. They have got their freedom. And they have no more wish to work than a bunch of children let out of school. And the Freedmen's Bureau keeps reminding them that they don't have to work for us any longer."

Jeff's laugh was short and harsh, like the bark of a dog. "The blacks can be kept in line, and they will be. Takes a strong hand to do it, that's all. And as for those damned scoundrels at the Freedmen's Bureau—your pardon, ladies—why we'll take care of them soon enough. Teach them a lesson they'll never forget and send them running back up North with their tails between their legs—those that're still able to run."

"Don't be too sure," Clay interrupted. He looked at his former neighbor, now overseer at Montrose, with barely concealed contempt. "The Yankees will be down here for a long time. The Freedmen's Bureau, the Army of Occupation. The Radical Republicans will see to that."

"You ought to know," Reed said, his face taut with anger. "They're your friends."

"Reed, please—" Samantha began.

Megan braced herself, expecting Clay to lash out at Reed, but instead he only smiled faintly. "Tell me, Reed, have you heard from your mother lately? Has she written to say how much she enjoys Boston society?"

Reed flinched. His mother was Abigail Taggart now. She had chosen the winning side, had kept Montrose supplied with all the comforts of life throughout the last years of the war, and had departed with the major for his home only a few months before. Megan braced herself. There must not be a family quarrel here at Montrose, not on the night of her wedding, of all times.

Samantha, still beautiful, in spite of her advanced state of pregnancy, in a loose, skillfully cut gown of rose-colored silk, went to Reed's side and put a restraining hand on his arm. But it was Jessica who spoke first. "I'm sure there are no cooks in Boston as good as our Rachel. Megan, my dear, isn't the wedding cake a masterpiece?"

"Oh yes—yes, indeed. It looks lovely," Megan replied quickly.

"Rachel's a treasure," Violet Shepley put in, looking at the white, three-tiered cake with its satin-smooth frosting and garlands of pale-pink sugar blossoms.

"I'm sure she had outdone herself this time," Jessica said. "Clay, don't keep us all waiting. It's time you and Megan cut the cake."

And Clay put his hand over Megan's to cut the first slice of cake. But his touch was impersonal, automatic, and when Megan smiled up at him, she saw no answering smile.

At least the threat of a clash between Clay and Reed had been warded off, Megan thought. And she was a little surprised when, after the champagne glasses had been raised in a toast, Reed had kissed her and said, "Welcome to Montrose, Megan." He sounded sincere enough, and Megan was grateful until a disturbing thought insinuated itself into her mind. Perhaps Reed would not have been so cordial under other circumstances.

Maybe he was seeing Megan, whatever her background, as a barrier between Clay and Samantha. Now that Clay had a bride of his own, perhaps Reed felt a sense of relief. An ugly thought but one not easily dismissed.

Was Clay still in love with Samantha, Megan had asked herself. But how could he be, now that Samantha was carrying Reed's child? She knew so little of Clay, of the years before the war when he and Samantha had been so often together.

And now, as she sat before her dressing table, a frivolous affair with an elaborate skirt of blue silk and creamy lace, and brushed her tawny hair down over her shoulders, she shivered. Soon she would be alone with Clay, who had been close to her only for those few brief hours months before in the warehouse office, who had changed into a stranger.

"Get hold of yourself, Megan," she told herself firmly. She was not a frightened virgin shrinking from her first joining with a man. Did Clay, perhaps, value her less highly because of that? But no, he was not a man to be bound by proprieties. He took what he wanted, and he had wanted her that night months before, had needed her in his arms to shut out the dark memories of Johnson's Island. Surely he would not now blame her for having answered his need.

Perhaps I should have gone out to see him at the railroad site, she thought. *Maybe then we would have been alone together again and he—*

But Aunt Kathleen had told her not to go, saying, "A pest hole, that swamp is, and plenty of strong men laid low every day with the fever. Sure, ye'd be out o' yer mind, goin' there. And ye'd be a worry and a burden to Clay, too."

She started slightly now as she heard the bedroom door open. Clay stepped inside, closed the door behind him, and came to stand behind her, his face reflected in the mirror over the dressing table. How handsome he looked, his black hair cropped short, his face tanned more deeply than ever by those months out at the railroad camps, his eyes a more intense blue by contrast. But there was no warmth in them. They were the eyes of a stranger.

"I'm sorry Rachel couldn't be spared to help you get ready for bed," he said. "As soon as I'm able to afford it, you'll have your own personal maid, of course. In the meantime, I'll speak to Rachel about Ludamae. She's only fourteen and untrained—

She's been helping in the kitchen, but perhaps you'll be able to make do with her until—"

"I'm perfectly able to make do with no maid at all," Megan said. "There's no need to inconvenience Rachel—"

"You're a Drummond now," Clay said. "As soon as the Natchez–Fort Worth Line has been organized and I'm drawing cash regularly, you'll have a well-trained personal maid. You'll have your own carriage and everything else suitable to your position. You can count on that."

Megan rose from the bench before the dressing table, bewildered, afraid. "Clay, what is it? You make our marriage sound like—like some sort of business arrangement."

"Isn't it?"

Clay was taking off his coat, folding it across the back of a chair, unfastening his cravat. His movements were controlled, deliberate, but she could sense the anger, the violence beneath the surface. "I don't know what you mean."

He turned away from her then and walked over to the fireplace. "The rain always makes the rooms damp this time of year," he said. Although he spoke quietly, her fear grew, for she could see the tensing of his heavy shoulders beneath the white-linen shirt; he thrust the poker into the flickering flames as if striking out at an enemy.

Megan went to him and grasped his arm. "Look at me, Clay," she demanded. "What's wrong? Are you—sorry you married me?"

He freed himself with one impatient movement. Then he turned, and his eyes raked over her body. She was conscious of the flimsy cambric, of the way that the firelight revealed the swell of her breasts, the lines of her thighs. "Sorry?" He laughed softly. "What man would be sorry to have so beautiful a bride?"

"Clay, don't—"

"You have what you wanted," he went on, and once more she was frighteningly aware of the violence under the soft drawl. "You spent all those years trying to better yourself, to talk and act like a lady. And your efforts have paid off. You're out of Natchez-under. Away from the stables and the warehouses. You are a Drummond—and mistress of Montrose."

"I don't care about that," she said, and realized that she meant it. Without Clay's love, what did it matter where or how she lived? "I don't want all that unless—"

"Do go on," he said, and there was no mistaking the mockery in his face.

"I want you to love me, Clay. I want us to be the way we were that first time. I want—"

"Don't ask for the impossible," he said. "You blackmailed me into marrying you. With the help of your aunt. I have to admit you were clever. You hit on the one way to force me into this marriage. You knew what the railroad meant to me, and you used your knowledge to get what you wanted."

His words made no sense at all, but there was no mistaking the anger, the cruel contempt with which they were spoken. Her skin prickled with mounting fear.

"I've had my share of experience with the sporting ladies of Natchez-under." He started to unbutton his shirt. "Pretty, some of them. But not one who can be trusted. The same wide-eyed little thing who'll sweet talk a man and get him drunk will lead him out into the alley and watch him being beaten or stabbed, then robbed, by her fancy man."

Now Megan's fear began to give way to anger. "How can you— I'm not one of those—"

"No, you're not. And that's why you're here at Montrose tonight, Mrs. Drummond." He dropped his shirt on the chair, and Megan felt her breath catch in her throat at the sight of his half-naked body, the skin as deeply tanned as that of his face, the scar high on his shoulder.

"Oh, yes, you were clever, sending your aunt out to end-of-track to tell me that unless I came back and asked you to marry me at once, she'd have your uncle take his crew off the job. You had it all figured out, didn't you? You knew that they'd have gone at a word from Jim Rafferty."

Megan tried to answer, but she could not speak. Now, at last, she understood the reason for Clay's coldness even when he had proposed to her, for his behavior at the wedding and, afterward, at the reception.

"Those Irishmen respect me, but their first loyalty is to your uncle. He speaks their language; he's one of them."

Still Megan could make no sound. Her Aunt Kathleen had wanted to give Belle a clear field with Gavin O'Donnell. And perhaps she had not been wholly selfish according to her way of looking at the matter, for she was determined that her niece would make a good match, too. Maybe Aunt Kathleen had even honestly believed that it was Clay's duty to marry Megan, having taken her virginity. She had spoken to Megan of arranged marriages, reminding her that they had been the custom back in Ireland.

But Megan would never have permitted her aunt to threaten Clay with the loss of his railroad and of Montrose. If only she had guessed at Aunt Kathleen's plans, she would have moved heaven and earth to stop her.

She was angry with her aunt, but that anger was unimportant compared with the realization that Clay believed that she had put Kathleen up to the scheme. Clay could not possibly know her if he could believe that she would have been a party to such a sordid plan. That night in the warehouse office, she had felt so close to him not only in body but in spirit. Now she felt betrayed, outraged, and fury welled up in her.

The bedroom was so silent that she became aware of small sounds: the rain lashing against the tall French windows; the splitting of a log in the fireplace; the wind in the live oak trees in the garden outside.

"You thought I knew," she said, her voice shaking. "You thought I planned it all."

"Spare me your indignation." Clay spoke with forced lightness. "I have what I wanted. I've finished the railroad spur, and I'm about to organize my own railroad company. And the Drummonds can go on living here at Montrose."

"And that's all our marriage means to you?"

"You underestimate yourself," he said, his hand reaching out for her. His fingers moved across her shoulder and downward, to cup her breast. "You are a beautiful bride."

His hand tightened on her breast, his other arm went around her, and he pulled her against him, then kissed her, his lips hard. She made a sound of protest and tried to push him away.

Clay took his mouth from hers. "Get out," she cried, her voice shrill with the beginnings of hysteria. "Get out of this room—"

"Oh, no. You've got yourself a husband, Megan, with a husband's rights."

She raised her arm, her fingers instinctively curving to claw at him, but he caught her wrist with a cold violence that drew an unwilling gasp of pain. He twisted her arm behind her.

"I won't let you—not this way—"

But a moment later, he had slid an arm around her shoulders, the other under her knees, and he was carrying her to the bed. She writhed and twisted in his arms, every muscle straining against him, but then she was on the wide mattress, and he was pinning her down easily, stripping off the rest of his clothing. Now she felt the heat of his flesh as he turned her on her side, fitting the length of his body against hers.

Her anger drained away, and her eyes burned with tears. Her wedding night, the night she had dreamed of for so long, ruined now. Numb with despair, she turned her face away, steeling herself for the brutal invasion of her body. She closed her eyes, but she could not stop the tears that came from between her lids. A few moments passed before she realized that Clay was lying beside her, unmoving, making no attempt to force himself on her.

Slowly, she opened her eyes again and looked up at him. He had raised himself on one arm, and now he reached out to brush the tears from her cheek. He still believed that she had betrayed him, forced him into marriage; she was sure of it. And they both knew that she was powerless to keep him from taking revenge here and now.

Instead, his fingers stroked her cheek again, and she felt the change in his touch. She did not want to respond, for she still felt a lingering anger. But somehow his arms were around her, and she knew that this man, with his hard, commanding hands, his powerful body, his hunger for her, was no longer her enemy. He was the other part of herself.

"Megan," he said softly. "Oh, Megan—"

And now he was above her, and her eyes held his. His mouth explored the softness of her body in ways that were unknown to her, that should have shocked and outraged her. But she made no attempt to stop him, for he was leading her through her anger, her fear, to a place where such feelings had no meaning.

He spread her thighs, and she arched upward to his searching mouth, and her hands stroked his hair and his shoulders. When he moved away, it was only long enough for him to move himself up over her. Then he was entering her with a slow thrust, and her arms tightened around him, for she was caught up with him in a swirling, pulsating darkness, shot with sparks that came faster and faster until her whole being burst into white-hot flame.

She went on looking up at him even as he began to thrust more quickly, more urgently, even as her legs wrapped themselves around his body as she arched upward in an instinctive need to draw him closer, to merge with him completely not only in flesh but in spirit. Only in the instant of fulfillment did she let her eyes close at last, pressing her mouth against his shoulder so that her cry was muffled against the hard, raised scar.

When she awoke, the golden light was pouring in through the windows, and the air was fresh with the scent of rain-soaked earth. She turned to see that Clay was no longer beside her. Startled, she raised herself and realized that she had been awakened by the entrance of a small, dark-skinned girl in a starched calico dress covered by a spotless white apron, both too large for her.

The girl carried a tray with a coffeepot and a single cup and saucer. She managed to bob a curtsy. "I'se Ludamae," she said shyly. "Rachel, she say t' bring y' de coffee dis mawnin'."

"But where is—"

"Mistuh Clay? He downstairs with de others havin' breakfast. Went down der soon as he finish packin' his trunk."

"His trunk?"

Ludamae nodded. "One o' de boys fum de stable, he took de trunk down t' de landin'. Goin' to signal de *Delta Lady* t' make a stop here."

Megan went cold inside. Surely, after last night, Clay could not be leaving her without a word. "Please—get my wrapper," Megan said.

As Ludamae hurried to obey, Megan remembered with a sinking heart the circumstances under which Clay had promised her a personal maid. He had been bitter and resentful at what he believed she had done to trap him into marriage. But surely, after what had happened between them here in this bed, his feelings had changed.

Or perhaps it had been only his physical need that had possessed him. For a moment, Megan wanted to remain where

she was. Perhaps, facing Clay again, she would once more see
the coldness in his eyes, hear the scorn in his voice. She couldn't
bear that.

But she had to face him, had to know the truth.

"Never mind about the coffee," she told the small black
girl. "I'm going downstairs to have breakfast."

Megan hesitated on the threshold of the small, sunny breakfast room at the rear of the house. She had thought that she
would have a chance to be alone with Clay, but she saw that
the whole family was already assembled.

She heard Reed saying, "I suppose once you and your Yankee friends have built your railroads, there'll be no more need
for boats like the *Delta Lady*."

"The *Delta Lady*'s a fine boat," Clay said calmly, "but
you're quite right. If we can get the subsidies from the state
legislatures—"

"The state legislatures. Carpetbaggers and blacks—" Reed
put in.

"If we can get their backing, we can run trunk lines flanking
both sides of the river. We'll haul freight faster and more
cheaply than the river boats. And carry passengers, too. It won't
happen overnight, I suppose. And there'll always be something
for the boats to carry: coal, maybe, and ore. But we'll get
cotton and grain. We'll give our customers speed—that's what
counts."

"Speed," Reed repeated scornfully. "You talk like a Yankee—"

Megan came into the room, and both men rose. There was
a murmur of "good mornings" around the table as Clay pulled
out a chair for Megan. But he did not interrupt his discussion.
"We'll be competing with the Yankees, so we'll have to beat
them at their own game. We have plenty of untapped resources
down here. Why there's enough iron ore up around northern
Alabama to build mills as productive as those in Pittsburgh."

"The prospect of another Pittsburgh in northern Alabama
doesn't particularly interest me," Reed said. "Immigrants pouring in, the sky filled with smoke, and houses blackened with
soot."

"The mills of Pittsburgh provided the material for the weapons that won the war for the Yankees. Those and the textile
mills of Massachusetts."

"Oh, for heaven sake," Lianne interrupted, her soft cheeks flushing with annoyance. "Must we have such talk over breakfast?"

"Let Clay finish," Reed said, his gray eyes hardening. "No doubt he'll tell us a lot we don't know about the glories of the North. Seems to me he's started thinking like a Yankee after all that time he spent up there."

Clay set his coffee cup down carefully, and Megan saw the white line around his lips. Was he still struggling with the guilt and shame he had confessed to that night in the warehouse office? She put a hand on his arm in a gesture of instinctive support. "Clay was taken prisoner fighting for the Confederacy," she said, "like hundreds of other loyal Southerners. He froze on Johnson's Island, and he starved, and the Yankee guards—some of them—were deliberately brutal."

"We don't need you to tell us how our men suffered in those dreadful prisons," Lianne said coldly. "You're not one of us—you—"

"That's enough, Lianne," Reed said. Megan looked at him in surprise. "It's only right for Megan to take up for her husband. And she *is* one of us now. She's a Drummond." Then, turning to Clay, he added, "I'm sorry, Clay. The morning after your wedding is no time for such talk."

Samantha smiled at Megan, but unlike Reed, there was no real warmth in her, and Megan knew it. "You're right, Reed, darling," she said sweetly. "We mustn't be forgetting that Megan's a new bride." She turned her huge, dark eyes on Clay. "And it's mean of you, Clay, to go running off to New Orleans. On business, of all things. Cheating poor Megan out of a honeymoon. But don't you fret, Megan. We'll all try to keep you in good spirits while Clay's gone." She wasn't even trying to hide her malicious triumph. Megan felt a chill in spite of the sun that poured into the breakfast room. Could Samantha have somehow guessed that Clay's marriage had not been made of his own free will? She could not possibly know about what Aunt Kathleen had done to force a proposal out of Clay, but she must have wondered why Clay would marry a girl from Natchez-under. Samantha, all of them, here in this room, had seen the coolness with which Clay had treated Megan during the wedding supper the previous night, and now he had packed his trunk and was preparing to leave Montrose for New Orleans.

Oh, yes, Megan thought bitterly, Samantha had every reason to gloat.

Unable to bear Samantha's pretense of friendliness and her false sympathy, Megan heard herself saying, "You're mistaken, Samantha. I'm going to New Orleans with my husband."

Samantha's face went white, and her dark eyes widened. Megan's shaft had hit home, but her triumph was short-lived, and she felt a wave of fear surging up in her, for she was sure that in a moment Clay would expose her impulsive lie, would leave her shamed and vulnerable in front of his family.

Oh, why had she let her pride, her quick temper, get the better of her? Megan heard a faint humming in her ears. The faces around the table appeared a little blurred. Never in her life had she fainted, and she would not let herself give way now. She folded her hands in her lap, digging her fingernails into her palms, fighting the sensation of weakness, forcing herself to listen to what Jessica was saying.

"Oh, you'll enjoy New Orleans, Megan. It's a charming city, and even now there are theaters, balls, the finest restaurants, and the French Opera House. You must have Clay take you there."

"Jessica, there hasn't been an opera company there since the city was captured," Lianne put in.

"Oh, but there is sure to be a benefit performance or a concert. There always is. Do you remember the night the opera house opened, Lianne?" Jessica turned to Megan. "We went for the first performance. *William Tell*, it was, and I can remember the chandeliers and the mirrors sparkling and the ladies all dressed so beautifully. And there were visits between the boxes and champagne in the private parlors behind the boxes. Papa said it was as fine as any opera house he'd visited in Europe. . . ."

Jessica's voice trailed off, for Megan was not looking at her. Instead, her eyes were fixed on Clay's face as she waited for the blow to fall. And then she heard her husband saying, "I'm sure that Megan will enjoy New Orleans, Jess." He had turned to Megan, one corner of his mouth lifted in a smile. "You'd better have Ludamae help you to get ready, Megan, my dear. You haven't much time if we're going to get down to the *Delta Lady*."

Megan's clenched hands relaxed, and she felt an overwhelming sense of relief and of gratitude to Clay. Then she made herself stand up and said a little shakily, "I'll be ready, Clay."

Chapter Ten

DURING THE month of her honeymoon, Megan tried to understand the man she had married, and although she found him baffling and unpredictable, she was determined that he should come to love her. Somehow she would make him forget that he had been forced into marriage. One day he would know that she had not conspired with her aunt, that she was incapable of such an action. In the meantime, she would enjoy her honeymoon with him in New Orleans, which was surely, even now in the year following the war, one of the most glamorous cities in the world.

The trip down river took forty-eight hours, partly due to the frequent stops, and then, after the carriage ride across the city, she found herself staring in awe at the regal Hotel St. Charles. "We'll be staying here," Clay told her, helping her down.

Her eyes widened as she examined the hotel's façade, with its fourteen Corinthian columns, topped by an impressive pediment, a circular colonnade of heavy marble, and above that, a white dome that gleamed in the sunlight.

"Like it?" Clay asked. And when Megan nodded, he continued. "A New York politician, Oakey Hall, was impressed, too. Hall said, 'Set the St. Charles down in St. Petersburg, and you would think it a palace; in Boston, and ten to one you would christen it a college; in London, and it would remind you of an exchange. In New Orleans, it is all three.'"

"It's splendid," Megan agreed. "But can we— I mean—it must be terribly expensive to stay here. Surely we could find cheaper accommodations."

Clay took her arm and escorted her inside. "I have to impress the men whose backing I'll need," he said firmly. Then, as they made their way through the crowded lobby to the registration desk, he added, "This is a business trip for me, Megan. Remember that."

She must not let him see how much his words had hurt her. Why, she asked herself, had he brought her along to New Orleans at all if he felt as he did? Was it that he had not wanted to humiliate her before his family? Or was it his own pride he was thinking of, not wanting his family to guess that he had been forced into this marriage even if it meant playing the conventional bridegroom, taking his wife off for a honeymoon? Or maybe, she thought unhappily, he only wanted her along because a man with a wife would impress prospective investors, who might think him more settled, a better financial risk.

Megan was still brooding over these questions that evening in their spacious suite, where she had finished dressing for dinner. She saw that Clay was looking at her critically.

"You'll need a new wardrobe," he told her.

She wore the same amber silk that she had made for the ball at Montrose last spring. "There's nothing wrong with my dress," she said.

"It's becoming," he said, "but you'll need many changes of costume while we're here. New Orleans is famous for its fashionable women."

She understood what he meant later that evening when they were seated in the hotel's huge dining room, for the women who strolled by were dressed in velvets and taffetas, in regal shades of wine red, jade green, purple, or midnight blue. Their gowns were designed in the latest mode, the necklines cut shockingly low, the bustles ornamented with ribbons, laces, and flowers. The gas lamps struck sparks from the diamonds in their elaborate chignons, from their earrings of emeralds, sapphires, or rubies.

Megan spoke to Clay in an undertone. "I'd have thought that since the war, Southern ladies—"

"These aren't Southern ladies," he told her, emphasizing the last word. "At least, few of them are. Most are carpetbaggers' women or the mistresses of Yankee officers. The ladies of New Orleans are wearing mourning, and you won't find them at the St. Charles."

"But where—"

"Some are living on the charity of relatives who have little enough to share. Others are hidden away in shabby boarding houses."

He broke off as the waiter appeared to put down the steaming tureen of spicy-smelling gumbo. Megan tried not to think of the poverty just a few streets away from where they sat, of the hunger and want that existed side by side with the luxury she saw all around her. But she could not forget the years of starvation back in Ireland.

"I'm told that Madame Helene's shop on Royal Street's the most fashionable these days. You can have your new wardrobe made there— I'll drive you to the shop first thing tomorrow morning and call for you at noon." He took a sip of wine, then went on. "I have business with Oliver Winthrop, a man from Boston. Major Taggart gave me a letter of introduction before he and my stepmother left Montrose."

She caught the look of self-mockery in his eyes. "You told Reed that the South needs railroads," she said. "If the Yankees are the only ones down here with money, you have no choice but to take their help."

"Maybe our marriage will be successful, after all," he said. There was no mistaking the bitter edge to his tone. "We're both opportunists, aren't we, my dear?"

Megan pushed back her chair and started to rise.

"Sit down," Clay ordered.

"I won't. I'm not hungry any longer. I don't want—"

"It doesn't matter to me what you want. You won't make a scene when you're with me. You'll behave like a lady."

She could feel his will, like a tangible force, beating hers down. She resumed her seat, but her face was hot with anger.

"Oh, but you've never considered me a lady. I'm only a girl from Natchez-under."

"You're my wife now. Mrs. Clay Drummond. If you don't understand what that means even now, I'll have to go on teaching you."

She remembered her response to his lovemaking on their wedding night, and she realized, with bewilderment, that even now she was stirred by the ruthless command in his tone. But she would not submit willingly.

"You'll find me a difficult pupil," she told him.

"Perhaps," he said, his eyes mocking her, "I don't mind a challenge."

Madame Helene's shop, on Royal Street, occupied a pink stucco building with a gallery of black ironwork that overhung the street. Here Megan spent the morning after her arrival in New Orleans being fitted for her new wardrobe. Clay had insisted that she spare no expense, and she followed his instructions, not letting herself think of how much money she was spending but choosing the most becoming colors and patterns: a walking suit of blue velvet and another of gray silk; a ball gown of lilac taffeta; a dinner gown of pale-green faille with a train of rose-colored faille trimmed with point lace; a dozen pairs of kid gloves in the latest shades, including a pale gray called "moonbeams on the lake," according to Madame Helene, a thin, dignified Frenchwoman.

Although Megan was sure that Clay had given her free rein in choosing these lavish clothes not to please her but because he wanted her to make a correct impression on his business associates, she felt her spirits lifting as she thought of how fashionable she would look in her new wardrobe. When he came to call for her at noon, he said, "I want you to have the dinner gown by Saturday night."

"I'm not sure—" Megan began, but Madame Helene interrupted.

"Oh, madame, the gown will be ready when you require it, I assure you." She pressed a bell set in the wall, and a dark-eyed, golden-skinned young woman came out from behind the velvet curtains at the rear of the shop.

"Opal will start work at once on the dinner gown," Madame Helene said.

Clay looked at Opal in surprise. His brows went up slightly.

"Mistuh Clay!" It was plain to Megan that Opal was startled, even a little frightened, and no wonder; if Clay refused to allow Opal to work on the expensive new gown, if he made a scene as he had back in Uncle Jim's general store that day last spring, Opal might well lose her job. Megan felt the tension in the air, and she braced herself for what might follow.

But Clay smiled, and turning to Madame Helene, he said, "Opal's a fine seamstress—she did all the sewing for the ladies of my family back at Montrose. If she's going to make the dress, I know that my wife will be pleased with the results."

"Yo' wife, suh?" Opal said.

"That's right," Clay told her. "Miss Rafferty is now Mrs. Drummond."

"Oh, Ah'm happy fo' yuh, Mistuh Clay." She curtsied to Megan. "Miz Drummond, ma'am, Ah'll make yuh a dress t' be proud of."

Opal looked visibly relaxed, her white teeth flashing in a smile.

"Perhaps you'd like me to take back some message to your mother," Clay said. "She's been worried about you—"

"If yuh please, Mistuh Clay—" She raised her head, and there was a look of dignity about her. "Ah'd like momma t' know that Noah an' me been married—all right and propuh by a preacher."

"She'll be happy to hear that," Clay said.

"An' mah Noah, he workin' in Mistuh Armand Dupré's carpenter shop."

"That's fine," Clay said. He reached into his coat pocket, and taking out his wallet, he counted out a few greenbacks. He tried to hand them to Opal, but she shook her head. "Noah an' me, we gettin' on fine—"

"Even so, you surely won't refuse to take this as a belated wedding gift." Clay put the bills into Opal's hand and closed her fingers around them.

"Thank yuh, Mistuh Clay." Megan knew that Opal was not thanking Clay only for the money.

Madame Helene, who had been watching the scene with interest, now said, "If you have the time, madame, you must

see our new selection of ostrich-feather fans from Paris. They're
the finest quality."

Megan threw Clay a questioning look.

"By all means," he told her. "I'll be waiting in the carriage
outside."

As he was leaving, Opal turned to Megan, saying, "Miz
Drummond—if yuh'd be so kind—please tell momma somethin' else fuh me. Ah'm goin' t' have a chil'."

"I'll tell her," Megan said. Then she added, "Mrs. Drummond—Samantha, that is—is expecting a child, too."

Opal's eyes clouded, and she was no longer looking at
Megan, but past her, at the shop door, which was closing behind
Clay. "Miz Samantha— When she goin' t'—"

"In a few months. March, I believe."

There was a silence between them that stretched out until
Megan felt uneasy without knowing why.

"An' Mistuh Reed?" Opal asked slowly.

"Why—I'm sure he's pleased." Every man wanted sons,
Megan knew, especially a man with land and a proud family
name to be carried on.

"Here they are," Madame Helene said, bustling up to Megan
and spreading a collection of fans on the counter. "This one
of Nile green would set off your dinner gown to perfection.
Notice the ivory handle. . . ."

Megan nodded, but she could not take her eyes from Opal's
face. The young octoroon was plainly troubled, and Megan
could not imagine what had caused her change of mood.

A half an hour later, when she was seated beside Clay in
the carriage, she still puzzled over the meaning of Opal's curious reaction. Then she told herself that she really knew little
about Clay and his family and about their relationships with
their former slaves. The tangled threads of those relationships
must stretch back over the years. For that matter, Megan thought
with a sigh, she did not really know Clay, even now.

"It was good of you to praise Opal before her employer,"
Megan said.

"I'm pleased that she's doing well," he answered. "She and
Noah are the exceptions, though. Many of the freed blacks are
worse off than they were before the war."

"But if Opal and Noah can make a decent life for themselves, surely it is only a matter of time before—"

"Noah can read and write. Few blacks can. It was forbidden by law to teach a slave to read and write in most parts of the South before the war."

"Then how did Noah—"

Clay laughed. "Jessica taught him. Pa was furious, but Jessica stood up to him. She pointed out that if pa wanted to make the best use of Noah's skills as a carpenter, Noah would have to be able to read blueprints and the bills from the lumberyard." There was no mistaking the fondness in Clay's voice when he spoke of Jessica. "She sticks to her guns if she believes she's right," he said.

"And can Opal read, too?"

"Not unless Noah's taught her. But my sisters and my stepmother always said that she was the finest seamstress in the county. You're sure to look splendid when we go to the Winthrops' dinner party on Saturday."

"Is it important to you—the party, I mean?"

"Oliver Winthrop's important," Clay said. "He has a great deal of capital to invest."

"Aren't there any investments to be made up in Boston?" Megan asked.

"Winthrop's after quick returns—like most of his Yankee friends," Clay said. "He didn't have much cash when he arrived in Louisiana last spring. He took a gamble, and he won. He now owns one of the finest houses in the Garden District. And a beautiful wife, twenty years younger than he is, to grace his home."

"You make it sound as if—as if he bought her along with the house."

"He did, in a sense. You see, many of these Creole sugar planters were desperate at the end of the war, completely bankrupt and demoralized. They couldn't believe that the freedmen could be trusted to make sugar, so they left the matured cane standing in the fields to rot. That's where Mr. Winthrop saw his chance. He bought the matured cane from the owners at next to nothing. And he promised to pay out of the returns from the crops."

Megan looked at Clay in surprise. "And they agreed to his terms?"

"They were in no position to refuse. Then Winthrop went

straight to the blacks. Told them he was a Yankee, that he'd
pay them a fair wage for their work if they would make the
sugar as they always had. By the end of the season, he'd turned
a handsome profit."

"But his wife—you said she—"

"Miss Angelique Vallière was the owner of one of the plantations Winthrop bought out of his profits. Her family was in
no position to oppose the match. Her father and brothers had
died in the war, you see, and she had two younger sisters to
provide for."

Seeing Megan's look of pity, he said, "Don't distress yourself, my dear. Marrying for love is a luxury few of us down
here can afford any longer."

Was he speaking of himself, Megan wondered, or was he
thinking of Samantha? Both of them, perhaps.

Megan fought down the hurt that threatened to force angry
words from her. One day he would know that she was the right
wife for him; one day he would tell her that he loved her.

The Winthrops' town house in the Garden District was a
handsome, white, two-story structure surrounded by towering
oaks. Vines twisted around the impressive ironwork of the
fence, and sweet olives and fig trees grew on the smooth, well-
kept lawns.

Inside, the furnishings were new and expensive, the guests
dressed in the height of fashion. Megan remembered what Clay
had told her of the poverty of the New Orleans Confederates,
and she found herself wondering where the former owners of
the house were living now.

Many of Winthrops' guests spoke with what Megan had
come to recognize as a New England accent. Oliver Winthrop,
although plainly older than his beautiful, dark-haired wife, was
a big, virile-looking man with genial manners.

The Winthrops' cook had prepared a magnificent meal, with
one delicious dish following another: Jambalaya, crawfish bis-
que, *daube glacé,* pompano fragrant with herbs, turkey simmered in wine, trays of pastries with pastel-colored sugar
frosting.

Megan looked at Angelique Winthrop and wondered if the
dark-haired young beauty regretted her decision to marry the
man who had profited so greatly by the downfall of her own

people. Or was she satisfied with a life of comfort, with fashionable clothes and a lavish table?

After dinner, the gentlemen remained in the dining room while the ladies withdrew to the parlor. Although within an hour most of the gentlemen had returned to join the ladies, Clay was still absent, no doubt deep in discussion with Oliver Winthrop about the advantages of making an investment in the Natchez–Fort Worth Line.

A few of the ladies entertained, and Megan tried to pay polite attention to an off-key rendition of "Lo, Hear the Gentle Lark," but her thoughts were on Clay. After the music had been politely applauded, Megan took part in the conversation, but her remarks were automatic. The new railroad line meant everything to Clay, and she was anxious to find out if he had succeeded with Winthrop.

"I don't see any sense in trying to educate these blacks." The speaker, a lean, horse-faced woman, had a New England twang in her voice, and Megan was bewildered. There was a tradition of abolitionism in New England—so she had read—and the Yankees had just fought a war to free the blacks.

"Quite right, my dear," said the lady's husband, a portly gentleman in a bright-blue waistcoat that accented his girth. "Give me a good, strong Irish girl any day. We have enough of those in Boston, I can tell you—glad to work like horses for a square meal and a place to sleep. We can get them right off the boat. They'll work seven days a week as long as they get time off for six o'clock Mass on Sunday, and they think four dollars a month's a fortune."

The horse-faced lady nodded in agreement, showing her prominent teeth in a complacent smile. "Oh, yes—I prefer Irish servants. If these blacks are taught to read and write, they'll come swarming up North, wanting to take work away from decent white people—"

"No fear of that," her husband said. "Blacks can't be taught. Their minds are not equipped to learn—"

"That's not true," Megan said. "Noah—he used to be one of my husband's people—learned to read and write. He has a job as a carpenter right here in New Orleans."

"An exceptional case," the portly gentleman said. "I trust you are mistaken, sir."

Megan turned to look at the speaker, a lean, sandy-haired man in his late thirties. "I have come down here to set up a school for the freedmen."

"Teaching school!" the portly man said with careless contempt. "You won't make your fortune that way." He turned back to his wife, and Megan remained looking up at the sandy-haired man.

"Where will your school be?" she asked.

"I'm not sure. There are a number of schools for freedmen here in New Orleans already. But farther up river, there are few as yet."

"My name's Mrs. Clay Drummond." Megan introduced herself. "My husband's plantation, Montrose, is up river, beyond Natchez."

A few moments later, Megan found herself out on the side veranda with Tom Langford, the Yankee schoolmaster. It was cool but not unpleasantly so, even now in January. A few of the hardier plants were already in bloom.

"Would your husband consider having a school for blacks at Montrose?" Tom Langford was asking. "So many planters are opposed to the idea."

"And many Yankees, too," Megan returned.

"I can't deny that. The war was fought for a number of reasons, and abolition was only one of them. Even those Northern citizens who wanted the slaves freed still believe that they are not capable of anything but the most menial labor."

"And you hope to prove them wrong?" Megan asked.

"I *will* prove them wrong." Megan knew that here was a man who, although he had no desire to make a fortune, as Clay did, was nevertheless filled with the same kind of inner strength, the same steely determination to accomplish what he had set out to do.

"I believe that you will succeed, Mr. Langford," Megan said. "I hope you will."

"Then you'll help me?"

Megan was taken aback. "But what can I do?"

"Perhaps you think I'm being presumptuous to ask for your help on such slight acquaintance."

"No. It's only that—" Megan thought that perhaps her fine clothes, her presence at this gathering, had led Tom Langford to believe that her husband was wealthy enough to offer financial support for a school. "You see, Mr. Langford, my husband wants to build a railroad from here to Texas. He would not be willing to spare any substantial sum of money for any other purpose."

"But he does have a plantation—you said that. Surely he might be persuaded to set aside a small piece of land, a building, however run-down, to be used as a school. My wages, such as they are, come from the Freedmen's Bureau, so that would be no problem."

Megan hesitated, for she was far from certain that Clay would go along with such a plan.

"Perhaps your husband is opposed to education for his ex-slaves," Langford said.

"I don't know. We've only been married for a week," Megan said. "We've never really discussed—"

"But you believe that the blacks can be educated," Langford said. "When you spoke out back there in the parlor, you made your feelings clear enough."

"I believe in education for everyone who wants it," Megan said. She smiled at Tom Langford and added, "You see, I'm one of those Irish immigrant girls those people were talking about."

Now it was Langford who was thrown off balance momentarily. "But you're not—I'm sure you weren't a servant up in Boston."

"Not in Boston," Megan told him. "In the home of our English landlord back in County Cork. I didn't even get four dollars a month. Only board and lodging. But that was more than enough, with my neighbors close to starvation."

"You're a most direct young woman."

"I'm beginning to think directness isn't a quality men admire in ladies here in the South."

Tom Langford laughed. "That's as may be. I approve of it. And I hope we may be friends, Mrs. Drummond."

Megan held out her hand, and he gripped it firmly.

"We're friends," Megan assured him. "And I'll speak to my husband. At the proper time."

The proper time did not come until a few nights before Clay and Megan left New Orleans. During the past weeks, Megan had grown accustomed to spending many of her evenings alone in their lavish suite at the Hotel St. Charles while the exciting life of the glamorous city swirled around her in the streets below. Clay told her only that he had to go out "on business," and she tried to fill the empty hours by reading or doing needle-work.

She believed that it was only business that occupied Clay on these evenings for when he returned long after midnight and got into bed beside her, he would take her into his arms and make love to her with tenderness and passion. Even in her inexperience, she was certain that he had not come to her from another woman.

After that first night at Montrose, he never showed her any violence, although he did initiate her into certain variations that were, at first, shocking to her. But she found that she was never able to refuse him, loving him as she did, although she did, at times, protest briefly.

"Oh, no—Clay—I can't—"

And then his voice, uneven and hoarse in the darkness. "Please—do it for me, love—" And his hands guided her, stroking the heavy, thick masses of her tawny hair as her lips found him. Later, when she lay resting her flushed, perspiring face against the lean, hard muscles of his thigh and heard him say softly, "Megan— Oh, Megan—" she could feel no shame, only a kind of pride at being able to meet all his needs so completely.

But tonight, when he returned to the hotel suite and let himself into the suite, there was something different about him. Although she was lying in bed, prepared for his lovemaking, he lit the lamp and moved about the sitting room as if driven by some powerful force that would not let him seek her arms.

Finally, she rose and lit the lamp, and it was only then that he came into the bedroom, his blue eyes bright under his dark, heavy brows. "It's done, Megan," he said. "Oliver Winthrop and three of his associates are going in with me on the railroad. They took some convincing, but we're ready to move ahead now. If Gavin O'Donnell's got the extra crews, we can start within the week."

"Oh, Clay—I'm so pleased—"

He went to her and stood looking down at her. His eyes searched her face. "I believe you are," he said. Then he smiled. "And why not? We'll be wealthy, Megan—really wealthy."

She felt her heart sink. Couldn . he understand that although, of course, she was pleased by the promise of wealth, she was even more satisfied to know that Clay was to fulfill his ambitions, that she drew joy from his obvious pleasure? No, he did not understand, but someday he would. And then she remembered.

"Clay, that night at the Winthrops' dinner party, I met a man—" She hesitated then, recalling her promise, and encouraged by Clay's obvious high spirits, she plunged ahead, telling him about Tom Langford and his plans for a school for the freed blacks.

"I wish him luck," he said when she had finished. "He'll need it. Men like Jeff Shepley—and even Reed, for that matter—will do everything they can to oppose him."

"But why?"

"Because, my dear, blacks who can read and write will be in a better position to fight for the vote—"

"They have the vote by law, don't they? Louisiana has a black lieutenant governor now—"

"It won't last, Megan. The South won't remain occupied territory forever, and when the Union troops move out, there'll be a backlash—even now it's beginning. But this is not time to talk about such things. Tomorrow, I want you to get yourself dressed in your prettiest gown, and I'll take you to Antoine's for dinner and then to the theater. And right now—"

His arms went around her, and for a moment she wavered, wanting nothing more than to have him lift her off her feet and carry her to bed.

But she refused to let herself give way to the swift, dizzying uprush of desire that always came to her when Clay wanted her. She had made a promise, and she was determined to keep it; and now, if ever, was the time.

"Clay, wait," she said. "Mr. Langford wants this school of his as much as"— she searched her mind, needing to make him understand—"as much as you want your new railroad. And—well—Montrose belongs to you. Surely, you can do as you please with the property your father left you."

"You want me to allow this Yankee idealist to set up his school on my property, on Drummond land?"

"Mr. Langford says there are several schools for freed blacks in New Orleans but none near Natchez, and I thought—"

"You know what this would mean? I don't need a family battle right now."

"Your whole family wouldn't object," Megan persisted. "You told me that Jessica taught Noah to read and write."

"That's true enough, but I—"

"Surely she'd be on our side."

Clay put his arm around her and drew her to him, and something flickered in his eyes as he looked at her.

"Our side," he repeated softly. She sensed a closeness between them that had not been there, not since that night in her uncle's warehouse when she had first given herself to him. Her heart lifted with joy. Surely, one day, he would come to know how much she loved him, would come to believe that she had not trapped him into marriage.

"There is an old building," he was saying slowly. "Pa thought he'd use it for a sugar mill when he was experimenting with the growing of cane, before he decided to raise nothing but cotton. It's in poor condition, I should think, but it's probably still usable." He shrugged. "I suppose the blacks will have to learn to read and write if they're not to be a burden on the state. I'll give this Langford fellow the use of the building." He dismissed the matter, and Megan relaxed, letting him lift her into his arms and carry her to the bed.

And this time, when he made love to her, it was better than it had ever been before, and she knew it was because of those words she had spoken and he had repeated a little while ago: *our side.*

As she lifted her body to his, as he entered her, she found herself longing for something more. For a child. Her whole being was filled with the need, and she clung to him after he had spent his passion and fell asleep in his arms.

Chapter Eleven

THE LAST of the guests were leaving Montrose after the celebration that marked the christening of Lucas Drummond, and Reed, standing tall and proud on the front veranda, was saying good-by to them as they started for their carriages. Samantha, in a gown of rose and white-striped organdy trimmed with lace, stood at the window of the upstairs nursery looking down at her husband. Her back was to the cradle in which her two-week-old son lay.

Then, hearing a familiar step in the hallway, she turned quickly; her face brightened as she hurried to the nursery door.

"Why Clay," she said. "Aren't you going to say good-by to me—and little Luke?"

Clay hesitated, then came inside. Already, in mid-March, the room was warm, filled with sunlight and with the scents from the gardens below: crepe myrtle, wisteria, flowering jasmine.

"You're mighty eager to leave Montrose again," Samantha said.

Clay made an impatient gesture. "I should have been gone

a week ago," he reminded her. "I only stayed on this long because of the christening." Then, seeing the reproachful look in Samantha's eyes, he added, "He's a fine boy, my new nephew." He went to the side of the cradle and looked down at the red-faced baby, whose small head was crowned with a fuzz of light-brown hair. Luke stared back, his eyes wide and dark blue.

"He's the first Drummond baby to use this cradle since Reed was born," Clay said. Then he added, "I haven't seen Reed looking prouder than he does today—not since he rode off with his cavalry troop in his fine new uniform with his brand-new sword." Clay's face clouded briefly at the memory. Then he said, "Reed's himself again for the first time since the surrender. And he'll make this place hum, now that he has an heir to work for; see if he doesn't."

Samantha quickly bent over the cradle and made an unnecessary adjustment of the baby's blanket, for she did not want Clay to see her face. Oh, yes, Reed was proud, all right. Strutting around like a turkey cock. She tried to suppress her mingled feelings of pity and contempt as she recalled how Reed had spent the afternoon showing off the baby to all their friends and neighbors: the Shepleys, the Hunters, the Surgets, and the rest. Jessica and Lianne had fussed over the baby, and so had Megan, and it had taken all Samantha's will power to fight back the urge to shout the truth, to tell all of them that Reed was not Luke's father, that it was Clay who should be receiving congratulations on the birth of a son.

"I'd better go and finish my packing," Clay said abruptly.

"Surely you won't leave before tomorrow."

"I'm leaving tonight," Clay told her. "I'll get a river boat from here to Jackson. I have to talk to the legislators in the state capital."

"Legislators! A fine word for that passle of carpetbaggers and scalawags—trash from up North and traitors from right here in Mississippi. Men who want the blacks to have the vote—"

"The blacks have the vote, my dear," Clay said quietly.

"But that—that's unthinkable. Clay, how can blacks who don't know how to write their own names have a voice in ruling our state?"

"As I recall, Samantha, you were completely opposed to my letting Tom Langford set up his school on Montrose land. Aren't you being a little inconsistent?"

"Certainly not. Blacks have no business learning to read and write, and they don't belong in politics, either. Jeff Shepley was saying only the other day—"

"Jeff Shepley! He's an embittered, angry man who wasn't able to make a go of his own plantation without unpaid labor, and he hates the idea of working for us as an overseer. And Violet's probably making it worse, never letting him forget he caused her to lose her place in the social order."

Samantha, remembering Violet's tight, set face, her reluctance to mingle with the other ladies at the reception, could not refute Clay's words.

"But Reed agrees with Jeff," she said, shifting her ground. "He says if we make the blacks do their work in the fields and here in the house, same as always—"

"Same as always." Clay did not bother to keep the irritation out of his voice. "When will Reed—when will all of you—realize that nothing will be the same at Montrose again? The changes we've seen so far are nothing compared to those that are coming. When Stevens and Sumner and the rest of the Radical Republicans have control of the government in Washington, not even President Johnson himself will be able to stem the tide. Those of us who can't bend with the wind will break."

"Oh, please," Samantha interrupted. "I don't want to talk about politics. Not now, when you're getting ready to go away again, when I won't be seeing you for heaven knows how long." She put a soft, white hand on his arm and raised her large, dark eyes to his. "It'll be so awful at Montrose with you gone. Oh, Clay—"

"Samantha, don't."

But although he drew away from her touch, he remained there beside the cradle. Samantha felt her hopes begin to stir. Ever since he had returned from his honeymoon, she had watched him with Megan, sick with jealousy because she sensed a new closeness between him and that trashy little Irish girl.

Night after night, she had lain awake, staring up at the canopy of her bed, trying to drive from her mind the picture of Clay and Megan, their bodies locked in passion, in their own bed in the opposite wing of the house. It was only a slight consolation to her that she had not allowed Reed to sleep with her, that she had been able to lie alone, her body heavy and misshapen in the last stages of pregnancy.

She had given herself to Reed perhaps half a dozen times to convince him that he was the father of her baby. After that, she had let him know, in a delicate, ladylike way, that advancing pregnancy would make marital relations dangerous to herself and to the baby.

Reed had not protested but had started sleeping on the dressing-room cot again. It was enough, he told her tenderly, that she was going to present him with an heir.

Of course, Samantha thought, she would not be able to keep him out of her bed for more than a few weeks longer. After that, he would want to make love to her again. Even now, he talked of their next child.

"A little girl, maybe," he'd said only that afternoon. "As beautiful as you, my dear."

The thought sickened her so that she shuddered slightly. "Samantha, are you feeling ill? Maybe the reception, all those people—"

Clay put a hand on her arm, and the touch of his fingers, even in so impersonal a gesture, stirred her. She felt the warmth of his fingers, and they sent a tingling through the nerves of her body, evoking a swift response. She was shocked. Surely, it wasn't decent for a lady, one who had so recently borne a baby, to be tormented with these desires.

She tried to deny her feelings, but for once her talent for self-deception failed her. Motherhood meant little to her. She had resented the last months of pregnancy, hating the sight of her once-slender body, bloated and distorted by her burden.

Those violent bouts of morning sickness had been painful and humiliating but not nearly so dreadful as the process of childbirth itself— The long labor, when she had felt as if her body were being torn apart.

What little feelings she now had for Luke were only the result of her passion for Clay. She was perfectly happy to let Rachel find a black wet nurse for the child, for she was determined that no squalling, hungry infant was going to ruin the perfection of her smooth white breasts.

"Sit down here and rest," Clay was saying.

But she turned to face him, her eyes wide, her voice rising shrilly. "I don't want to rest. I don't want—"

"I'll call Jessica—or Lianne," he said quickly.

"No, stay here with me. Listen, Clay, you don't have to go to Jackson or to the railroad site after that. Why you can run the business from an office in Natchez. There are lots of men who can oversee the construction. Jim Rafferty or that other Irishman—the one who married Megan's cousin. There's no need for you to leave me—"

Samantha felt her spirits rising as her mind moved ahead. If Clay had an office in Natchez—or in New Orleans. Yes, New Orleans would be better. Then she could make excuses to travel to that delightful city. New clothes. Visits to the French Opera. She had heard that the French Opera was having a new company this fall. It was to be a gala season, with fifty-seven artists to be brought over from Europe. Reed had never cared for opera, but she could surely persuade him to allow her to attend. And once in New Orleans, she and Clay could meet . . .

"Clay, darling, listen to me," she began. But she saw that he was looking past her.

She stiffened and turned to see Clay's wife standing there in the doorway. "I've packed for you, Clay," Megan said quietly. "I don't think I've forgotten anything, but perhaps you should come and make sure."

Samantha lowered her eyes to conceal her anger and frustration as Megan entered the nursery and went to Luke's cradle. Gently, she touched Luke's tiny fist with one finger.

Clay was saying, "Did you know, Megan, that Grandfather Drummond built this cradle with his own hands? Back in Charleston, that was. Then he and my grandmother brought it with them across the country and down the Natchez Trace."

He was obviously trying to smooth over a tense moment, Samantha told herself. Megan was stroking the polished wood, a look of tenderness in her eyes. "I'm glad they brought it with them, Clay," she said softly. "Because when Luke doesn't need it any longer, I want our own child to—"

"Our own child?" Clay stared at Megan.

"That's right," Megan said, and there was pride in her voice, in the set of her head and shoulders. "Our child. Early in November, I think—"

"A son." Clay reached for Megan's hand. "Our first son."
Samantha flinched, seeing the unconcealed joy in Clay's face.
"Oh, Megan— How long have you known?"

"I've suspected it for a few months, but you were so taken
up with railroad business, and then, too—" She smiled at
Samantha. "This is Samantha's day, and Reed's—and little
Luke's, of course. I was going to tell you tomorrow, but since
you're leaving tonight, I—"

Samantha could not bear it any longer. Whatever Clay's
reason might have been for marrying Megan, he was plainly
overjoyed at the prospect that she was to give him a child.
Samantha watched as the two of them left the nursery, Clay's
arm around Megan. Then, feeling drained and miserable, she
sat down beside the cradle and stared without the slightest
warmth at her sleeping son.

Clay left Montrose that evening, and after his trip to Jackson,
he went directly to the site where the new railroad was to be
started. It would be linked to the spur line and would then go
on to cut through the swamps of Louisiana and on across the
arid plains of Texas.

For Megan, that spring and summer were lonely, for Clay
rarely wrote to her, and when he did, it was only to inquire
about her health and to tell her about the progress of the Natchez–
Fort Worth Line.

Without Clay, she felt like a stranger among the Drummonds, who treated her with cool courtesy but nothing more.
Jessica was less distant than Lianne and Samantha, but she was
occupied with running the household and handicapped by the
drastically reduced domestic staff.

In desperation, Megan began going down to Natchez-under
to visit her cousin, Belle, who was also lonely, for Gavin had
returned to New York City to round up additional men for the
railroad crew. The Drummonds were openly critical.

"I don't think it looks proper for you to go down to that
dreadful place, especially in your condition," Lianne remarked.

But when other ladies from neighboring plantations came
to pay social calls, Megan found herself shut out from their
gossip. She knew nothing of the people they discussed or the
events they reminisced over, and they did not take the trouble
to enlighten her. Once, when Lianne spoke of the young man

to whom she had been engaged and who had died at Antietam, some of her friends had responded with sympathy, mentioning the names of other Confederate soldiers—brothers, husbands, and sweethearts—lost in the war. Megan had tried to show that she understood and had mentioned her brother Terence, killed by the British in the Fenian raid on the garrison back in County Cork. But Winona Hunter had given her a freezing look and said, "That is not the same thing at all. The Confederate soldiers were gentlemen, not a gang of lawless cut-throats."

Because she did not want to stir up tension in the household, Megan did not go down to Natchez-under often, but she occasionally visited Tom Langford's small, whitewashed school-house at the edge of the Montrose property near the cypress swamp. Tom had built a small lean-to beside the schoolhouse, a modest two-room affair that served him as his living quarters.

One sultry July afternoon, when she was returning from a visit to the school, Megan found Jessica seated alone on the side veranda, busy with a pile of needlework; on impulse, she spoke of Tom's problems in getting the necessary equipment for his pupils.

"He tells me that two or three children often have to share a single book," Megan explained, "and nearly all the books are worn to tatters."

Jessica looked up from the dress she was making for Luke. "I'm sure our old schoolbooks are still packed away upstairs," she said.

Lianne, who had just come out for a breath of air, bridled at Jessica's words. "You're surely not going to give our books to be pawed over by a flock of woolly-headed little—"

"We don't need our old copies of *Webster's Speller* for ourselves," Jessica said, adding, "although your spelling, my dear, still leaves something to be desired."

"If you could spare some books, I know that Mr. Langford would be most grateful, Jessica," Megan said. "Some of the older boys and girls have made remarkable progress during the past few months."

Jessica's eyes brightened with genuine interest, and Megan

remembered how Clay had told her that his sister had taught Noah to read and write.

"Have they really been learning?" Jessica asked. "Arithmetic, too? I think I can find a few arithmetic books, the ones Reed and Clay used. And our slates and the globe papa brought us from New York."

"Why don't you come to the school with me tomorrow?" Megan asked impulsively. "Then you can ask Mr. Langford what he's teaching. Maybe"— she hesitated, then went on— "maybe you could find the time to teach one of the girls' classes—"

Lianne turned on Megan, her eyes flashing anger.

"How dare you even make such a suggestion? Have you no sense of decency at all? The very idea of my sister going to help that—that—"

"Mr. Langford doesn't have horns," Megan said, her temper rising. "His father was a minister back in New Hampshire, and he is a perfectly respectable gentleman."

"You would think a Yankee could be a gentleman," Lianne said scornfully.

Megan's eyes burned amber-gold as she tried to force back her anger over the implied insult against herself. But it was Jessica who intervened, saying, "That's not fair, Lianne. And, as a matter of fact, I happen to know that Mr. Langford is a gentleman. He's a pleasant-spoken man, and he—"

Lianne turned on her sister. "You've talked to him— Oh, how could you?"

"I only said good morning when I passed him. I was on my way down to the quarters. I could scarcely refuse to answer his greeting, could I?" Jessica looked thoughtful. "Mr. Langford must be lonely, living in that lean-to, next to the school, speaking only to his pupils—and Megan—"

"Then he ought to go back up North where he belongs," Lianne snapped. "Why he wouldn't be here at all if Megan hadn't sweet talked Clay into letting him use that old sugar mill—"

Jessica smiled. "I doubt that Clay has ever been sweet talked into doing anything against his will."

Lianne's eyes were narrow slits, and her voice was tight with barely concealed resentment. "Oh, I'm not so sure of that," she said, tossing her head. "After all, when a man's on his honeymoon, when he's carried away by his—his feelings— it's easy enough for a girl like Megan to get anything she wants from him."

"Lianne, that's downright indecent," Jessica said sharply. "And unfair. Megan is Clay's wife. She is carrying his child."

All at once, Lianne's eyes began to gleam with tears, and her soft, pink mouth quivered. "It's—it's easy enough for her kind to get a husband—even now—when there are so few eligible men left—" She turned, and lifting her full skirts, she hurried back into the house.

"You must not mind Lianne," Jessica said. "She can't help envying any married woman. Her own beau was killed in the war."

"And you? Wasn't there ever someone you—"

"Oh, no," Jessica said, smiling, as if the notion was faintly ludicrous. "I was never a belle like Lianne. I suppose some of us are born to be spinsters."

"I don't believe that," Megan said firmly, moved as always by Jessica's uncomplaining acceptance of her unmarried state, and aware of the warm, womanly tones in Jessica's voice that belied the severity of her appearance. Jessica would be a good wife and mother; Megan was sure of that.

But Jessica had already dismissed the subject, saying, "Why don't you come upstairs with me right now, Megan. We'll see if we can find those books and other schoolroom articles for Mr. Langford."

Although that particular conflict had been smoothed over by Jessica, who even went so far as to help Megan get the books, the globe, and the rest of the needed material down to Tom Langford, Megan could not help but feel the mounting tension all around her. The weather had become hot and sultry, without even a trace of a breeze from the winding yellow river.

The cotton crop would be a good one, Reed predicted, if only the hired freedmen could be counted on to do their work and not wander off.

"If we have a good season," he said, "we ought to produce at least twelve hundred bales, and at the going rate—one hundred dollars a bale—we'll be doing well for the first time since the war, even allowing for what we have to pay the laborers."

"Violet says that Jeff thinks we've overpaying our people," Samantha remarked. "Fifteen dollars a month—"

"That's only for the prime hands," Reed pointed out. "The women, even the best of them, get ten."

Megan had seen the black women, their skirts tucked up, laboring in the fields along with their men back as early as February. The river bank had been misty blue, as smoke rose from the piles of burning briars and logs from those fields that had been neglected during the war. Women worked in the log-rolling gangs, thrusting their handspikes under each log, while Jeff Shepley, seated on his horse, shouted at them to urge them along. Megan flinched at the obscenities he used and, even more, at the barely restrained violence in his tone. Clay had been right about Jeff—a frustrated man, angered by the loss of his own plantation, resentful that these laborers were freedmen, who could, if pushed too far, simply walk off the job.

At the beginning of April, when the clearing and plowing were finished, the planting had begun. And now, at the end of August, the picking was well under way, and the cotton gins, which had fallen into disrepair, were put to work again. Each Saturday, the cotton that had been baled during the week was hauled to the river bank, to be shipped to New Orleans. Lianne and Samantha talked eagerly about the probable returns on the crop, about new drapes for the upstairs windows, a new set of china, perhaps from England, to replace the tableware that had been broken during the past four years.

"And I must have a maid for myself," Samantha said. "And a really well trained nursemaid for Luke." She gave Megan an envious look, for neither Samantha or Lianne had been able to forgive the fact that only Megan had her own personal maid.

But although Megan liked Ludamae and appreciated her services, she was uneasy because the child had become another source of friction here. Samantha had hired and dismissed several black girls, complaining that they were unsatisfactory, lazy, or "uppity," prone to disappear when they were most needed.

Samantha also criticized Megan for insisting that Ludamae must attend Tom Langford's school. Ludamae was more than willing, and Megan could not repress a smile, seeing the girl trot off each afternoon, wearing a clean starched dress and clutching a cracked slate that Jessica had found for her.

"If Ludamae has so much free time, she could take care of
Luke," Samantha remarked peevishly. She had no patience with
her small son, and although he was a fine, healthy baby, his
occasional fits of crying drove her frantic. But Megan was
firm, insisting that as many of the children of the freedmen as
possible must learn to read and write, and the adults as well.

"You don't understand these people," Samantha told Megan. "And you're putting the wrong ideas into their heads.
Why only the other day, Rachel spoke of going to that Yankee
school in the evening. I put a stop to that."

"But you have no right to—" Megan began, her amber eyes
beginning to narrow dangerously.

"I have every right. I have no intention of losing the best
cook in the county simply because you and that—Mr. Langford—want to fill her head with a lot of foolish notions. Don't
meddle in matters you don't understand, Megan."

After one such discussion, Megan, her nerves strained to
the breaking point by her effort to keep from quarreling with
Samantha, hurried upstairs and wrote to Clay, pleading with
him to let her join him at the railroad camp, which had now
moved as far as western Louisiana, close to the Texas border.
But Clay's reply, which came early in September, caused Megan's heart to sink.

She sat in their bedroom, and although twilight had already
fallen, she did not take time to turn up the lamp but read Clay's
words by the faint glow that came in through the tall windows.

"A railroad camp . . . no place for a lady . . . living conditions
are primitive . . ."

She pushed back a strand of hair from her damp forehead,
for even sunset had brought no relief from the heat. "The crew
lives in three-tier bunkhouses," she went on reading. "They
roll along the track as soon as it is laid. There are flatcars with
tools and one that houses a blacksmith's shop . . . we call the
whole work train the perpetual train because it never stops for
long . . . As for the men, they are hard working but a rough
lot . . ."

Had Clay chosen to forget that Jim Rafferty, her uncle, was
one of those men? Did he believe that when she had married
him, she had turned her back on her own people?

". . . must remain at Montrose . . . I want my first son to sleep in that cradle built by Grandfather Drummond . . ." And then, her sense of depression deepening, she read on: "I can't promise to return in time for the baby's birth . . . the railroad has to keep moving . . ."

Yes, for Clay, the railroad came first. Maybe if he had married Samantha, he would have felt differently. But she must not let herself think about that. Clay was her husband, and one day, he would come to love her as she loved him. He would—

She heard a sound at the bedroom door, and turning, saw it open. A moment later, she was on her feet, Clay's letter slipping from her fingers.

Ludamae had not returned from Tom's schoolhouse at the usual time to help Megan dress for supper, but Megan, immersed in Clay's letter, had not given the child's tardiness any thought. Tom Langford often gave extra time to those pupils who were bright and eager to learn, and Ludamae was both. Now Megan cried out, for she saw that the slim, dark-skinned girl was shaking violently, that her dress had been torn so that her small, budding breasts were revealed. Her face was bruised and swollen.

Megan turned up the lamp and stared at Ludamae, and even before the child could be persuaded to give her account of what had happened, Megan guessed the truth; she knew what had delayed Ludamae's return from school.

Chapter Twelve

"REED, WAIT! I must speak to you."

Samantha and Lianne had already gone into the dining room, but Megan had been waiting in the hall to intercept her brother-in-law, who was returning from a trip to Natchez-under-the-Hill, where he had gone to place an order for new equipment for one of the cotton gins. Since the end of the war, many of the buildings in Natchez-under-the-Hill, which had been seized by the federal government, had been returned to their former owners, and business was gradually being revived.

Reed removed his hat and said, "We can talk over supper. Come along, Megan. I understand that Rachel has prepared her turtle soup—one of her finest dishes."

"Oh, Reed—please—" Megan's face was white and taut with strain. In spite of the humid heat that filled the house, she felt cold inside and sick with revulsion as she remembered her talk with Ludamae.

Reed looked at Megan anxiously, his eyes moving to her thickening waist before he averted his glance. "Are you ill?" he asked. "Is it—the baby—"

Megan shook her head impatiently. "I'm quite well," she

told him. "But you will have to dismiss Jeff Shepley at once." She was far too upset to be tactful. "He'll have to leave Montrose. It's far less punishment than he deserves—"

Reed took Megan's arm and propelled her into the dining room, but she went on speaking. "There's no need for Violet to know what Jeff has done—"

"And what has Jeff done?" Samantha asked, her dark eyes wide with curiosity as Reed and Megan came to the table. Reed drew out a chair for Megan, and she sank down into it, her legs unsteady. Jessica had not yet come to the table.

"Yes, Megan, you must calm yourself and explain. I don't know what's upset you so, and as for dismissing Jeff, that's out of the question," Reed said.

Megan began to tremble, and she had to exert her will power to maintain her self-control. She drew a deep breath, grateful that now, in the latter stages of her pregnancy, she no longer had to wear stays.

"It's about Ludamae," she said. "Jeff saw Ludamae returning from the schoolhouse—perhaps he was watching for her, I don't know— He dragged her into the cypress swamp and he—he forced her—"

Lianne's face went deep pink, and her lips parted as she gasped with outrage. Samantha was listening intently.

"I realize that the Shepleys and the Drummonds have been neighbors for years," Megan went on, "but it makes no difference. Jeff will have to go."

Reed filled his wine glass and drank, and then set it down. "Now, Megan, you don't know these darkies like we do—you can't be expected to. They'll make up all sorts of outrageous tales. Perhaps Ludamae was out in the swamp with one of the field hands and—"

"Ludamae was raped," Megan cried, too indignant to choose her words carefully. "Jeff Shepley raped a child of fourteen."

Lianne put one small white hand to her throat, her breath coming quickly. "Never have I heard such vile talk at this table," she said. "I feel quite faint." She fumbled in the pocket of her ruffled organdy dress and brought out her smelling salts. But Megan was not concerned with Lianne's vaporings.

"Well, Reed? Are you going to tell Jeff to leave Montrose?" Reed looked at Samantha as if for support, but his wife remained silent. He turned back to Megan, saying, "That's hardly possible. I know you're unfamiliar with the workings of the plantation, but you do know that we've already begun the picking—the first good crop we've had in three years. We need Jeff. He's the only one who can get any work out of these free blacks."

Rachel came in at that moment and carefully set down a large tureen of steaming turtle soup. Her dark eyes were completely impassive, although she knew about Ludamae, for Megan had asked Rachel to get one of the older women from the fields to sit with the girl and try to soothe her. Perhaps such incidents had been commonplace on some plantations before the war, Megan thought. But Vance Drummond had never tolerated such behavior, not here at Montrose. Clay had told her so, and she believed him.

"You'll have to hire another overseer," Megan told Reed. "Or manage by yourself. But Jeff must leave." Her hands were clenched in her lap, and she had to drive her nails into her palms as she struggled to keep from losing control of herself. She was shocked to see that none of the other Drummonds at the table shared her feelings.

"You mustn't distress yourself, Megan, not in your—your delicate state," Reed said, his voice placating, indulgent. "Perhaps if you went up to bed, Rachel could bring you your dinner there. Or a pot of herb tea. Rachel brews an herb tea that's most soothing—"

"I don't need to be soothed," Megan cried. "Ludamae has been—"

"Oh, please," Lianne interrupted, clutching at her green cutglass bottle of smelling salts. "I really cannot stand such talk. Megan, I must insist—"

"I'm sorry if I've offended you," Megan said quietly. "But I want Reed's promise that Jeff will leave here. He deserves far worse, and if it were up to me—"

"It's not up to you," Samantha said. "Reed will do whatever he feels is necessary. Really, Megan, you can't be expected to understand the situation, since you're—well, since you're a foreigner. But even you should understand that we've been counting on the money from the cotton crop to refurbish Montrose and buy some decent clothes for ourselves."

Megan did not answer for she had not really expected support from Samantha. But Reed was a courteous man, and sensitive as well. She must make him understand, must appeal to his sense of decency.

"Reed, what would your father have done to an overseer who was guilty of—" she glanced at Lianne and went on— "of such a crime?"

The look in Reed's eyes told Megan that she had struck a chord. Vance Drummond had not permitted his overseers to take their pleasure with the black slave women, and he had forbidden his sons to visit the quarter to slake their needs.

"You're sure Ludamae was telling the truth?" Reed asked.

"I'm sure," Megan said.

"I'll go and speak to Jeff," Reed said, pushing his chair away from the table, leaving his soup untouched before him. "And if I'm convinced that he—I'll take whatever action is necessary." He got up and left the dining room.

"How dare you?" Samantha demanded. "Ordering my husband about as if he were a field hand? You don't know anything about Montrose, and you don't care about it."

"You're wrong," Megan said, anger starting to rise within her. "Montrose belongs to Clay. His father left it to him. I have as much of a stake in it as any of you, more perhaps. But I can't pretend that I never heard Ludamae's story."

"Megan, these are matters for gentlemen to deal with," Lianne said primly. "And since Clay isn't here, we must trust Reed to do what is proper. Now we won't say another word about the whole unfortunate business. No decent woman would even sully her lips with the words you have used here tonight."

"Considering Megan's background," Samantha said, "we should not be surprised by her outburst."

Megan felt the heat rising up along her throat and face, felt the blood begin to pound in her temples. "Common decency is the same everywhere," she said, her voice shaking with barely repressed rage. "I can remember the British soldiers stationed in my village back home. No girl coming home through the fields alone after dark was safe."

"Really, Megan, you must learn to forget your unfortunate beginnings," Samantha said. "You have already embarrassed us before our neighbors by speaking about—"

"If you're saying that I ought to be ashamed of being Irish, I'm not. I never will be. Or if you mean that I should forget that Uncle Jim lives in Natchez-under, I can't do that, either. It's a bad place, Natchez-under, but my uncle's not bad. He's a decent, hard-working man. I'm sorry I shamed you before your neighbors by talking about my people." Pride stiffened her spine as she went on speaking, and words came swiftly, for she had held them back too long, trying to keep peace in the house, and she could restrain herself no longer. "I see no reason why I should hide the truth about myself. After all, Clay married me, knowing who and what I was."

She did not flinch before the naked resentment in Samantha's eyes. "Clay is master of this house. Since he is away, I'm doing what I feel he would want—"

"You—you don't know what Clay would want! You don't understand him. You don't know how he thinks and feels and you never will. You know nothing about Clay or any of us." She stopped speaking abruptly, and Megan heard a curious, almost gloating tone in her voice. She stopped speaking for a moment, and Megan felt a nameless fear stirring inside her. Then Samantha went on. "Clay came back from the war, confused, shaken by all that happened to him. He was not himself. He went down to Natchez-under, and he saw you there. I don't know how you managed to trap him, but then I suppose your kind have their little ways."

"Samantha! That is enough." Jessica had come into the dining room, unnoticed.

"Jessica, you don't understand," Lianne began.

"I understand well enough," Jessica told her sister. "I met Reed a moment ago. He told me about his errand to Jeff's cottage. And Megan's right. We can't have such a man as our overseer."

"We don't know that Jeff did anything to Ludamae," Samantha said. "If the girl was—attacked—it might have been by that Yankee schoolteacher. He kept her late, didn't he?"

Megan was sickened by the accusation, for Tom was an outsider here, as she was, and if Samantha spread her ugly suggestion, he might be driven from Montrose. Reed would be only too eager to believe that it had been the Yankee stranger, not Jeff, who had raped Ludamae.

"I know how you feel about me," Megan told Samantha. "But I didn't think that you would take out your spite on an innocent man."

"Innocent? Perhaps you think so. You made it possible for Mr. Langford to have his school here. You wheedled Clay into—"

But before Samantha could go on, Jessica confronted her and said, "Tom Langford is innocent. I was with him this afternoon. He kept Ludamae late, and I helped her with her reading. And then"— Jessica hesitated, but only for a moment—"I stayed to talk with Tom—with Mr. Langford. And he drove me back from the schoolhouse because it was getting dark. I'd have asked him in for supper, only I know how you and Reed—and Lianne—would have treated him." Jessica glared at Samantha. "But if I ever hear you breathe one word against Tom, I will call you a liar in public."

"Jessica, honey, you're not yourself," Lianne said.

"Of course, she's not," Samantha said bitterly. "Everything has changed in this house since Megan came. Clay never should have married her—"

Megan stood up, and all at once she felt steady and in control. "He did marry me, though, and I am carrying his baby. And you can't forgive me for that, can you, Samantha?"

Samantha flinched, but Megan went on. "You needn't be troubled by having me here at Montrose any longer."

A faint gleam of hope came into Samantha's eyes.

"You're going back to your uncle's home? Perhaps that would be best." She sounded almost cordial now, but Megan was not deceived.

"No," Megan said. "I'm going to my husband. As soon as I'm sure that Ludamae will be properly cared for, I'm going to join Clay at the railroad camp."

The elation that Megan had felt when she had left Montrose on the morning after her quarrel with Samantha had long since faded. True, she was satisfied with the arrangements that she had made for Ludamae, sending her off to stay with her grandmother on a plantation near Selma. But she was by no means certain that Reed would dismiss Jeff Shepley even though he had questioned the overseer about the attack on the black child. Jeff had denied his guilt, and Reed had insisted that although he might dismiss the man after the cotton had been gathered, the success of the crop came first.

Megan had packed a carpetbag with her clothes and had

also taken a small horsehair trunk. She took the river boat down to Natchez and then prevailed on one of Uncle Jim's teamsters, Pete Callahan, to drive her to the railroad camp, since he was making the trip that morning with a load of supplies. Callahan was not happy about the arrangement. He looked at Megan and shook his head.

"Sure, now, a female in your condition has no business traipsin' about the countryside. And the weather due to turn bad any hour now—"

Both Aunt Kathleen and Belle, who was herself expecting her first baby, joined in trying to dissuade Megan from making the trip, but she remained adamant, assuring them both that old Dr. Purvis, who had treated the Drummond family for years, had said that her baby was not due to arrive for at least another month.

"I'm perfectly all right," Megan told her aunt and her cousin. The truth was that having left the tense atmosphere of Montrose, she was beginning to feel her spirits rising as she thought about being with Clay again, lying beside him, holding him close. She had not realized until now how much she had missed him during these long months when they had been apart.

She pushed to the back of her mind those things he had told her in his letter, about how the railroad camp at end-of-track was no place for a lady. She did not need luxurious surroundings, for she was not one of those soft, fluttering plantation ladies like Samantha. Hadn't she spent the first years of her life in a one-room, thatched-roofed cottage and endured the fetid misery of the steerage passage from Ireland to get to America?

But now, as she sat in the heavy supply wagon that rocked and jolted its way across the countryside, along the deeply rutted trail through the Louisiana swamp country, she felt a stirring of uneasiness. Callahan's prediction about the bad weather had been fulfilled, and the fine, misty rain that had, at first, been welcome after the heavy, sultry heat of the past few weeks had changed now to a hard, pelting downpour. The rain, driven by the rising wind from the Gulf, hit against the canvas top of the supply wagon with growing force. Megan sat braced against one of the wagon's sides, on a folded blanket, surrounded by lashed-down sacks of potatoes, crates of tea, bags of flour, and sugar. As the force of the wind increased, the canvas began to sway ominously, and she felt the rain dripping down through a few small tears in the heavy material.

"I warned ye, Mrs. Drummond," the huge, broad-backed teamster shouted over the rising wind. "No turnin' back now."

Once, they halted to rest the horses, and Callahan pointed out the gleam of a section of rain-wet rails through the thick stand of scrub oak and palmetto. Megan realized, as never before, why Clay insisted that a railroad was so necessary in this untamed swampy stretch of the Gulf Coast country. She managed a smile as she realized the irony of it: Clay Drummond's wife jouncing along a muddy road, blocked by branches torn loose by the wind, while he was busy building a railroad. . . .

But the smile froze on her lips, for she felt a curious, sharp sensation in her swollen abdomen. The baby, kicking. She had felt it many times before, and each time she had been thrilled at the feeling of life inside her. Clay's child and hers. But this sensation was somehow different. An ache in the small of her back moved until pain encircled her like a steel corset, causing her to sink her teeth into her lower lip.

A whole month to go, she told herself firmly. Surely Dr. Purvis should know about such things. The ache subsided, and she told herself that it must be due to the jouncing of the wagon. As soon as the horses had rested and she and Callahan had shared a meal of bread and cold pork, with cold tea for her and whiskey for him, they started off again.

On the following morning, the wind blew harder, and she could hear Callahan swearing under his breath each time the team of horses shied and reared when a branch came crashing down into the path of the wagon. He was an expert at handling his team, as were all of Uncle Jim's men, but even he had to fight with all his strength to keep the horses in check.

Late that afternoon, the sky grew black with the high-piled thunderheads, and Megan, crouched in the back of the wagon, ached in every joint from the rough ride. She felt damp and chilled in spite of the traveling cloak she had wrapped around her, and she edged forward to ask Callahan if it was much farther to end-of-track.

She rose, bracing herself against the crates, and inched

toward the front of the swaying wagon when the huge, moss-hung branch of a live oak tree cracked and then came crashing down directly in the path of the wagon.

The horses reared up and whinied in panic, and Pete Callahan had to exert all the strength in his heavy, powerfully muscled body to fight the team to a halt. The wagon tilted, the wheels spinning, for there was no traction in the road, which had been turned into a muddy bog by the heavy rain.

Megan felt the wagon sway to one side, and she lost her precarious footing; she was flung, face down, against the rough boards. She screamed, trying unsuccessfully to break her fall with her hands. Then she lay still, hearing Callahan's hoarse shout and the sound of ripping canvas. He came to her, turned her over, and she saw through the tear in the canvas a blur of gray-green, rain-soaked foliage: live oak, Spanish moss, palmetto, and tangled vines that became a spinning kaleidoscope, that moved faster and faster, then dissolved into darkness. . . .

Pete Callahan's powerful arm supported her as he tried to force the neck of a whiskey bottle between her teeth. The rain was soaking through the dark, heavy poplin of her traveling dress, the thin wool of her cloak. She shivered, swallowed a little of the whiskey, choked, and then felt the heat of the liquid burning through her and reviving her.

"Are ye all right now, Mrs. Drummond?"

"I think so." But as she spoke, the ache formed again in the small of her back, and the pain encircled her and tore at her before it relaxed its grip. "Is it much farther to end-of-track?"

"Only a few hours and we'll be there." Pete Callahan shook his head. "I warned ye, Mrs. Drummond. Ye know I did."

"I'll explain that to my husband when we arrive at the railroad camp." Pete started to get to his feet, but Megan gripped his arm. She hesitated for a moment, then told herself that this was no time for false modesty.

"Perhaps we'd best stop at the nearest town first," she said. "We—you—if you know of a midwife there—"

"Town, is it!" The words exploded from Pete, and he stared at her in mingled amazement and dismay. "There ain't no town anywhere near here."

"Then perhaps one of the women in the camp, a wife of one of the men in the crew could—"

"Mother of God," Pete said softly. "No man of the crew has a wife along. The only women at end-of-track are—" Then, seeing the look of panic in her face, he patted her shoulder awkwardly. "Don't you worry," he said. "We'll manage somehow."

He pulled off his heavy coat, wrapped it around Megan, settled her back on the blanket, and then went to the high seat and whipped the team forward, his heavy shoulders hunched against the force of the wind and the driving rain.

"Callahan, why the devil did you bring her out here?"

Megan, lying in the back of the wagon, heard Clay's voice, and in spite of her pain, she felt her heart lift at the knowledge of his nearness. She would be safe now. Clay would take care of her.

"Sure, now, Mr. Drummond, I told her, and so did Mrs. Rafferty, but there was no stoppin' her."

Megan managed to sit up, setting her teeth against the pain, her hair clinging to her forehead in damp tendrils.

"It isn't Pete's fault," she said, and she was dismayed by the weakness of her voice. A moment later, Clay was lifting her down from the supply wagon and carrying her to a boxcar a short distance away.

"But where's your house?" she asked as he carried her through the half-open door. Pete Callahan stood on the threshold, looking uneasy.

"This is my house," Clay said, his voice hard with anger. "My house, my office. It moves along with the rest of the work train. Megan, I wrote you. I told you that this was no place for a lady. You got my letter, didn't you?"

She nodded. "Yes, but I thought—"

He set her down on his cot, the sheets damp and mildewed from the humidity of the surrounding swampland, the blanket coarse. "You didn't think," he said, his heavy eyebrows drawn together in an angry frown. "You were determined to have your own way as usual. But it's no good, Megan. As soon as this storm lets up, you're going right back to Montrose, and you're going to stay there—"

He broke off, seeing her body stiffen under the onslaught of pain, and he stared down at her, his eyes darkening until they looked almost black. "The baby." It wasn't a question. He knew.

"I wanted to be with you, and Dr. Purvis said— Oh, Clay, I'm sorry—"

He pulled up a packing crate and sat down beside her. "Don't try to talk now," he said, the anger gone from his voice.

"She'll be needin' a woman with her, Mr. Drummond," Pete Callahan said.

"And where would I find a woman out here?" Clay demanded.

Pete looked down at his huge, mud-caked boots, not wanting to meet his employer's eyes. "There's—Miss Nadine."

"Miss Nadine?"

Megan lifted her head, the pain having abated, and looked from her husband to Pete. She remembered what Pete had said back in the wagon. "The only women at end-of-track are—"

She understood, and she could sympathize with her husband's dilemma.

"Miss Nadine's a female, and she's had plenty of experience. I guess her kind knows a lot about— What I mean t' say—" Pete said.

Megan felt a sudden gush of warm wetness against her thighs and was grateful for the heavy petticoats, the poplin skirt, and the coarse blanket that covered her. Even so, she sensed that there was little time to be lost.

"Get Miss Nadine—" she said, her voice filled with urgency.

"But you don't understand," Clay began.

"I think I do—but get her—quickly—"

Clay turned to Pete Callahan. "Do as she says," he ordered. "Carry Miss Nadine down here if you have to—if her tent hasn't been washed away by now. Get moving."

Pete Callahan nodded and disappeared, sliding the boxcar door shut behind him. Another pain caught at Megan, and she reached out. Clay's hands closed around hers, his strong, warm fingers giving her reassurance by their grip.

Looking into his face, she saw no anger there, only helplessness. And fear. For her safety? Or the baby's? She did not know, and it did not seem important.

"Don't worry," she said. "I'll give you the son you want."

Brant Drummond was born in the hour before dawn, and Megan was grateful for the help of Miss Nadine, a stout, rouged woman whose blue-black hair was obviously dyed and whose heliotrope perfume filled the boxcar with its heavy, musky smell. Miss Nadine, who ran a thriving business in a tent where her girls gave comfort and relief to the hard-working men of the railroad crew, was calm, efficient, and skillful.

"I'm sorry—we can't put the baby in the cradle that your grandfather made—" Megan spoke a little disjointedly, worn from her ordeal, her eyes fixed on Clay's face. Miss Nadine had just allowed him back inside the boxcar, and now he was moving about, setting down a wooden crate beside the cot. He smiled at Megan, touching her cheek lightly.

"Maybe this is more suitable for my first son," he said, his fingers curving around her damp face. "It's a box that was used to store the dynamite we use for blasting out here."

Miss Nadine had contributed a small, lace-trimmed pillow of her own to make a soft bed for the new arrival.

"I wanted your son to be born at Montrose— I wanted—"

"It doesn't matter," Clay said gently. "You're safe, and my son, too. That's what matters."

Her eyes closed then, and she let herself drift into sleep, but not before she heard him say, with a kind of wonder in his voice, "My wife and my son. . . ."

Chapter Thirteen

ALTHOUGH REED had not dismissed Jeff Shepley, Clay had done it for him. After Megan had recovered from the birth of Brant, named for Clay's paternal grandfather, she had stayed on for a time at the railroad camp, until Clay was able to make the arrangements to escort her home. During the return trip, Megan told Clay that she could not stay on at Montrose any longer, that she did not want to raise her son in an atmosphere of tension and unending conflict. She made no mention of Samantha's personal attack on her, but she did tell him about Jeff Shepley's brutal assault on Ludamae.

"All right, Megan," Clay told her. "I'll get you a home of your own, and you may run it to suit yourself."

Immediately upon their return, Clay went down to the overseer's cottage, where he confronted Jeff, questioned him briefly, then told him that his services were no longer needed.

"You're throwing me off the place because I tumbled that little black bitch?" Jeff stared at him in disbelief. "She was begging for it." His voice grew bitter. "Maybe that wife of yours is turnin' you into a psalm-singin'—"

"Leave my wife out of this. My father had certain rules here at Montrose. He never touched a black woman himself, and

Reed and I were forbidden to take our pleasure with them. The same rule applied to our overseers."

"But look here, Clay—"

"I'm only doing what my father would have done under the same circumstances. I want you off Montrose land by tomorrow."

Clay was unmoved by the resentment in Jeff's eyes. But after Jeff and Violet had packed up and left, Clay was faced with a serious problem, for he doubted Reed's ability to run Montrose at a profit.

Clay's worries were not unfounded, for now, three years later, in the fall of 1869, Reed had hired and fired a long succession of unsatisfactory overseers. Now he was trying to manage the plantation with only the help of a couple of black drivers. He had admitted to Samantha that this year's crop would be a poor one, and even before the picking was over, he had started spending time in Natchez-under, which had changed little since the end of the war. The noisy, dilapidated gambling shacks, set on pilings that jutted out into the river, the raucous taverns, and the sleazy brothels were still going full blast, catering to the Yankee soldiers, the Carpetbaggers, and the ex-Confederates alike.

Now, as he rode his bay mare home from an afternoon of drinking at a Silver Street tavern, he hoped that Samantha would be in a good mood. She had been distant and irritable lately, for she chafed over the constant lack of money and often pointed out to Reed the difference between their way of life and the one enjoyed by Clay and Megan in their handsome new house, Azalea Hill, set high on a bluff in the finest section of Natchez-on-the-Hill.

The house had been built in the style known as Steamboat Gothic, with a double staircase of two flights leading to the veranda. The low-pitched, hipped roof was pierced with dormer windows, whose diamond-paned glass caught the rays of the sun. Inside, Megan had chosen light colors: white woodwork, pale-yellow walls, and drapes of soft yellow Liberty silk. While several of the rooms had been furnished in the conventional rosewood and mahogany, the breakfast room and Megan's dressing room were done in wicker and bamboo.

Megan had her own carriage, her coachman, and Ludamae, who, at seventeen, looked every inch the well-trained lady's maid in her gray silk uniforms with their lace-trimmed aprons. All Natchez turned to look at Clay Drummond's lovely young wife when she went out driving with her two sons, three-year-old Brant, dark-haired and tall for his age, and the new arrival, Terence, who had been born only a few months before.

All the Drummonds had attended the christening and the reception in the new house, but Samantha had been distinctly cold toward Megan, and pleading a sudden headache, had made it a point to leave early. Lianne, Jessica, and the other ladies had stared with fascination at the fine furnishings, for there were few families in the Delta country that could afford such luxuries these days.

Clay's railroad venture was paying off, but Reed knew that the Natchez–Fort Worth Line was not his brother's only source of income these days. Now, as Reed turned the bay mare off the road bordering the bluffs and onto the path leading to the Montrose stables, his mouth tightening into a thin, hard line, he thought of the ways in which Clay was making his money— working hand in glove with Yankee speculators.

Clay had invested in great tracts of timberland in Texas and Louisiana; he had gone into partnership with Oliver Winthrop, a Bostonian who had settled in New Orleans, and the two men were building cotton mills and were preparing to tap the iron and coal deposits in the hills of Alabama.

Reed did not begrudge Clay his growing wealth, for Clay was working hard for it; but Reed did resent having to listen to Samantha's litany of complaints, her comparisons between her own situation and Megan's.

"That trashy Irish girl can flaunt herself like a queen. I have to scheme and scrimp to get enough money for a couple of decent dresses to wear to the French Opera House."

Reed had not wanted to accompany Samantha to the French Opera House in New Orleans for even a few performances, and he had definitely refused to stay there with her for the whole opera season. He had only consented to a week in New Orleans because he did not want Samantha to go alone or even with Jessica as a chaperone. He could not bear to be separated from his wife even for so short a time, for in spite of her outbursts of temper and her coldness, he still loved her. He would force himself to sit through a few operatic performances, although he found the entertainment in Natchez-under more satisfying these days.

Although he had only visited the brothels of Silver Street a few times as a boy, now he was driven to seek solace there; for Samantha had complained of vague ailments after Luke's birth and had kept Reed from her bed once more. She was the only woman he had ever really wanted, but he could not force himself on her, and so he had been driven, in desperation, to visit the narrow, shuttered houses of Silver Street where the girls were accomplished and agreeable.

This afternoon, after leaving a brothel, he had gone to a tavern. There he had met Jeff Shepley, and although he would not have been surprised if Jeff had either ignored him or picked a fight, his former overseer had done neither; instead, he had insisting on standing Reed to a drink. Reed, in turn, had ordered a bottle, to be served at one of the tables, where Jeff had told him of several not particularly lucrative positions he had held since he had been dismissed from Montrose.

He was now working for a dealer in plows and harnesses in Natchez, he explained. He made it plain that he did not blame Reed for his dismissal from the Drummond plantation, but he was careful not to criticize Clay openly, for he knew that Reed and Clay had always been close and that their family loyalty was not to be challenged by outsiders.

Instead, Jeff turned the conversation to politics, to the election of Ulysses Grant to the presidency and to the triumph of the Radical Republicans.

"Grant still has a lot to learn, him and his Republican friends," Jeff said. He spat, missing the nearby brass spitoon by several inches. "If he thinks we'll stand for having a bunch of Carpetbaggers and Scalawags and their trained black apes running our state, we'll teach him a lesson he won't forget. And soon."

"The Fourteenth Amendment—" Reed began, but Jeff cut him short, pouring himself another drink.

"To hell with that lawyer talk," he said. "Giving the blacks the vote is one thing. Letting them have the right to use it's another."

And Jeff, leaning across the stained wooden table, went on to tell Reed about the organization that had been formed recently, adding that he himself had been elected leader of the local chapter. Reed was troubled by what he heard, and when Jeff urged him to join, he said that right now the picking season at Montrose took all his time and energy.

Reed had no intention of joining Jeff's organization, the Knights of the White Camellia, for their activities, as set forth by Jeff, were thoroughly repugnant to him.

But Samantha did not share Reed's views, and she made that plain to him while she finished dressing for supper that evening.

"But you've got to join—you've just got to," she insisted. "If all our neighbors belong and we don't, they'll think we're no better than Scalawags—Republicans—"

"All our neighbors don't belong," Reed said. "Jeff's the leader, and Seth Hunter's second-in-command, but there are plenty of decent citizens around here who'll have no part in it. I agree with the goals of the Knights, but I can't go along with their methods."

"They're doing what they have to do to protect their women," Samantha began, her dark eyes stormy. "I should think that if you cared for me as much as you say—"

"Damn it, you know I'd kill any man, black or white, who affronted you in any way. But this organization was not formed for the protection of our women. Jeff and the others want to keep the blacks out of the schools and away from the polling places."

Samantha rose from in front of her dressing table, her full skirts of pale-rose poplin swaying about her. Her delicate features hardened. "And you don't want those things?"

"Of course I do—but not if it means terrorizing and torturing helpless blacks—"

"You don't care that we have a Yankee schoolteacher, that Langford man, right here at Montrose, filling the heads of our field workers with all sorts of foolish ideas. Influencing your own sister."

"Langford's teaching some black children and a few of the older folks to read and write. I asked old Elijah—he's sixty-five if he's a day—why he wanted to learn to read. He said he wanted to be able to read the Bible for himself. I can't see what's so disturbing about that."

"And I suppose you're not disturbed by Mr. Langford spending all that time with Jessica, unchaperoned."

"My dear Samantha, I learned when I was about ten years old that Jessica would do as she pleased no matter what anyone said. Clay and I used to go climbing down the bluffs to the river. Jessica insisted on tagging along. We tried to stop her, said it would be dangerous. All those skirts and petticoats. But she put on a castoff pair of my trousers and went on following us. Almost broke her neck one time—"

Samantha struggled to control her rising irritation. "Jessica's not a little girl any longer," she said. "She and that Langford man are alone together."

"Oh, for—Jessica's past the age when she's going to get involved in a flirtation with any man. She's thirty-one. She goes down to the schoolhouse for the same reason she taught Noah, our carpenter, to read and write years ago—she's a born teacher. A bluestocking. But as for anything personal between her and Langford, the whole idea's ridiculous."

"Maybe so," Samantha said. Reed had the most provoking way of changing the subject, of dodging any issue with a bunch of fancy words. "But you've got to join the Knights, Reed. You've got to. I won't be able to hold my head up if you don't. Our neighbors'll say you're disloyal to the Confederacy. To our state."

"And that's more important to you than my own feelings on the matter?" Reed asked.

Samantha longed to cry out that it was, but she kept her voice soft, appealing. "It's not easy for me, Reed. I have so little social life as it is. None of our friends give the kind of big parties they used to."

"They can't afford to. You know that," Reed said impatiently.

"I know. And that's all the more reason why I don't want to be shut out of the little entertainments. I don't want to be shunned by folks I've known all my life because you won't even join a patriotic society. It's no different from the Mardi Gras crewes in New Orleans and Mobile."

"Oh, but it is. Jeff, Seth, and the rest of them didn't organize the Knights to give fancy dress balls and parades, Samantha. You don't understand. Black men have been flogged and—

mutilated—and hung. A black woman who was carrying a child was attacked up near Selma. She was killed—she and her unborn child." He stopped abruptly. "Forgive me. But I have to make you see why I can't join a society dedicated to violence, to killing."

"I guess I understand," Samantha flung back at him. "I think you're afraid that you'll be arrested by the Yankee militia. I think you don't have the backbone to stand up and fight alongside our friends, our neighbors—"

"I fought for the Confederacy," Reed said quietly, "and I'm not ashamed of my war record."

Samantha was silent, for she could not deny that Reed had served in his cavalry regiment with distinction. He had been cited twice for exceptional gallantry by his commanding officer. But her pride in her husband's wartime exploits had dimmed, and now, goaded by her bitterness, her frustration, she lashed out at him.

"The war's been over a long time. Maybe it would have been better if you'd never—if you—" She broke off, and then she took a backward step, frightened by something she saw in his eyes.

"Go on," he said. His voice was deceptively soft, but there was no mistaking the violence that she had stirred to life within him.

"Reed—I never meant—I—"

"Finish what you started to say." His fingers closed on her smooth white shoulders, bared by the low-cut neckline of her dress. "It would have been better if I hadn't come back at all. Because then you could have married Clay."

His fingers tightened, and she felt the arrows of burning pain shooting down her arms. Never before had he hurt her this way. She was terrified, frantically seeking an escape.

The tears of agony that filled her eyes were not feigned, but she made no attempt to blink them back. Instead, she gave way to sobs that shook her body.

"Samantha—"

"Let me go. You're hurting me."

Reed released her, and she slumped down on the wide bed. When he took a step in her direction, she cringed even though she saw the shame, the regret for his action, plainly in his face. She had the upper hand again.

"Please go down to supper," she said.

"We'll go down together."

"I'll have to put on another dress. Something that will cover my shoulders. I don't want Lianne and Jessica to know that you—"

Once again, she let the sobs come. Then he was beside her, holding her in his arms. "Forgive me," he said. "I love you— I'll never love any woman but you—"

She let her body rest against his. He went on speaking softly, pleadingly. "I'd do anything in the world to make you proud of me. But you're asking me to go against my principles. The things Pa stood for all his life—"

"How do you know what Vance Drummond would have done if he'd lived through the war?" Samantha asked. "His world was different. He could afford a lot of—of high-flown principles. But we're fighting for survival. Reed, you don't want to see our state represented by blacks. You don't want them making our laws, grinding us down into the dirt—"

"You know I don't!"

"Then you will join Jeff and the others."

He drew her closer and pressed his lips to her soft, shining hair. Even before he answered, Samantha knew that she had won.

That night, for the first time in months, Samantha shared her bed with Reed and found that she felt a slight stirring of response to his tender lovemaking. He touched her body with his hands, his mouth, carefully, gently, as if she were too delicate and fragile to bear the full force of a man's need. But later, when she lay beside him in the darkness, she thought that maybe if he had ever once possessed her with the driving hunger that Clay had shown her that night in the summerhouse, she might have responded completely.

By the end of November, when the last of the cotton had been shipped down river to market, Samantha knew that she was pregnant again, and she felt only resentment, for she had counted on the week in New Orleans that Reed had promised her. Dr. Purvis's warning that she ought not to travel in the early stages of her pregnancy went unheeded. There was little enough money to spend on new dresses, for the cotton crop had been a poor one, but Samantha attended every performance at the French Opera House. Her pleasure in the week's stay was somewhat lessened by regular bouts of morning sickness. She had not suffered from that malaise when she was carrying Luke, and she resented her second pregnancy fiercely.

In February, Hiram Revels, a black man from Natchez, took his seat in the U.S. Senate as a representative from Mississippi, the seat previously held by Jefferson Davis. A wave of indignation arose, and Reed was frequently absent from Montrose, attending meetings of the Knights of the White Camellia. He was away on such an errand on the night when Samantha suffered a miscarriage. Jessica, unable to get Dr. Purvis, who was also a member of the organization and therefore absent from his home, brought in young Dr. Mark Burnett, who had recently set up practice on the outskirts of Natchez.

The round-faced, stocky young doctor had a calm, kindly manner about him, and he was skilled at his calling. He stopped the bleeding that had terrified Samantha, gave her something to ease the pain, and did whatever else was necessary.

When he came out into the hall, Jessica was downstairs, and it was Lianne who confronted him.

He put a reassuring hand on her arm. "I'm sorry I was unable to save the baby," he said. "But your sister-in-law will recover." Lianne, shaken by the experience, her long, dark curls loose about her small, heart-shaped face, clutched her pale-blue wrapper more closely about her and fumbled for her handkerchief at the same time.

Dr. Burnett handed her his own, and she dabbed at her eyes. "Mrs. Drummond will need good nursing care for the next few weeks, of course, but I am sure that you—"

Lianne, who had never nursed so much as a sick cat in her whole life, looked up at the doctor, her blue eyes sparkling with tears, and said, "I'll do whatever is necessary for dear Samantha, doctor. But you will have to give me your instructions most carefully."

When Jessica returned carrying a steaming pot of coffee, she saw Lianne seated close to the stocky young doctor on a loveseat in the hall outside Samantha's door. Lianne was listening intently, her eyes fixed on Mark Burnett's face. Because there had been no time for Lianne to twist up her hair in its customary chignon or put on a proper dress, she looked far younger than her years, and there was no mistaking the warmth and admiration in the doctor's manner.

Even though Samantha made a swift recovery, Dr. Burnett found it necessary to call at the house nearly every day for the next two weeks, and it was no surprise to anyone at Montrose when, after the patient was up and about again, the doctor continued his visits.

"Surely it's time you spoke to Dr. Burnett," Samantha said to Reed one afternoon when the doctor had taken Lianne out for a drive. "He can't expect that Lianne would consider him seriously as a suitor."

"She appears to be fond of him," Reed replied, and poured himself a glass of brandy.

"But that's not what I mean, and you know it," Samantha said impatiently. "He might begin to think that she would marry him, and that is out of the question."

"Is it?"

"Reed, don't be difficult. Dr. Burnett's not at all suitable. Why he—"

"He saved your life," Reed reminded her.

"And I'll always be grateful, naturally. But that doesn't mean that I would welcome him into the Drummond family." And when Reed remained silent, she went on. "If you won't speak to him about this, I'll ask Clay to do it."

"Mark Burnett's a Southerner and a gentleman," Reed said. "He fought for the Confederacy."

"I know that," Samantha said. Reed could be so contrary at times, she thought, trying to keep her annoyance out of her voice. "But his father ran the hay and feed store on Silver Street."

"Perhaps Lianne doesn't care how Mark's father made his living." Now there was a trace of sadness in Reed's voice. "Maybe our unmarried ladies here in the South don't think such things are as important as they used to be. So many eligible young men died in the war, and Lianne's desire for a husband is perfectly normal, isn't it? She wants to be the mistress of her own home. And, of course, she wants children. Every woman does."

Samantha turned her face away. What a fool Reed was. She never wanted to become pregnant again. She shuddered every time she thought of her miscarriage, the wracking pain and the bleeding. She had borne Luke, and he meant little to her. Indeed, she was quite content to allow him to spend his time in the kitchen with Rachel or down in the stables.

"All right, then," she said. "Clay's off with the surveyors, looking over new land for his railroad, and heaven knows when he'll be home. If you won't take the responsibility of preventing this match, I'll speak to Lianne myself. Perhaps she doesn't realize how strongly attracted poor Dr. Burnett has become. And really, it isn't fair to him, either. She has no intention of marrying him, and it's thoughtless of her to allow this flirtation to continue when nothing can come of it.

But Samantha's talk with Lianne was fruitless.

"I have every intention of marrying Dr. Burnett," Lianne said. "And don't think it will make any difference if you get Clay to try to talk me out of it when he gets back home." Lianne tossed her head, her eyes narrowing with defiance and perhaps a touch of malice. "If it comes to that, you've no reason to be sure that Clay would oppose my marrying Mark. Why should he? He married Megan, didn't he?"

Samantha had dominated her unmarried sisters-in-law ever since she had come to Montrose as a bride, and now Lianne struck back. "I'm sure that Clay does not have cause to regret his choice of a wife. She's given him two beautiful little boys, and now, Jessica tells me, she's in the family way again."

Samantha did not want any more babies, but she was sick with jealousy at the picture that came into her mind: Clay and Megan, locked in each other's arms, in the bedroom at Azalea Hill. She turned and swept out of the room with what dignity she could muster. She did not appeal to Clay when he returned to Natchez; she did not ask him to try to prevent Lianne's marriage to the young doctor.

Lianne and Mark were married in the parlor of Montrose in late spring when the breeze from the gardens carried the fragrance of wisteria and roses. The whole Drummond clan attended. Reed was cordial to his new brother-in-law, for he would never forget that the doctor had saved Samantha's life. Clay, too, welcomed Mark into the family, and Megan stood beside her husband, looking radiant and proud. Opal had designed her gown of yellow silk to conceal the lines of her body, for it was considered shocking for a lady to flaunt her condition, but there could be no doubt that Megan was happy. She carried herself with dignity, her eyes glowing warmly each time they rested on Clay.

Little Luke, who had been dressed for the occasion, much against his will, in a blue-velvet suit with a lace collar and cuffs, came running over to Clay and Megan the moment that the ceremony was over. Samantha watched, pain clawing at her, as Clay swung the sturdy, dark-haired child up in his arms. "Did you miss me?" he asked Luke, and the child nodded vigorously.

"Never mind—when you get a little older, I'll take you, along with Brant and Terence, to end-of-track. I'll let you see how we lay a railroad. Would you like that?"

Luke wriggled with delight, his arms around Clay's neck. "Will you—honest?"

"It's a promise," Clay said. Megan smiled at her nephew affectionately. Samantha had to look away, for she could not stand the sight. Luke was Clay's first-born son, but Clay would never know; he would never be able to claim the boy as his own.

Chapter Fourteen

MEGAN'S THIRD child was a girl who even now, at six months, already gave promise of growing up to be a beauty, for she had thick jet-black hair like Clay's and her mother's eye coloring: an arresting shade of amber-gold set off by long, dark lashes. Clay, with Brant and Terence to carry on his rapidly expanding business empire, which now stretched from Mississippi on through Louisiana and Texas and up into the hill country of Alabama, was delighted that the newest arrival was a daughter.

Megan was both touched and amused when Clay insisted that Deirdre, named for Megan's mother, have the finest embroidered dresses trimmed with yards of imported lace and that the Drummond cradle, brought from Montrose, be draped in silk and lace as well.

"I've packed away all of the boys' baby things," Megan protested. "Surely there's no need—"

"Deirdre's a girl. A little princess. She will be dressed like one. And order a new wardrobe for yourself, too," he told Megan. "That will keep you happy and occupied while I'm away."

He put an arm around her, and his mouth covered hers. Even now, after nearly five years of marriage, his caresses stirred her to swift response.

Clay was leaving for Chicago to inspect the plans for the remarkable new refrigerator cars that were being built there. "The inventor, a Mr. William Davis, calls the refrigerator car his 'ice box on wheels'," Clay explained. "Fresh air is forced over ice, then circulated through the storage compartments. If it works as promised, I'll be able to make a fortune shipping meat and fresh fruits and vegetables to the East."

Megan thought, as she so often had in the past few years, that they had more than enough money already; besides, she hated sleeping alone in the wide bed upstairs while her husband was off in Chicago or in New York to confer with men who were only names to her: Jay Gould, J. P. Morgan, August Belmont, and John Jacob Astor; or to Washington, where he was well known now to members of President Grant's cabinet, to the senators and congressmen who were willing, for a consideration, to push for subsidies and land grants for his railroads.

But although Megan would have preferred that Clay spend more of his time with her here in Natchez, she knew better than to express her feelings openly, for she had learned how strongly Clay was driven by relentless ambition, how any opposition to his goals, no matter how well meant, would only cause him to withdraw into cold silence.

On a May morning, a few days after his departure for Chicago, Megan was both surprised and pleased when she had an unexpected visitor: Opal. But the octoroon was strangely subdued as she told Megan that she had been up to Montrose to visit her mother. She had asked for work as a seamstress there, but Samantha had turned her away.

"Miz Samantha, she said she had no money for new clothes. She said the cotton crop was real poor last year. But then Miz Jessica, she said Ah should come and see you, ma'am. She said you might have work for me, what with your new baby and all."

Although Megan had planned to order her wardrobe from New Orleans or even New York, she sensed the desperation in Opal's voice and manner.

"Yes, indeed," she said quickly. "I'll be needing new clothes for little Deirdre. And for myself, too. I'll want at least two new ball gowns and a walking suit."

The look of intense relief in Opal's dark eyes was unmistakable, but when Megan tried to question her about her own affairs, Opal quickly changed the subject. Soon the two of them were poring over the fashion plates in *Godey's Lady's Book* and *Madame Demorest's Mirror of Fashions,* conferring on which materials would be most suitable.

A few days later, when Megan had made her selections and had had the materials delivered, Opal came for the first fitting, but the octoroon was still obviously unwilling to speak of her personal affairs. Deftly, she draped the yards of applegreen watered silk, measured carefully, then knelt down to place the pins in the skirt. She paused only to consult Megan on the number of flounces she wanted and the length of the train that was to be attached to the bustle.

"Is Noah here in Natchez with you?" Megan asked.

"No, ma'am."

"I suppose he couldn't get time off from his work at the carpenter's shop," Megan said, then stopped abruptly as she saw the swift pain in Opal's eyes, the tightening of her full lips. The hand that held the pins trembled slightly.

"Opal, what's wrong? Can't you tell me?"

"Nothing's wrong, Miz Drummond, ma'am."

"I don't believe you," Megan said gently.

Opal dropped a pin and bent her head to search for it. "Noah—he don't work at the shop no more."

"Then where is he working?"

"He ain't been working for a long time now. He—he just hangs around one of them shanty-town places in New Orleans—drinking and—"

"But Noah's a fine carpenter and a hard worker. My husband has often said so."

"He ain't never going to be a carpenter again. He can't. But Ah sure am thankful to you for all this sewing work. It'll take care of us. Ah got three little ones now. All girls—"

"But Noah—what about him? I don't understand—"

"He was working two jobs to get extra money for us. Days he worked in the carpenter shop and nights in a lumberyard.

Hardly got no sleep at all—That's why he had the accident in the lumberyard."

"Accident?"

"Noah, he lost his right hand and part of his arm and now he ain't the same man. It appears like he don't care about me. Like he don't want to—to—come near me—like a husband should. Been months since he—I'm sorry, Miz Drummond."

Megan understood and her heart went out to Opal. "But surely there's other work Noah can do," she began.

Opal shook her head. "Too many free black men lookin' for work down in New Orleans. Strong men with two good hands. And all them white gentlemen back from the war. They're lookin' for work, and—Noah, he can read and write and figure, but no one needs a black man for that. And it's takin' away his pride. A man needs to take care of his wife and little ones."

"I know," Megan said. She remembered the bitterness of the men back in Kilcurran, the ones who had been unable to provide for their families, who had watched their wives and children starving, and who had often turned to drink to blot out, if only for a little while, their sense of helplessness and humiliation.

"I'll speak to my husband when he returns from Chicago," Megan promised. "Perhaps he will be able to find work for Noah."

"Noah—he don't want no charity," Opal said. "We're free now. No concern of the Drummonds what happens to us. Miz Samantha, she said Ah had no business goin' off like Ah did, and she said—"

"Never mind what she said," Megan told Opal firmly. She made a swift resolve to find some way of helping Opal and Noah and their children without further damaging Noah's already shaky self-respect.

On an afternoon three weeks later, Jessica Drummond went down to Tom Langford's schoolhouse with a new mathematics textbook that she had ordered from New York for one of his students who had shown unusual promise. Now she lingered with the Yankee teacher out behind the small whitewashed building. Dusk was approaching, and the air was heavy with the elemental smell of the earth and of growing things in the cypress swamp.

At this particular hour, Jessica found these mingled odors, familiar since childhood, oddly disturbing. Although it was not yet June, she felt unusually warm, and her dress, a gift from Megan and made, by Opal, of fine blue broadcloth, clung to her body. She was aware of the firm swell of her breasts as they pressed against the closely fitted bodice, of the soft curves of her hips, the roundness of her thighs, under all the layers of cloth and tight whalebone corseting.

Even Tom's voice, gentle and quiet, sent a curious tremor through her. But his words were commonplace enough.

"It's getting late, Miss Jessica," he said. "I'll drive you back to the house."

Jessica's small, rather shabby little buggy stood a few feet away, the sway-backed horse cropping at the thick grass. "Oh, no! I can drive myself perfectly well," she said. Then, realizing that her answer might have sounded ungracious, she added quickly, "It's almost quitting time in the fields. The older folks will be coming for their evening lessons, and you haven't had your dinner yet."

"There's plenty of time," Tom assured her. The lean, sandy-haired man shook his head, and his deeply set hazel eyes were troubled. "I wonder that the older folks keep coming. Why should they want to get an education? Why should they try to exercise their right to vote when it could cost them their lives? When the White Line, or the Klan, or the Knights of the White Camellia—" He broke off.

"I heard about the burning of that schoolhouse up near Jackson," she said sadly. "But I'm sure that the Knights had no part in that." She wanted to be sure, for she knew that Reed was a member of that secret society, and she wondered now if Tom Langford knew it, too.

She stood in silence for a moment at his side, and she became aware of the small sounds all around them: the croaking of a bull frog, the sighing of the wind in the tall grass, the plop of an alligator slipping into the stream.

"I won't irritate your family by driving you up to the front door. I'll let you out behind the summerhouse in the garden."

"There's no need," Because of her confused emotions and

the unfamiliar stirring of her senses, she spoke more sharply than she had intended. "I won't go skulking about as if I—"

"Why, Miss Jessica, what's wrong? I didn't mean to offend you."

She was unable to speak, and she turned away, fixing her eyes on the green thickness of the cypress swamp, on the gnarled old trees twisted about with broad-leafed vines. She heard a quail sound its plaintive cry and felt something move deep within her.

"I don't want either of us to have to go skulking about," he said, and now his voice was hard. "I only wish I could drive you up to your front door. That I could come calling on you, to sit with you in the parlor and to—to speak openly of my feelings for you. I wish I could go to Reed and tell him that— that I want to court you."

She stared at him, not sure for the moment that she had heard correctly, but his meaning was plain in his face.

"Oh, Tom. I never thought that you—"

Then, somehow, his hands were gripping her arms, and he was pulling her against him, hard, holding her with an urgency that she had never known in any man before. For a moment, she stiffened in fear, but then her hands reached for him, her arms encircled him, and she welcomed the hunger in him, for it answered her own. She responded to the pressure of his lean thighs pressing against her own.

Her back rested against the trunk of one of the cypress trees, and she made no protest when he opened the top buttons of her high-necked bodice, when she felt his warm mouth against the curve of her throat. A swift, tingling sensation moved along her nerves, from her hardening nipples downward to her loins.

Then, with a sudden movement, he thrust her away.

"Not like this, Jessica. No—not like this."

It was a moment before he could speak again, and then he said, "It's been so long, and I've wanted you so much." He looked down into her face. "Are you angry with me?"

"No—not angry—I—I don't know what I feel—"

"That isn't true," he said quietly. "You do know—"

"All right, then. But we can't—we mustn't—"

"Jessica, my dear, please say you'll marry me."

For one instant, she felt joy surging up within her, an eager hope, a promise of a future she had never imagined for herself. Then stark reality forced its way into her mind, and she said, "You know it would be impossible."

"Because I'm not wealthy? Because I can't give you a home like Montrose or—"

"Tom, no. I don't want a home like Montrose. I only want to be your wife and share your work. But I can't." Close to tears, she turned and fled, climbing into the buggy.

"Jessica, wait—Don't leave like this—please—"

Her eyes blinded by unshed tears, she brought the reins down on the horse's back with more force than usual, and the startled animal moved off at a trot, the buggy jolting over the road.

"Jessica—wait—You mustn't leave this way—"

But she did not even turn to look back at him, for she did not want him to see the tears that were spilling over onto her lashes.

"But why did you refuse him?" Megan demanded. "You love him—you've told me so—and he loves you."

Jessica was seated with Megan a few days later in Megan's boudoir, adjoining the master bedroom at Azalea Hill.

"Tom's lonely. Perhaps he's mistaken his loneliness for— And then, the idea of a woman my age—marrying for the first time—Why it isn't decent—"

"Tom Langford is a mature man and a sensible one," Megan said. "He knows what he wants in a wife—"

"Even so, Megan, if I were to marry Tom, I'd have to break with my family, my friends, people I've grown up with—"

"Clay and I are part of your family. If I talk to Clay when he gets home, I'm sure I can make him understand—" She smiled wryly. "He married me, and that hasn't made him an outcast."

"It's different for a man—especially a man like Clay. People have to accept you because you're his wife, and they need him, they need his money and his political influence and—" Jessica broke off, her eyes widening with the realization of what she had implied. "Oh, Megan, my dear—I'm so sorry— I never should have said—"

"You said what you thought, and you were right. A man has more freedom, and a man in Clay's position can force people into accepting his wife even if she is an Irish immigrant girl from Natchez-under. Don't you suppose I know that?" Megan forced herself to keep her voice light. "It's you we're talking about, and I won't have you dodging the matter of you and Tom. Lianne didn't marry a wealthy man. Her husband's people weren't planters, and yet she—"

"Mark Burnett is a Southerner. He served with distinction in the Confederate army. Lianne would never accept my marriage to a Yankee, particularly one who works for the Freedmen's Bureau, who is against everything she believes in. And Reed and Samantha would never let me enter Montrose again. And little Luke—"

"Oh, now surely you aren't going to tell me that a five-year-old has any sort of prejudices—"

"Samantha would make certain that I never went near him again. And, Megan, he's like my own child—Try to understand. Samantha has never really been a mother to the boy. I don't know why that should be. Luke is such a beautiful child and so bright. If I had a little boy like him, I'd consider myself the luckiest woman in the world."

"You can have children of your own," Megan said. "Marry Tom and I'm sure that in time Reed, Samantha, Lianne, and your friends, too, will come to accept the marriage."

But although she went on trying to reason with Jessica, her arguments were useless, for Clay's sister shared his stubborn disposition. Still, Megan was not willing to let the matter drop.

"Even if you don't decide about the marriage at once," Megan persisted, "you could help him in his work. You would make an excellent teacher."

Jessica's face reddened, and she looked away. "Oh, Megan, no! Why if I were working in the schoolhouse with Tom, the two of us together, he might—"

"Tom wouldn't force himself on you."

"I know that," Jessica said. "It's myself I don't trust, because I—want him, too."

Megan's heart ached for Jessica, who not only shared Clay's stubbornness but his passionate nature. But it was wrong that such passion should be forever held in check. There must be a way to bring about a marriage between Jessica and the man she loved.

Megan spoke carefully. "Tom must be dreadfully overworked at the school."

"He is," Jessica said, looking relieved that Megan had shifted to a less embarrassing topic. "He teaches the children during the day, and then the old folks come for lessons in the evenings. They do try so hard to learn, but it's so difficult for them. They must start with the alphabet, the same as the children. They must be taught to count and do simple sums."

For the moment, Megan forgot her immediate goal of bringing Tom and Jessica together. "Noah," she said slowly. "I think perhaps Noah could help Tom."

"Noah? Opal's husband?"

Megan explained Noah's difficulties. "I'm paying Opal well for her sewing, but it isn't only money that she needs. Noah is a proud man. He wants to do useful work, to support his wife and children. He isn't a qualified teacher, but he can read and write and do sums."

"I know that," Jessica said eagerly. "I taught him."

"Then why can't he take over at least one of the evening classes at Tom's school? All he needs is a chance to work again. Jessica, won't you ask Tom to take him on?"

"I haven't been down to the schoolhouse since Tom and I—since he asked me to marry him. It was so difficult for me to refuse him. I could not hide my feelings." She looked away. "You must think me shameless. Maybe Tom does, too."

"Surely you can put aside your own feelings and do this to help Noah," Megan persisted. "You'll have to see Tom again sooner or later, since he's right there on the grounds of Montrose."

Jessica hesitated, then said, "You're right, of course. I was being foolish and selfish. I'll speak to Tom if it will help Opal and Noah."

Chapter Fifteen

❧

"I'LL BE pleased to have Noah's help in the adult evening classes," Tom Langford said. He and Jessica were seated in the small, sparsely furnished parlor, one of the two rooms that made up his living quarters in the lean-to next to the schoolhouse. There were no curtains on the windows, a shabby, faded rag rug on the floor, and the only ornament was the miniature of Tom's wife, who had died in the first year of their marriage: a delicate, doll-like face surrounded by soft, blonde ringlets. Jessica had seen the miniature before, and she had always forced her eyes away, pained by the contrast between that pretty, girlish face, and her own, which was plain and angular—a spinster's face, grown haggard with self-imposed restraint.

"I'm sure Noah will prove useful," she said, rising from the bentwood rocker. "I'll have Opal send him to see you."

Tom stood up quickly and put a hand on her arm. "Surely there's no need to rush off so soon."

"There's every need," Jessica told him, trying to keep her voice firm and steady.

"Jessica, do you think I would try to persuade you—or to force you—against your will—"

"Perhaps it would not be against my will," she said, unable to hold back the words. But even as she spoke, she started for the door. Tom moved swiftly to block her way.

"But if that's how you feel, surely you'll reconsider. Give me permission to speak to Reed. I know how he feels about me, but he must want your happiness. And I'll do everything in my power to make you happy. Let me go to Reed and tell him—"

"No!" It was a cry of pain and self-denial. "I forbid you to go to my brother about this."

"But when will I see you again?" The hunger and the longing in his voice tore at her, but she would not allow herself to weaken. Reed had often spoken of his dislike for Tom Langford, his resentment of the man's presence on the grounds of Montrose. So far, Tom had not faced the open persecution from the Knights of the White Camellia; his schoolhouse stood intact. But other schoolhouses had been burned; teachers had been attacked, beaten. Even if she were willing to risk an open break with her family, she would not risk Tom's safety. "I'll speak to you if we should meet by chance here on the grounds— or in town. But I won't come down to the schoolhouse again. Believe me, Tom, it's better that way."

In the months that followed, through the stifling, humid heat of summer, Jessica kept to her resolve, and the pain of her self-restraint took its toll. She grew thin and gaunt, and the bones of her face became more visible, the flesh stretched tightly over the jutting line of her jaw, her high cheekbones. She went about her household duties, speaking only when it was necessary but driving herself every moment of the day, rising at dawn, and not going to bed until after midnight. She took over the keeping of the household accounts from Reed, who had always disliked that chore, and she drove her shabby buggy to town for supplies for the kitchen and medicines for the field hands and their families, for although she was no longer obligated to do so, she looked on the Montrose blacks as "our people," as she had before the war.

In autumn of the following year, a few days after Ulysses S. Grant had defeated Horace Greeley in the presidential election, to return to office for a second term, Clay came back to Natchez to pay off his crews and make plans for his new feeder line. The new line was to stretch up into New Mexico, and Gavin O'Donnell was already sending down the first gangs of newly arrived Irish immigrants for the additional jobs. Clay himself insisted on interviewing the surveyors and foremen, using one of Jim Rafferty's warehouses as a headquarters, for he had an office of his own there now. But the day after his return, he rode out to Montrose for a visit, and he noticed at once the change in Jessica.

"Are you ill?" he demanded.

"Certainly not," she said quickly, but he remained concerned, putting a hand under her chin to tilt her face upward.

"Working too hard, perhaps. Taking care of Luke, running the house while Samantha goes gallivanting off to New Orleans for the opera season."

"You know how much Samantha enjoys attending the performances at the French Opera House."

"What Samantha enjoys is decking herself out in the latest fashions and holding court in a private box between the acts," Clay said. Although he still felt a lingering tenderness for Samantha and was still stirred by her beauty, he had few illusions about her character. "You're the one who has always had a real love for music."

Jessica did not deny it but said quickly, "Someone must stay here to—to supervise the house and look after Luke."

"Luke's not your child."

Jessica twisted her head, freeing herself from Clay's hand beneath her chin but not quickly enough to hide her feelings. Clay was startled by the look of pain his words had evoked. "Let me hire a nursemaid—half a dozen if you like—and you can go down to New Orleans, too. Get yourself some new gowns—go to the opera, the theater. Lord knows, I can afford it now, with the Natchez–Fort Worth Line completed and the iron-ore mines up in Alabama—"

"I'm perfectly satisfied here at home," Jessica said. "And Luke's not a bit of trouble."

Clay smiled. "Every six-year-old boy is trouble," he said. "Our Brant's a real hellion. Terence is better behaved, but he's no angel, either. Besides," he went on, the amusement leaving his voice, "it isn't right for you to spend your whole time acting as an unpaid nursemaid and housekeeper for Reed and Samantha. And keeping the accounts. Oh, yes, I recognized your handwriting when I went over the expense accounts. Can't Reed even be bothered adding up a column of figures?"

"And what would you have me do?" she demanded impatiently. "Fill my life with useless pastimes for ladies of leisure? Make mosaics of shells and seaweed? Feather pictures? Flower paintings on velvet? Shall I embroider needlecases and doilies and contribute them to be sold at charity fairs and bought by other leisured ladies who haven't the slightest use for them?" She drew a deep breath and went on more quietly. "At least, caring for Luke, planning meals, keeping accounts—those are real. They make me feel that I am not completely useless."

Clay stared at his sister in silence, realizing that he never stopped to think how limited her life must be, hedged around by endless rules of propriety and social custom. And because Jessica had intelligence, she found it impossible to be content with frittering away her time on the pursuits she had just spoken of so scornfully. He felt ill at ease, helpless, and these feelings, so unfamiliar to him, made him angry. "All right, if you won't go down to New Orleans for the opera season, at least go to visit Lianne for a few days. Surely Rachel can look after Luke that long. Or let me take him home with me—Megan loves children; she'll be happy to have him, and he can get acquainted with his cousins."

"I would like to visit Lianne," Jessica admitted wistfully. "Especially now when she—" She hesitated. "Oh—I didn't realize—you only arrived in Natchez last night, and Megan probably hasn't had time to tell you. Lianne is—in the family way," she finished, her cheeks growing pink.

"A baby—that's fine."

"Opal told me about it," Jessica went on. "Lianne visited Opal's dress shop in Natchez to have a new dress made because she'll be needing—that is—"

Clay would never understand why the facts surrounding pregnancy had to be expressed by ladies in such circumspect terms. Their sister, Lianne, had been married over a year now; she was pregnant, and naturally she would need a dress that would accommodate her thickening waistline. But not wanting to embarrass Jessica, he changed the subject swiftly.

"So Opal has a shop now. I guess I've got a lot of catching

up to do now that I'm back. I hope she's doing well in her new business."

"Oh, she is. Our friends can't afford many new gowns. All the ladies I know are wearing twice-turned dresses. But the wives of the Yankees down here are getting themselves fitted out splendidly." She stopped, remembering Clay's association with the Carpetbaggers, his partnership with Oliver Winthrop in the iron-ore mines. "And Noah's working at the school-house," she said.

"Is Langford satisfied with Noah's ability as a teacher?"

"Yes, indeed. Opal says that Noah has proved most useful and willing."

"Opal says?" Clay was puzzled. "What does Tom Langford have to say about Noah's work?"

"I haven't spoken to Mr. Langford in—in some time."

"But you and Langford used to be good friends. As I recall, your friendship with him infuriated Samantha. And Reed wasn't too happy about it, either, although I thought perhaps he—"

Once more, Clay saw the naked pain in his sister's eyes, saw her flinch as if he had struck her. What the devil was wrong with her? He had always assumed that she had resigned herself to spinsterhood years ago and now . . .

Good Lord! he thought. *Jess has fallen in love with Tom Langford. And he doesn't love her.*

Clay's thoughts moved swiftly. Jessica was too proud, too reserved to force her company on a man who had let her know that he did not return her feelings. That would explain her obvious unhappiness, the loss of weight, the haggard look on her face.

Hadn't Megan said something about Jessica's bringing books down to the schoolhouse? Jessica, thrown into the company of a personable man, a gentleman for all he was a penniless Yankee. No doubt they shared many of the same interests: books, music, that sort of thing.

Why had he allowed Megan to talk him into giving Langford the use of the old sugar mill for a schoolhouse? But then, he told himself, trying to be fair, Megan had had no way of predicting that Jessica would be attracted to Langford, and the Yankee teacher was not to blame because Jessica had fallen in love with him. All the same, something had to be done.

"Jess, I—look here, you're going to visit Lianne. The change will do you good. And before you go, I'm going to buy you a new buggy and a fine new mare to pull it—"

"But I have a buggy, and Dolly is—"

"High time old Dolly was put out to pasture before she drops in the traces. And that old wreck of a buggy you've been using is a disgrace."

Clay felt more in control now that he was giving orders, offering material gifts, for he could not deal with his sister's torment directly, could not offer any other solace. At least he could see to it that she got away from Montrose for a few days and that she traveled in style.

Lianne was impressed by the new buggy, with its fine red-leather upholstery, its polished-brass trim, and by the sleek, high-stepping little mare that had replaced the sway-backed Dolly. Jessica's horse and buggy had been put in the shed behind the small house, a few miles above Natchez, to which Dr. Mark Burnett had brought his bride after their wedding.

"Clay's doing well for himself," Lianne observed as she and Jessica sat sipping tea and nibbling at small sandwiches in the boxlike, low-ceilinged parlor. The room, the whole house, were in such contrast to the spacious elegance of Montrose, Jessica thought.

"And Megan must be proud of him," Lianne added. She spoke without the slightest trace of envy or bitterness.

"No doubt she is," Jessica said. "Clay's ambitious and successful. He's going to start extending his feeder line into New Mexico in a few months. And the Natchez–Fort Worth Line has already made him a great deal of money. Then there are those refrigerator cars and—Why, there's no end to his plans."

"Megan's a fortunate woman," Lianne said, but to Jessica's surprise, there was, for once, no envy or bitterness in Lianne's voice when she spoke of her brother's wife. She was plainly satisfied with her own role of wife to Dr. Mark Burnett and mother-to-be. She radiated quiet happiness, and there was a calm, matronly air about her, for she no longer used those girlish mannerisms that had been characteristic of her before her marriage. Even her high, tinkling laughter was softer now, but she smiled more often.

"And the children—Brant and Terence and little Deirdre— how are they?"

"Thriving," Jessica told her. "But why not visit Megan now that Clay's home and see them for yourself?"

"I doubt that she'd want to see me," Lianne said. "I guess I wasn't very pleasant to her when we were all living at Montrose. And now—"

"Oh, but you're quite wrong," Jessica assured her. "You don't know Megan. She never expected the Drummonds to welcome her with open arms when she married Clay. She's not a fool. But she doesn't hold grudges. She's much too happy being Clay's wife and bringing up his children."

"I can understand that," Lianne said softly. "Oh, Jess, when I found out that I was—that Mark and I were going to—I can't tell you what it's like to love a man and know that he loves you." She smiled. "You know, when I first set my cap for Mark—oh, yes, I did—it was only because I wanted a husband, because I didn't want to wither away at Montrose—" She gave Jessica a quick look and then stared down at her teacup, obviously embarrassed by the implication, but then she hurried on. "What I mean is, after we were married and he brought me home here—even that first night, it was so wonderful, just the two of us, and Mark was so understanding and patient, and then, when I got over being nervous, he was so—" She paused once more. "I don't suppose you'd understand, but it's not like anything I'd ever known. This house—it's not like Montrose—and Mark will never be rich, and Samantha looks down on him because his family weren't planters—But all of that isn't important, because when he comes home late at night, after he's been out on an emergency call, and he comes upstairs—he tries not to wake me, but I'm only half asleep because I'm so eager to have him home. It's so wonderful with him beside me and—"

Carried away by her own feelings, Lianne now saw the look in Jessica's eyes, but she misunderstood it completely. Of course, she told herself, it was not proper to speak to an unmarried lady so frankly even if the lady happened to be one's sister. But Jessica had always been so realistic and straightforward. All the same, Lianne was sure that she had gone too far, for how else was she to explain the spots of color that now burned on Jessica's high, jutting cheekbones, the way in which her jaw line was thrown into prominence with the swift tightening of her mouth.

Lianne rose swiftly. "The tea's getting cold, and Suky's out doing the marketing. I'll go and get us another pot."

"I don't want any more tea." Jessica's voice, sharp and strained, only confirmed Lianne's belief that her conversation had offended her spinster sister. "I'm going upstairs to lie down."

"Oh, Jess, dear, I'm sorry. I never should have run on so about Mark and—and—"

"I have a headache." Jessica lied. "I'll rest for a while before dinner."

"Oh, let me go with you. I'll get some eau de cologne for your forehead."

"I don't need—"

"And when Mark comes home, I'll ask him to prescribe a cordial for you. Your appetite has been so poor all the time you've been here. And you have lost weight."

"I don't want a cordial—or the eau de cologne. I don't want you to come upstairs with me. Please, dear, don't fuss. Let me go up and rest for an hour by myself."

When Jessica appeared at the dinner table, she was outwardly composed, and she managed to eat enough to calm Lianne's concern about her appetite. She politely refused Mark's offer of a cordial and made conversation with him about his growing practice, asking his advice on a few of the more difficult ailments of the blacks at Montrose. And she spoke, too, of Megan, urging Lianne to go and pay a call on her sister-in-law. "We'll make a family party of it if you like. Mark, you must come, too, if you can spare the time from your practice."

Jessica left the following afternoon, driving off in her smart new buggy, smiling and waving back at Lianne and Mark as they stood together in the doorway. But on the drive back to Natchez, in the damp chill of the November afternoon, moving along the winding red-clay road, under the trailing gray moss, she could not get Lianne's words out of her mind.

I can't tell you what it's like to love a man and know that he loves you...

It's so wonderful with him beside me...

But I know, I understand, Jessica thought, her strong, capable hands tightening on the reins as she remembered that afternoon in the cypress grove behind the schoolhouse, remembered Tom's lean, hard body pressed against hers, the warmth of his mouth, and the swift answering passion that had stirred to life inside her.

Lianne could not know that although Jessica had never given herself completely to Tom, to any man, she knew, with every nerve of her body, the fierce hunger, the aching need between man and woman.

The buggy wheels made a rustling sound as they rolled over the dead leaves. The river mist softened the outlines of the trees on the bluff overlooking the Mississippi. Another autumn. And then spring again. And season following season, and one day Luke would go off to school. He would write an occasional duty letter to his maiden aunt back at Montrose, would think of her kindly, no doubt, but only rarely. She would go on doing Samantha's work around Montrose and some of Reed's as well, rising at dawn, riding through the fields, seeing to the needs of their black tenant farmers.

"No!" She realized that she had spoken aloud, and she knew that the word, coming from a place deep in her mind, could not be taken back. She was only a year older than Lianne, and although everything was against her, she wanted to be Tom Langford's wife. Childbirth at her age and for the first time might be difficult, even dangerous, but she wanted that, too. She wanted to bear a child for the man she loved.

She turned the buggy on to the esplanade, but she could scarcely see the tall houses because of the mist. Her mind moved eagerly now that the decision had been made. There was so much she could share with Tom besides the physical relationship, she told herself. She could help him in his work. She could teach at his school. Her life would be busy, active, meaningful.

But maybe Tom no longer wanted her. How long had it been since that afternoon in the cypress grove? Almost a year. Since then, there had been one brief meeting when she had asked him to hire Noah to work at the school. She had seen him since then, of course, for their meetings were inevitable, but she had confined herself to a formal greeting and ridden on quickly.

How could she still be sure that Tom wanted her. She was not young; she had never been pretty. Maybe he had changed his mind. Maybe he had found another woman.

She had to know. She thought briefly of riding down to the schoolhouse, but she could not risk a direct confrontation, with the searing shame, if she discovered that he had turned to someone else or that he simply had lost his desire for her. Suppose she offered her love and he turned her away. He would be gentle, kind, but she could not bear it if he no longer wanted her.

A wide, towering house loomed ahead with a double staircase of two flights leading up to the veranda: Azalea Hill. She had planned to stop here, to suggest that Megan send an invitation to Lianne and Mark for the small reception to be given in a few weeks to mark Clay's homecoming. If Lianne received an invitation, perhaps with a personal message from Megan, she would realize that Megan was more than willing to overlook their past differences.

Now, however, Lianne's desire to visit Megan was only secondary. The reception would be the ideal opportunity, Jessica told herself, for her to see Tom again. Megan had been completely supportive last spring when Jessica had spoken of Tom's proposal, even offering to persuade Clay to accept the Yankee schoolteacher as a prospective brother-in-law—in case Clay should need persuading. And there would be several of Clay's Yankee business associates there, so that Tom would not feel like an outsider.

She drew rein in front of Megan's house, and it was as if she already found strength in knowing that Megan would be her ally. As she went up the flight of steps to the wide veranda, she thought how strange it was that she, who had befriended the shy young Irish girl from Natchez-under on that first night that Clay had brought her to Montrose, should now be turning to her for help.

But Megan had changed during these years of her marriage to Clay. She had grown confident, self-possessed, and secure in her position as Clay Drummond's wife, the mother of his children.

Jessica knew that there were still ladies here in Natchez and on the up-river plantations who would refuse to accept Megan as a social equal. But Megan had made a beginning, and now she received invitations to take tea, to go driving along the esplanade. Perhaps, Jessica thought with a wry smile, some of those invitations had been issued because of pressure from husbands who needed Clay's financial or political backing. But others, she was sure, had come because of Megan's own qualities: her generosity, her lack of pretension, her kindness.

And now it was Jessica who needed her help.

If Megan would invite Tom to the reception, they could be together without constraint or embarrassment, and Jessica would know if Tom still wanted her as he had last spring. For a moment, she had a cruel, taunting vision of what the rest of her life would be like if he had changed in his feelings toward her: the emptiness, the gray, meaningless years that would stretch ahead for her. But she blotted out the picture. She would not let herself think of that, not yet. Not while there was still a chance for her to reach out for what she wanted.

Chapter Sixteen

IT WAS a little after nine on the evening of Megan's reception, and Jessica, in a new gown of blue silk trimmed with lace flounces and black-velvet ribbons, lingered in the wide downstairs hallway, tense and anxious. Megan had assured her that Tom would be there, for he had sent a note of acceptance; but now, with the dancing in full swing upstairs in the ballroom, he had not yet appeared.

Jessica kept her eyes fixed on the door, but no more guests were arriving, and Clay and Megan had already gone upstairs to lead the first waltz. Now Lianne was saying impatiently, "Do come along, Jessica. I've heard so much about this ballroom. I'm eager to see it for myself." And so, with Lianne and Mark, Jessica reluctantly climbed the staircase.

But although the ballroom, recently completed was indeed splendid, Jessica was in no mood to appreciate it. Lianne, however, exclaimed with pleasure, for the room, over sixty by seventy feet, was surrounded on all four sides by a balcony and was lighted by crystal chandeliers. The candlelight caught the gleam of jade and amber, azure-blue and purple, in the stained glass of the high, pointed clerestory windows. It shone down on the dresses of the ladies, the jewel-colored velvets and taffetas that were so popular that season with those who could afford such luxuries.

Jessica sat with Mark and Lianne, who could not join in the dancing and had only come because she was not yet beginning to show her condition. Reed had not come and had sent his regrets, saying that since Samantha had chosen to remain in New Orleans, he did not care to attend without her. He had, in fact, left Montrose shortly after the noon meal and had not reappeared when Lianne and Mark had come to call for Jessica and take her along to the reception.

Jessica thought sadly that Reed had no doubt gone down to Natchez-under to visit the taverns, the gambling houses, and the sporting houses, too, for she had overheard enough quarrels between her half brother and his wife to know that he was spending more and more of his time in such places. Perhaps, Jessica told herself, if Samantha had been a real wife to Reed, as Lianne was to Mark, there would be no need for him to seek comfort elsewhere.

Jessica forced herself to put aside such distressing thoughts and to make polite conversation when Mark Burnett waltzed with her and later, when Clay asked her to dance. She could not help noticing that few of the guests were known to her, that even those Natchez ladies who had shown Megan some friendliness during the past few years were not present here tonight; and neither were their husbands.

Maybe, Jessica thought, their absence was related to the mounting tension that had followed the re-election of President Grant, for the ex-Confederates had made no secret of their bitter resentment when the stocky, bearded man who had captured Vicksburg went to the White House for a second term. It had been Grant, after all, who had ordered federal troops, some of them black, to keep the peace in Mississippi and several of the other Southern states. And in his first term in office, he had signed the bill that gave him the power to suspend the writ of habeas corpus and to proclaim martial law; and he had used federal troops to make arrests and to enforce the hated law.

Perhaps Clay's former friends and neighbors were avoiding the reception to show how they felt about his working hand in glove with Republican politicians. But if Clay was troubled by their absence, he did not show it. Instead, as he moved decorously about the polished floor with Jessica, he spoke enthusiastically about his new railroad, which would cut its way through New Mexico. "I plan to start work early in spring," he said. "The crew here in Natchez has been paid off, and a lot of them plan to hole up in Natchez-under to spend their wages. They'll have themselves a big time for a few months and sign on again when I'm ready to start work. I already have my surveyors out there—" He stopped, realizing that Jessica wasn't listening, that her eyes were moving from his face to the doorway of the ballroom. "I'm sorry if I'm boring you," he said with a smile. "I guess railroading isn't—"

"I'm interested in your new railroad—you know that—in anything that is important to you." Then, seeing disbelief in his face, she said quickly, "I was admiring the new ballroom, that's all. Those magnificent stained-glass windows and the murals on the ceiling."

"A fit setting for my elegant sister," he responded. "That dress is most becoming, Jess."

The dress had been chosen to catch Tom's eye, to make her look as attractive as possible, she thought sadly. And Megan had insisted on paying for it. For once, Jessica had not been able to bring herself to refuse, and she knew that she had never looked better. The silk, in a deep, glowing peacock blue, brought out the color of her eyes, and the style had been copied from a fashion plate in *Harper's Bazar;* with flowing, lace-trimmed sleeves and wide flounces of lace on the bodice, it had a dignity suited to Jessica's personality. It was charming without being girlish.

"Opal made this dress," she told Clay.

"She did a fine job of it. I dropped in at her shop, you know," Clay said. "She's doing well, and as for Noah, his work at Tom Langford's school is—" He stopped short, for he did not want to distress Jessica by speaking of Langford. Why had the man accepted the invitation to the reception if he had not intended to come?

The same question went on plaguing Jessica. Perhaps, she tried to tell herself, it was better this way. Better for both of them if they never met socially again.

At ten, when supper was served, she tried to make a pretense of eating and let Mark heap her plate with the lavish delicacies that had been spread out on the long buffet table. But she had no appetite for the ducklings simmered in Burgundy, the oyster gumbo, the hothouse pineapples.

"We'll have to do something about this," Mark told her. "You must spend more time out of doors, Jessica. Take a brisk walk each morning before breakfast. And at bedtime, cream and sherry, with a beaten egg and a dash of bitters—"

At the other end of the table, Megan, who was carrying on a conversation with Oliver Winthrop and his lovely young wife, Angelique, could not help glancing over at Jessica from time to time, and she felt a pang. Jessica had so looked forward to the reception, and Tom had not come. It was not like him to send a note of acceptance and then stay away. Had he perhaps been taken ill?

Reed's absence was easier for Megan to understand, for there had been a growing coolness between Clay and his half brother during these past few years as Clay's enterprises had flourished, money rolling in not only from the railroads but also from the iron-ore mines in Alabama, from the new textile mills he had built in partnership with Winthrop.

Reed could not help but resent taking money from Clay, to keep Montrose in repair, to hire one overseer after another, to buy seed and farming equipment, to keep the tenant farmers' cabins in decent condition. How had he felt, Megan wondered, when he knew that Clay's money was paying for the dress Jessica wore here tonight, for whatever luxuries Samantha was able to enjoy? That last must have inflicted a particularly stinging blow to Reed's pride.

"It's most kind of you to invite us to your summer home," Megan said in reply to a remark from Angelique. "I'm told that Lake Pontchartrain is delightful in summer, and I know the children would enjoy it." But she could not stop her thoughts from wandering.

Even if Reed did resent Clay's success, he might have come here tonight, since Clay had been away from Natchez for so long. And those others, too. Megan had not been able to bring herself to invite Jeff and Violet Shepley; indeed, she never wanted to see the man again, remembering his assault on Lu-

damae. But she had invited Seth and Winona Hunter and several
other local people from the vicinity of Montrose, and none of
them had accepted, not even old Dr. Purvis.

Megan stood a little straighter, her chin held high, her shoulders squared above the pale-green watered silk of her gown,
for she was determined to pretend that the reception was the
complete success she had hoped it would be. Then she turned
as Ludamae, in her black uniform, topped by a starched, lace-
trimmed apron, approached her timidly. " 'Scuse me, ma'am,"
she said quietly. "There's somebody t' see yuh."

"Another guest?"

Tom, perhaps, at last.

But Ludamae shook her head. "Oh, no, ma'am. Ain' no
guest. She in de kitchen, an' Ah tol' her yuh din' have no time
t' talk t' her, but she say—"

"Who is she?" Megan demanded impatiently.

"Opal, ma'am. Opal Carpenter."

Noah, having gained his freedom, had not taken the name
of his former owners, as had many of the other former slaves;
instead, he had adopted the name of the trade he had been
following at the time.

"But Opal knows I'm having this reception tonight," Megan
said, puzzled and faintly disturbed. Opal had been told the date
of the reception when Megan had ordered her own gown and
Jessica's. Something urgent must have brought Opal to the
house tonight. Megan felt a nameless fear begin to stir inside
her.

"I'll go down and speak with Opal," she said.

She excused herself to the Winthrops and saw Clay's surprised look as she went out after Ludamae. She hurried downstairs and through the short brick passageway that connected
the kitchen quarters to the main house.

One look at Opal's face made Megan go cold with apprehension.

"What's happened? Is one of your children ill?"

Opal shook her head. "No, ma'am—they fine—Oh, Miz
Drummond, ma'am, Ah didn' want t' come here tonight, to
trouble you, but Ah didn' know nowhere else t' go, and you've
always been good to me and mine—"

Opal shuddered, and the whites of her eyes were visible all

around the dark-brown irises. Her skin, usually a warm apricot, had turned a peculiar grayish color.

"Tell me!" Megan demanded.

Opal's words came quickly then. A customer had come to Opal's shop only a few hours ago and had told her.

"A raid—" Opal said. "The schoolhouse at Montrose—the—" She swallowed and went on with an obvious effort of will. "The Knights—an' Noah—he's there—said he'd be there 'til late cause Mr. Tom was comin' here to the party—"

Megan pressed her hands together, forcing herself to remain calm. "Ludamae, go upstairs to the ballroom and tell my husband that he is needed here at once." And when Ludamae stood frozen as if Opal's words had struck fear into her, too, Megan gave her a slight push. "Go on—hurry—"

Ludamae went streaking out of the kitchen and down the brick passageway while Megan continued to question Opal.

"It's after ten. Why didn't you come here sooner?"

"Like Ah tol' you—didn' hear 'bout it 'til this customer, she come t' my shop, 'round nine o'clock—"

"You have customers so late?"

"Ah—Ah got two kinds o' customers, ma'am. Respectable ladies like you and Miz Jessica—they come in the daytime. But the others—'Scuse me for speakin' so plain—the—the sportin'-house ladies. They come after closin' time to the back door of the shop. Ah need the money—an' they buy a lot o' fancy underwear an' satin wrappers and—This one—she tol' me that there wasn' many customers at the—the sportin' house where she works—'cause so many white gennelmen are out ridin' with the Knights—Ridin' t' Montrose—An' Ah thought, Mistuh Reed bein' one of them and Mistuh Clay bein' his brother, maybe—"

"Opal! What the devil are you saying?"

Clay's voice was harsh, cutting her short. He had come into the kitchen in time to hear her last words.

"It's true, Mistuh Clay, suh—My momma, she told me las' time she come t' see me—Mistuh Reed, he didn' wan' t' join the Knights, but Miz Samantha—she tol' him if he didn' join, he wasn't no real man an'—"

"Never mind that now," Clay said. "I'll—do what I can."

"If you only would, suh. My Noah, he's a good man, hard

workin' and respectful—He ain' no troublemaker. An' Mistuh Tom Langford's been real good to him, and the Knights—they'll hurt Mistuh Tom, too, like they did that white man that worked for the Union League up in Jackson—"

Megan pressed her fist to her mouth to keep back a cry, for she had heard of the white worker who had tried to encourage the blacks to exercise their right to vote and had been found a few days ago, his body washed up on the river bank.

"All right, Opal—I'll go out to Montrose."

As Clay spoke, Megan's fear for Tom Langford and Noah was swallowed up in an even greater terror. "Clay, the militia is up near Jackson, but it would take far too long to reach them there and—"

"I'm not going to call in the militia," he said quietly. She looked at the hard, set face of her husband and thought what it would be like if he were hurt, perhaps even killed. The old, painful memories of her brother's death, which she had pushed to the back of her mind all these years, came alive. Her hand tightened on Clay's arm.

"You can't face those men alone—you mustn't—"

"I won't," Clay told her. "My railroad crew's down in Natchez-under, remember?"

"But they're not trained to fight—"

He turned and looked down at her, putting his hand over hers so that she felt his vitality, his assurance, flowing into her. "They're Irishmen," he said. "They don't need training to fight. You should know that, my dear."

Megan understood. Clay was determined to handle this without calling in the authorities so that if Reed was involved, he would not face trial and possibly imprisonment. She pitied Clay, knowing that he was being torn between his need to protect Reed and those of his neighbors who might be mixed up in this and his desire to help Tom and Noah.

He drew Megan into his arms, and his mouth came down hard on hers. When he released her, he said, "I don't want word of all this to get around. You'll have to carry on with the reception—"

"I can't—Oh, Clay, don't ask me—"

"You can, and you will. Make some excuse for my absence. Business—anything. And you, Opal, stay right here." He turned to the terrified octoroon, and his eyes held hers. "I'll do everything I can for Noah. I give you my word on that."

Even before he opened his eyes, Tom Langford smelled the thick, acrid smoke; he coughed and choked. His insides churned, and his head throbbed. Someone had smashed him across the back of the skull with a club, or perhaps it had been a pistol butt. He could not think clearly. Memory came and went in confused bits and pieces.

"On your feet, you nigger-lovin' bastard," a harsh voice ordered. He felt himself being pulled to his feet. He knew that voice; he'd heard it before—Jeff Shepley. The overseer who had raped Ludamae.

He fought down the anger stirred by the memory. He had to keep his thoughts clear. Noah. Where was Noah? Something had happened to the black man, something too terrible to remember.

When the Knights had descended on the schoolhouse, Tom had already dismissed the last of his students, letting them go early so that he could dress to get to the reception. He had put on his best suit—he had only two—and a newly purchased pair of white kid gloves. He was eager to see Jessica tonight, to make one more attempt to change her mind about marrying him.

All these months, seeing her only at a distance, he had hungered for her. They were so right for each other in every way; there was so much they could share, so much they could accomplish together. And he longed to hold her against him during the nights, to satisfy the passion that he knew was there, beneath her calm, controlled surface.

Cecelia, his first wife, had been a child of seventeen when he had married her. Pretty, winning—but a child, and although she had submitted to him dutifully, she had never really understood a man's needs. She had not been able to share his ambitions, either, and he had learned soon after their wedding that her interest in books, in music, had been superficial. He had loved her for her charming, kittenish ways, but even before she had died of typhoid, he had known that there could be no depth to their relationship. . . . But Jessica was different. Jessica was all he wanted in a woman.

"You look real fine, Mistuh Tom," Noah had been saying as Tom had prepared to start for the reception. A moment later, both men had heard the hammering of hoofs, the shouts of the riders. They had thrown open the door of the schoolhouse to see the glare of torches reddening the dark sky, turning the gnarled cypresses into monstrous shapes.

He had tried to reason with his attackers but had known that it was useless, and then he and Noah had fought, side by side, as the white-robed riders set torches to the old, dried wood of the schoolhouse. And then something had happened to Noah. Something had been done to him—obscene, unspeakable. . . .

Now he heard himself croaking hoarsely. "Noah—"

"That black ape isn't goin' to help you." Shepley's voice came from behind the white hood, his small, pale eyes glinting through the slits in the fabric. "He's not goin' t' strut around here again, teachin' those other apes t' act uppity—"

"Where is—Noah?" Tom demanded, his throat burning from the smoke he had breathed. Turning his head, he saw that the schoolhouse still burned, heard the crash of timber. He reeled and would have fallen, but another robed, hooded figure caught his other arm, holding him upright. "Noah—"

"Better worry about yourself, you Yankee bastard. Before we're finished with you, you'll wish you were dead along with your nigger friend."

Dead. Noah was dead. Tom managed to wrench himself free, anger welling up, overpowering him. He swung at Shepley, but a moment later, his head reeled, his knees sagged, and once again, the rough hands closed on his arms.

Someone was tearing off his coat. His best suit—the thought, senseless, idiotic, came from the depths of his mind . . . Jessica . . . the reception . . . Jessica would be waiting. . . .

Then Shepley and the other man dragged him to a tree with a thick, heavy branch that grew outward almost at right angles to the trunk. His hands were being tied, the rope biting into his wrists. Someone jerked the rope upward, looping it around the branch, and a moment later, he cried out, feeling that his arms were being jerked from their sockets. His feet left the ground. For a moment, rage blotted out all other emotions. Then he saw that Shepley had picked up a mule whip.

Tom felt a film of ice on his perspiring flesh in spite of the scorching heat of the burning schoolhouse. His insides tightened with animal fear.

"Shoot him and get it over with." He heard a harsh voice shout from somewhere in that crowd of white-robed men. Several had dismounted and were closing in, forming a semi-circle about the tree.

"Toss him back into his schoolhouse—let him burn—" came another voice.

"No—for God's sake, no! We agreed that there would be no killing—"

Another voice, one known to Tom. He tried to think, his brain swimming as he hung by the rope from the tree branch.

"—no killing, not here at Montrose—"

Reed Drummond. Jessica's half-brother.

"Maybe we'll fix him like we fixed the nigger and ship him back up North," someone said.

"Not until I'm finished with him." That was Shepley. "If he lives through it, that is."

Shepley laughed, and a moment later, Tom felt his shirt torn away, felt the damp chill of the night wind from the river raw against his bare back. He closed his eyes and braced himself for what he knew was to come. The whip whistled, then struck, tracing a line of fire across his flesh. The pain snaked its way upward into his brain. He heard one of the horses pawing the earth, whinnying. And then he heard his own hoarse cry, torn from him against his will as the whip descended again and again. He tries to press his body against the tree, to escape the slashing agony.

"That's enough!" Reed Drummond's voice again, sounding far off, through the mist that was enveloping his brain. "I don't want—"

"The hell you don't! It's you should be doing this, Drummond—"

"That's right—Yankee scum daring to go after your sister—"

Jessica, Tom thought. They were speaking of Jessica. . . .

"But it's nearly midnight," Jessica was saying to Megan. "It's not like Clay, leaving a reception in his own home, leaving his guests."

Megan fought for control and was surprised that she was

able to speak calmly, to force a smile. "I've already explained to you and to the others. He had to go out on a matter of business."

"I don't believe you," Jessica said stubbornly. "Surely, whatever the business, it could have waited until morning."

From the ballroom came the lilting melody of a Strauss waltz. The air was sweet and heavy with the mingled scents of flowers from the conservatory.

Megan searched her mind frantically for a believable excuse. Jessica was no fool, but she must not even suspect what might be happening out at Montrose.

"It's about the money for the payroll," Megan said. "There wasn't quite enough to cover it, and Clay had to get the rest of it. Those men won't wait, and they're a rough lot. . . ."

"I see," Jessica said slowly, and Megan's hand tightened around the ivory sticks of her fan. For although Jessica appeared convinced, her blue eyes—so like Clay's eyes—were still fixed on Megan's face. "But he'll surely return before the guests have to leave, won't he?"

"He'll do his best," Megan said.

A red mist enveloped Tom, and beyond it was a black whirlpool. He wanted to sink into the whirlpool, to find oblivion there, but he was dragged back again and again by the crack of the whip and the pain that followed. . . . His body jerked spasmodically, and he no longer screamed. He heard animal sounds, and he was only half aware that they came from his own throat. From time to time, he gasped, fighting for breath. . . .

"Stop! Now!" Not Reed's voice—another—familiar—but he couldn't remember, couldn't think—he slid through the red mist into the dark whirlpool and was swallowed up in its depths. . . .

Clay Drummond's powerful body was rigid with his sense of outrage, of revulsion. He had not ridden like this since he had led a cavalry troop during the first years of the war. With the men of his crew at his back, he had covered the distance from Natchez at top speed; some of the others were mounted, some crowded into wagons provided by Jim Rafferty, who had accompanied the rest. They had cut across the fields, skirted the cypress swamp, using every short cut known to Clay. They came pounding into the clearing now. In the last dying flames from the ruins of the schoolhouse, Clay's face looked as if it had been carved in granite; his voice was hard and commanding, but inside he felt sick with anger and disgust. For he was remembering, for the first time in years, Johnson's Island. Remembering his own helplessness there and the indignities, the brutalities that had been visited on him by the guard about whom he had made a complaint.

"Cut him down," Clay ordered.

The white-robed men were startled. But they stood their ground. "Get out of here and take those damn Irish Paddies with you—"

The crew needed no more. They began to clamber down from their horses and out of their wagons, armed with pick handles, with iron pipes. Clay raised his hand to signal them to hold back.

"Cut Langford down and ride out of here fast. Montrose is my land."

"You aren't fit to own it—lettin' this Yankee set up a school for—"

"I threw you off Drummond land once, Shepley, and I'll do it again. Take off that hood—or are you ashamed to show your face?"

Jeff pulled off the hood, but he stood his ground. He turned on Clay and swung the mule whip, but Clay side stepped and caught hold of it. He tore it from Shepley's grasp, then swung down from his horse.

"You damn traitor," Shepley called him. "Bringing in a gang of foreigners to fight your own people. Oh, I'm forgetting. You married an Irish biddy from Natchez-under. Thought you could make that trashy wench into a lady."

Clay heard a wordless roar from Jim Rafferty, and he made no attempt to restrain Megan's uncle or the other Irishmen who came surging forward, swinging pick handles, hammers, iron pipes, and huge, work-hardened fists. Within moments, those of the Knights who had not yet dismounted were dragged from their horses. Clay heard the crack of a pistol; turning, he saw Jim Rafferty bearing down on the white-robed man who had fired the shot. Rafferty knocked the pistol from his hand and sent him crashing into the gnarled truck of a cypress.

The bullet had slammed into one of the charred timbers of

the schoolhouse. Clay tore off his coat. Although he had come
out here for practical reasons, the slur against Megan had changed
all that. He smashed his fist into a hooded face with grim
satisfaction. The fight was soon over, with many of the Knights,
their robes bloodied, stretched on the blackened, fire-scorched
grass, while the rest remounted and took flight into the cypress
swamp. But Clay, who was preparing to pursue them, stopped
when he caught sight of one of them, who was about to get
back on a tall gray stallion. One look at the man and the horse
and Clay knew that Opal had been speaking the truth about
Reed.

Clay seized his brother, tore the hood away, and the two
men faced each other. "Clay, I didn't mean for things to go
this far. I swear it. I thought we'd only scare Noah and the
Yankee off Montrose. You know I never wanted—"

Clay drove his fist into Reed's face. Blood spattered down
the white robe. Reed raised his arm to protect himself, but he
did not strike back. Again Clay lashed out, putting all his weight
behind the blow. Reed slumped to his knees, and Clay hauled
him back up on his feet again.

"Fight, damn you! You led those men here. You disgraced
Pa's memory." He gave Reed a hard, back handed slap across
the face. "Fight!" he said.

Reed shook his head. "You don't understand—Shepley—
his idea, not mine—thought we'd chase that Yankee off—
You don't know—about Langford and Jessica—"

"Say one more word about Jess and I'll break you in two."
Clay released Reed and gave him a shove in the direction of
his horse. Reed managed to mount, to spur the horse forward.
He rode off, not toward the swamp into which the other Knights
had fled but back toward the plantation house.

It was Clay, his face set, who cut down Tom Langford and
laid him on the grass, face down, and felt for a pulse. It was
there, but faint and erratic. He lifted the man, carried him to
one of the wagons, and settled him, face down. When one of
the teamsters put a coarse shirt over Tom's bloodied back, he
groaned faintly, then lapsed into unconsciousness.

Clay walked to the smouldering ruins of the schoolhouse.
The fire was nearly out now. Only the smell of charred wood
hung over the clearing. He was turning to go back to his horse
when his foot struck something in the rubble. Noah's body.

No need to feel for his pulse. The body was already stiffening. He would have to take Noah back to Opal for burial, he thought bleakly. Then, as Jim Rafferty came to stand beside him, holding a lighted torch, Clay rolled the body over on its back. For one moment, he felt the muscles of his throat constrict and thought he was going to vomit. Nothing he had seen in battle or on Johnson's Island had prepared him for this.

He could not take his eyes from the naked body, the mangled flesh, like so much bloody rubbish, between the black man's muscular thighs, the dried blood on the legs and belly.

"Mother of God!" It was Jim Rafferty's voice that brought Clay back to the need for immediate action. He could not take Noah back to Opal, not after what had been done to the man; no woman, black or white, should ever have to see her man so mutilated.

"Have two of the crew bury Noah here. Under that big cypress behind the schoolhouse." Behind the place where the schoolhouse had stood, Clay thought, for it was now a blackened ruin. "And tell the men, all of them, to say nothing about—what was done to him. Understand?" Such stories had a way of getting around, and if Opal were to hear . . .

Rafferty nodded. "I'll see to it. But ye'd best be gettin' that Yankee schoolteacher back t' Natchez—quick. If he lives through the ride, he'll be needin' a doctor."

Mark Burnett was at Azalea Hill, Clay thought quickly. Mark was a good doctor, and he would do whatever could be done. Clay mounted his horse. He refused to allow himself to think about what would become of Jessica if Tom Langford did not survive.

Chapter Seventeen

CLAY CARRIED Tom Langford into the house by way of the kitchen. The Yankee schoolteacher was still alive but unconscious, and Clay had hefted him across one shoulder. Opal was crouched in a chair beside the huge cast-iron stove, Ludamae beside her, while Becky, the cook, a stout, middle-aged black woman, went about her chores.

At Clay's entrance, Opal sprang up from her chair. "Oh, dear Lord—" she whispered at the sight of Langford's torn body. "Is Mistuh Langford—"

"He's still alive," Clay said tersely. "You, Ludamae, come upstairs with me—up the servant's stairs—"

"An'—my Noah?" Opal asked. "Did he come back with you—"

Clay shifted his burden. "No, he—" He looked straight ahead, unable to meet Opal's dark, frightened eyes. "Noah—"

"He—he's dead, ain't he, suh? You didn' get there in time t' save my Noah—" Her voice was rising shrilly now.

Clay nodded. "I'm sorry, Opal." The words sounded hollow

and meaningless even as he said them. Later, he would try to comfort Opal, to assure her that she and her children would be provided for.

"I've got to get Mister Langford upstairs," he told her. "There's still a chance for him. You—Becky—take care of Opal—"

"Yessuh, Mistuh Clay," the cook said.

"And not a word to anyone about any of this, understand?"

"Yessuh," Becky said, putting a stout arm around Opal's rigid body.

Clay left the kitchen, moving quickly in spite of his burden, with Ludamae scurrying behind him, down the bricked passage from the kitchen to the main house, then up the servants' stairs and into the nearest guest chamber in the west wing. After he had put Tom Langford down on the bed, heedless of the ruin of the elaborate pink-silk spread, he turned and spoke quietly.

"You go down and find my wife, girl. Tell her to come up here with Dr. Mark Burnett, right away. If you're questioned, say that one of the ladies had a dizzy spell. And tell Dr. Burnett to bring his bag."

Ludamae left the room, and while Clay waited, he stripped off Langford's remaining clothes, bloody rags now, and drew the spread over the lower half of the man's body. Then Megan and Mark Burnett were at the door, with Ludamae at their heels. Clay blocked the doorway for a moment, hesitating, wanting to spare Megan from the sight of Langford's torn body, but knowing that he would be needing her full cooperation in the hours ahead. She had the inner strength to do what would have to be done.

He stepped aside, motioning to Megan and the doctor to follow, and Ludamae as well. He told them briefly what had happened to Langford.

Megan caught her breath sharply when she saw the schoolteacher, then pressed a fist to her mouth. Her whole body was rigid under the folds of the green, watered-silk gown. Mark, his face grim, went about his duties, examining Langford carefully, then sending Ludamae off to get soft, clean rags and a pitcher of hot water. Megan held a lamp close so that he might be able to see better.

"He has a chance," Mark said. "I can't promise anything,

of course. A mule whip, you said?" He shook his head. "There could be some internal damage. Kidneys may be smashed or—"

The lamp wavered in Megan's hand, and her face was nearly as white as Langford's. For the first time, Clay was able to imagine what she might look like years from now when she was an old woman. Then he saw her take a deep, steadying breath and set her mouth in a hard line. The lamp did not waver again.

Ludamae returned with the rags and the pitcher of water. "Good thing I always keep my bag in my carriage," Mark said, beginning to wipe away the dried blood from the deep welts on Langford's back. Tom groaned faintly, then lapsed back into unconsciousness.

Ludamae, who had moved like a small, terrified woods creature since she had first seen Clay walk in, carrying the Yankee schoolteacher, now spoke timidly.

"Please, Mistuh Clay, suh—Opal, she be wantin' t' know 'bout Noah. 'Bout how he died an'—"

"You go and tell Opal to stay right where she is. Tell her—" He paused. "Tell her I'll be down to talk to her as soon as I can. Then get back up here."

But when Ludamae returned again, Jessica was with her. Clay moved swiftly to the door, putting out his arm to hold his sister back, trying to interpose his tall body between his sister and the man who lay face down on the bed. "Jess, honey," he said, "no need for you up here. Why don't you go down and help to entertain our guests?"

But his gentle, soft-spoken sister moved with the speed of a cat, thrusting his arm aside. She dropped to her knees, pressing her face against the bed. "The Knights," she said in a voice he had never heard before. "They did this. They've killed Tom—Oh, Tom—Oh, my love—" And then she raised her head, and Megan heard a sound like the keening of the women back in Kilcurran when they had mourned their dead.

"Jess, don't," Clay said, reaching down and closing his hand around her shoulder. "Langford's alive. Mark's going to fix him up—"

"Clay, I've already told you I can't promise," Mark began. Then he looked across the width of the bed at Jessica's face.

"I'll do everything I know how, Jessica," he said.

Clay spoke quickly. "Listen, Jess, I've seen men in worse condition than Langford here during the war and on Johnson's Island, and they pulled through. Why I escaped with a Yankee bullet in me, and I'm here to talk about it."

"But you're so strong," Jessica said. "Tom—"

"There are different kinds of strength," Clay said. He raised her to her feet and held her, his arm around her shoulders. "Ludamae, take Miss Jessica into one of the guest chambers. See that she rests and—"

"I'm not leaving Tom," Jessica said.

"But honey, it would be better if—" He broke off, for he saw a familiar look in Jessica's eyes that warned him that it would be useless to try to reason with her; she would remain at Tom's side until he recovered. Or until he died.

"I have had a good deal of experience nursing our darkies," Jessica told Mark. "I can do whatever has to be done."

Mark nodded. "Very well, Jessica."

Clay turned to Megan. "Come along, then," he said. "I've got to change, and then we've both got to get back to our guests, if only to bid them good night."

"I can't. Not after this."

"You must," Clay said. "And no one must guess from your manner that anything has happened to disturb you. They don't suspect anything's wrong, do they?"

She shook her head. Clay led her from the room, closing the door behind them, and hurried her down the long hallway to their own bedroom. "I—told them you'd gone out on business—something about paying the wages of the railroad crew—But Clay, how can we keep it from them?"

"We must. At least until our guests from the North are on their way. Villard and Seligman and the others."

"You want to give Reed time to make up an—an alibi? Is that it?" Megan's eyes flashed golden fire. "Clay, you're not going to try to protect Reed and those others. Not after what they did to Tom!"

"They did worse tonight—and probably will again." He drew her into their room. "And I am going to keep this quiet as long as I can."

"Because of Reed?"

"Only partly," Clay said. While she was finding a clean

shirt, a fresh cravat, and clean white gloves for him, he went on, his voice controlled, reasonable.

"Megan, listen to me. Men like Villard and Seligman and those other financiers are naturally reluctant about investing capital in areas where law and order can't be maintained, where there is constant civil disorder. And I need their backing. I have to have it. And as for the politicians, I need them, too. The South needs their support. Favorable banking laws. Rebates. Land grants. Those politicians want a strong, well-organized Republican party here in the state. That means the black vote. An end to terrorism and violence. My railroads—"

"What do the railroads matter? A man is lying here in our own home tonight. He's been tortured, he may die, and you— you—"

"Control yourself." Clay's voice was hard now. "Mark's doing his part to help Langford. You'll have to help me." He poured her a glass of brandy and forced it between her lips. "Drink it—all of it," he ordered.

She managed to swallow the brandy, and it steadied her a little. She tried to tell herself that it was her duty to help her husband, that his goals must be hers, also; that she must help to further them in any way possible. But she felt revulsion as she looked up at the big, hard-faced man, composed and handsome, with his starched white shirt and dark-blue satin cravat. Only the deepening of the lines around his mouth showed that anything out of the ordinary had happened tonight.

She had always known the strength of Clay's ambition, his need for wealth and power. But she had never before been repelled as she was now. Nevertheless, she let him take her arm and lead her back through the long gallery and into the ballroom. There he ordered the leader of the black orchestra to play a reel, something lively and fast, for the last dance of the evening. They crashed into the first bars of the music, and Clay led Megan out on to the polished floor, the rest of the guests forming two lines.

"Lianne will be wondering about Mark," he said softly.

Megan shook her head. "Lianne retired a couple of hours ago—her condition, you know—she should sleep soundly."

They moved apart again, but each time they joined hands for another and yet another figure of the reel, she tried not to meet his eyes, fearing that he would read her feelings and be angered by them.

Somehow she got through the short time that remained, before she could stand at Clay's side in the front hallway and say good night to their guests: to the Winthrops, Mr. Villard and Mr. Seligman, and the rest.

When they were alone, he put an arm around her. "You did well tonight," he said. "I'm proud of you." Then, all at once, his eyes were bleak. "You go up to bed," he said. "I'll be along after I've spoken to Opal."

Opal. Megan had not wanted to think about that, but now a new fear flooded over her. "Didn't Noah come back with Uncle Jim and the others—didn't he—"

"Noah is dead," Clay said, his voice carefully expressionless. But Megan could feel the muscles in his arm tighten where it curved about her waist.

"I'll come with you," Megan said.

"As you wish. It won't be easy for you—"

"I'm coming along."

But when they reached the kitchen, they discovered that Opal had slipped away, unnoticed, in the confusion of clearing up after the reception supper.

It was mid morning, the sunlight gilding the fields of Montrose, but a chill breeze caused Reed Drummond to shiver. He stood on the side gallery while a black servant carried his suitcases to the waiting carriage. He would go down to New Orleans, to join Samantha, would squire her about to the opera, the theaters, the restaurants. He would explain to her why she had to say that he had arrived at least a day before he actually would get there.

He had slept fitfully for a few hours last night and then had finished more than half a decanter of brandy to give him strength for the journey and to blot out the images branded on his mind during last night's raid.

It would be better once he was away from Montrose. Perhaps Samantha would even be willing to end their long estrangement. Perhaps she would...

Reed started as he saw the slim shape of a woman coming around the curve of the side path: Opal.

Elijah, the black coachman, carried Reed's luggage out to

the carriage. In a few minutes, Reed had thought to be on his way. And now here was Opal. He braced himself, wishing that he had drunk a little less brandy.

She approached slowly, and when she spoke, her voice was soft, almost expressionless. Standing at the foot of the veranda, she said, "Mr. Reed—Ah come for Noah's remains." He felt somewhat relieved, but as she mounted the veranda steps, he found himself drawing back instinctively.

"Ah got me a ride with a peddler," she explained. "He promised he'd stop by here tonight on his way back t' Natchez and give me a ride with him—and he'd take Noah's—he'd take Noah along in the wagon."

"Noah has already been buried, Opal," Reed said quickly.

Less than an hour ago, he had returned from a ride down to the cypress swamp and had seen the marker behind the ruins of the schoolhouse. Someone had cut the name Noah Carpenter, carving out the letters crudely, probably with a pocket knife.

"Y' had no right t' bury Noah here," Opal said, her eyes cast down, her tone respectful. Reed flinched, hearing the accusation beneath the surface, however. "My Noah is—was— he was a free man, suh. Your own Papa, Mistuh Vance, he let Noah buy his freedom, y' know that."

Reed did not want to think about his father, not now, of all times, for he knew what Vance Drummond would have said about what had happened on Drummond land the night before.

His father would have done what Clay had done; he was sure of it. But then Clay and papa had always been two of a kind, while he had been the outsider. Papa's own flesh and blood, but still somehow alien. He put up a hand in a useless attempt to conceal his bruised face from Opal's gaze.

"I'm sorry," he began. "I'm truly sorry about—last night— the schoolhouse—dry as—when it caught fire, there wasn't anything—"

Opal was on the veranda now, facing him, her dark eyes fixed on his. "No need t' cover up what you done las' night, Mistuh Reed. Ah know all 'bout the raid."

If only she would cry or swoon, he would know how to handle her. But her face was set like a copper mask, her voice quiet, even.

"Ah'm the one brought word t' Mistuh Clay 'bout the raid

las' night. Heard 'bout it from one o' my customers. An' Ah
was in the kitchen at Azalea Hill when Mistuh Clay come back,
carryin' Mistuh Tom Langford. That Yankee—his back was
like raw meat. Never saw no man, black or white, cut up worse.
Whip cuts near down t' the bone."

Reed caught sight of Elijah, who, having loaded one trunk
onto the top of the carriage, was now returning for the rest of
the luggage. Quickly, Reed grasped Opal by the arm and drew
her inside the house. "We'll talk in here," he said, leading her
into his mother's old office, unused since she had married and
left Montrose.

For the first time he could remember, he felt a need to
justify himself, not to another white person but to a former
slave. Or, perhaps, to himself. The brandy had left a bad taste
in his mouth. His lips were sore where Clay had struck him,
and there was a livid bruise under his right eye from another
blow. His head throbbed remorselessly. If only he had been
able to get away from Montrose before Opal's arrival.

"Ah wanted t' take care of Noah's buryin' myself, suh.
Ah'm—Ah was his wife. Y' had no right—"

"Oh, for God's sake, I didn't have anything to do with the
burial. It must have been Clay or—"

"He shouldn' have done it, neither."

The throbbing in his temples was getting worse, and his
stomach began to churn. He shut his eyes briefly, as if to try
to blot out the memory of Noah's mutilated body, but he could
not forget the black man's cry of agony when that outrageous
thing had been done to him. That cry had tormented him during
the few hours of fitful sleep he had had before dawn; it had
driven him down to the ruins of the schoolhouse earlier this
morning. He had been somewhat relieved at seeing the freshly
dug mound of earth, for he knew that if Clay or one of Clay's
men had not buried Noah, he himself would have dug the grave
with his own hands.

"Finish what ye' were sayin'—" Opal's voice was tight with
pain now. "Mistuh Clay wanted t' keep me from seein'—What
did you an' those other—those night riders—what did you do
to my Noah 'fore he died?"

Reed swallowed. "Now, girl, I've told you it was an accident—"

"Accident? Like what they done to that black man down near Pass Christian—or the other one at Pascagoula? Is that what you done t' my—"

Reed looked away. Both those men had been castrated as Noah had. But the Knights had not been involved. That had been the work of another group of night riders who called themselves the White Line.

"Look at me, Mistuh Reed! Ah want t' know—"

"Opal, you're forgetting yourself. I realize that you are deeply distressed, and I—But you must not go around making these accusations. For your own sake. And the sake of your children. You have three little ones now, don't you?"

Opal did not answer, and Reed went on, speaking quickly. "Listen to me, girl. I'll see to it that you and your children are provided for. Even though Montrose is no longer your home, I'll see that you have enough to live on. I give you my word—"

"Don't want your word—or your money. Ah have a good business. Ah can take care of my own."

"Well, then—in case you change your mind—remember my offer and—Now why not go out to the kitchen? Your mother's there. You'll want to see her. She'll be a comfort to you in this time of—of—I can't stay any longer, Opal. I'm leaving for New Orleans. To join my wife."

"Ah seen the carriage," Opal said. Her eyes narrowed, and her voice took on a cutting, sarcastic tone. "Ah 'spect your wife'll be pleased t' see you, Mistuh Reed."

Good Lord, was his estrangement from Samantha common gossip? Did the servants here at Montrose, the blacks in Natchez, know?

In an effort to maintain his dignity, he said, "I am sure Miss Samantha will be pleased to—"

"Ah ain' sure," Opal interrupted. One corner of her mouth lifted in a mocking smile.

"That's enough. I warn you—"

"No, Ah ain' sure at all. 'Cause Miz Samantha, she never did care nothin' 'bout you. Not from the beginnin'. An' even when you joined up with them night riders—Ah know 'bout that, too. You joined 'cause you thought it would please her, but she ain' never—"

"Get out." Reed's voice shook with anger.

"You ain' never pleased Miz Samantha—she never cared nothin' for you. It's always been Mistuh Clay. Everybody knows that—"

Reed advanced on her, a red mist swimming before his eyes, his shoulder muscles tensing. He drew back his arm, but Opal stood her ground. Her voice rose, shrill and filled with an anger that matched his own.

"Miz Samantha don' belong to you—she never did—an' that little boy you so proud of—Luke—ain' yours. He's Mistuh Clay's child—" She looked at him with contempt. "Hit me if you've a min' to—kill me like you killed my Noah—but it won' change nothin'. Luke ain' yours—"

The mist dissolved, and Reed fought his way back to sanity. "You are demented. You've lost your wits—the shock of Noah's death—" Then, speaking more quietly, he went on. "There is no way you could possibly know—"

"Ain' there? Didn' Ah pass the old summerhouse that night after the ball? The night Ah ran off from here to marry Noah?" Her voice broke, but she went on. "Nearly three in the mornin', it was. Ah saw Mistuh Clay's horse in front of the summerhouse—and Ah heard the noises inside—heard Miz Samantha cryin' out like a woman does when she's been pleasured—when she—"

Reed felt the floor move under his feet, and he put out a hand to steady himself, resting it on the back of a chair. "Luke is—"

"He come early, didn't he? An' Miz Samantha, she made up a story 'bout trippin' on the stairs. But that baby, my momma say he wasn' no early-born baby. Big, he was—a big, strappin' boy—"

The rapping on the door startled both Reed and Opal. A moment later, in response to a word from Reed, Elijah came in.

"Carriage all ready, suh," he said respectfully. "Bes' we get started now. That river boat won' wait."

"Yes," Reed managed to say. "Thank you, Elijah. I'll be out directly."

He could not look at Opal. He straightened his cravat, and turning, he walked from the room.

The December air was damp and chilly, and there was a coldness inside him. Before he could reach the carriage, Rachel came forward, leading Luke, who had come to see his father off. The child pulled away from Rachel and flung himself against Reed. "Take me along, Papa—please—take me—"

At any other time, he would have lifted the boy in his arms, comforted him, and placated him by promising to bring back a special present. Now Reed drew back and stood looking down at Luke. And he saw, really saw for the first time, how the child's hair had darkened so that now he had a mop of thick, black curls. He saw the jutting cheekbones, too, the full lips and the eyes. Vivid, arresting, dark blue. Clay's eyes.

Reed spoke sharply. "Rachel, take Luke back to the kitchen with you."

Luke stared up at him in surprise. "But Papa, I want—"

"You go along with Rachel. Right now," Reed said in a tone he had never used before in speaking to the child. Luke's eyes began to fill, and his mouth quivered.

Quickly, Rachel lifted the child into her arms.

"Yuh come 'long with me, Mastuh Luke," she said firmly. "Can' yuh see yo' Papa's in a hurry? Got a boat t' ketch." She carried the boy off, saying over her shoulder, "Hopes yuh have a good trip, suh."

In the kitchen, Opal was waiting. Rachel set Luke down and automatically put a piece of cake into his hand. "Now go out an' play, there's a good chil'," she said.

He hesitated. First Papa and now Rachel. Didn't anybody have time for him this morning? She gave him a gentle little push in the direction of the door, and he went out, clutching the cake.

A moment later, Rachel embraced her daughter, holding her close. "Ah knows—we all do—po' Noah. Nevah ought t' have learned t' read an' write—Settin' hisself up t' be mo' than he wuz—"

Opal's body stiffened. "Ah won' have you talking 'gainst Noah—"

"Ain' talkin' 'gainst him—"

Opal freed herself and began to pace the kitchen.

"Terrible night we had heah," Rachel said. "Thought them night riders might burn the cabins—All the folks kept inside. But they smelled the smoke from the schoolhouse an'—Oh,

Lord, if only Mistuh Clay had got heah sooner—"

Opal gasped. "Mistuh Clay—Oh, what'd Ah say—what'd Ah do—"

"What yuh talkin' 'bout?" Rachel demanded.

"Mistuh Reed—seein' him tryin' t' make like he didn' have nothin' t' do with the night riders—lyin' t' me—Ah must'a' gone outa my head—an' Ah tol' him—and Miz Megan, she been so good t' me an' Mistuh Clay, he did try to save Noah— Never meant no harm t' Mistuh Clay nor Miz Megan—"

Rachel stared at Opal wondering whether the loss of Noah had unhinged her mind. "What y' talkin' 'bout, honey?" she asked anxiously. "'Yuh ain' makin' sense."

Quickly, Opal explained what she had told Reed about Luke. "An' now if Mistuh Reed go an' tell Mistuh Clay—if they fight—Miz Megan's sure t' find out the reason. An' she got spirit, that woman. She loves Mistuh Clay, but she got too much spirit to keep her mouth shut if she finds out that Mistuh Clay and Miz Samantha—An' Ah never meant to make no trouble for Miz Megan or—"

Rachel put her arm around Opal's shoulders and led her to a chair. "Yuh ain' made none," she assured her daughter. "Yuh got enough t' grieve yuh this day. Don' go frettin' 'bout somethin' that ain' goin' t' happen."

"But Mistuh Reed—"

"He ain' goin' t' say nothin' t' Mistuh Clay. Nor t' Miz Samantha, neither." Rachel sighed. "Ah been with the Drummonds fo' de las' twenty-five years, ain' I? Ah know dem. Mr. Reed, he ain' neveh been able t' look the truth in de eye. If he did, he'd never have married Miz Samantha, knowin' she didn' care 'bout him an' never had. He got t' make things like he wants them t' be in his head—"

"But how can he still believe Luke's his own after Ah told him—"

"He b'lieves what he's got t' b'lieve t' keep on goin'." Rachel spoke with calm certainly, her lined face impassive. She moved away to the window beside the stove and looked out. Luke was still standing a few feet from the kitchen quarters, the cake crumbled in his hand. He kicked at a stone beside the path.

"No, Ah ain' worried 'bout Mistuh Clay an' Miz Megan.

It's that chil' there I'se sorry fo'. Mistuh Reed goin' t' pretend t' himself that Luke's his. But he ain' goin' t' be able t' ferget whay you say t' him, neither. Those words yuh say, they goin' t' be like poison in him—like poison from a cottonmouth. An' that little boy there, he goin' be the one t' suffer."

Chapter Eighteen

THE EARLY-SUMMER sunlight streamed in through the tall bedroom windows and glinted on the Waterford goblet, now filled with a spray of Cherokee roses. Over the years, Megan had become used to seeing the chip in the goblet's base, the crack halfway up the stem, so that now these flaws were like an integral part of the design to her. She smiled and went about finishing the packing of Clay's trunk, her motions quick and neat, as they had been all those years before when she had worked as a maid back at the manor house in Kilcurran.

She had a dozen servants now at Azalea Hill who could have done this chore for her; but as always, when Clay was leaving on a long business trip, she preferred to pack for him herself. This summer, he would be in Colorado to examine the advances on the newest of his lines and the possibilities of joining the new line with one that ran directly to Denver. She had been careful to pack several white ruffled shirts and two suits for evening wear.

"Denver's no raw mining town, not anymore," he had explained when he had been outlining his plans. He went on to tell her that now, in this summer of 1882, Denver boasted the finest luxury shops, a palatial hotel called the Windsor, where he would be staying, and the Tabor Grand Opera House, where such famous stars as Sarah Bernhardt, Madame Modjeska, Maurice Barrymore, and Lillie Langtry had appeared. "The hotel—and the opera house, were both built by Horace Tabor, the Silver King," Clay had said. "The man's overextended himself, they say. Likes to cut a wide swath, to impress that blonde mistress of his with the outlandish name—what is it now? Oh, yes, Baby Doe."

But Clay's interest was in railroads, not silver, and he was filled with almost boyish excitement at the prospect of inspecting his newest line. Yes, Megan thought, even now that Clay was forty-three, he still had that driving ambition, that enthusiasm that had attracted her from the beginning. But now her love for him, although still strong, was tempered with a more realistic view of the man. And their lovemaking, although still satisfying to her, was no longer the overwhelming, dizzying experience it had been during those first years of marriage.

That was only natural, Megan told herself firmly, for she was occupied with running Azalea Hill, raising three lively, strong-willed children, and taking part in the social activities of Natchez. And when Clay was at home, the house was always filled with guests; there were balls and receptions, breakfasts and musicales, important men, and their wives, from New York and Washington, form Chicago and San Francisco, to be entertained.

Megan refused to let herself admit that there was any other cause for the distance between herself and Clay, for the fact that even when they were locked in each other's arms in the large, ornate bed, they were no longer completely one. She shut the thought away as she closed down the lid of the trunk; then, turning, she left the bedroom and went downstairs, to find two envelopes, resting on the silver tray on the hall table, addressed to her.

The first one she picked up bore the name Opal Carpenter. A bill, no doubt, for her own summer dresses and the six new frocks ordered for Deirdre. Even at eleven, Deirdre was a beauty, her black curls thick and glossy, her eyes a deep amber-gold. Already Deirdre had thrown several tantrums, demanding to be allowed to put up her hair instead of wearing it loose over her shoulders, as was proper for a girl her age. Megan had ignored her outbursts, for on some matters she could be fully as stubborn as her daughter. But she could do little enough to curb Deirdre's other desires when Clay showered the child with luxuries. It was Clay who had given her permission to get the six new summer dresses, lavish confections trimmed with yards of imported lace and ruffles. Five of the dresses were suitable, Megan supposed, for they were of cambric, muslin, and lawn, but the sixth...

"White silk, imported from Paris! For a child!" Megan had protested.

But Clay had given permission, and he had been backed up by Miss Amy, a thin spinster whose once-blonde curls had faded to gray but who still spoke in a girlish voice that set Megan's teeth on edge. Miss Amy was a distant Drummond cousin from Charleston who had come to make her home at Azalea Hill when Deirdre had just turned six. She was the little girl's governess, properly speaking, but because of the family relationship, she took her meals with the rest of the Drummonds and made her opinions known. She invariably sided with Deirdre, and although she was courteous to the mistress of the household, Megan suspected that Miss Amy deplored Clay's marriage to an Irish immigrant girl. But it was not Miss Amy's private opinion of her that troubled Megan.

"She fills Deirdre's head with a lot of fancy notions," Megan had protested to Clay only a few days before and not for the first time. "She spoils her, treats her like royalty."

"Deirdre is a princess," Clay had replied with a smile. He had looked over at his daughter. "See the way she carries herself."

Megan had not been unable to deny that Deirdre did indeed move with a grace and poise that would have done credit to one of Queen Victoria's daughters. But she had snapped at Clay, "Stuff and nonsense. Princess, indeed. She is a headstrong child who needs a firm hand."

With Clay's spoiling her and with Miss Amy in attendance, it was not likely that Deirdre would get the right kind of discipline, however. And Megan had to admit that in other ways Miss Amy was satisfactory enough, having taught Deirdre not only to read and write but to sketch, to play the piano, and to follow all the intricate rules of deportment, which would one day be valuable to her. Deirdre already knew how to enter a ballroom, how to curtsy, how to serve tea and make conversation with other girls from the finest families in Natchez. But Miss Amy, at the same time, had filled Deirdre's head with notions about the superiority of the Drummonds back in Charleston and, going farther back, had told her about the Drummonds who had fought and died at Colloden in the last vain attempt to regain the throne for the Stuarts.

Yes, there was a rift between Megan and her daughter, although she loved the child and felt the force of her charm. Deirdre could be charming, even affectionate, when it pleased her.

As for the boys, Brant, at sixteen, was beginning to spend much of his time away from the house, hunting, riding, indulging, Megan suspected, in flirtations with the daughters of tenant farmers up river. Or, perhaps, if he took after his father, he had already progressed beyond the stage of flirtations. Terence was a little on the bookish side, serious, studious, and outstanding in his schoolwork. Both had been enrolled in a fine preparatory school near Natchez, and Clay was already talking about which college they should attend. Harvard, perhaps, or maybe the Massachusetts Institute of Technology. "A classical education won't be much use when it's time for them to come into the business," Clay had said. Megan, although she had remained silent, had privately thought that unless Brant applied himself more closely to his studies, there was little likelihood that he would be accepted by either school.

She set down Opal's bill, to be paid with the rest of the household accounts, and found herself thinking that oddly enough, it was Luke, of all this younger generation of Drummonds, to whom she felt closest.

A tall, gangling boy, he was shy and a little too quiet. Although he was a few months older than Brant, he showed none of Brant's easy self-assurance, his winning charm. Luke would be a big man—that was already plain—for his shoulders and chest were broadening out, and he was almost six feet tall. He could ride and hunt with the same skill as Brant, but there was something in his eyes, a brooding, vulnerable quality, that made Megan's heart go out to him.

For she could understand well enough at least some of the

things that troubled her young nephew. Ever since he had been a little boy, he had preferred Azalea Hill to his own home, and who could blame him, she thought. Even when Reed was at Montrose, he was often the worse for drink. And many times he did not bother to come home to Montrose to sleep at all. There were plenty of beds in Natchez-under and plenty of girls willing to share them with Reed Drummond.

As for Samantha, ever since that summer—when had it been? Oh, yes, the summer of 1872. Ever since then, Samantha had stopped spending her summers at Montrose. That summer, she had gone off to White Sulphur Springs, and gradually she had started going farther afield. This summer, she had already set off for New York State, where she would stay at the fashionable and lively resort of Saratoga.

Samantha had explained to Lianne, who had passed the information on to Megan, that the climate of Mississippi in summer was far too trying. Lianne had laughed. "She spent all her summers in Mississippi when she was a young girl and was never any the worse for it."

It was Clay's money that paid, indirectly, for Samantha's summer jaunts and the trunks of clothing she took along with her. Not that Clay gave her the money. He sent it to Reed for the upkeep of Montrose, which, in one way or another, was always a source of trouble and expense and which could never be made to pay for itself. Reed had given up even the pretense of managing the place himself and had gone on hiring overseers, none of whom had proved equal to the job.

Megan pushed away her thoughts of Reed and of Samantha and picked up the other letter on the tray, smiling as she recognized Jessica's angular handwriting.

Jessica. Mrs. Tom Langford these past ten years. Walking quickly, lightly, Megan went out to the downstairs gallery to read her sister-in-law's letter.

Jessica had married Tom during that winter of 1872. Even now, Megan could not forget the weeks when none of them could be sure if Tom would live to make Jessica his wife. He had lain upstairs in the guest chamber, with Mark Burnett visiting almost daily and Jessica remaining at his bedside, nursing him devotedly, pausing only to catch a few hours of sleep in an armchair beside his bed.

It had taken all of Megan's determination to persuade Jessica to take time for food. Then, one rain-swept evening, Jessica had stumbled down the hall and had, at last, given way to tears, and Megan had feared that Tom was dead.

"No—" Jessica sobbed when Megan held her in her arms. "The fever's broken. He recognized me—he's going to live."

The wedding had taken place only a week later, with Jessica repeating her vows at Tom's bedside. Neither Reed nor Samantha had been invited, and even now, although Jessica wrote to Samantha once a year, at Christmas, she had not returned to Montrose. After Tom's recovery, the couple had set out for Tom's new post, a school near Birmingham, in Alabama. A year later, Jessica had borne a son, Evan.

Now Megan unfolded the letter and began to read.

> My dear Megan,
> Tom and I are quite taken up with this great new plan of ours, and so I must ask your forgiveness for not having replied to your letter sooner. Think of it, a college for young black men. Tom believes that an agricultural institute would be most useful, but later, perhaps, we could include studies in mining engineering. And then there is my own particular dream, that one day we will have another institution for black women, a normal school where those of sufficient intellect can be trained as teachers . . .

Jessica went on to speak of her appreciation for Clay's generous contributions to the school she and Tom were running now and for Clay's promise of even larger sums when the college should become a reality.

> ". . . and we owe Clay so much more, Megan, dear, for how can I ever forget that dreadful night when Clay rode out to save Tom's life. . . ."

Megan could not forget that night, either, but her feelings were rather different from Jessica's. For although Clay had, indeed, saved Tom's life and would have saved Noah's too, if he had been in time, he had refused to make out a complaint to the authorities. Because of his loyalty to his family and also because he did not wish to call attention to the fact that the outrage had occured on Drummond land, fearing to alienate his Northern financial and political backers, Clay had remained silent.

Even though he had lashed out at Reed himself—Megan had seen the bruises on his knuckles and had questioned him at the time—he had resumed the family relationship, riding out to Montrose each time he returned to Natchez. And, at his insistence, Megan had accompanied him, had spoken to Reed with distant courtesy, had made polite conversation with Samantha. The Drummonds must present a united front to the world no matter what their differences.

Megan looked up from Jessica's letter, hearing the clatter of hoofs on the long, curving drive, and she smiled when she saw young Luke. No matter how she might feel about Reed and Samantha, she had always had a warm liking for her quiet nephew, with his dark-blue eyes, his shy smile.

One of the grooms hurried forward to take Luke's horse, and he came up the steps to the gallery to kiss her cheek lightly, to compliment her on her appearance, on the new sprigged muslin dress she was wearing. He was nearly as handsome as her own Brant, with the same wide shoulders and chest, the same black, curling hair.

"Is Uncle Clay at home?" he asked.

She nodded. "He's in his study. He's busy making preparations for his trip to Colorado, but he'll be happy to see you, I know. And, of course, you'll stay to dinner."

"Thank you—I will. I—is it all right if I go in and talk to him now? I didn't know he'd be leaving so soon—but when Papa mentioned it this morning, I started right over. I was afraid he'd be gone before I could—"

"Is something wrong, Luke?"

"No, Aunt Megan. It's only—now school's out, I have made plans."

"Of course you have. I'm sure that you and Brant will be out on a hunt before the week's over. And perhaps you'd like to join us at Lake Pontchartrain. Your uncle will be gone by then, but your cousins and I—"

Luke shook his head. "That's mighty kind of you, Aunt Megan, but I want to go to Colorado with Uncle Clay—I want to work on this new railroad."

Megan's eyes widened. "But there's no need. I mean, railroad work is hard and taxing. And if you do want to work,

I'm sure that your father would be glad of your help at Montrose. His new overseer is not entirely satisfactory, I'm told."

"I'm not interested in becoming a planter," Luke said with quiet firmness. "I never have been." There was a set to his jaw that reminded her of Clay, who had said the same thing, in almost the same words, that summer when he had returned from the war.

"You could not hope for a supervisor's position," Megan said. "Even though you are a Drummond, I'm afraid your uncle would refuse to put an inexperienced young man in over experienced workers."

"I would not expect favors," Luke said, flushing slightly. "I'm strong—I could start as a section hand—"

Megan tried to imagine her soft-spoken, shy young nephew swinging a pick side by side with rough Irish immigrant laborers. "Are you sure you understand the difficulties?"

Luke laughed. "If you mean, can I hold my own with the other men on the crew, don't worry."

"But you're not—not one of them, and they know it—they might make it difficult for you—"

The laughter faded, and he spoke with calm assurance.

"I'm a man now," he said. "And I'll prove it. If you'll back me up. If you'll tell Uncle Clay that you think I should go."

"If it's what you want, I'll back you up," she said.

As Luke and Megan went into the house together, she wondered, as she had so many times before, how Samantha could be so indifferent to her only son. How could Samantha have cared so little about Luke's feelings that she had gone off to Saratoga without even waiting to greet Luke when he returned home from school for the summer?

"Why Samantha, honey, are you sure you want me to leave you all alone?" Violet Shepley asked. "With one of those awful headaches of yours? I feel downright mean going off like this."

Samantha had to make an effort to keep her set smile in place. Violet, even after all their summer vacations together, still insisted on going through this silly charade. The woman would have to be an idiot not to know why Samantha was urging her to leave their cottage at the fashionable Grand Union Hotel.

"Now you go along, dear," Samantha urged sweetly, her

hands clenched so tightly that her nails bit into her palms. "You know how much you enjoy the carriage promenade to Moon's Lake-House. And you can come back and tell me what everyone was wearing."

"Well—if you're sure. Shall I put a handkerchief soaked in cologne on your forehead?"

Was Violet deliberately trying to torment her, Samantha wondered. At least she did not have to worry about Gilbert Marshall's arriving before Violet had left. He was too experienced for that. Right now, she was sure, he was somewhere nearby, watching for Violet to make her departure.

"Don't fuss over me," Samantha said, smoothing the folds of her thin silk wrapper. "Once you're gone, I can lie down and take a nap. That's all I need."

"Whatever you say, honey," Violet said. She picked up her lace-trimmed parasol, which, like most of her wardrobe, had been given to her by Samantha. It matched her dress, and both were cast offs from last season. Unfortunately, that shade of green, so becoming to Samantha, gave Violet a sallow look. "I'll be back in time for supper," Violet said, leaving the cottage.

Samantha watched Violet making her way across the stretch of grass to the hired carriage. Samantha would have preferred a carriage of her own, but she had learned to make do with what she could get. And that included Gilbert Marshall.

Samantha had long since learned that it was not necessary to love a man in order to take pleasure with him. She had met Gil, the younger son of a New York shipping dynasty, at a ball here at the Grand Union Hotel only a few days after she had arrived at Saratoga. He had let her know that one day soon he would have to marry and settle down, to take his place in his father's business, but this summer he was here to enjoy himself.

He had ignored the unmarried young ladies at the ball, even the prettiest of them, who had been brought to Saratoga by their anxious mothers to make a good match; instead, he had danced with Samantha several times before escorting her back through the garden to her cottage.

He probably would have tried to make love to her that same night, but Samantha explained that she was staying with another lady, a close friend from Natchez. At the same time, her eyes had made promises, and he had asked if he might call on her—and her friend, of course—the following afternoon.

When he had called, Violet had been conveniently absent, having been sent into town to buy a new fan for Samantha.

That first afternoon had been good, better than Samantha had let herself hope, for Gil knew how to arouse and satisfy a woman. He was tall, muscular, perhaps five years younger than she, but thoroughly experienced.

Thinking about that first time, Samantha felt her body go taut with expectation, felt a tightening in her rounded thighs, felt her breasts, still high and firm, begin to tingle. The light rose-colored silk of the wrapper was like a caress against her bare white skin.

She took the pins out of her heavy dark-brown hair and brushed it down over her shoulders. Ignoring the eau de cologne Violet had recommended, she picked up a flask of jasmine perfume and dabbed it not on her forehead but in the deep shadowed cleft between her breasts, then down along the insides of her thighs.

A few minutes later, she was opening the door to admit Gil Marshall, who entered the cottage, his eyes moving over her hungrily. He lifted her into his arms and carried her to the bed. His hands moved swiftly, baring her body in the shadowed room. She watched while he undressed, her lips parting as she saw the lean body: the muscular arms, the narrow hips, and the long, hard legs.

Then he was beside her on the bed, and she felt the heat of him. She needed this—how she needed this. How else could she bear to live through the long, empty months back at Montrose, how else could she play the role of the respectable matron who had had the misfortune to be married to a man who drank too much; who spent many of his nights in Natchez-under; who was letting the plantation go to seed? All that made her life bearable were the summers....

Gil's hand cupped her breast, his fingers playing with the nipple until it grew firm and hard. She moaned as he put his mouth where his fingers had been, drawing the nipple in between his lips. His hands moved downward, stroking, exploring the clefts and crevices of her body. She arched herself upward, ready, eager to receive him.

He laughed softly, teasingly. "Not yet, my dear. Not until you do something for me...."

He twisted his hands into her hair, guiding her downward. Once, the mere thought of what he wanted from her would have shocked her. But she was no longer a young girl. And she needed what he had to give her.

He lay on his back, his hands sliding from her hair to caress her throat, her shoulders. She heard his harsh gasp of excitement as her lips sought him, as her mouth, her tongue, claimed him.

And then he was kneeling over her, entering her and thrusting fiercely while her hands clutched at his back, drawing him deeper and deeper into herself.... Her legs encircled him, tightening around him until, at the moment of climax, she pushed her mouth against him to stifle her cry, sinking her teeth into the hardness of his shoulder.

A few hours later, as twilight moved across the lawn, turning the great elms into black shadows, she felt the beginning of a familiar sadness. Although her eyes followed Gil's figure until it was lost from view, there was no warmth, no tenderness in her. He had pleased her and would again. He had satisfied her need. But that was all.

It was always the same with the men that she found during her summers away from Montrose. Even that first time, at White Sulphur Springs, she had felt no sadness at parting. The big, florid man from Kentucky—or had it been Tennessee— had gone back home to his wife, a lady suffering from "a nervous indisposition," as he had put it, and unable to travel.

But Samantha had decided that White Sulphur Springs was too dangerous even with Violet, along as her companion, giving an air of respectability, for there had been too many belles from Mississippi and Louisiana.

Saratoga was a little less conventional in this summer of 1882, and there were few Southern visitors since the war. But there were plenty of wealthy men, some from New York, like Gil, or from the West.

And although the Grand Union Hotel still retained its reputation as a respectable hostelry, there was a little more leeway for those guests who chose to stay in the cottages. Her lips

twitched in a smile as she remembered the story that was going
the rounds about the wealthy New York businessman who
required no fewer than two secretaries, both young and attractive, in his cottages, to deal with his correspondence.

Her smile faded. She remained at the window, staring into
the darkness, remembering. Oh, if only she and Clay had married before the war. If only she and Clay . . . She had never
loved any other man, and she never would. But although his
money, which she diverted from the upkeep of Montrose, paid
for her vacations, for her lavish wardrobe, his behavior was
friendly, courteous but no more. Still, although she did not
have him with her now, she thought, with a touch of malice,
neither did Megan. Not this summer.

She had received a letter from Luke only yesterday saying
that he and his uncle were going out to Colorado. His uncle.
Let him go on believing that Clay was his uncle. Only in that
way could she preserve her unblemished reputation. Even Clay
himself would never know the truth.

She had begun to feel a little guilty about her neglect of
Luke. She had taken no interest in him when he was a child,
but now he had begun to remind her of what Clay had been at
sixteen. Sometimes she wished that she might be closer to her
son. But it was too late. He treated her with respect and wrote
her dutiful letters, but she knew that it was Megan he went to
with his problems, Megan who comforted him. Oh, why had
it all worked out this way? That Irish nobody, that interloper,
had Clay, and now, in a sense, she had Luke, too.

Samantha rose and went to the closet to choose a dress for
the evening. It was better that Luke spent so little time with
her, she told herself. For although she looked youthful, a tall,
broad-shouldered son at her side would destroy the illusion.

As she stood before the open door of the closet, with its
row of satins, taffetas, and silks, she felt a chill deep inside.
Now, in her thirties, she had no difficulty in finding a lover.
But what would happen in the years ahead? For a brief moment,
she was shaken, afraid.

Chapter Nineteen

THE FOLLOWING summer, Clay, accompanied by Megan and their three children, made a trip to New York City, traveling in Clay's private railway cars. The cars were of black walnut, with silver mountings and decorations, and Deirdre reveled in the luxurious accommodations: the marble wash basins, the ice-water fountains, blue-velvet carpets and well-upholstered seats, the curtains of pale-blue silk, and the doors of ingrained glass. There were three separate staterooms, with curtained beds: one for Deirdre and Miss Amy, one for Brant and Terence, and the third for Clay and Megan.

"Now remember, this is a business trip," Clay warned Megan. "I hope you won't be disappointed if I have to spend a good deal of time away from you and the children."

Megan understood, for she had been listening for the past year to Clay's terse, angry comments about the railroad rate wars, and he had told her of the tactics being used by such financial giants as J. P. Morgan and William Vanderbilt, who employed every means at their disposal to destroy or swallow up the smaller lines. Railroad men like Henry Villard were being pressed into bankruptcy, while in the West, railroad gangs fought with fists, clubs, and guns to capture the right-of-way to the great mining sections. "They won't push me to the wall," Clay had said grimly. "But I've got to get more financial backing. Perhaps from Seligman and his associates."

Then he had added, "So you see, it'll mean business meetings in New York, and I'll be occupied at all hours." He smiled ruefully. "Fact is, I'm somewhat overextended. I'll need a great deal of extra cash if I'm going to go on with this new line out in Colorado. And that's exactly what I intend to do."

She felt a coldness, seeing the ruthless determination in his face, in the lines of his body, hearing it in his voice. Would Clay never be content? Was there no limit to his need to increase his holdings? She could not find fault with his drive, his ambition, for it made him what he was: the man she loved and always would. But she could not help but be unhappy when his dreams of future conquests took him away from her so often.

Even now he was saying, "Perhaps this time it would be better if I went to New York alone. Then, next year—"

"Next year you'll be off in Colorado. Or starting to build a railroad into Canada, for all I know. Please, Clay, this trip would mean so much to me. And you need not feel concerned about not spending much time with me. Now that Cousin Belle and Gavin O'Donnell are living in New York, I'll be visiting them. Why, do you realize that I have six nephews and nieces I've never even seen?"

Clay smiled. "Are there really six now? Belle's certainly been keeping that man busy—"

He broke off abruptly as Deirdre came into the room, and Megan knew that whatever he had been going to say about Gavin's reproductive zeal had been unfit for the child to hear. Megan covered the awkward moment by saying, "And I would so like to visit those New York shops I've read about in *Harper's Bazar*. A. T. Stewart's department store and Lord and Taylor. And all those wonderful stores on what they call 'the Ladies' Mile'."

The truth was that Megan had always been perfectly satisfied with the handsome dresses made for her by Opal Carpenter, and she could have managed quite well with her present wardrobe. But she could not bring herself to speak of her real reason for wanting to go to New York with Clay. Certainly not in front of Deirdre. And even when she and Clay were alone, her pride made it difficult for her to tell him how much she hated their long and frequent separations. She dreaded those nights when she must lie alone in their wide, canopied bed, her body hungering for his, those times when she turned, at dawn, still half-asleep, and reached out, only to find that he was not there.

Now Deirdre ran to Clay's side and smiled up at him, her amber eyes pleading. "Oh, Papa, let us go with you. Oh, please—I want to visit the—'the Ladies' Mile,' too."

Clay smiled down at her with amused tenderness.

"And what would you like to buy there, my lady?"

"Oh, lots of things." She was so pretty, Megan thought, with her black curling hair, her flushed pink cheeks. "A feather fan, a big one with real ostrich plumes. And—an enamel case for calling cards. And a topaz necklace like mama's, and—"

"You're a bit young for the ostrich-feather fan," Clay said, ruffling her dark curls. Her eyes filled, and her full underlip trembled. "Oh, now, I'm sure that Miss Amy will be able to find enough fripperies in New York that are suitable for a girl your age," he said quickly.

Megan repressed a sigh for she had hoped to go on the trip without Miss Amy, whose presence often irritated her. But she said nothing, and it was Deirdre who spoke up. "Papa, I'm twelve. I'll be putting up my hair and letting down my skirts next year."

"Oh, no you won't," Megan said firmly. "You're still a little girl—"

"Your mother's right," Clay agreed. "But since this trip means so much to both of you, I suppose I'll have to give in and take you along. And the boys, too."

Although Megan could not help wishing that it had not been necessary for Deirdre to tip the scales in favor of the trip, she was so pleased at the prospect of accompanying her husband to New York that she refused to let anything spoil her pleasure, even the presence of Miss Amy. She felt sorry for the thin, aging spinster, and she did not begrudge her a place at Azalea Hill. Miss Amy had so little in life, for all her airs and graces, her frequent references to the importance of the Charleston branch of the Drummond family. It was right that Clay should provide for this woman, who would otherwise be living in genteel poverty in some boarding house, like so many of her kind. If only Miss Amy would not fill Deirdre's impressionable young mind with all those false and snobbish notions.

But during those precious hours when Megan and Clay retired to their private compartment and he drew the heavy velvet curtains around the bed that was set into the wall, she managed to forget everything else. When she rested her head on his shoulder, as they watched the dark countryside rushing by, she forgot that she was the mother of three children. It was as if she and Clay were young lovers once more, discovering each other, exploring the delights of passion for the first time. For Clay, at forty-five, was still handsome and virile, without a touch of gray in his thick, dark hair; and the hours he had spent on horseback in New Mexico and Colorado, overseeing the expansion of his new railroad lines, had kept him hard, lean, and tanned. Megan shivered with sensual pleasure as she caressed his body, as she held him close in her arms, pressing the length of her body to his, molding herself against him.

There was a special excitement in their lovemaking here in these new surroundings, with the movement of the train rocking their joined bodies and the roar of the train like thunder in her blood. When, at last, she was fulfilled, it was so good, so satisfying, to drift off to sleep with Clay's powerful arms around her, with his face pressed against the thick, golden cascade of her hair or resting against the swell of her breasts, to have the warmth, the scent of him enfolding her.

Perhaps, she thought, it was even better than her honeymoon in New Orleans, for now Clay knew her so well. He knew each touch that would arouse her, knew when she wanted him to enter her with leisurely gentleness, when she would welcome the swift, fierce thrust, the demanding violence that made her arch upward to him, her body demanding, and receiving, the ultimate satisfaction.

She began to wish that this trip would go on endlessly. But soon enough they were in New York, and they were taking a carriage to the Fifth Avenue Hotel, where Megan and the children were startled and impressed by their first ride in a steam elevator, which bore them up to their rooms.

Clay had engaged three adjoining suites, one for himself and Megan, one for the boys, and the third for Deirdre and Miss Amy, who was obviously nervous during the ascent, her thin, sharp features tense, one gloved hand clutching at the handle of her silk umbrella. Even Deirdre forgot that she was, in her own opinion, a young lady, and she made a little squealing sound when the elevator started to rise. Brant and Terence did their best to look nonchalant, causing Megan and Clay to exchange amused smiles.

Each of the suites was made up of a separate parlor, bedchamber, dressing room, and bathroom. After the Drummonds had dressed for dinner, they descended again, this time to the grand dining room, which was filled with fashionable men and women. The boys ate heartily, trying as many of the elaborate dishes as Megan would allow them to have and sampling two of the desserts with the ravenous appetites of boys in their teens. Miss Amy picked at her duckling in Burgundy and pronounced it quite acceptable, although not, of course, in a class with the cuisine of her native Charleston. No dinner, not even those at Azalea Hill, could ever rival the meals she had enjoyed back in Charleston, she insisted.

Megan was not surprised when Clay told her that he had set up a business meeting for the following morning. "At least you'll get the chance to spend plenty of time with Belle," he reminded her. "And you'll get to meet all those nieces and nephews."

"And Gavin's younger brother, Michael," she said. "Belle wrote me that he's just come over from Ireland."

Belle had grown stout during the years since Megan had last seen her, but unlike Aunt Kathleen, she wore her corsets tightly laced, and on the afternoon of Megan's first visit, she had encased her heavy body in a smart, if somewhat overornate, dress of gray brocade grenadine trimmed with Spanish lace, braiding, and jet beads.

She and Megan sat over their afternoon tea in a parlor so crowded with plush and rosewood furniture and china knick-knacks that Megan wondered how Belle's lively, active brood had not wreaked havoc there. Perhaps, Megan thought, the parlor was kept closed except when Belle entertained guests.

"Oh, we didn't live this fine, not when we first came to the city," Belle admitted, sipping her tea. "First, we was—were—down on Cherry Street. That's all the way downtown, near the waterfront, and a rough place it is, too. Brawlings and stabbings and streetwalkers flauntin' themselves, bold as ye please. But then, what with the children growin' up and starting t' notice things and Gavin doin' so well for himself, why I got him t' move us up here. Ever seen anythin' like it, Megan?"

"Never," Megan said, still a little dazed by the bustle and clamor of New York, so startling after the slow pace of Natchez. She had certainly never seen an apartment house before, although she had read about them.

The Victoria was one of the finest of these new multiple dwellings, a massive building at Twenty-seventh Street that occupied the whole block between Fifth Avenue and Broadway. The suite in which Belle and the rest of the O'Donnells lived was one of eighteen on the third floor of the eight-story, red-brick, marble-trimmed structure, with its imposing mansard roof. Belle had beamed when she had shown Megan through the rest of the suite: the dining room, with its huge, heavy mahogany furniture, the kitchen, butler's pantry, the bedrooms, dressing rooms, and bathrooms.

"Of course, the servants' quarters are in the attic." Belle sighed, putting a plump hand to her swelling bosom. "Such trouble as we have gettin' good servants here. And trainin' them. And no sooner do I get them trained when like as not they're after runnin' off t' get married."

Megan tried to look properly sympathetic, barely repressing a smile as she remembered the cottage opposite the warehouses and the livery stable, back in Natchez-under, where Belle had scrubbed the kitchen and emptied the slops out into the alley. But Belle, cheerful and amiable, had gone on talking as she escorted Megan into the parlor and rang for tea and sandwiches and cakes. She had obviously put from her mind everything having to do with Natchez-under. Her shocked talk of the brawling and the streetwalkers on Cherry Street had made it plain that she did not remember those same sordid conditions that had been a part of her everyday life down South. She had apparently forgotten, too, that she had been angry with Megan and bitterly jealous during the time when she had feared that Megan, not yet married to Clay, would take Gavin away from her.

Now, with six children and a devoted husband, Belle O'Donnell was the picture of matronly complacency, proud of her husband and his success, doting on her good-looking high-spirited brood of children and wanting to give them all the advantages that she and Gavin had missed.

At the moment, Deirdre, Brant, and Terence had gone off to Central Park with their cousins. "Are you sure it will be safe?" Megan had asked, and Belle had reassured her. "Miss Amy can take the girls to the Casino on the Terrace for ice cream, and the boys'll go rowing on the lake. They'll be fine, with Michael to keep an eye on them."

Michael O'Donnell, Gavin's younger brother, was a tall, powerfully built youth of twenty-one with an air of self-confidence that made him appear older. Megan was content to send the children off with Michael riding herd on them.

Deirdre, however, had surveyed her O'Donnell cousins with a cold, distant expression and had joined them in the outing with obvious reluctance. Brant and Terence, to Megan's relief, had hit it off quickly with Belle's boys, Pat, Keith, and Vincent, and with Michael.

As for Belle, she settled into her plush-covered chair, prepared for a long, cozy chat with Megan, to bridge the gap of the years since they had last seen each other.

"Michael looks like a fine young man," Megan said. "I suppose Gavin's pleased to have him over here."

"He's a good lad, Michael is," Belle agreed, helping herself to a third cream-filled cake. "But he's a problem, too. He don't take t' city life—a born farmer, y' see. And when Gavin got him a job clerkin' at Tammany Hall, he didn't keep it long. Said he couldn't stand working indoors—"

"Tammany Hall?"

"Oh, that's where all them bigwig Democratic politicians hang out," Belle said. "Gavin's got political ambitions of his own—he's got big plans."

"But I thought that being a labor contractor—"

"Sure, an' we ain't forgettin' it was your man that gave Gavin his chance t' better himself, bringin' laborers over from Ireland. But now Gavin wants to go higher. Like I say, he's got plans."

"What sort of plans?"

Belle leaned forward. "Ye see, there still all these Irish

comin' over by the thousands. Things ain't much better back there than they were when my folks came over. And Gavin, he got t' know a lot of those newcomers when we were livin' down on Cherry Street." She wiped her lips with a damask napkin and went on. "Gavin used t' go right down t' the boats t' collect up the men he'd had brought over t' work on Clay's railroads. And Gavin, he had t' find places fer their wives and young ones t' stay." She shook her head and sighed. "Sure, some o' them tenements were awful. But folks were thankful to have a roof against the cold and a basket o' food t' tide 'em over. It ain't easy bein' a stranger in a city like this."

"I can well believe it," Megan said, remembering her arrival in Natchez and her gratitude at having relatives to take her in.

"After a while, those folks started comin' t' Gavin with their troubles. He knew where t' get a district nurse if a woman was havin' a hard time in labor. An' if a young lad got himself into trouble with the law on account o' gettin' in with one o' them awful gangs—lots of them down near the waterfront, y' see— why Gavin'd do what he could to smooth things over with the law.

"An' these bigwig politicians at Tammany, they got t' know Gavin, and they liked him. He's in good with 'em now 'cause he can deliver the votes. An' lately they been tellin' him that he ought t' run fer alderman himself. Think o' that, Megan. My Gavin, an alderman. If only Michael would settle down. Otherwise, he's liable t' get into trouble. He's a good lad, strong and smart, a born farmer. A fine hand with cattle an' horses. But here in the city—" She shook her head.

"Why did he leave Ireland?" Megan asked.

"He was the assistant to the estate manager fer one o' them English landlords. But he wouldn't help drive his own people out o' their houses when they couldn't pay the rent—There was a fight an'—Ye understand how it is over there."

"I understand," Megan said quietly, her mind slipping back over the years, remembering her own brother, killed fighting with the Fenians against the tyranny of the English landlords.

In the Casino on the Terrace in Central Park, Deirdre was finishing her serving of strawberry ice cream. "Let's have some more," said Hortense, her fourteen-year-old cousin, a well-developed girl with a mane of flaming red hair and Belle's loquacious disposition. "Then we'll get the boys to take us rowing." The boys were already out on the lake, below the Casino terrace, having finished their refreshments more quickly and grown restless. "I expect they won't want to take us," Hortense rattled on. "I guess your brothers'd like to see a lot of other places in New York besides the park."

"It's a charming park," Deirdre said politely, remembering Miss Amy's lessons in social conversation. "And I'm sure both my brothers are looking forward to their visit to the Natural History Museum and the Meteorological Observatory."

"Maybe Terence is," said Hortense with a wicked grin. "But Brant—my, but he's good-lookin'—I'll bet he'd a lot rather go off for a visit to the concert saloons."

"How you talk," said Euphemia, giving her sister a little poke in the arm and giggling.

Deirdre said, "I love concerts. Papa took me to a recital in New Orleans once, and I—"

Hortense and Euphemia giggled together. "Girls don't go to concert saloons," said Hortense, still laughing.

"Not unless they work there," Euphemia put in. "We had one of them right around the corner from where we lived, on Cherry Street—and Ma and Pa moved away as soon as we could afford it. She said it would give us bad ideas."

"The girls that work in those places—they're supposed to get the men to buy them drinks, see. And they dance for the customers—in tights—"

"And some of them don't wear nothing except tights. I heard pa say that some of them didn't have a thing on above the waist and—"

Miss Amy choked on her lemonade, her pale, sharp-featured face flushing crimson.

"I don't believe you," Deirdre said. "You're making it all up."

"Oh, no, we ain't. That Cherry Street was a rough place. I'm glad we're away from there now." Euphemia turned, snapped her fingers, and a waiter hurried over. "I want another dish of ice cream—chocolate, this time."

"So do I," said Hortense. "How about you, Dee?"

Deirdre disliked the nickname her cousins had given her. She was embarrassed by their free-and-easy manners, their loud voices; but most of all, she was shocked by their talk of girls in tights with nothing to cover them above the waist. Even if they had heard of such things, they should never had spoken of them.

"More ice cream, Dee?"

She shook her head. "I've had quite enough, thank you." She looked at Miss Amy, hoping for support, but the woman sat frozen, her eyes fixed on her empty glass.

"Oh, Cherry Street wasn't so bad," Euphemia said as the waiter went off. "Remember that Fourth of July—Mrs. O'Brien and the firecracker?"

Once more, Hortense began to shriek with laughter, so that a few ladies at the next table turned to look at her. Deirdre writhed with shame.

"See, Mrs. O'Brien, she was a fat lady—near three hundred pounds, wasn't she, Hortense? And when she went into the back-yard privy—there was one for all the families in our building—why my brother Pat, he slipped a firecracker under the privy door. It was lit, and when it went off, Mrs. O'Brien was in there. Well, she came runnin' out, screamin' like a stuck pig. She didn't take time t' fasten her drawers up right, and they fell down around her ankles—"

Deirdre wanted to sink through the floor of the Casino in her agony of embarrassment. The waiter, who was returning with the order, had heard every word, and his lips twitched under his moustache.

The sunlit lake below the terrace swam sickeningly before Deirdre's eyes. Privies. Drawers. How could any decent female speak of such things? The shame of it! And these awful, vulgar girls were Mama's relations. A wave of nausea swept over Deirdre. Although Miss Amy had never said it in so many words, she had often implied, ever so delicately, that Papa, as a Drummond, had married beneath him. And she had been right.

Deirdre took a deep breath and regained a measure of control. "I declare, I'm quite overcome by the heat and the noise in here. And I do believe you are, too, Miss Amy. Let's go down to the lake and wait for the boys there."

"And I'm not going back to Cousin Belle's, not ever. And you can't make me!"

Deirdre confronted her mother in the parlor of their hotel suite that evening. Clay, who had returned a few minutes before, had gone into the bedroom to change for dinner.

"You can't possibly offend Cousin Belle and her family that way," Megan said. "Perhaps the girls should not have spoken as they did. But you must remember that they have not had your advantages, and they—"

"They're awful! I can't stand them! I'm never going to talk to them again!"

"Oh, come now," Megan said gently. "We're only going to be here in New York City for a few weeks. Surely you can overlook—"

Clay had just emerged from the bedroom, freshly shaven and dressed for dinner. Deirdre ran to his side and caught his hand. "I don't have to see my cousins, do I, Papa?"

Clay, who had earlier received a sketchy version of what had taken place that afternoon, shook his head. "Not if you don't want to. Your mother will make some excuse for your absence—a heavy cold or an attack of la grippe. And you may see the city in Miss Amy's company. I'll tell you what—you may take a carriage and help to select gifts for Aunt Lianne and Aunt Jessica. And for yourself, naturally," he added with a doting smile.

"Oh, but Clay, I don't think—" Megan began.

"Run along now," Clay told Deirdre, "and change for dinner." And when the girl had gone, he turned to Megan.

"I made it clear that I'm here on business, important business," he said, his voice tight with suppressed irritation. "I don't want to get involved in foolish domestic squabbles."

Megan pressed her lips together, thinking that she was perfectly capable of handling such "domestic squabbles" if only Clay did not insist on taking Deirdre's side, of giving the child her way in everything. No matter what Belle's girls had said, Deirdre would not be irreparably damaged by associating with them during this brief visit. And had they really said anything so dreadful, after all?

"I suppose you don't mind if Terence and Brant go on exploring the city with Belle's sons and Michael O'Donnell?" Megan asked quietly.

"Certainly I don't mind. Boys are different. They don't have to be sheltered from the—earthier facts of life, as girls do. Deirdre's a sweet, innocent child, and I want her to stay that way."

"Deirdre will be a young woman soon enough," Megan said. "She'll marry, and then she'll be forced to discover the—earthier facts. I've always believed that—"

"It's time you were dressing for dinner, too," Clay said, and it was plain that he considered the conversation closed.

In spite of their clash over Deirdre, Megan managed to enjoy much of her visit to New York, for on those evenings when Clay did not have to meet with business associates, he escorted Megan to the opera, to the theater, and to the fine restaurants for which the city was famous. She saw the plump, voluptuous Lillian Russell, who was playing the leading role in Offenbach's operetta *Princess of Trebizonde;* afterward, she and Clay feasted on steak, lobster, and corn on the cob in lavish surroundings: walls covered with tapestry, red plush upholstery, and huge, glittering crystal chandeliers.

During the afternoons, she attended matinees with Belle and went shopping on "the Ladies' Mile" and at the impressive department stores. She bought a handsome gold watch for Luke at Tiffany's store, and, at Lord & Taylor, a length of heavy black silk to be made into a fine new uniform for Ludamae; a set of the works of Sir Walter Scott for Jessica and Tom, the books bound in red leather; a cashmere shawl for Aunt Kathleen.

Then, a few days before they were to leave New York, Clay arranged for a dinner at Delmonico's Restaurant for Gavin, Belle, and Michael. Megan, seeing her husband's high spirits, was not surprised when, earlier that evening, he had told her that he had succeeded in getting the financial backing he needed. "Now I can go full speed ahead with the Colorado line," he told her.

"I'm pleased for you," she said.

He glanced at her sharply. "For us, my dear," he said. "Whatever I do is for us. And for our children. My father left me only Montrose, and Reed's letting that fall apart. But I will leave my children an empire."

At dinner, Megan had reason to remember Clay's words about Montrose. She knew that Reed, through his indifference, his lack of ambition, was apparently content to see the plantation slide toward bankruptcy, to give the overseers a free hand, rarely checking on their expenditures or their output. And now, with the price of cotton falling, it was only Clay's continuing financial support that kept Montrose in the hands of the Drummond family.

It was Gavin who mentioned Montrose over the heavy, elaborate meal, and almost at once, Michael O'Donnell, who had been silent, even withdrawn, brightened, his gray-green eyes alight with interest.

He asked Clay how many acres there were and how many workers, what crops were grown.

"Only cotton?" Michael shook his head. "Forgive me, sir. I'm not pretendin' t' know about farmin' over here. But why have ye not thought of puttin' in other crops. Fruit trees, maybe. Ye can grow fruit down there in—Mississippi, is it?"

"Why, yes. Certainly. Melons and figs—"

"Fancy stuff. Should be a good market for them things here in New York." Michael's brow furrowed. "Sure, though, there'd be the problem of getting them up there before they spoiled—"

"That's no great problem," Clay said. "I have my own rail lines and my own refrigerator cars."

"Yer own cars t' ship 'em in!" The young man leaned forward, his face intent on Clay's. "Then why don't ye—"

"Now, my lad, easy there," Gavin said. "Mr. Drummond's got bigger things on his mind these days."

"Sorry, sir," Michael said. "Still, I would think that—But then, yer brother, him that runs the place, he must have his own good reasons for not puttin' in other crops."

Clay's eyes were troubled, and Megan knew that he was quite aware of why Reed did not put all his efforts into making a go of Montrose. And that Reed's apathy, his drinking, the time he spent in Natchez-under were a source of concern to Clay.

"But what of cattle?" Michael was asking. "Do ye raise cattle on the place? All those acres of land—"

"Now, Mike, stop talkin' like a farmer," Gavin told his younger brother.

Michael pushed out his jaw. "It's a farmer I am and proud of it," he said.

On the drive back to the hotel from Delmonico's, Clay, relaxed and expansive, put his arm around Megan and drew her head down on his shoulder; he was more relaxed than he had been since their arrival in New York.

"He's a fine young man, Gavin's brother," she said.

"And an ambitious one. He'll go far, I think," Clay said.

"Perhaps. But Belle thinks that he may get himself into trouble here in New York. He hates city living, you see, and there are so many chances for a young man with drive and energy to get himself into trouble if he doesn't find the right sort of outlet for those qualities."

"That would be a pity," Clay said. "Do you think he might want a job on the railroad? He'd be out in the open, working with his hands."

"I think he'd far rather work at Montrose," Megan said cautiously, not wanting to bring up family problems tonight but anxious to do what she could to help Michael.

"Montrose? As an overseer, you mean?"

"Why not?"

"He's bright enough—but he's only twenty-one."

"He's had experience, though," Megan said. "Belle told me that he was the assistant to the estate manager for an English landlord back in Ireland."

"And what made him leave?"

"He—had some trouble. But only because he refused to have any part in helping to turn out tenants who were behind in their rent. He could not tumble the cottages of his own neighbors and see them sent out on the roads to starve."

Clay nodded thoughtfully. "I can't blame a man for that," he said. "It's to his credit, that kind of loyalty."

"Then you'll give him a chance?"

Clay laughed. "I haven't said—Lord, Megan, you do know how to get around me, don't you? You know what will move me."

"I should after all these years," she said softly. "Clay, the overseer Reed has now is a thief. Even Reed admits that. Padding bills for seed and farm equipment, cheating the share-croppers at that store of his—Surely, it's time he got his walking papers. And Michael has so many ideas for improving Montrose—and he hasn't even seen the place yet—"

Clay's arm tightened around Megan's shoulders.

"All right, darling," he said. "We'll give young Michael O'Donnell a chance at Montrose."

Chapter Twenty

CLAY NEVER regretted having agreed to hire Michael O'Donnell; under the young Irishman's management, Montrose flourished for the first time since the years before the war. Its most important crop was cotton, as always, but during the past four years, Michael, financed by Clay, had planted fruit trees, pecan trees, and melon vines. He had bought fine new horses for the Montrose stables, traveling all the way up to Kentucky to get the best stock, and only a few weeks ago, when he had come to Azalea Hill to celebrate Christmas with Megan, he had discussed buying a few of the powerful Brahman bulls he had seen on a farm near Pass Christian.

Reed had no objections to Michael's innovations, for he spent little time at Montrose these days; and he was relieved to be able to leave the running of the plantation to Megan's energetic, hard-working young cousin. On those nights when Reed returned to Montrose too drunk to get himself to the house, Michael saw that he got to bed, pulled his boots off, and covered him with a blanket, for Michael was a tolerant young man who pitied the master of Montrose.

Megan had been disappointed when Luke had refused to go

to college and, instead, had taken a full-time job with the Natchez–Fort Worth Line. But she knew that Luke had a passion for railroading, and an enthusiasm that reminded her of Clay's.

When Clay had urged Luke to go to Princeton with Brant, the boy had refused, saying that he wanted to work for his uncle. Luke had always listened with fascination when Clay had talked about his own beginnings: the building of the spur, the beginning of the Natchez–Fort Worth Line, the dangers that he had overcome in laying track through the swamps of Louisiana and the plains of Texas.

Luke had soon gained firsthand experience in dealing with these obstacles. Only last year, Clay had made him foreman of a construction crew, and Luke had proved his worth in clearing away the wreckage left by the hurricane of October 1886, when the Gulf waters, driven by gale winds, had devastated the Texas coast.

"Luke—a common railroad laborer," Samantha had said bitterly during one of the rare occasions when she had entertained Clay and Megan at Montrose.

"There's nothing common about young Luke," Clay had said. "He's got a good future with the railroad, Samantha."

"Grubbing around in the mud like an Irish railroad hand," Samantha had retorted. "Swinging a pick, hammering spikes."

Megan had shrugged off the implied insult, for she had long since become inured to Samantha's snobbery, and the two women saw little of each other socially. Since Clay's passion for Samantha had long since cooled, Megan did not care about her sister-in-law's scornful treatment.

"Brant is off at Princeton," Samantha had persisted. "He is being educated like a gentlemen, while Luke . . ."

As it happened, Brant did not graduate from Princeton. He was well able to do work there, but he refused to apply himself consistently, for the school was too close to New York City, and his weekends there often stretched into a week or more. There were plenty of eager young ladies from good families who were delighted to dance with the handsome, charming Brant Drummond, and whose mothers were well aware that the young man was heir to one of the largest fortunes in the country. There were also brash, beautiful girls in the Tenderloin who had no mothers to guide them but who adored the free-spending Mr. Drummond. With these, he did not stop with a chaste good-night kiss, and even at twenty-one, he knew how to please them in bed.

Clay had tolerated Brant's exploits, saying that it was only natural for a lad his age to raise a little hell. But members of the Princeton faculty were less tolerant, and although Brant had not been formally expelled, he had been informed that he would not graduate with his class and that, indeed, he would not graduate at all unless he repeated several courses.

Brant refused and returned to Natchez, where he had been the subject of a good deal of local gossip. When the daughter of a sharecropper became pregnant and insisted that Brant was the father of the baby, Clay had paid the girl off even though he had told Megan that the girl had been so free with her favors that there was no way of knowing if Brant or some other man was responsible for her condition. It was more difficult to smooth things over when Brant kept a young lady, a relative of Winona Hunter, out driving after dark, and even Brant's plausible story about the horse having thrown a shoe was a flimsy one. Megan suspected that it was only because Miss Maryellen Hunter's father was heavily in debt to the bank in which Clay held a controlling interest that the man chose to accept Brant's version of the story.

But last summer, when Brant had become involved with the restless young wife of a plantation owner who was twenty years her senior, and the husband, too angry to care about Clay's financial power, had threatened to shoot Brant on sight, Clay decided it might be advisable to take his elder son with him to Colorado to look over the new line out there.

"Why not?" Brant said with an indolent smile. "From what I've heard, Denver's quite a lively town these days."

Megan had expected Clay and Brant to return home in the fall, but they had not done so, but as Christmas approached, she was certain that her husband and her son would come home. She had spent the early part of December in New Orleans with Oliver and Angelique Winthrop, who had given a ball, the first that Deirdre had been allowed to attend. The girl had been besieged by partners and had accepted invitations to the opera, the theater, and a round of local parties. Megan had protested that she was far too young but had at last agreed to allow her to stay in New Orleans over the Christmas holidays.

Megan, however, had returned to Azalea Hill, still hoping that Clay and Brant would surprise her by returning for Christmas. Two days before the holiday, when she had received a wire saying that they would not be able to make the trip because of pressing railroad business out in Colorado, she had been bitterly disappointed. Nevertheless, she had managed to make it a festive holiday for Luke, who had come up from Texas; for Terence, now in his freshman year at Princeton; for Uncle Jim and Aunt Kathleen; and for Michael O'Donnell.

Jim Rafferty had been out in Colorado with Clay but had made the trip back to Natchez to spend Christmas with Kathleen and, at the same time, to check the efficiency of the men he had hired to run his business in Natchez-under. Kathleen had grown stouter and was as blunt in her speech as ever.

"If I was you," she said to Megan after the ample Christmas dinner, "I'd not let my man go rovin' about without comin' home for a visit from time to time. Clay's still a fine-lookin' man and not the kind t' sleep alone fer too long."

Terence had flushed, and Jim had said, "Mind yer business, woman. When Megan wants yer advice, she'll be askin' fer it." But Megan saw the troubled look in Jim's eyes, and she felt uneasy, for she knew that Kathleen was right about Clay: he was not the man to live in celibacy, and he was still attractive to women.

Luke, anxious to save his aunt further embarrassment, changed the subject. "Michael, I hear you have some new horses at Montrose," he said.

"I didn't think you railroad men were interested in horses," Michael said with a good-natured grin. "But yer right. Yer father agreed t' let me buy some of the finest beasts ye'd ever want t' see. Got a stallion from up in the blue-grass country in Kentucky—a real beauty he is. Put him with the right sort of mares and ye'll have a line that yer father'll be proud of."

"How is my father?" Luke asked quietly, his eyes shadowed.

"Why he's—well enough. Ain't ye been up t' see him yet?"

Luke shook his head, and Michael went on. "Why not come up with me when I go back there tomorrow mornin'? And ye can get a look at the stallion. He's got a coat as black and glossy as—as cousin Deirdre's hair. Beggin' yer pardon, ma'am," he added hastily with a smile in Megan's direction.

Megan felt a touch of sadness. At least Deirdre might have come back to Azalea Hill for Christmas, but she had insisted on staying in New Orleans and since she was being chaperoned by both Miss Amy and Angelique Winthrop, Megan had not been able to find any real reason to thwart her daughter's wishes. She had become close friends with Geneviève Vallière, a cousin of Angelique's, a pretty, lively little thing of Deirdre's own age.

It was not until the middle of January that Deirdre returned to Azalea Hill, and when she did come back, her homecoming brought Megan cause for concern. It was an overcast morning, and Deirdre came sweeping into Megan's boudoir, a room that was free of the usual clutter preferred by so many women, and that, even in winter, had a cheerful, springlike look, having recently been redecorated, the walls painted pale green, with off-white woodwork. Megan's Waterford goblet stood alone on a small bamboo table and held a few sprigs of holly, its red berries blazing against the deep-green leaves.

Deidre's skirt brushed the table as she moved swiftly into the room, and Megan stared, realizing how much the girl had matured during this past year. The changes in her appearance were emphasized by a new costume, no doubt paid for out of the too-large check Clay had sent for Christmas. She had pinned her jet-black hair up high on her head, a few ringlets escaping from under her small, dashing, plush hat with its high crown of deep amber and its bow of primrose satin. Her walking costume was of yellow faille, and the jacket, of amber velvet trimmed with sable, emphasized her full breasts, her hand-span waist.

Megan kissed Deirdre lightly, but Deirdre drew back, saying, "Mind my dress, mother," as she evaded the warm embrace Megan would have given her.

"It's good to have you home, darling," Megan said. "We missed you at Christmas dinner."

"We?"

"Luke and Terence—and Aunt Kathleen and Uncle Jim—and Michael—he was here, too."

Deirdre's eyes narrowed with annoyance. "That dreadful, vulgar old woman—and Michael—an overseer—"

"They are part of our family," Megan said, keeping a tight rein on her temper, for she did not wish to quarrel with her daughter. "And Michael has done wonders for Montrose."

"No doubt he has. He was a farm laborer back in Ireland, wasn't he?"

"He helped to manage an estate for one of the English landlords—" Megan began, but Deirdre was plainly indifferent.

"You should have stayed in New Orleans over the holidays," Deirdre said. "Oh, it was lovely. The opera and the theaters and all those shops. And since Papa wasn't able to come home, anyway—" She put her head to one side, a wicked gleam in her eyes. "Now what sort of railroad business do you suppose he had in Colorado in midwinter?"

"I'm not sure," Megan began.

"I wouldn't have my husband out there all by himself—not if he were as good-looking as Papa."

The girl was showing off, trying to sound sophisticated, but Megan found her words irritating, echoing, as they did, Aunt Kathleen's observations at Christmas dinner. "I'll thank you to speak respectfully of your father, young lady," Megan snapped.

Deirdre shrugged. "Papa's a man, isn't he? When I'm married, I'll make sure that my husband doesn't go off without me—"

"Your husband!" Megan did not know whether to be angry or to laugh. "It'll be a while before you've a husband to worry about, my girl."

Deirdre slanted a smile at her mother. "You were married when you were seventeen," she said. "Maybe I won't wait that long."

"What on earth are you talking about?" Megan demanded.

Deirdre perched on a small white wicker chair.

"I'm talking about Lord Sutcliffe," she said calmly.

"Lord Sutcliffe?"

"Sir Allen Reginald Herbert Sutcliffe of Yorkshire. You remember, mother. You met him at the Winthrops' ball."

"But he—why he's more than twice your age. No doubt he turned your head, dancing with you more than once that night—"

"He danced with me six times. And we went into the conservatory together and he kissed me. He's in love with me, and I adore him—"

"I've never heard such nonsense. You know perfectly well that your father is sending you to finishing school next fall and then to Vassar College—"

"Papa will have to change his plans. I'm not going to waste years and years in school. Let Terence be the family bookworm if he wants to. Genevieve Vallière says that college is only for plain girls who can't get husbands, anyway—"

She stood up as if too filled with energy to stay in one place for long; there was the look of a beautiful, untamed young animal about her. "I'm going to marry an English lord and live in England on an estate—I'm going to have a title, and everyone will call me 'Your ladyship'—Allen's estate's been in his family since the time of Henry the Eighth—"

"That's fine," Megan said dryly. "No doubt it is in need of repairs by now and that's why—"

But Deirdre went on, doing a little pirouette. "Oh, we're not going to live in Yorkshire all year 'round. There's a townhouse in London, too. And I'll get to meet all sorts of fascinating people—and I'll be presented at court. And perhaps I'll meet the Prince of Wales—I've heard he has an eye for pretty young girls—"

"I've never heard such foolishness in my life," Megan said. "You're an American, and you should be proud of it. Those titles, what do they mean? There are a lot of titled Englishmen over here these days, I'm told. Looking for brides from wealthy families. Fortune hunters, many of them."

Deirdre shrugged. "I suppose Allen's impressed by Papa's money—Who wouldn't be? But I don't care so long as I get what I want. Allen's handsome and has such elegant manners. And he'll take me out of Natchez and—"

"What about love? Oh, darling, you're such a child. Don't you understand what marriage means? Without love, it can be a bitter thing, a curse."

"Like Aunt Samantha's marriage? Oh, I know she doesn't love Uncle Reed—it's always been Papa she loved—and she'd have married him if he hadn't been reported dead back then during the war." Deirdre laughed, seeing Megan's startled expression. "Surely you know I've heard about all that. People do gossip, and here in Natchez no scandal about the Drummonds will ever be forgotten."

"Scandal?" Megan could not look at her daughter; instead,

she kept her eyes fixed on the sprays of red berries and glossy green leaves in the Waterford goblet.

"Girls hear these things from their mothers, and they're only too eager to pass them along, the spiteful cats. I know how you came from Natchez-under and got papa to marry you. You must have been smart, trapping him like that—"

Megan began to tremble with the anger that was rising in her, the white-hot rage, not so much against the girls who had spread the malicious stories heard from their mothers but against Deirdre, her own daughter, who was taunting her now.

"I've never tried to hide the fact that I came from Natchez-under—"

"No, you haven't. Shaming me—shaming all of us by inviting Jim and Kathleen Rafferty here to Azalea Hill—and—and bringing Michael O'Donnell to Montrose—"

Megan chose to ignore the slur against her people.

"Never mind that. How could you have taken the words of those girls—how could you think I trapped your father—"

"Why else would he have married someone like you?" Deirdre's golden eyes narrowed. "I think you were really clever. But then you must have picked up a lot of little tricks from the ladies of Natchez-under—the ones in the taverns and the sporting houses—I didn't have your advantages." Deirdre smiled sweetly. "Miss Amy couldn't teach me about such matters—"

Megan took a step forward, her legs unsteady. "That's enough—"

"Oh, but I mean it," Deirdre said. "Maybe if I get into bed with Allen, he'll propose right away—he is a little slow—"

Without realizing what she was about to do, Megan drew back her arm and struck Deirdre on the cheek, a hard, stinging blow with her open palm. The girl drew her breath in with a gasp, her eyes filling with tears. For a moment, mother and daughter stared at one another.

Then Deirdre set her jaw, the mark of Megan's hand red against her white skin. She lifted her skirt, turned, and struck the corner of the small bamboo table with her hip, whether accidentally or on purpose Megan would never know. The table toppled over, and the Waterford goblet landed on the thick carpet; the holly berries were scattered like drops of blood at Megan's feet.

Deirdre did not hesitate, but turned and left the room, her head high, and Megan saw her hurrying down the hall to her own room. Then Megan dropped to her knees and picked up the goblet. The deep pile of carpet had kept the glass from shattering; except for the old damage, the chip in the base and the thin crack running halfway up the stem, it was the same as it had been when she had stuffed it into her bundle and carried it onto the ship that long-ago day when she had fled from Cork.

She held it in her hands, her fingers, stiff and cold, curving around it.

"But Charleston is so far away, Miss Amy," Megan said. Two days had passed since her clash with Deirdre, and the girl had refused to take her meals with her mother and Miss Amy, having a tray sent to her room instead. Megan's attempts to talk to Deirdre were met with cold politeness. Even when she humbled herself, saying, "I never should have struck you—I was too angry to think what I was doing—Deirdre, it's only that you're so precious to me. When I think of that man, that fortune hunter—"

"I think you've made your feelings plain, mother," Deirdre said, her eyes remote.

And now Miss Amy was suggesting that it was time to send Deirdre away and coming up with the name of an exclusive school in her native Charleston.

"The school is run by Miss Evelynne Pembroke," Miss Amy said. "She and I grew up together. Her father owned one of the finest rice plantations in the Carolina low country. But since the war . . ." Miss Amy sighed. "Poor, dear Evelynne has been forced to turn her family's townhouse into a school for young ladies. Only young ladies from the best families, you understand."

"Clay did speak of sending Deirdre to finishing school before she enters college," Megan said slowly. "But I'm not sure that he would approve of my making such a decision alone."

"There is no telling when he'll be back from Colorado, though, is there?" Miss Amy asked. "And if he were here, I know that he would approve, for Miss Laurette Drummond— she is his great aunt—married a Pembroke. Evelynne's third cousin, on her mother's side."

Miss Amy had a formidable memory for the genealogical records of most of the families in Charleston who had any social standing. To her, the fact that the Pembrokes were related, however remotely, to the Drummonds of that city was a completely satisfactory recommendation. Megan was a little amused; nevertheless, she realized that if Deirdre could be persuaded to leave Natchez, she would have plenty of time to get over this ridiculous infatuation with the visiting English nobleman.

"I'm not sure Deirdre would go willingly," Megan said. "This business about Lord Sutcliffe—Really, Miss Amy, I trusted you to chaperone my daughter."

"Oh, but—surely—" Miss Amy's lips quivered slightly, and she looked guilty and a little frightened. And well she might, for if Clay heard of this matter, he might well hold Miss Amy responsible, might even send her away. Here, at Azalea Hill, the spinster had lived in comfort and dignity, a member of the family; she could have no illusions as to what her future would be if she had to make her own way in a world that no longer had room for genteel but penniless spinsters. "Lord Sutcliffe was attentive to Deirdre, but he never in any way— Young girls of her age are given to flights of fancy. And she was, naturally, dazzled by his station—"

Megan could not help feeling sorry for Miss Amy.

"No doubt Deirdre misinterpreted Lord Sutcliffe's kindness for a—a more personal attachment," Miss Amy said.

"No doubt," Megan said dryly. "But if I were to write Clay and tell him about all this, I think he would put aside whatever business he has out there in Colorado and come back here. And if he did, Lord Sutcliffe would be lucky to escape without being horsewhipped—or worse—"

"Oh, dear. That must not be allowed to happen. Why that would cause a scandal—it would ruin the dear child's chances to make the right sort of marriage," Miss Amy said. "Oh, you must not write to Clay—The Drummond men are so hot-blooded. Why Clay's uncle, Vance Drummond's brother, fought a duel with a gentleman who was attentive to his wife—it happened at White Sulphur Springs in the summer of fifty-three, or was it fifty-four—and Clay's uncle killed the man, but he, too, died as a result of his wound, and his wife had to go to live abroad—" Miss Amy shuddered. "Oh, no, there must be no scandal for Deirdre. I'll be ready to leave with her within the week if you are willing."

"She may not be willing," Megan said.

"Let me speak to her," Miss Amy said. "I'm sure that I can make her see reason. It's for her own good—"

Whatever was said between Miss Amy and Deirdre, the girl agreed to go, to Megan's surprise. Perhaps Miss Amy had impressed upon her the fact that a scandal would ruin her chances not only with Lord Sutcliffe, but with other eligible gentlemen in the future.

Miss Amy sent a telegram to her friend, Miss Pembroke, in Charleston, and the lady wired back saying that she would be pleased to receive the daughter of Clay Drummond and the granddaughter of Vance Drummond among her select group of young charges. Within the week, Deirdre and Miss Amy had departed. Megan had provided Clay's spinster cousin with a handsome sum of money so that she might remain in Charleston for a few months to visit her relatives and friends there.

Once Deirdre and Miss Amy were gone, Azalea Hill was bleak and lonely. Terence was back at Princeton, and Luke had returned to his job on the Natchez–Fort Worth Line. For once, the coming of spring brought Megan no joy, only a painful restlessness. The azaleas burst into bloom, flame color, orange, copper, pink, and mauve. The gardenias and the camellias gave their heady fragrance to the soft air, and the wisteria, its lavender clusters covering the wooden trellises, added its more delicate scent. To Megan, walking the garden paths alone, the beauty that surrounded her brought a poignant, all-pervasive sense of longing.

It was Opal who pointed her toward a solution. She had gone to Opal's shop, although she really did not need anything new to wear, and had ordered a simple gray faille walking costume and half a dozen new cambric nightdresses.

"Been a long time since Mistuh Clay been home," Opal remarked softly as she pinned the hem on the gray faille.

"He's in Denver on business," Megan told her. His letters, less and less frequent over the past eight months, had spoken of trouble between himself and Samuel Barstow, a New York financier and railroad owner, over the right of way between Denver and several of the small, outlying mining towns. Barstow belonged to the new breed of railroad men who were determined to push their competitors into bankruptcy, to swallow up the smaller lines and make them part of their own giant empires. And, Clay had written, if men like Barstow could not gain their ends through rate wars, watered stocks, and political lobbying, they were quite prepared to send in railroad gangs, their numbers swelled by hired gunmen, to wage their private wars for control of a particular right-of-way. He had told her years before of the battle for the Leadville Line, waged between the Atchison, Topeka, and Santa Fe and the competing Denver and Rio Grande, back in 1876. He had spoken of men hired to burn railroad bridges, to move the survey stakes of the rival line, to bury the roadbed under carefully planned rock slides. Railroad stations had been turned into fortresses, Clay had told her, and the men in one roundhouse had been commanded by the notorious Bat Masterson. Station by station, the two forces had battled for control as if "the damned war had started all over again," and only the intervention of Eastern financiers, who finally had seen the need to put an end to the expensive violence, had forced peace on the battling railroad men.

And now Clay was bending all his efforts to avert another such costly conflict between his line and the one controlled by Barstow. That was why he had been gone so long, or at least so Megan tried to tell herself.

"It isn't any good, Miz Drummond," Opal was saying.

"What isn't—what do you mean?"

"Isn't any good for a woman t' be one place an' her man miles away all this time. Y' got no little ones hangin' on t' your skirts no more, keepin' y' busy. An' Mistuh Drummond so far away." Opal shook her head. "No, ma'am—that's not good at all."

Megan was not offended, for over the years she had come to know Opal well enough to accept such personal observations. Opal knew what it was like to be without a man, for although she had had her chances, she had not remarried after Noah's death. She had expanded her small shop on Federal Street, and her excellent work was much in demand. She had raised her three daughters and had been filled with pride when she had sent her eldest, Rebecca, off to the normal school established by Tom and Jessica in northern Alabama to become a teacher.

"Miz Megan, y' got that there fine private railroad car settin' in the yards. Why don't y' go on out there to Mistuh Clay now? Nothin' t' keep y' here."

Nothing to keep me here.

Opal was right, and Megan knew it. True, Clay had told her that he would be involved in business dealings in Denver and had promised to return as soon as possible. But that was not good enough.

She would not write to him, for if she did, she knew quite well that he would put her off, telling her that he would soon be home, that he did not want her to follow him. But it was one thing for her to stay in a boxcar at the end-of-track and another to travel cross-country in a parlor car and stay at a hotel in Denver. Surely he could have no objections to that.

The pent-up hunger that had been building in her for so long could not be denied, not now. She was Clay's wife, and her place was with him. She would have to make him understand that.

Chapter Twenty-one

❧

"LOOK AT this, Mr. Drummond," said the jeweler, holding up the sapphire necklace so that the brilliant blue stones glittered in the light. "You couldn't find anything better, not in New York or Paris. Sapphires of such fire, such depth of color are rare, and the workmanship—"

Sapphires the color of Kirsten's large, vividly blue eyes. A real beauty, Kirsten was, with those eyes of hers and that hair, so pale a shade of blonde that it looked like silver gilt.

"I'll take it," Clay said, feeling at once taut with anticipation, yet uneasy. Not that he hadn't strayed before during those long separations from his wife. A man had his needs, and those girls in the parlor houses in New York, New Orleans, Fort Worth, were quickly forgotten. An hour after he'd left their beds, he could not have described them.

Kirsten Nordstrom was different.

She was twenty-one, and in spite of her virginal airs, Clay was willing to bet she was not a virgin. All the same, she worked for a living, waiting tables in a respectable hotel, the

Blue Spruce, near the Denver depot. A soft-spoken girl with a body that was enticing even under her prim, starched waitress's uniform, she wore her blue and white striped bodice buttoned up to her chin, but what man could ignore those large, shapely breasts that thrust against the square top of her starched apron, the movement of those rounded hips as she went about her work, bending over to set down a laden tray?

She was accessible—of that Clay was certain—and would be willing enough to give herself to a man who had experience with women—and money to buy her expensive gifts. She had made no secret, even in their brief exchanges, that she had come to Denver to better herself. "To be a farmer's wife," she had told him scornfully, "to be old before my time—that is not for me. Here in Denver—" she had added with a sidelong glance, "anything could happen. . . ."

And she had flashed a smile at him, leaning closer than was necessary to put down the tray, so close that he caught the delicate yet stirring female scent of her.

She had come where the money was—and where the men with money were, men who had earned fabulous fortunes and were starved for the company of a pretty girl, men who had wrested wealth from gold mines, the silver diggings.

Women who had taken in laundry or waited on tables in mining tent camps now rode through the streets of Denver in fine landaus and broughams with uniformed coachmen; they ordered their gowns from Paris, and they had even launched a campaign to raise the moral tone of the city, having formed a society called the Denver Protective Association. This worthy group had demanded an ordinance to prevent the women from the sporting houses on Holladay Street from showing themselves on Exposition Row on Sundays. Denver was taking on the aspects of cities to the east.

"I can show you something else," the jeweler was saying, interrupting Clay's reverie. "I have a fine pair of ruby earrings—"

Clay shook his head. "This necklace is exactly what I want," he said.

He had not seen Kirsten for several weeks, having been traveling to the railroad camps higher in the mountains, beyond Leadville, to see for himself the damage that had already been done by the skirmishes between his men and those who worked for Samuel Barstow. But now there would be a pause while he and Barstow waited for the arrival of associates from New York and San Francisco, financial titans whose interests would be threatened by an all-out war for the right-of-way between Denver and such settlements as Horseshoe Gulch, Yellow Pine Peak, and Bitter Foot. It was a time that could pass pleasantly in the suite Clay planned to engage for Kirsten at the Windsor Hotel.

Kirsten might be reluctant at first, but Clay was sure he could overcome her reticence.

"Would you like to write a card to be enclosed with the necklace, sir?" the jeweler asked, arranging Clay's purchase carefully on the white and gold satin lining of the box. Clay shook his head. The necklace would speak for itself.

He wrote out a check while the jeweler wrapped the box. He would have to be careful, of course, until Brant returned to end-of-track. But in a few days, when the boy had left Denver, he could move Kirsten into the Windsor; until then, her room in the annex behind the Blue Spruce Hotel would have to do.

"Kirsten—sweetheart—let me—" Brant Drummond was saying as he held the girl against him, his lean young body trembling with the urgency of his need. "You're driving me out of my mind—"

"No—I can't—please try to understand—"

"You want to; you know you do," Brant said softly, his mouth warm against her throat.

But Kirsten, having allowed Brant to strip off her outer clothing so that she now wore only her thin cotton chemise and her drawers, still held back. "I'm so afraid," she whispered. "It hurts so much and—"

"I won't hurt you—I swear I won't." How could she possibly compare him with that clumsy lout of a farmer's son she'd told him about, her tongue loosened by her third glass of wine. That ham-handed clod who had cornered her in a barn, thrown her down, torn her clothes off, and raped her, leaving her bruised, bleeding, and filled with shame and revulsion.

Brant was determined to help Kirsten to forget that first miserable experience that had made her run away from the farm. He had no lack of confidence in his own skills, for he had been pleasing members of the opposite sex since he had turned fifteen. And he had learned plenty in those fancy parlor houses during his weekends in New York City. His stay at Princeton had given him the opportunity for a liberal education, although not the sort of education his parents had had in mind.

"I won't be rough with you, dearest," he said, trying to steady his breathing. It was not the thin air of this mile-high city that was making it difficult for him to draw air into his lungs at the moment. "I'll be patient," he promised. And he would, because he loved Kirsten; he really did. He hadn't been able to sleep last night thinking about her, and now here she was in the wide bed in his room at the Windsor Hotel. He was stroking her long silver-blonde hair, drawing her closer, and feeling the softness of her breasts against him. Her breath was fragrant with the fine French wine he had ordered with their dinner; her lips still tasted of its sweetness.

He moved his tongue between her parted lips, and he could only hope that the tremor that ran through her body was not caused by fear, that his own overpowering desire had communicated itself to her. Although he still wore his shirt and trousers, he was sure that she was aware of his mounting passion.

Carefully, he slipped her chemise down from her smooth white shoulders. Her breasts, now that they were not hidden by her waitress's uniform, were even more impressive, large and round, the nipples deep pink; under his caressing fingers, they grew firm and pointed. She caught her breath and made a sound deep in her throat, then lay back, letting him take off her prim cotton drawers. Lord, but she was beautiful, her legs long, her thighs strong and rounded, her body like silver in the moonlight that shone in through the half-drawn red-velvet drapes.

For a moment, he hesitated, his eyes moving over the soft curves and shadowed crevices of her body, awed by her loveliness. Then his need, almost painful now, overpowered him, and he stripped off his own clothing and drew her against him.

At the touch of his male hardness against her, she stiffened for a moment. "It's nothing to be afraid of," he told her, moving her hand so that her fingers encircled him. He taught her the motion and was somewhat startled at how quickly she learned it. And moments later, when he turned her on her back and parted her legs, she was more than ready for him, her body arching upward, her legs encircling him, her hips beginning to move rhythmically.

Her strong fingers clutched at him, drawing him into her, and her head was thrown back, her eyes half closed. How simple it had been to overcome her fears, after all, Brant thought with a glow of pride. And then he did not think at all but gave himself up to the primitive, mindless hunger that built and built to a shattering climax. He heard Kirsten cry out, and he knew that it was a cry of delight, of fulfillment. . . .

Later, much later, they sat side by side in the great walnut bed, finishing what was left of the wine. Kirsten's pale silver-gilt hair half covered her breasts, and she rested her head against Brant's shoulder. He felt a sense of male pride and complacency, remembering how completely he had overcome her fears, making her give herself without the slightest reservation. His body felt pleasantly relaxed.

He drew her closer, and the swell of her hip against him made him feel a new stirring of desire. "No, Brant. Not now. I must get back to the Blue Spruce before closing time."

"But why?"

"A girl has to watch her reputation." She sighed. "Once we're married, of course, it will be different, but for now—"

Brant was startled. He loved her, she was beautiful and enticing, but as for marriage . . .

With his ability to dismiss serious matters at will, he kissed her lightly.

"No," Kirsten said, pushing away the red-satin quilt and swinging her legs over the side of the bed. "Please, darling—you must take me back now."

Brant sighed. "Whatever you say. I'll get dressed and have the buggy sent around to the side of the hotel—"

Clay entered the Windsor through the huge black walnut doors, with their hand-tooled and engraved brass hinges, part of the flamboyant decor demanded by the owner, Horace Tabor, the Silver King. Tabor had been a miner, struggling for twenty years to find a strike, and when he had done so, he had changed the face of Denver with a magnificence that reflected his personal style.

The ceilings were twenty feet high, and the frescoes in the

hotel's public rooms were of frolicking cupids. The lobby was lavish with red plush, decorated with full-length diamond-dust mirrors like those found in the fancier sporting houses Clay had visited in New York and San Francisco.

He would not have to seek relaxation in Denver's bordellos now, he told himself. Although tonight Kirsten had not appeared for her dinner shift at the dining room of the Blue Spruce Hotel, he could wait. The jeweler's box was in his pocket, and the slight delay might be all to the good, for he would have time for a talk with Brant after which he would send him out to one of the towns in the foothills of the Rockies, telling him to make himself useful, to keep his eyes open for any signs that Samuel Barstow's men were getting ready to break the precarious truce.

Mounting the stairs, Clay smiled. He had to admit that although Brant had not distinguished himself for scholarship at Princeton, he had proved invaluable as a trouble-shooter here in Colorado. Brant had a way with people, a natural easy charm of manner. He could get men to talk freely, and he knew instinctively how to deal with their grievances, how to smooth over the potential conflicts that might slow the progress of the railroad.

The men respected him, too, not because he was "the boss's son" but for his own capabilities. He could drink an Irish laborer under the table and be up at dawn the next morning, ready to ride over narrow, twisting mountain trails. Yes, Brant had proved his worth out here, and Clay was proud of him.

He walked quickly down the hallway now and opened the door to his suite. He and Brant would go down to the bar for a few drinks and then . . .

The bedroom door opened, and Brant, who was fastening his belt, heard Kirsten's cry before he turned and saw his father. He was startled to see his father's face turn dark red under its tan, to see the swift fury in the older man's eyes. His father had never been really angry over Brant's exploits with girls. If anything, he'd been amused and perhaps a little proud.

But now—In spite of his twenty-one years, Brant felt like a child again, caught in a forbidden act.

Kirsten's fingers were frozen on the ribbons of her chemise so that her full breasts and her bare legs were revealed.

Brant heard his father make a wordless animal sound deep in his throat, and there was something frightening in it and in the swift tensing of the powerful shoulders and heavily muscled arms.

"Pa, I—"

"Get out. And take that—take her with you."

"I'm sorry, Pa—I didn't think you'd mind—"

"Get out," Clay repeated. He took a step toward his son.

"Kirsten needs time to—to dress—"

"Five minutes—I want you gone in five minutes, and I don't want to set eyes on you or that little slut again—"

Brant's sense of protective masculinity was outraged. What the hell was wrong with Pa? He'd been the one who had introduced Brant to Kirsten in the dining room of the Blue Spruce.

"Kirsten and I love each other," Brant said with what dignity he could muster. "I can't allow you to speak of her as if—"

Then Clay was upon him, was grasping his shoulders in a brutal grip. Clay flung Brant against the wall with such shattering force that he was momentarily stunned.

Before Brant could recover himself, Clay drove a fist into his stomach, putting all his weight behind the blow. Brant gagged and fell to his knees, then looked up to see his father locking his hands together, raising his arms in a motion that Brant recognized from a dozen railhead brawls. He tried to move aside, but the blow from those interlocked hands caught him on the back of the neck, knocking him face down on the floor. A blackness, shot with red sparks, moved before his eyes. His insides twisted, and he tasted the wine, sour in his throat.

He was only vaguely aware of his father turning, stalking out of the suite, slamming the door behind him, of Kirsten helping him to his feet. He pushed her away, sick, humiliated, and stumbled into the marble and walnut bathroom.

Kirsten dressed, trying to ignore the retching sounds from the bathroom, only partly covered by the noise of the water running in the sink. Damn the luck, she thought!

She'd never had any luck, not really. Momma and Papa dying, leaving her alone to slave as a hired girl on that miserable, drab Minnesota wheat farm, feeding hogs and chickens, doing all the heaviest chores, helping to prepare meals for old

Gunderson and his six sons and the hired men, too. And then Olaf, one of those sons—he hadn't raped her, of course. He hadn't had to because she'd wanted it real bad even then.

But that stupid fool, Olaf, had starting talking about marriage. As if she wanted to be a farmer's wife, her belly swollen with a baby every year, her hands turning red and cracking from scrubbing diapers and overalls with lye soap, her face growing lined and weather-beaten, her gleaming silver-blonde hair losing its sheen, her body becoming gaunt and shapeless.

Oh, no! That wasn't for Kirsten Nordstrom! She would use her body, yes—but to get her what she wanted. And her first step was to leave the farm.

She had given herself to the ticket agent at the nearby depot in exchange for a ticket to Virginia City. She shrugged, remembering those months at the saloon. She could have gone directly into a parlor house or a crib, but she quickly realized that would have been worse than marrying Olaf. She had learned, however, from a former inmate of one of those places how to avoid getting pregnant—a bit of sponge soaked in vinegar.

But a saloon in Virginia City was a dead end. Men gave her presents, and a few, desperate for a wife, had even proposed marriage, but the life they offered was little better than the one she could have had on the farm—a cabin on a squatter's claim or a tent in a mining camp.

She had come to Denver to make a fresh start, to find the right kind of man. And such a man would only want to marry a decent, respectable girl. Brant Drummond, with a wealthy father who had always indulged him, was exactly the right kind of man.

Now, remembering Clay Drummond's anger, his savage attack on Brant, she felt a tremor of uncertainty. Had she been a fool, going after the son instead of the father? A fine-looking man, Brant's father was, and strong as a bull. He'd probably be as good a man in bed as his son was. Maybe better. She felt a curious excitement, remembering the violence Clay Drummond had revealed in his attack on Brant.

And she realized that Clay Drummond must have been attracted to her, for she was willing to bet that the savage beating he had inflicted on his son had not been the result of moral scruples. Was there, perhaps, a chance—

She shook her head. Too much of a gamble. Clay Drummond already had a wife, while Brant was free to marry her, to make her into a wealthy, respected lady.

Brant came out of the bathroom as Kirsten was fastening the top button of her bodice. He must have doused his face and head with water. His thick brown hair was still wet. He looked pale but in control.

"Let's go," he said.

"Not yet. Brant, I can go back to the Blue Spruce alone. You must go and talk to your father. You must explain to him that we are going to be married. You must convince him that I am not—what he called me. Say that you were foolish, that you could not wait until after the wedding. Ask him to forgive you and—"

"The hell I will! Forget my father, Kirsten. We don't need him."

"But your job with the railroad company—"

"That's finished."

Kirsten had to use every ounce of will power to keep from turning on Brant and reminding him that he had a great deal more at stake than his job. There was his inheritance, the Drummond fortune.

She had to make this foolish, spoiled young man understand the importance of avoiding a permanent break with his father. But how could she expect him to understand when he had grown up in luxury?

She sighed. Men had their stupid pride. Plainly, this was not the proper time to urge a reconciliation between father and son. She put a light hand on his arm. "Whatever you wish, my darling," she murmured softly as they left the ornate suite with its red plush, gilt, and marble.

"But Clay, I don't understand. It's been nearly two weeks since your quarrel with Brant. Surely it's time you made up and sent him back out on the railroad again. All your letters said that he was doing such a splendid job."

"Megan, I told you back at the depot, I don't want to talk about Brant."

"He's our son, Clay. Whatever he's done to anger you, surely you can forgive him. He's young and headstrong—"

Clay turned away from her and stared at the elaborate marble fireplace in the sitting room of their suite at the Windsor.

Megan's heart sank, for he'd been withdrawn and taciturn since he had met her at the station in response to the wire she had sent him from Pueblo. She had tried to explain his behavior, reminding herself that he was distracted by business problems. This talk of the possibility of a railroad war...

And he could scarely have been expected to embrace her publicly with Ludamae looking on. But now Ludamae had helped her to change from her traveling costume and had gone off to the quarters set aside for servants here at the hotel. She was alone with Clay, and still he remained cool and distant.

The excitement she had felt as the train had approached Denver, her awe at the savage beauty of the view from the train window—inky pines etched against a golden sky, the splendor of the distant, snow-capped mountains, the purple gorges—all were forgotten as she tried unsuccessfully to find the slightest indication of Clay's pleasure at her arrival.

Instead, he went on speaking of his break with Brant over a girl. "I'm not saying Brant did the right thing bringing her here," Megan began. "But there have been so many—unsuitable—girls in his life. He'll probably lose interest in her."

"Says he's in love with her. In love!" Clay repeated, anger and disgust in his voice. "He's living with her down at the Blue Spruce Hotel near the depot. He—"

"You've made inquiries?"

"I didn't have to. One of my railroad foremen told me all I wanted to know." He turned back to her. "Now would you prefer to have dinner sent up here, or shall we go down to the dining room?"

"Clay, we're talking about our son."

"There's nothing more to be said."

"Oh, but there's a great deal more to be said, and you're going to listen. You spoiled Deirdre. But she's a girl and more easily controlled. Now that she's settled down in that school in Charleston—But Brant's a young man. Headstrong. And you've always given him his own way. Laughed at his escapades with girls. Most of them as—as unsuitable as this hotel waitress. This Kirsten. Now, without warning, you turn on him—"

"That's enough," Clay said, and although he did not raise his voice, his cold stare, the hard set of his jaw, deepened her uneasiness.

"Clay, you'll have to see Brant sooner or later," she began.

"If he wants to see me, he knows where to find me. And he'd better come alone. I don't want to set eyes on that little trollop of his again."

"But he says he loves her. Surely just because she has to earn a living as a waitress doesn't mean—There are worse ways for a girl on her own to—"

"And I'm damn sure she knows most of them. That foreman of mine, he recognized her when he saw her at the Blue Spruce Hotel. Said she'd worked in a saloon in Virginia City."

"Even so, we can't judge her without knowing her. I can't believe that Brant would have any serious feelings toward a girl who was—"

"He wouldn't be the first man to be taken in by that wide-eyed, angelic look of hers." Clay jammed his hands into his pockets. "When he comes to his senses, if he wants to come and talk to me, I'll listen to what he has to say. Unless he's fool enough to marry her first."

"And—if he marries her—"

Clay's face flushed with anger. "Then I'll disinherit him."

"You don't mean that—You can't—"

"I can and I will."

Megan went cold inside. "Clay, no!"

"I mean what I say. Brant can give that slut the Drummond name. He can go where he pleases and take her along—I can't stop him from doing that—but she'll never see one cent of the Drummond money, and neither will he."

Megan had no appetite for the excellent dinner served in the Windsor dining room. As for Clay, he ate stolidly, pausing now and then to point out one of the local celebrities. There was a brief stir, a turning of heads, when a stocky, moustached man in his fifties entered accompanied by a small blonde woman at least twenty years younger, splendidly dressed—over-dressed, Megan thought—in a gown of peach-colored satin with a train that might have been more suitable for a presentation to Queen Victoria. The gown was embroidered with pearls, and the woman's fingers were laden with rings. A ruby and diamond brooch the size of a saucer glowed between her ample breasts.

"Horace Tabor—he owns the hotel," Clay said. "And that's his wife—his second wife. Baby Doe."

"What an odd name," Megan said.

"Real name's Elizabeth," Clay explained. "Horace dotes on her. She's never been accepted in Denver society—The respectable married ladies can't forget that he divorced his wife for her."

"I see," Megan said quietly. "I suppose they can't forgive her for being so young and pretty, either."

"Probably not. Although from what I've heard, that wasn't the whole reason why Tabor divorced his first wife."

He went on to explain that Horace Tabor's first wife, Augusta, had been a puritanical New Englander. "She stuck by him through all the lean years when he was out here looking for a strike," Clay said. "Then, when he made his pile, she nagged him mercilessly. She didn't know how to enjoy their money—and how to play—"

"Play?" Megan repeated. "I should think that a man of his age—"

"A man of his age, if he's worked hard all his life, wants a woman who can make him forget his business, who can join him in having a good time. I guess he—" Clay shrugged. "Horace Tabor likes a good time, that's sure. Wait until you see his opera house. It cost him one million dollars. Carpeting from Brussels, tapestries from France, Italian marble for pilasters and lintels." He broke off. "Ah, there's James Fair, in from San Francisco. Made his fortune in the Comstock Lode."

Fair approached their table, and Clay introduced him to Megan. He was a mature, good-looking Irishman, and Megan remembered that Clay had spoken of him before, that he was taking part in the talks aimed at smoothing out the difficulties between Clay's new line and that of Samuel Barstow. But although Fair accepted Clay's invitation to join them at their table, he made a point of not talking business. "I wouldn't think of it, not in the presence of your charming wife," he said, looking over Megan appreciatively. He gave her a warm smile. "Seen anything of Denver yet, Mrs. Drummond?"

"Not yet—my husband is far too busy right now to take me sightseeing."

"No man should ever be that busy," Fair said. "Wait until

this business with Barstow's settled, and then, if he doesn't squire you around, I will."

Later, in the sitting room of their suite upstairs, Clay told Megan that Fair, too, was divorced and that he had a reputation as a womanizer. "Smart as they come in business," Clay added.

"But what has he to do with your railroad—and Mr. Barstow's?"

"A railroad war is wasteful—it impedes progress. It's to the interest of Fair and his partners to keep the silver moving from the mines—and he'll put pressure on Barstow to come to terms for that reason." Clay took off his coat, tossed it over a chair, and loosened his shirt collar. "Look here, Megan, why don't you go off to bed—get a good night's rest?"

So many months apart, and now . . .

"You've had a long trip. You must be tired. And I've got papers to go over. I'll be up until all hours."

But long after she had gone to bed, she lay awake looking at the sliver of light under the door that separated her from Clay. She might as well have remained back home at Azalea Hill. Perhaps even now she could cut short her visit, return to Natchez. . . .

Her spirit rebelled at the thought. She would not retreat, not now, with Clay so cold, with her whole family moving apart, the structure, built over the years, crumbling. Deirdre off in Charleston . . . Brant estranged from his father. . . .

At least she could do something about that. Tomorrow, when Clay was busy with his meetings, she would go to Brant. She would bring about a reconciliation between her husband and her son. When that had been accomplished, she would turn her attention to Clay, would find a way to break down the barrier between them.

For the first time since her arrival in Denver that afternoon, she felt a new confidence flowing through her. She turned on her side and let herself relax into sleep. . . .

Chapter Twenty-two

THE NEXT morning, after Clay had left for his meeting, Megan put on a handsome new walking suit of brown velvet and went off to speak to Brant at his room at the Blue Spruce Hotel. But after they had exchanged greetings and Brant had gotten over his surprise at seeing her here in Denver, she found herself feeling constrained, even embarrassed. For it came to her with swift realization that her son was a man now, six feet tall, and there was a new hardness to the planes and angles of his face.

He took her jacket and invited her to sit down on the couch, in the clean, impersonal little room, but when she tried to convince him of the necessity of a reconciliation with his father, he refused to consider the possibility.

"But dear," she said, "you really must listen to reason. It won't be so difficult once you've made the first advances. We're going to a performance tonight at the Tabor Grand Opera House. If you will join us there, if you'll speak to him afterward. Tell him you're sorry."

"Apologize? After he—he humiliated me—after he—"

"What did he do to you?" Megan asked quietly.

"He hit me—I wouldn't have taken a beating like that from any other man without fighting back, but he's—"

"He's your father. I don't say that gave him the right to strike you, but such things sometimes happen." She was remembering her confrontation with Deirdre, their quarrel over Allen Sutcliffe, and the slap that had left the imprint of her hand on Deirdre's cheek. "I'm sure he regrets what happened—"

"Are you? I'm not. Mother, you don't understand. A woman can't be expected to understand—"

"I understand a lot more than you think. Your father told me—"

"My God! He couldn't have told you. Not about—"

"Brant, your father and I have been married for twenty-two years. Of course, he told me. About you and Kirsten. But it's not important enough to cause a permanent rift in the family. And the longer you stay away, the more difficult it will be for you to repair that rift."

Brant went on pacing, his hands thrust into his pockets, his shoulders forward. So like Clay, Megan thought. Useless to appeal to his sense of filial duty. Instead, she decided to take another tack. "This railroad trouble—I don't understand all the details, of course, but I'm sure that you do. You're a man now, and your father needs your help."

Brant stopped pacing, and there was something in his eyes that made Megan feel hopeful. A momentary change from the cold, distant expression she had seen there each time she had spoken of his father. "He said that? He said that he needs my help?"

Should she lie? No, not even in a good cause. She hated anything devious, anything that bore the taint of deception. "Your father is like you," Megan said. "He won't humble himself; he won't admit that he's in the wrong. But every time he wrote to me, he told me how useful you'd been to the railroad. The best trouble-shooter he'd ever hired, that was what he wrote. And now, if you were to go out along the right-of-way, if you were to keep your eyes and ears open and report back about what's happening up there in the mountains—if you were to seek out the trouble spots where a shooting war

between your father's men and Barstow's is most likely to
break out—You could do that, couldn't you? You know the
terrain, and you know the men—you could—"

"I could, but since I'm no longer working for my
father—" He looked away. "He shamed me. In front of Kirsten."

She forced herself to speak lightly. "You've the devil's own
pride, the both of you," she said. "And the Lord have mercy
on the poor female who must try to make peace between you."
She managed a smile, but Brant did not smile back. Instead,
he dropped down on the couch and put his arm around her.

"Mother, I don't want to make things difficult for you. I
know how this hurts you. But I can't do what you ask. Even
if I could forgive the things he said to me—the things he did—
I couldn't forgive the way he treated Kirsten."

"Kirsten," Megan said quietly. She would have to feel her
way carefully. "Yes, there is the matter of Kirsten. But perhaps
your father needs to know her better. She must have many fine
qualities if you've come to love her." She looked at her son
closely. "You are in love with this girl, aren't you?"

"I'm going to marry her."

But where was the warmth, the tenderness that should accompany such a declaration? Megan heard determination and
defiance. A spoiled, arrogant young man's gesture of defiance
against a father who had humiliated him, who had opposed his
wishes for the first time. Such a marriage could have disastrous
consequences not only for Brant and Kirsten but for the whole
family. A loveless marriage. . . . She thought of Reed and Samantha, of Luke. One such marriage in the Drummond family
was enough.

"I tried to tell Pa I was sorry when he found Kirsten and
me—in his hotel suite—" Brant flushed, the color spreading
under his deeply tanned skin. A young man should not refer
to such matters to his mother, but since she already appeared
to know . . .

"I can't believe your father became so furious with you only
because he found you and Kirsten together." Clay, when he
had been younger, had been much like Brant, and Megan remembered that night in the office above Uncle Jim's warehouse
back in Natchez-under and the hot, driving need with which
he had taken her.

Once more, Megan sensed that there was something hidden, nameless but threatening, in this clash between Clay and his son. Why had he been so outraged at finding Brant making love to a girl? Why?

"I guess Pa thinks Kirsten's not good enough for me," Brant said as if in answer to her unspoken question. "Just because she's a waitress here in the hotel. And that's so unfair. She has no family, no money, and the Blue Spruce dining room is every bit as respectable as those restaurants on the Atchison, Topeka, and Santa Fe, where the Harvey girls work. Those Harvey girls, a lot of them, marry wealthy ranchers and businessmen and—"

Megan bit back the desire to tell him that she knew Kirsten had been a saloon girl in Virginia City before coming to Denver. Perhaps he already knew, and if not, it was up to Kirsten to tell him when she wished to.

But, Megan thought uneasily, Clay had not known about Kirsten's past when he had found Brant with the girl in his suite at the Windsor; he'd only learned the facts from his foreman afterward. Why, then, had he struck his son in anger?

Megan forced herself to consider Brant's last remark. "Yes, I've heard of the Harvey girls," she said. "And I agree, they're earning a decent living and doing nothing to be ashamed of."

"Pa doesn't see it that way, I guess," Brant said. "But it doesn't matter, because I'm of age, and I don't need his permission to marry."

There was a knock at the door, and he broke off and went to admit a young girl, tall with a magnificent figure; her eyes, a deep, vivid blue, widened at the sight of Megan. While Brant was introducing them, Megan had time to give the girl a swift appraisal.

Kirsten was at least Brant's age, perhaps even a few years older. Her walking dress of blue and silver plaid taffeta was obviously cheap, the material sleazy. The bodice was too low for daytime wear. And the sky-blue hat, laden with yellow plumes and blue-velvet blossoms, topping her silver-gilt curls, was definitely vulgar. But, Megan reproved herself, a girl could not be condemned solely for a lack of good taste in matters of dress. That sort of discrimination had to be learned gradually, and no doubt Kirsten had not had the opportunity to pick up the fine points.

Megan came forward and took Kirsten's hand. "My dear, I'm so pleased to meet you," she said. She hesitated, then added, "My son has told me that the two of you are going to be married."

"That's right," Kirsten said, and now, after the first moment of surprise at finding Clay's mother here, her manner changed to one of defiance. Or was it a flicker of contempt Megan caught in those wide blue eyes before Kirsten lowered them. Contempt for what? Perhaps for a woman she believed to be the naive, pampered wife of a wealthy man, a woman who had had no contact with the seamy side of life. Maybe Kirsten was thinking that it would be far easier to win over such a woman than she had feared. And if she could win over Brant's mother, she could use her as an opening wedge to force acceptance into the immensely wealthy Drummond family.

Megan drew the girl down on to the couch beside her while Brant began again his restless pacing. "I only arrived here in Denver yesterday," Megan said. "I was sorry to learn of the quarrel between my husband and my son."

"It'll blow over," Kirsten said confidently.

"I hope so," Megan said. "Naturally, it is most distressing to me, finding Brant and his father at odds with each other. We'd expected that he would go into partnership with his father."

"Oh, yes—of course," Kirsten agreed, nodding so that the yellow plumes on her hat swayed. "And he will. If you speak to your husband, if you would try to make him understand how much Brant and I regret what's happened—how sorry we both are—"

"Kirsten—" Brant began, but the girl went on.

"And you, Mrs. Drummond. I don't want to be the cause of your unhappiness—"

"There is more than my unhappiness to be considered," Megan said. "My feelings are not important at the moment. It is Brant's whole future I'm concerned about."

"I'll make my own future," Brant said. "I don't need Pa's money. I'll get work on another railroad doing the same sort of job I did for the Colorado and Western. I'll—"

"That may not be easy," Megan told him. "Your father is bitter and angry, and he may use his influence—"

"To hell with his influence. I'll work as a laborer if I have to. I can swing a pick with the best of them—like Pa did when he was getting started—"

"Don't talk like a fool!" Kirsten's voice was shrill, her dark-blue eyes blazing with anger. "Swing a pick! You are Clay Drummond's son."

"I'm not going to trade on that," Brant retorted. "I'm used to rough living. This past year, moving from one railroad camp to the next, I wasn't sleeping in a feather bed. Tents and shacks, that's all I found at those towns up in the mountains, and they were plenty good enough—"

"Not for me!" Kirsten's lips tightened. "I'm not going to live like a laborer's wife in a leaky old tent or a broken-down shack. I'm not—"

. Megan put a hand over Kirsten's in a soothing gesture, and she laughed. "Oh, it's not so bad. Brant was born in a railroad boxcar at end-of-track. Did you know that, my dear? And his first bed was a box that had been used for storing dynamite. That may account for his explosive temper."

"That was years ago—before Clay—Mr. Drummond—had made his fortune—"

Megan caught the slip. But Kirsten went on, oblivious to everything except her own desires. "Brant, you have to go to your father—"

"I've already told you, I won't—" Brant began.

Kirsten spoke softly now, her voice wheedling. "But darling, think of your mother. She wants you to make up with your father, too. She wants what is best for you. We both do—"

"Surely you don't expect me to go crawling to him—Even if I could forget the way he treated me, you don't expect me to forget those things he said to you."

"I've heard men say a lot worse when they're fighting over—when they are angry," Kirsten finished lamely.

Swift pain lanced through Megan, for she could guess, she was sure, what Kirsten had been about to say. The pieces began to fall into place. Not only a young man like Brant would be taken with Kirsten's charms: the large, firm breasts, outlined now by the tight bodice of the sleazy blue and silver dress; the swaying hips, under the rustling skirt. Not only a young man . . .

"But you must forget all about those things your father said,"

Kirsten was saying. "After you've made up with him, after we are married, everything will be fine."

"And suppose my father doesn't change his attitude toward you even after we marry. What then?" Brant demanded. "Would you expect me to stand by in silence, to hear my wife insulted—"

Kirsten laughed, and Megan heard the smug, easy confidence in the laughter; she caught something coarse in Kirsten's tone when the girl said, "I'll be able to handle your father. Don't you worry about that."

Megan struggled to conceal her response. She had come here out of concern for her son, out of her desire to heal the breach between Brant and his father. But she had discovered something more. She needed time to think, to sort out her impressions of the girl Brant wanted to marry.

"No doubt you're right," Megan said gently to Kirsten. "But I want you to make me a promise, my dear."

"And what is that?"

"I want you to promise to put off your marriage until Brant and his father are reconciled. I want both of you to promise—"

"What's the point?" Brant said. "I'm not going to Pa and beg him to forgive me. And I'll choose my own wife. Go and tell him that, Mother."

"But the money—If he were to carry out his threat to disinherit you—"

"Let him do it," Brant said. "Let him leave his money to Terence—to Deirdre. I don't want it. You tell him that, too!"

But Megan told Clay nothing about her visit to Brant. They had dined together in their suite, and now, as the light changed from rose and gold to purple behind the distant mountains, she busied herself in laying out Clay's evening clothes. This was a chore that Ludamae would have performed willingly, but Megan took pleasure in doing such small services for Clay herself.

She was already dressed in a gown of honey-colored French faille trimmed with black lace; a topaz necklace, sparkling at her throat, set off the costume, accenting the tawny richness of the expensive fabric and Megan's own coloring.

Clay, who had returned later than expected from his meeting

with Samuel Barstow, James Fair, and the other men, was still bathing in the walnut and marble tub in the adjoining bathroom. Megan gave a final check to Clay's garments. She had been so preoccupied by the scene that had taken place back at the Blue Spruce Hotel that she had been forgetful. Clay's cravat— the new gray one that she had packed for him, months before, when he had left for Denver. That one would go well with his suit.

Swiftly, she went to the chest where he kept his clothing, thinking, as she often did, of how methodical he was. Every piece of wearing apparel was neatly folded and in its proper place. She went through the pile of cravats, and then her fingers brushed against something hard, and she drew out a tissue-wrapped box with silver ribbons that had been carelessly shoved under the neckware.

Silver ribbons and a spray of white and silver flowers to set off the bow.

She had not been the only one who had been preoccupied tonight, she thought with a smile; Clay had bought her a gift and had forgotten to give it to her. She removed the tissue and saw the square velvet box with the name of the jeweler's shop imprinted in silver. She would wear Clay's gift at the Tabor Grand Opera House, she thought with pleasure.

She opened the box and drew back, her lips parting. A diamond and sapphire necklace glittered in the light from the chandelier. Never had she seen sapphires of such a deep, brilliant shade of blue.

But Clay had such good judgement in choosing her jewelry. For her, he had always bought topaz stones. Pearls, perhaps. Diamonds. Never sapphires. And even if he had forgotten to present her with the gift, why, she asked herself belatedly, had it been tossed carelessly under a pile of his cravats?

There was no avoiding the answer, not any longer. Everything fell into place now: his fury at Brant when he had found the boy with Kirsten; the savage beating he had given his son; the ugly names he had flung at Kirsten.

What was it Kirsten had said? In her mind, Megan completed the phrase the girl had cut short.

When two men fight over a woman . . .

Anger clawed at Megan's insides. Clay was a virile man, strong, passionate. And he had been away from her for so long.

She tried to make excuses for him. If he had gone to one of the sporting houses for a few hours' release, she would have hated the notion, but she would have been realistic enough to accept it. But men did not give the girls in such places valuable jewelry, like the necklace she held in her hand. The color chosen with great care, the same care he had used in choosing jewelry to compliment her own eyes, her hair.

She would not stand for this. She would confront him with the necklace the moment he entered the bedroom. She would not listen to any explanation he might offer because no explanation would be plausible. And then she would leave at once. She would have Ludamae pack her suitcases. She would change to a traveling costume and go back to Azalea Hill.

She paused, trying to collect her whirling thoughts.

Back to Azalea Hill, and what then?

Kirsten was no fool. If Brant persisted in his decision not to seek a reconciliation with his father, Clay would carry out his threat: he would disinherit his eldest son.

And Kirsten would not want to settle for a life of struggle with a penniless young man. She would be far more likely to try to trap an older man who could give her a fortune. If Clay had already bought this necklace for her, he must have planned to make her his mistress. That thought, in itself, was terrible enough to Megan—but if she were to quarrel with her husband now, if she were to return alone to Azalea Hill, might Kirsten not try for higher stakes?

A husband thirty years older than Kirsten but one who was wealthy, one who would leave her well provided for. All at once, Megan's thoughts, which had been chaotic a few moments before, became clear. For her own sake and for Clay's, she had to put aside her anger, to think calmly, even with detachment.

Horace Tabor had been clever enough to make a fortune, but he had divorced his first wife to marry Baby Doe, a pretty young blonde with a reputation that had already been tarnished before she had become the second Mrs. Tabor, a young girl who fed his male ego and who—perhaps—made him feel young again.

There, in the red plush and marble hotel suite, Megan fought a swift, silent battle with herself. She would not stand by and see the Drummond family torn apart by Kirsten Nordstrom.

She would not let her outraged pride drive her back to Azalea Hill.

Even at this moment, when her first impulse was to give way to hurt and fury, when she longed to throw the necklace at Clay, to accuse him in bitter, angry words, she was held back by a stronger, deeper emotion.

Clay was capable of being drawn to other women. He had loved Samantha once. She was not sure of what his feelings toward Kirsten might be. But she knew, with unshakable certainty, that although she had not been the only woman for Clay, he was the only man for her.

And it was that certainty that gave her the strength to do what had to be done, to act in a way completely contrary to her impulsive, forthright nature. She made herself unfasten the topaz necklace she was wearing, to put it down on the dressing table. Then, a moment later, when Clay emerged from the bathroom in his robe, she forced a smile.

"What a lovely gift," she said.

"Megan, I—"

"Would you put it on for me, dear?" She handed him the velvet box, then turned around. "Such beautiful sapphires," she said. It was easier to play out the charade when she did not have to look at him. "I want to look my best tonight at the opera house," she rattled on. "I want to be a credit to you."

"You—you always are," he said. Was his voice a trifle hoarse, or did she imagine it? She felt his fingers touching the skin of her neck, and in spite of herself, her body tensed briefly.

She knew that the sapphires were not particularly becoming, worn with her honey-colored dress and the gold and amber combs that held her tawny hair in place, but that was not important. When she turned back to Clay, she was able to say quietly, "I have your clothes all laid out, dear, and you'd better dress quickly. We don't want to keep Mr. Fair waiting."

They had arranged to have dinner with James Fair and then to share a box with him at the opera house. Megan managed to get through the evening without betraying her inner turmoil, but she was only vaguely aware of the splendors of the opera house: the Italian marble pilasters and lintels; the heavy silk imported from France to line the three tiers of boxes.

She showed suitable admiration for the impressive stage

curtain, remarking on the painting that depicted a Roman ruin, complete with crumbling pillars and lions crouching among the rubble. She listened with a smile to Mr. Fair's telling of a story, now familiar to all the natives of Denver, about how Horace Tabor, when he had been shown his office above the opera house, had criticized the painting hung over his desk. He had demanded to know the name of the portrait's subject and had been told that it was a likeness of William Shakespeare.

"What the hell did he ever do for Denver?" Tabor had demanded, and then he had ordered that the artist take back the picture and paint his own rugged features in place of Shakespeare's.

Megan laughed and encouraged Fair to tell more stories about the eccentricities of Horace Tabor. She leaned forward when Fair pointed out Horace Tabor, with Baby Doe and a collection of Tabor's friends and hangers-on, who were seated in Box A, drinking champagne. The popping of the corks from Box A provided an accompaniment to the efforts of the singer, a well-upholstered Italian soprano. She had no memory afterward of whether the woman sang well or badly, for her thoughts were fixed on her own difficulties, her desire for the evening to end so that she could return with Clay to their hotel suite.

But when at last they were back in the suite, when Megan was lying in bed in the darkness while Clay was still in his dressing room, she found herself more miserable than before, unable to still her jangled nerves. Then she heard his footsteps as he approached the bed. She made herself lie perfectly still, her eyes closed. If he thought she was asleep, he would not touch her. She did not know, she could not predict, how she would respond to his touch.

"Megan?"

For the first time since she had known him, Clay sounded unsure of himself, and although this should have given her satisfaction, it did not. She felt, instead, the awakening of tenderness. But she kept her eyes closed and did not move. A moment later, he was in bed beside her, and she could feel the heat of his body.

"Megan, you're not asleep."

She did not answer.

Then, with one swift movement, he reached out for her, drawing her against him. His face was pressed against the swell of her breasts, his lips moving against the silk of her nightdress. "My love, I need you."

And in that moment, the years fell away, and she was back with him in the office over Uncle Jim's warehouse, when he had reached out to her for the first time and she had sensed his need for more than physical release. Then, as now, he had needed her acceptance, her understanding, had needed the solace of her freely given love.

Did he suspect that she knew the truth about the necklace, about Kirsten? She did not know; she would never know, and it did not matter at all. Only Clay mattered, her love for him, strong, changeless, sustaining both of them.

She reached out and drew his face closer against her breasts, and then she was stroking his hair, thrusting aside the bodice of her nightdress so that there was no longer a barrier, however fragile, between her flesh and his, between her taut nipples and his seeking mouth. He took one of her nipples between his lips, and the contact sent shock waves of pleasure out along the nerves of her body.

Although she had been tense and rigid only a few moments ago, now her body came alive, pulsating, aching, wanting. She molded herself against him, lifting her hips, encircling him with her legs, taking him into herself, deeper... and still deeper... And her cry, at the climax, was one of fulfillment, of triumph.

Chapter Twenty-three

❧

BRANT DRUMMOND glanced at the nickel-plated pocket watch that had replaced the fine silver watch given him by his father on his twenty-first birthday. "The train for San Francisco will be here in half an hour," he told Kirsten. "If it's on time," he added.

Kirsten did not answer. She had been unusually silent for the past few days. Indeed, she was sullen at times, which was a side of her that she had never shown Brant before; now she was less eager to charm him, to please him. He was handsome, surely, and he never failed to satisfy her in bed. But he was such a fool! All because of his stupid, senseless male pride, he had thwarted her plans. Even this morning, right up until the moment when they had left the Blue Spruce Hotel, she had kept hoping that he would seek a reconciliation with his father. Then she and Brant could have been married in style with the approval of the Drummond family. Here in Denver, perhaps, or back at his fine home in Natchez. Azalea Hill, it was called.

How many times she had visualized the scene: herself in a fashionable white-satin wedding gown with a sweeping train

256

and a lace veil—silver lace, perhaps, to accent the unusual color of her silver-blonde hair. And wedding gifts. And receptions and parties in honor of the new Drummond bride. Then a wedding trip to Europe, a stay in Paris, where she would be outfitted by the finest of the French dressmakers.

But Brant had ruined everything by his stubborn refusal to go and see his father, to ask, to plead if necessary, to return to work for Clay Drummond's newest railroad, the Colorado and Western. Even as late as this morning, she had continued to cling to the hope that Brant might be made to change his mind, but his determination to make the break with his father a permanent one, to succeed on his own, could not be shaken.

Oh, why hadn't she tried for the father instead of the son? Too late now. Brant's mother was youthful and attractive, still in her thirties. Each morning since Megan Drummond's arrival in Denver, Kirsten had read in the Denver *Tribune* of the latest social activities of Mr. and Mrs. Clay Drummond, of Megan's immediate acceptance by the ladies of Denver society. Every dinner, every reception, every visit that Megan had made at the Tabor Grand Opera House, had kept the *Tribune*'s society editor rhapsodizing over "the lovely and charming Mrs. Clay Drummond of Natchez." He had gone into great detail over the magnificent dinner given at the Windsor Hotel by James Fair, one of the "Bonanza Kings," for Mr. and Mrs. Clay Drummond. Kirsten had heard of Mr. Fair, for who had not? Fabulously wealthy, divorced, and a womanizer. Other important men had attended the dinner: Mr. Seligman from New York and Mr. Henry Villard, a railroad tycoon. And always there was Megan Drummond at her husband's side. Kirsten had missed her chance there.

She tried to console herself. At least she had talked Brant out of the ridiculous notion of taking a laborer's job on another railroad. She had managed to persuade him that he could at least get some sort of position in San Francisco working in the offices of one of the other railroad companies, perhaps, or with one of the cable-car lines.

If no such opportunity materialized, she told herself, she would at least be in San Francisco, where she would have a chance to attach herself to a wealthy man. And this time, she would not consider age a barrier. In fact, an old man, really old, might be best— If she could inveigle such a man into marriage, she might be left a well-off widow. . . .

"Kirsten. Look there—it's my mother's carriage."

Megan alighted and came hurrying down the platform toward them. Kirsten felt a surge of excitement. Had Clay Drummond relented? Had Brant's mother talked his father into making the first advance? She turned her sweetest smile on Megan Drummond, but Megan gave her a cool, appraising look before going directly to Brant.

"I inquired at the Blue Spruce. They told me that you and Kirsten were leaving—going to San Francisco, one of the waitresses said."

"I'd have come to say good-by to you, mother," Brant said a little awkwardly, "but I didn't want to run into pa. I was going to write you as soon as we got settled, though."

"What will you do in San Francisco?" Megan asked.

"Brant will get a fine job there," Kirsten said. "In an office. And we'll live in one of the new hotels. The Grand or maybe even the Palace Hotel. Not one of those dirty little railroad camps—"

"All that will take time," Megan said, speaking to her son. She had scarcely acknowledged Kirsten's presence after that first long look. "And money. How much money have you saved?"

She knew Brant's lavish, careless way with money only too well.

"I'll manage," Brant said.

"On what?" Megan demanded.

"I—sold a few things. My watch and my—"

"You sold the watch your father gave you for your birthday?"

"What does it matter?" Brant said. "Pa and I—"

"Listen," Kirsten interrupted. "The train's coming."

But it was not the expected passenger train bound for San Francisco; it was not a passenger train at all but one made up of boxcars, each marked with the name of the Colorado and Western. Clay's railroad. Megan caught her breath in shock when she saw the crew clambering out of the cars: bruised, bloodied, their clothing dirty and torn. And there were others on improvised stretchers, their faces covered with blankets.

"Oh, dear God, what—" Megan began, but Brant left her

with Kirsten and ran to the train. He seized one of the men by the arm, and Megan's eyes widened with recognition.

"Jim—Jim Rafferty—tell me what happened—"

Uncle Jim had a dirty bandage wrapped around his head, and his shirt was ripped to tatters; there was a long gash on the side of his face. Megan, hurrying up to join them, caught only a few words: ". . . put up a divil of a fight . . . hired guns . . . lead pipes . . . all hell's broke loose . . ."

Then Brant was speaking, his eyes hard, his face grim. "Get the wounded over to the Blue Spruce," he told Jim Rafferty. "Get rooms for those who've been most badly hurt and take over the lobby for the rest. They can put up cots—tell the manager that we'll pay for the inconvenience. Then send one of your men for a doctor—fast." Brant looked at the dead men on the stretchers. "If any of those have—had—wives here in Denver, the women'll have to be told. We'll take care of the expenses for the burials—and for a little extra cash for the—the widows. They never have much put aside—"

This was her son, but now he was somehow unfamiliar. A man taking charge of the family's business affairs. And Megan was impressed by the speed with which her uncle hurried off to obey Brant's orders.

Brant turned back to face Megan and Kirsten, who had come running up.

"That sneaking son of a—That Barstow! We never trusted him. Talking settlement with Pa and getting his bully boys rounded up for a surprise attack." Brant's eyes were hot with anger. "But we'll take care of Barstow once and for all."

He started off, then turned. "I'm taking your carriage back to the Windsor— Come along, mother—hurry—"

"But the train to San Francisco—" Kirsten began.

"To hell with San Francisco. I've got to find Pa—to tell him what's happened. Then we've got to get together a new crew—reinforcements—and get them up into the mountains—Horseshoe Gulch and Yellow Pine Peak— I can help round up the men. Come along, mother—"

"And me—what about me?" Kirsten's voice was shrill with anger. "You can't just go off and—"

"You wait here," Brant told her. "Or take the train to San Francisco—" He reached into his coat and took out the tickets. "Cash mine in and use it for your expenses if you want to—"

"But when will you come out to join me?" Kirsten persisted.

"How the devil do I know? When we've won the right-of-way from Barstow's crew—" Brant took Megan's arm. "Are you coming, Mother?"

Megan hesitated but only for an instant. "I'll wait here with Kirsten," she told him, her brain working swiftly in spite of her inner turmoil. "You take the carriage and go to your father." She reached up, standing on her toes to kiss her tall son while she tried to ignore the fear that she felt at his leaving. No use to plead with him to be careful. When had Brant or his father ever been careful? When had they ever weighed the odds in the face of danger?

He held her hard for a moment, then turned and hurried off. Moments later, he was springing into the carriage and driving off.

"Now Brant and his father will make up," Kirsten was saying. "They're bound to—"

Kirsten's eyes gleamed with triumph, and Megan, to whom anything devious was repellent, had to choose her words carefully. "And that pleases you?"

"Why yes! Yes—of course, Mrs. Drummond." Kirsten stared at Megan in surprise.

Megan reminded herself that this girl represented a threat not only to her son's future but also to her own relationship with her husband, to the solidarity of the Drummond family. Kirsten was not in love with Brant; Megan was sure of it. She had not shown the slightest concern for him, knowing that he was going into mortal danger.

And as for Brant, his parting words to Kirsten had been careless, offhand; if he did marry Kirsten, it would only be out of defiance, the desire to prove his independence.

But troubled as she was, Megan forced a smile and said, "You're most generous, Kirsten. You must love my son very much to put his happiness before your own."

"Before my— I don't understand. Brant and I are going to be married as soon as this foolishness of the railroad war is settled. He'll go back to work for his father, and I'll come to live at Azalea Hill, and one day—"

Kirsten broke off, but Megan knew what she had been about to say. One day, Brant would inherit the eldest son's share of the great Drummond fortune: the railroads, the steel mills, the coal mines, the timberland. All of it. One day, as Mrs. Brant Drummond, Kirsten would be a fabulously wealthy woman.

"My dear," Megan said with a gentleness she did not feel, "you must understand that my husband's not a man to make a decision lightly. He has already said several times that if Brant marries you, he will be disinherited. My husband will not change his decision."

"Oh, but surely if you were to talk to him—"

Megan shook her head. "I know my husband—after twenty-two years of marriage. He is a stubborn man."

"But Brant loves me—" Kirsten's voice faltered slightly, for Megan had seen Brant's casual good-by to her.

"Ever since Brant turned sixteen, he's been in and out of love with—all sorts of pretty young things. But he is a Drummond. You don't understand what that means perhaps. When he marries, he will want his father's approval. Oh, he's had these little differences with his father before. But you saw how quick he was to go to his father's aid now that there's real trouble. And he went of his own free will, not because of my pleading—or yours." That much, surely, was true. "Forgive me, my dear," Megan went on. "I know how painful it must be for you to accept the truth. But since you love Brant so deeply, you surely want what's best for him."

Kirsten's fair skin had gone a sickly greenish color, and her soft mouth drooped at the corners. Under other circumstances, Megan might have pitied her, but the family came first. It had to.

Now, from around the bend in the track, the long, piercing sound of a train whistle sounded. Smartly dressed men and a few women emerged from the depot's waiting room. Others were getting out of carriages and hurrying down the platform.

"The train to San Francisco," Megan said. "You have your ticket, and as Brant said, you can cash in his. I haven't brought much with me, but I can let you have—"

"Don't bother." Again, Megan heard the hard, coarse tone in Kirsten's voice. "I'm not leaving Denver until Brant gets back."

"But I've already told you—"

"Let him tell me." The girl's first shock at the realization that Brant would not marry her was giving way to sullen stubbornness. "He owes me something. He—he took advantage of me. I came here to Denver from a farm in Minnesota, and I knew nothing about—"

"From Minnesota?" Megan's eyes narrowed slightly. "By way of Virginia City?"

Kirsten's lips parted in surprise. But she was still not willing to surrender. She smelled money, a great deal of money, and she was not about to give up the chance of getting her hands on it, not without a struggle.

"Why Mrs. Drummond," a man's voice boomed. Both women started slightly. "I didn't expect to find you here." Megan turned to face James Fair, stocky, self-assured with his alert, deeply set eyes, his rugged good looks. He swept off his hat and bowed. And Megan knew that she had one card left to play.

"Mr. Fair. It's good to see you again. Are you returning to San Francisco?"

He nodded. "They'll hold the train long enough to couple my private car to the others. A nasty piece of double-dealing, this trick of Barstow's. I'm going to go on putting pressure on the man—waste of time and money, these railroad wars. But I can do what needs to be done back in San Francisco, and I have other pressing business there."

"You heard about the—the fight for the right-of-way—"

"Of course. Spoke to that boy of yours before I left the Windsor. Fine lad. And a fighter, like his father."

Then, as if realizing that his words might be frightening to Megan, he added quickly, "Now don't you worry, Mrs. Drummond. Brant's rounding up a crew of the best fighting men here in Denver. He and Clay are going to settle this once and for all."

"Oh, but I—saw those men being carried off the boxcars—"

"No need for Clay or Brant to take part in the fighting. That's what hirelings are for." He smiled reassuringly. "Now it'll take time to have my car joined with the train—plenty of time for luncheon on board. My chef always travels with me, and he's as good as any at the Windsor. So if you and Miss—" His eyes raked Kirsten appreciatively.

"Miss Nordstorm," Megan supplied.

"If you two ladies would join me over a meal of venison—
or pheasant, if you'd rather."

"But the train—" Megan began.

With easy assurance, he said, "They'll hold the train if I
tell them to."

"I must refuse," Megan said. "I want to get back to the
Windsor to speak with my husband. But Miss Nordstrom—a
dear friend of our family—is leaving for San Francisco, and
it is so difficult—an inexperienced young lady, traveling
alone—you understand—" Megan looked appealingly at Fair.
"I would consider it a great favor if you would look after her
on the journey."

"I'd be honored, ma'am," Fair said.

The two women exchanged a swift look of understanding.
Then Kirsten gave the man her most charming smile, her blue
eyes radiant. "I shouldn't want to impose, sir—" she said
softly.

"Nonsense, Miss Nordstorm. My pleasure."

And a few minutes later, Megan watched as Kirsten, escorted by James Fair, boarded his private car. She felt a brief
sense of relief, for she was sure that the Drummond family
would not be seeing Kirsten Nordstrom again.

But her relief gave way to anxiety when, on returning to
the Windsor, she learned that both Clay and Brant were gone,
and they were out rounding up men for the fight and were
determined to go along into the mountains. And Jim Rafferty
departed, too, after getting Megan's promise that she would
take care of the comfort of the men wounded in the first skirmish
and aid the wives of those who had been killed.

"But Uncle Jim—at your age—" she protested.

"I'll thank ye t' keep a respectful tongue in yer head, girl,"
said Jim, bristling. "I can fight with the best of 'em—" Then,
his action belying the severity of her words, he drew her close,
gave her a bearlike hug, and hurried off.

In the days that followed, Megan tried to keep busy, taking
charge of the arrangements for the burial of those men who
had died in the first skirmish. She found a priest and looked

after the immediate needs of the widows. Some had relatives back East, and Clay's lawyer here in Denver advanced the money for train fare at Megan's orders. Those others, some with small children, who chose to remain in the city received enough ready cash to take care of their expenses until the pensions could be arranged for by Clay himself. She knew that he had a strong sense of responsibility to his employees and that he was liked and respected by their families.

The days stretched into one week, then two, and every night she lay awake in her bed in the hotel suite, tossing sleeplessly, waiting for morning. Early each day, she hurried down to the telegraph office, where, along with the wives of some of the other men who were out there with Clay, she waited for the latest word of the fighting. But the news was confusing and often contradictory. There had been a fight near Horseshoe Gulch. Clay's men had taken the station. No, Barstow's men had won it back from them. Places that had been only names to Megan were now desperately important: Yellow Pine Peak. Bear River. Rabbit Ears Mountain.

The wealthy ladies with whom Megan had become acquainted now made a point of calling on her at the hotel suite, where Ludamae, in her best black-silk uniform and starched apron, served tea and cakes. Megan found these visits a strain, for her callers tried to distract her with gossip about the latest fashions from the East, the juiciest local scandals, the steps they were taking as members of the Denver Protective Association to close down "those dreadful places," the sporting houses on Holladay Street, and the deplorable lack of cooperation from their menfolk.

Then, early one morning, when Megan, with the help of Ludamae, had just finished dressing for her regular trip to the telegraph office, there was a knock at the door, and Ludamae went to admit Jim Rafferty. He did not look Megan in the face, and she felt an icy chill surge up inside her. Uncle Jim sank down on the red plush couch, and Ludamae offered him a shot of whiskey without being asked. He gulped it gratefully. "We won," he told Megan. "A hell of a fight, but we licked 'em. Right down the line."

His clothes were filthy, and his heavy boots had soiled the thick carpet. He kept his eyes fastened to the empty glass in his hand, and his voice was unnaturally controlled now. Megan sat motionless beside him, her eyes growing wider, her hands clenched in her lap.

"Both sides were usin' the same telegraph wires, ye see. And so Barstow's people were able to decode our messages—to know what our plans were. We did the same, of course."

"And Clay?"

He went on as if he had not heard her. "Barstow garrisoned the important stations on his line. He packed the roundhouse at Yellow Pine Peak with his hired guns—all the worst scum from Dodge City to Pueblo. But Clay knows how to lead men—remembered that from back during the war, I guess—an' he had us climbin' aboard Barstow's trains—bootin' his bastards right off—clubs, it was, an' pick handles and bare fists. Up an' down the line we went. Capturin' one station after another—one hell of a fight—"

He poured himself another shot of whiskey and drank it, tilting back his head in one swift motion. He shifted on the couch, his eyes bleak. "An' then, when it shoulda been all over—then—"

"Clay? Where is he? Why isn't he with you?"

"He's still—up there."

"He's dead—"

"No, darlin', no. Not a scratch on him. But your boy—Brant—" He cleared his throat loudly. "Brant was shot. Doc said no use t' move him—easier to leave him up there, y' see."

Megan rose, moving stiffly, jerkily, like a marionette.

"Take me to him."

"Passenger trains ain't running yet—not up there—Beaver Creek—"

"Wagon, then. Get one of the teamsters to drive me."

"I'll drive ye, darlin'—if yer set on goin'."

In the years to come, Megan was never to remember the details of that journey, only small, isolated memories that came back to torture her: Ludamae forcing a heavy cloak into her hands. "Be cold up there in them mountains, Miz Megan"; the endless, jolting ride in the wagon under a blazing sun; sentinel peaks of granite, huge, fantastic, against the deep brilliant blue of the Colorado sky; a mud-roofed log cabin, covered with lynx and beaver pelts laid out to dry; a thin gaunt woman with

a brood of children clutching at her skirts as she offered Megan
a drink of spring water; the blue-green of the spruces and the
gold of the aspens; and then, at last, at sunset, a stream running
red—not blood but the rays of the setting sun; the canyons
shadowed with purple; and, at last, the first stars coming out,
clear and dazzling in the thin mountain air.

Past and present were one. She relived that other journey
by wagon to join Clay at end-of-track. Her body had ached
then, too. Swollen with her first pregnancy.

Megan's body was stiff, numb, when Jim Rafferty pulled
up at the camp and lifted her down. In silence, he led her into
the boxcar, set apart on a slight rise, close to a swiftly running
stream.

Inside, Megan saw her son stretched out on a low cot and
then Clay, who rose from the crate on which he had been sitting
and came to her. Clay's face was haggard, and there was a
dark stubble along his jaw.

"Brant's not—" Megan could not go on.

"Not yet," Clay said in a voice she had never heard before.
"He's—not in any pain—the doctor gave him laudanum—"

"But there must be something—if we can get him to
Denver—"

Clay shook his head. "The bullets smashed his spine. He
said—he could feel nothing from the waist down—he—"

Megan moved to Brant's side and dropped to her knees.
She took his hand. It was hot and dry. He opened his eyes,
and she saw that the expression in them was vague for a moment. "Brant—"

There was a flicker of recognition then, a brief tightening
of his fingers around hers. Then his lips moved.

"We won," he said. "Pa'll tell you—we won—"

He was talking about the railroad line, and for a moment,
Megan wanted to cry out, to curse the line and Clay, with his
consuming ambition—then she felt Brant's hand clutching at
hers. She bent forward, touching her lips to his burning forehead. His head rolled to one side, and she watched the light
fade from his open eyes.

Then Clay was lifting her to her feet. She bent to draw the
blanket over Brant's face. When Clay tried to lead her outside,

her body stiffened, the hot words springing to her lips. But then she saw her husband's face, and the words would not come. Brant had been like his father, reckless, quick to take up a challenge.

In silence, they left the boxcar and went out into the night, to stand together in the icy wind that blew down from the mountains. In silence, they turned and clung to each other.

And when, at last, she heard his broken words, "My fault— I should have let him go off with—that girl—anything—only not this—" she found that she was able to put aside her own pain, the grief that tore at her.

"It was his choice," she said, her arms tightening around Clay. "A man has the right to make his own choices—"

"But it was for him—the railroads—all of it—for him—"

"And for Terence—and Deirdre," she said. "For their children—and their children's children. For the Drummonds."

Chapter Twenty-four

MEGAN, who was returning from a shopping expedition to the business section of Natchez, shivered slightly as she got down from her carriage in the drive at Azalea Hill. The breeze from the river below the bluffs carried the raw dampness of early winter.

Winter. More than a year had gone by since she and Clay had brought Brant's body home to be laid to rest in the Drummond family graveyard at Montrose, where three generations of Drummonds had been buried. And only a few weeks ago, Megan, at Clay's urging, had agreed to stop wearing black since the year of mourning was over.

The walking suit she wore today was pearl-gray velvet trimmed with bands of lilac satin; most appropriate for half mourning, according to Opal Carpenter, who had copied the style from a fashion plate in *Harper's Bazar*. And Opal was knowledgeable about such matters, for now, in 1888, her dress shop on Federal Street was a mecca for the most fashionable ladies in Natchez as well as other customers who came to her from the towns and plantations as far up river as Jackson.

At Clay's urging, Megan had agreed to give a ball, the first to be held at Azalea Hill since Brant's death. "You can't grieve forever, love," Clay had reminded her gently. But, as always, he had a practical reason for wanting to give the ball, too. He wished to entertain a visitor from up North, a man named Richard Whitaker.

"Whitaker's been buying up thousands of acres of timberland all through the South," he had told her. "I think he's prepared to pay a handsome price for the stretch of pine and cypress down in Louisiana."

Megan was relieved to see that Clay was involved in business again, driving himself with fierce energy. She suspected that his grief over Brant's death was mixed with guilt, for the boy had died fighting for the right-of-way for Clay's railroad. No matter what Clay's motives, however, it was reassuring to see that his ambition was still strong, that he had shaken off the black depression that had followed the death of his eldest son.

She could even feel gratitude toward their Yankee visitor, although there were those, like Reed, who still bitterly resented the invasion of Northern speculators. Richard Whitaker, a personable man in his late forties, had come South to add to his already considerable fortune, as had so many other Northern businessmen. Indeed, the stampede of Yankee speculators had been so great during the past decade that the Illinois Central Railroad had run a series of special trains from Chicago to Mississippi and Louisiana just to accommodate them. These men had lost no time in carving out huge holdings from the rich timberland, the coal and iron regions of the lower South; and now Richard Whitaker of Grand Rapids had joined in the race to buy up an enormous tract that was a part of Clay's original land grant for the Natchez–Fort Worth Line. The railroad line itself, Clay had assured Megan, was another matter; that would stay in the Drummond family.

She no longer tried to persuade Clay to curb his ambitions, so great was her relief at seeing him active and busy again. It had been because of her concern for her husband that she had permitted Deirdre to remain at Azalea Hill after the funeral instead of returning to Miss Pembroke's school for young ladies in Charleston.

Deirdre's presence had been a comfort to Clay during those first few months after Brant's death, for the girl, subdued by the loss of her brother, had stayed close to home. In the eve-

nings, after dinner, she had played the piano and sung for her
parents, and had accompanied them on drives to Montrose.
She had made no reference to the reason why she had been
sent off to school, and Megan had said nothing about it to Clay.
There was no point in troubling him about the matter now,
particularly since Allen Sutcliffe had left New Orleans, presumably to continue his tour of the United States.

Gradually, as Clay's interest in his far-flung business holdings had revived and he had begun to spend more time away
from home, Deirdre had started to take part in the more restrained social activities in and around Natchez. Because she
was still in mourning, she could not go to balls, but at a small,
sedate dinner party given by Mark and Lianne, she had drawn
the eyes of several likely young men in the county. There was
no doubt that Deirdre made a striking figure in her black-silk
mourning gowns, which set off her flawless white skin and
emphasized the golden lights in her amber eyes.

After that first dinner party, there were several young men
calling at Azalea Hill. And, Megan told herself, there could
be no possible harm in a drive along the bluffs, with Miss Amy
along to act as chaperone. It was acceptable, too, for Deirdre
to attend an afternoon musicale or bazaar given to raise money
for a charitable cause.

Then, only a few weeks ago, since the year of mourning
was over, Megan had agreed that Deirdre might go to visit
Angelique Winthrop's pretty young niece in New Orleans.
Deirdre had promised to return to Azalea Hill in time for the
ball, to which Genevieve Vallière had been invited. Perhaps,
Megan thought, Deirdre would be attracted to a suitable young
man at the ball, a young man from a good Natchez family,
one of whom she and Clay could approve. The young man
would not only have to come from the right sort of family to
satisfy Clay, but, Megan thought, he would have to have a
forceful disposition, for Deirdre needed a firm hand. Clay had
spoiled his daughter shamelessly.

Now Megan put aside thoughts of Deirdre as she entered
the house. She was beginning to feel the first stirrings of anticipation about the ball. Lengths of silver ribbon and others
of white satin would be draped in the hall; masses of holly,
the red berries brightening the decor. Then there should be
swags of greenery to be looped along the sides of the buffet

table. Becky, Megan's cook, would prepare a turkey, simmered in wine, and her delicious fruitcake. Perhaps, if Becky needed help, Megan could borrow Rachel from Montrose for the evening. . . .

On the evening of the ball, two days before Christmas, Reed, Samantha, and Luke, who had come home for the holidays, drove down from Montrose to Azalea Hill. Samantha stared out of the carriage window, occupied with her own thoughts, while Reed asked Luke about his work on the Natchez–Fort Worth Line. Luke was proud of his new position as foreman of the repair crew, and he described his work to Reed in great detail.

Samantha, after a few minutes, did not bother to listen, for she was preoccupied with her own concerns. She had not wanted to accept Megan's invitation, seeing it as an opportunity for Clay's wife to flaunt her affluence. Clay's wife. Even after all these years, the thought had the power to hurt Samantha.

"I don't see why you insisted on our attending this party," Samantha said.

Reed turned from Luke and said, "My dear, you've been complaining because you couldn't go to one of those watering places up North these last two summers. This ball will raise your spirits."

Samantha looked away, her eyes fixed on the river beneath the bluffs. True, she had been angry when Reed had refused to allow her to spend money on a visit to Saratoga for two summers in a row, for she had not dared to become involved with another man close to home. But she needed her summer affairs. Reed had his bottle, and she had her liaisons with men she would never see again after summer's end.

Although, she told herself, trying to be fair, Reed had been drinking far less recently and had begun to take an interest in the cultivation of the Montrose acres.

"A visit to Azalea Hill is scarcely a substitute for a summer in Saratoga," she said.

"That's as may be," Reed told her. "But Clay's kept Montrose going all this time; he's been handing us money whenever we needed it. Now that young O'Donnell is running the place at a profit, we must do our part. Clay's been more than generous."

"And why not?" Samantha's voice was tinged with bitterness. "Clay holds title to the plantation, doesn't he? It's to his interest to keep it going."

"That's not quite fair," Reed said. Luke had lapsed into silence, for he had grown up listening to such wrangling, and he hated it.

"Clay doesn't need the profits from Montrose crops," Reed went on. "He's given us help because we are family and Montrose is the home place. And I won't have you frittering away Clay's money on those summer excursions. Every year, you go up North with enough clothes to outfit a dozen women— and for what? To sit on the piazza at some Saratoga hotel with a lot of Yankee women, trying to impress them."

Not the women, Samantha thought, feeling contempt for her husband. But then she quickly reminded herself that she should be thankful that he did not suspect the real reason for those eye-catching gowns, those provocative bonnets that she had taken with her on her vacations. "I like pretty clothes," she said with forced sweetness. "You can't blame me for that. Is it a crime for a lady to want to look attractive?"

"Of course not." He looked at her for a moment with the adoration that she had seen in his face so often during the days of their brief courtship. "Samantha, you're beautiful— You always will be no matter what you wear or— All the same," he went on, "you must understand how important it is for me to be able to start paying Clay back, and that means economizing. Montrose can at last be self-supporting, now that we have Michael O'Donnell managing the place. He's got a real feeling for farming, and he's a good hand with horses."

"That's scarcely surprising," Samantha said with contempt. "He's an Irish peasant, isn't he?"

"You can't hold that against him. Do you dislike him, Samantha?"

"I don't think about him one way or the other," she said quickly. "Why should I?"

But she was lying. She had resented Michael's presence at Montrose from the beginning because he was Megan's relation by marriage. She had avoided him whenever possible and had scarcely exchanged more than a few words with him. But now she had even more reason to keep away from him, for she could not forget a certain incident that had taken place at Montrose on a sultry afternoon last summer. Frantic with boredom and frustration, she had gone out riding and had reined up beside the corral on her return to watch Michael O'Donnell breaking a new mare to the saddle.

Even now she could remember the warm weakness that had swept through her at the sight of his muscular body; the sweat had plastered his shirt to his back and chest, and his powerful thigh muscles stood out against the cloth of his breeches as he fought to get the mettlesome young animal under control.

She had remained motionless, watching him climb down at last from the mare's back, had listened, her insides tight with frustration, as she heard the soft brogue. Michael had patted the mare and said soothingly, "Ah, now, my beauty, ye'll do nicely, now ye know who's master. And 'tis a little beauty ye are, too—"

Samantha, aching with her unsatisfied need, was appalled by the hunger that shook her. The shame of it, to feel such stirrings, looking at Michael O'Donnell, a young man scarcely older than her own son. Sick with self-loathing, she had spurred her horse and ridden back to the house.

After that, she had taken care to avoid Michael O'Donnell. Next year, she told herself, she would go to Saratoga or Newport or perhaps White Sulphur Springs; but she would not stay at Montrose with a husband who had ceased to matter to her at all.

The ballroom at Azalea Hill was filling with guests, but Megan and Clay were still receiving latecomers in the drawing room off the wide downstairs hall. Samantha returned Megan's cordial greeting with frigid courtesy. Reed was friendlier, and as for Luke, Samantha could not help but see the warm affection in his eyes when he greeted his aunt, the way he pressed her hand.

"Where's Deirdre?" Luke asked.

"We're expecting her at any moment," Megan said with a small, worried frown. "She promised to return home for the ball. And to bring her friend, Genevieve Vallière."

But an hour later, Deirdre still had not arrived. Megan, feeling a growing uneasiness, left the ballroom and went downstairs to watch for her. Clay remained in the ballroom, and

Samantha caught sight of him, standing near the holly-wreathed punch bowl, speaking with Richard Whitaker.

No doubt he was concerned with the reception that his Yankee visitor might receive, for many of the local guests were resentful of the Northern investors who were still swarming down to buy up Southern land for speculation. Reed had been particularly bitter on that subject, but Samantha no longer listened to his diatribes.

She was still loyal to the South, but her attitude toward money had changed gradually. For Reed had shown openly his resentment of the Yankees who had come South to enrich themselves, while Clay, more realistic, had worked with them from the beginning of Reconstruction. And Samantha could not shut her eyes to the fact that Clay had made a fortune, created a showplace here at Azalea Hill, had bailed out Montrose a dozen times over before the arrival of Michael O'Donnell. If not for Clay, she and Reed might have had to let the place go; they might have been forced, like so many other families they knew, to live in some dismal boardinghouse, some backwoods dogtrot cabin.

Clay was introducing Luke to Richard Whitaker as Samantha approached them.

"Luke Drummond—my nephew," Clay said.

Whitaker shook Luke's hand; then, looking from Luke to Clay and back to Luke again, he said, "This young fellow's enough like you to be your son. He's the image of you."

"Is he?" Clay looked surprised, and Samantha, a few feet away, caught her breath, her eyes widening with apprehension. Whitaker, unaware of the effect of his words, went on. "You mean no one's remarked on it before? Same hair, eyes. And his features— I'll wager you looked exactly like him when you were a young man, Clay."

For one terrible moment, the buffet table, laden with silver trays and covered dishes of food and bright with holly and white and silver Christmas baubles, began to swim before Samantha's eyes. But she made herself walk forward. "Why that's only natural, sir," she said to Richard Whitaker with a tinkling little laugh. "Vance Drummond was Clay's father—and my husband's, also. Reed and Clay are half brothers, you see, and Luke resembles his grandfather. Haven't you noticed how these resemblances often skip a generation?"

Whitaker had turned to Samantha when she had started speaking, and it was plain to her that he had lost interest in the resemblance between Clay Drummond and his nephew, that his eyes were all for her, now. Samantha accepted the tribute with complacency, for she was used to the admiration of men.

Now in her early forties, she was still a beautiful woman, a woman whose sensuality was scarcely concealed by her ladylike manners. She was looking her best, and she knew it. Her wine-red velvet dress was cut modishly low over the bosom to reveal the swell of her breasts, still high and firm. The bustle of the dress was lavishly ornamented with silver roses, and the cut of the gown emphasized her waist, which was as small as that of any of the young belles here tonight.

"Mr. Whitaker, this is Samantha Drummond, my brother Reed's wife," Clay said. But even as he introduced them, she saw that his eyes were shadowed. What was Clay thinking? Had he forgotten that night in the summerhouse so many years ago? No, he could not have forgotten that. More than twenty years had past, but he must still remember, as she did.

Would he begin to wonder about Luke? Would he ask questions? No, he must not do that. Knowing Clay's disposition and her husband's fierce jealousy, she dreaded the scandal that might ensue. Clay must not know that Luke was his son—and Reed must never suspect, either.

Samantha was scarcely aware that the orchestra had struck up the opening bars of a waltz. Richard Whitaker bowed and asked, "Will you do me the honor, Mrs. Drummond?"

Samantha gave him her most gracious smile, and then she was in his arms, whirling about the floor. Looking up at him from under her long, dark lashes with the automatic coquetry that was so much a part of her, she saw that he was gazing down at her in rapt fascination. Such flattery from a male never failed to please Samantha.

Richard Whitaker danced well, leading with easy, practiced skill. Samantha tried to remember what little she knew about this stranger from up North, the gossip shared with her by Violet Shepley. Whitaker had lost his wife a few years before and had not remarried. He was extremely wealthy—so Violet had said—and he came from someplace called Grand Rapids, in Michigan. He had already bought up great tracts of timberland in Texas and others rich in coal, in Alabama, before buying the Louisiana land from Clay.

He's not handsome, but he's strong and—and there's something about him. Samantha did not want to admit, even to herself, that she was drawn instantly by the man's obvious virility, the strength and power of his rugged features.

"Have you heard this waltz before?" he asked, and when she shook her head, he went on. "It's quite new, I believe. I heard it in Paris last summer."

"Paris?"

"I was there on business," he said. "I travel a good deal," he added.

"How I envy you," she said with just the right note of wistfulness in her voice. "I've never been any farther from home than Newport—and Saratoga."

"A lively town, Saratoga," he said heartily. "Are you and your husband going there next summer, perhaps?"

"I hope to," she said. "My husband is absorbed in running our plantation, Montrose. But he insists upon my leaving Natchez during the hot months. The heat down here is quite unbearable in Natchez in summer, and I find it—overpowering. . . ."

Whitaker looked down at her, smiling. "If I could hope that you would be at Saratoga next summer, I would arrange my business affairs so that I could be there, too. . . ."

The waltz swirled to an end, and Samantha was relieved, for although she was physically attracted to this man, she felt that the situation was moving too swiftly. She wanted to be in control, and she sensed that with a man as forceful as Richard Whitaker, this might be difficult. She sensed that he was a man who decided quickly what he wanted and went after it, and she found this quality exciting and at the same time disturbing.

Seeking to play for time, she looked about the crowded ballroom, her eyes coming to rest on a pair of new arrivals.

"Oh, there's my niece, Deirdre," she said. "She's a lovely little thing, isn't she?"

"Charming," Whitaker agreed. "And the gentleman with her?"

Samantha thought she saw something familiar about the tall, slender man with the sandy-blond hair who stood at Deirdre's side. Was he one of Deirdre's many suitors? Then her lips parted in surprise. "Why it's Lord Sutcliffe," she exclaimed, remembering the visiting English nobleman she had met in New Orleans last winter. "I thought he'd gone back to England months ago. . . ."

"Deirdre, whatever possessed you to do this thing?"

Megan tried to remain calm and controlled, but she had been badly shaken by Deirdre's revelation. And she was not the only one, for Clay, his face dark with anger, stood before the library fireplace, his eyes moving from her daughter to the Englishman seated on the leather sofa beside her: the man who was now her husband. Samantha and Reed were down here in the library, too. As members of the family, they had been asked by Clay to remain after the other guests had departed. Miss Amy was perched on the edge of a chair, moving restively, like a frightened squirrel. And Genevieve Vallière, who had accompanied the newlyweds to Azalea Hill, looked equally nervous.

There was no fear in Deirdre's face, although she was obviously under strong tension. Her mouth was set, her golden eyes blazing defiance. She did not have the air of warm contentment, of fulfillment, that should have sustained her as a happy bride even in the presence of her shocked and troubled parents.

"I ought to break you in two," Clay had told Allen as soon as the library doors were closed behind them. "Deirdre's a child, and you—you sneaking son of a—"

"Clay. No! You must not say such things. Deirdre is still our daughter, and this man is her husband. All the same—" She turned to her daughter. "Deirdre, how could you?"

"It wasn't difficult," Deirdre said. "The Winthrops are away visiting their kin up in New England. Genevieve and I had the house to ourselves except for the servants. And Miss Amy, of course."

"Oh, Clay—you must not blame me—" Miss Amy quavered, fumbling for her smelling salts. "I meant no harm— The child was so desperately in love, and Lord Sutcliffe— Surely you can find no fault with his family—"

"To hell with his family," Clay said, his voice tight with barely controlled fury. But Megan noticed that even as angry as he was, he did not blame Deirdre directly but turned his wrath on the man who had been her husband for the past two weeks. "This isn't England. I don't care if his great-grandfather was knighted as King George's royal panderer or—"

"Sir, I must insist—" Allen began.

"You'll insist on nothing while you're under my roof," Clay told him. Megan was aware of her husband's deep anger, for she knew that, under ordinary circumstances, he would never have spoken as he had in the presence of ladies. Samantha looked down, feigning an embarrassment she did not feel, while pert little Genevieve stared, round-eyed, at Deirdre's father. As for Miss Amy, she was close to tears.

Surprisingly, it was Reed who made the first effective attempt to bring the situation under control. He went to Clay's side. Putting a restraining hand on Clay's arm, he spoke quietly. "I understand your feelings," he said. "Deirdre is my niece. She is a Drummond. But I'm afraid we'll have to make the best of the situation now."

"Deirdre's a child— I'll have the marriage annulled."

"Oh, Clay, no! You must not even think of such a thing. Remember, Deirdre and Lord Sutcliffe have been living together as man and wife— It's possible that she— Oh, think of the scandal. Think of her future. If there should be a child—" Samantha said.

Clay looked startled, then sickened by the realization that his daughter might, indeed, be carrying Allen Sutcliffe's child.

"Samantha's right," Megan said. She did not have to add that if the marriage was annulled now, Deirdre would run the risk of bearing a bastard child. And even if Clay could arrange for a divorce, Deirdre would have to bear a terrible social stigma. Divorces were more common since the war, but even so, here in Natchez a divorced woman faced ostracism among respectable people.

Miss Amy, somewhat encouraged by the words of Reed and Samantha, stammered out the facts surrounding the marriage. The Winthrops had departed for New England, feeling secure enough in leaving Deirdre and Genevieve together in their home with Miss Amy acting as chaperone.

"Clay, please—try to understand—" Miss Amy pleaded, dabbing at her eyes with a small, lacy handkerchief. "This was no light infatuation. Deirdre has been deeply in love with Lord Sutcliffe since their first meeting—back last winter in New Orleans. It was Megan who tried to thwart them. She insisted on sending Deirdre off to school, and you were away in Colorado, and so I—I cooperated. But I never understood her reasons— She was quite unfeeling." There was a quaver in her voice now. "It was useless to separate them. True love is the most beautiful—the most sacred emotion—"

"That's right, Mr. Drummond," Genevieve ventured, torn between her fear of the formidable Clay Drummond and her desire to give moral support to her friend. "Deirdre and Allen were swept away utterly by their—their deep and sincere feelings."

"Be still, both of you," Clay thundered. "You, Miss Vallière, are a child— And you, Miss Amy— You should have had the good sense to— True love my—foot. Sutcliffe's not the first down-at-the-heels Englishman who has come over to this country to trade his title for the dowry of an American heiress. It takes money to keep up those estates over in England, and there are plenty of wealthy men who don't mind putting their daughters up for sale in exchange for a title. But I'm not one of them. And if you're looking for a fortune, Lord Sutcliffe, let me tell you—"

"Mr. Drummond I assure you, I—" Lord Sutcliffe began, but Clay cut him off.

"I don't want to hear your assurances," Clay said. "What do you do for a living? Have you ever earned an honest dollar? What's the condition of your estate over there in England? Mortgaged up to the hilt, I'll bet—"

Samantha said quickly, "Deirdre's always been headstrong, Clay. High-spirited and willful. Perhaps if you had been more strict with her— No matter, we must think of the future."

"What future?" Clay demanded, but Megan noticed that he now spoke somewhat more quietly. "If this—gentleman thinks that his marriage to Deirdre will give him a share in my railroads or any of my other holdings, he's mistaken. Unless," he added with a touch of irony, "he'd like to start as a clerk in one of my offices."

Allen Sutcliffe drew himself up with a quiet dignity that even Megan was forced to admire, however reluctantly. "I have no such intention, sir," he said. "My wife and I will be sailing for England next week on one of the Cunard Line steamers."

Chapter Twenty-five

THE STEAMER *Callista* cut through the icy waters of the Atlantic, while Deirdre, seated at a small writing table in the ladies' parlor, paused over her letter to Genevieve Vallière. The ship was to arrive in Southampton on the following morning, and it was high time, Deirdre decided, that she should take care of her social obligations to her friends and family back home.

> We had some rough weather—only to be expected this time of year, Allen says. Many of the ladies, and some of the gentlemen, too, suffered greatly from seasickness, but I am happy to say that except for a slight touch of that malady the first day out, I have been enjoying excellent health and a most unladylike appetite. The *Callista* is one of the newest vessels to make the Atlantic crossing. There is a music room, a splendid first-class dining saloon. And our cabin is most comfortable and tastefully decorated, with matching William Morris wallpaper and fabrics and a fine brass bed. . . .

Deirdre hesitated, then scratched out the last phrase. It was highly improper to write about beds in a letter to Genevieve, who was still an unmarried young lady. Then she threw down the pen and crumpled the sheet of notepaper. A moment later, she was tearing the paper to shreds and dropping it into the wastebasket. Her lips were pressed together in a tight line. For all the difference it had made in her life, she might as well be unmarried, too.

Of course, she had told no one, not even her mother, that during the two weeks she had been Allen's wife back in New Orleans, he had not made any attempt to consummate the marriage. She had not dared to let her parents know, for when Aunt Samantha had suggested that she might be pregnant, Deirdre had realized that it would be best to let her aunt and all the family believe that this was, indeed, a possibility; in that way, she could keep them from trying to have the marriage annulled.

It had worked, for her father had finally settled a handsome dowry on her, saying, "You'll be going to England in style, able to hold your head up with the best of them over there." He had arranged for Deirdre and Allen to go to New York in his private railway car, and there they had embarked for England. And Eula Carpenter, Opal's youngest daughter, had been hired as Deirdre's personal maid.

Once aboard the ship, Allen had made no attempt to make love to her, but instead had slept on the couch in their cabin, leaving her alone in the wide brass bed. He had been courteous, even solicitous, always quick to put her shawl about her shoulders if it was cool in the dining saloon, to stroll around the deck with her each morning, steadying her against the motion of the ship.

"This is not the season I would have chosen for taking a lady on such a voyage," he had said. "Most trying, I'm sure."

She had assured him that she felt fine, that she found the brisk ocean breezes bracing, but he had continued to treat her as if she were a delicate creature, to be pampered and cosseted. Deirdre, at eighteen, was strong, vital, and passionate, and the only strain she suffered was that of living in close quarters with her husband and remaining untouched by him.

She discovered that he had a passion for cards, and he made it a point to send her off to bed while he remained at the gaming table until the small hours. She found herself growing increasingly tense and frustrated. True, she knew little of the physical side of marriage, but she did know that other married women had survived the ordeal of the wedding night, had borne children, and appeared none the worse for it. Her own mother. . .

All at once, seated in the ladies' parlor on a ship moving toward the coast of England, Deirdre found that pictures were going through her mind, half-forgotten memories. Her parents, in the garden at Azalea Hill, where she had come upon them one evening. They had been standing beneath one of the live oak trees, locked in an embrace. Her mother's body was bent backward, pliant, responsive, her eyes closed, her lips parted. And other pictures came now. Her father's hand lingering on her mother's shoulder, his eyes resting on her with that special look.

It was different with Aunt Samantha and Uncle Reed, but everyone knew that Uncle Reed had been her aunt's second choice, that Aunt Samantha had wanted to marry Papa. But there had never been anyone else that Deirdre had loved. Was she in love with Allen? The question frightened and shocked her. Of course she loved him. And he must have loved her passionately to have eloped with her. Then why had he not yet made her his wife—really his wife?

Had there been someone else for him, perhaps? A girl back in Yorkshire? Had they been forced apart by an unfeeling father, a cruel guardian? Deirdre's ideas of love and marriage among the English nobility had been garnered from the novels of Ouida and Mrs. E. D. E. N. Southworth. But even if there had been someone else in Allen's life, he had married her, and she knew that she could make him forget any other girl he might ever have loved if only he would give her the chance.

For Deirdre had no doubt about her power over men. As soon as she had gone into long skirts and pinned up her hair, she had had a dozen beaus from the best families in and around Natchez. They had paid her extravagant compliments, had pleaded for a kiss, had crowded around her at dances. One, who fancied himself a poet, had written her verses, praising her golden eyes, her blue-black hair, her magnolia-white skin, her grace of movement.

And several times, she had locked the door of her bedroom and stripped off her nightdress to study the contours of her body. Her breasts were well developed, high, firm, and enticing; her waist was tiny, her hips softly curved, her legs long and shapely. But Allen had never seen her unclad body, not once.

She started slightly when she heard the soft chiming of the gong announcing luncheon. She rose from the writing table with a sigh and went out on deck. Other passengers were moving toward the first-class dining saloon, and she joined them.

Then she stopped, frozen, for she heard Allen's voice. He was speaking to someone, and his tone was warm, tender, a little teasing. Never had he spoken to her in that tone, and she stiffened with instinctive jealousy. A moment later, she turned and went to the railing, wanting to laugh at herself for her own foolish notions. For Allen was talking to a child, a dainty little girl, no more than eight, with masses of blonde ringlets.

"Mama's still down in our cabin—she's been seasick the whole voyage long—and I can't find Nanny—"

"I'll help you find her, my sweet," Allen said. He lifted the little girl in his arms, and she put one arm around his neck in a trusting gesture. "Look about now," Allen said. "Do you see her?"

"Oh, yes—over there—"

A moment later, the stout woman in her black silk dress and starched white apron had come bustling up. "Oh, Evelyn, dearie," she said, "I was that frightened." She reached out and took the little girl from Allen, then set her on her feet. "I'm so sorry, Lord Sutcliffe—Miss Evelyn's mother has been wretched with seasickness, and I was caring for her, and the child slipped past me—"

"I heard the gong," Evelyn said. "And I was hungry." She turned back to Allen and made a prim curtsy. "Thank you for helping me, sir."

"My pleasure," Allen said. His hand rested lightly, briefly, on the golden ringlets. "You'd best get her down to the dining saloon," he told the nurse. "She'll take cold in that thin muslin frock."

The woman hurried off with her charge, and only then did Allen become aware of Deirdre. He took her arm.

"What a lovely little thing she is," Deirdre said, looking after Evelyn.

Allen made no response, but all the same, Deirdre felt heartened, for she was sure now that Allen was fond of children. And he had spoken before their marriage of his desire for a family, particularly an heir to carry on the Sutcliffe name. But Deirdre had never regarded patience as a virtue, and she was determined to speed up the process even at the cost of forgetting her modesty and those virginal airs taught to her by Miss Amy.

It was nearly dawn when Allen finally came down to their cabin that night, for he had left Deirdre shortly after dinner to play cards with a group of other male passengers. Deirdre had not tried to keep him from his card game but had spent the time taking a long, leisurely bath in warm water scented with perfumed oil and in having Eula brush her dark hair until it gleamed with blue-black highlights. Eula had been pressed into service just before Deirdre and Allen had left Natchez. There was no question of traveling without a personal maid, as Megan had pointed out. Someone had to keep Deirdre's wardrobe in order, had to lace and unlace her corsets and fasten the endless tiny buttons that were a feature of every garment. Someone had to arrange the elaborate coiffures that were now in fashion and to take them down again at bedtime.

Eula had found the nightdress Deirdre had thought exactly right for tonight: a garment of pale-green silk—so thin and delicate that Deirdre's body was visible through the fabric and trimmed with delicate Brussels lace. Then Deirdre had dismissed the girl and had gotten into bed, but not to sleep.

Now, hours later, she made herself lie still in the shadowed cabin until she saw that Allen had stripped down to his trousers. Then, reaching over, she turned up the night light.

"Deirdre—I'm sorry I woke you. The game lasted longer than I'd expected. Go back to sleep, my dear."

But instead, Deirdre sat up and swung her legs over the side of the bed. Allen looked at her, his eyes remote.

Her body tensed. "I'm not at all sleepy."

"Are you feeling ill? Shall I have the steward bring a pot of tea? Or warm milk with honey, perhaps. That will soothe you—"

"I don't need soothing," she said, and, in spite of herself, her voice was sharp. The next words came unbidden. "Allen—

back in New Orleans you said—I thought— You do want children, don't you?"

He looked wary. Was it possible that he hesitated to make love to her out of a mistaken sense of chivalry, a fear of shocking or hurting her? Remembering certain whispered conversations she had overheard back in Charleston at Miss Pembroke's school, she said, "Oh, Allen, I'm not afraid, truly I'm not. I understand that the first time can be—difficult—but I—"

"Understand?" He looked down at her with a mixture of pity and contempt. "You understand nothing," he said softly. "Nothing at all."

"Then teach me," she whispered. "You're my husband—help me to understand—"

But when he approached the bed, she found herself drawing back before the cold, remote look in his gray eyes. Mechanically, he stripped off the rest of his clothing. She should have been stirred by his fine, lean body, the wide shoulders, the narrow hips and muscled flanks. Instead, she grew rigid, the desire draining from her. She put out a hand as if to hold him off, but he pushed it aside, and then he was beside her. She heard him saying softly, contemptuously, "This is what you wanted, isn't it?"

She felt his weight upon her. He pushed the nightdress up around her waist, and a moment later she felt the first hard thrust. He took her quickly, without the slightest trace of tenderness, without the least consideration for her complete lack of experience. Tears welled up in her eyes, and she turned her head away. There was no possibility of responding to this cold, driving invasion of her body, this outrage to her sensibilities. She could only lie still, listening to her husband's harsh breathing. Her nails cut into her palms, and she bit her lip to keep from crying out. Then she heard him groan, felt the shudder that shook him. A moment later, he lifted himself from her and moved to the far side of the bed. She turned away, burying her face in her pillow.

It was not possible. Could this be what it meant to be married? The charming gowns, the dancing lessons, the training in deportment—and all to end in this brutal, animal coupling? But maybe the fault had been hers; maybe her lack of modesty, her forward behavior, had repelled Allen, had angered him. She should have waited until he had been ready to claim her. She should have played the part of the shy, reluctant bride.

She forced back her tears. She would make things right between them. She had to, or what hope did she have of any sort of future happiness?

"I can't believe it," Megan told Clay as they stood on the veranda in front of their home, waiting for the carriage to take them to the train. "First Deirdre and now Terence."

"Terence isn't married yet," Clay reminded her. "And you may be sure, he'll wait until he gets his law degree, before the wedding. This is only the engagement party."

He put his arm around Megan and drew her close, his eyes warm with affection. "You don't have to be afraid of becoming a grandmother, my love. You'll be the most beautiful grandmother in Natchez—in the whole state—and people will refuse to believe you have grandchildren. 'That slip of a girl,' they'll say."

"Girl, indeed." Megan laughed. "And me forty-one, my last birthday—"

"And lovelier than ever," he said, helping her into the carriage. But once they were settled inside, Megan went back to her concern over her family. "I don't mind in the least if I have a dozen grandchildren," she told him. "But I want to be sure that my children are happy in their own marriages, as I am in mine."

"Deirdre's happy," Clay reassured her. "She's obviously delighted at playing lady of the manor over there in Yorkshire."

Deirdre's one letter, which they had received only a week ago, had been a long one, filled with detailed descriptions of Ellesdonfield, her husband's estate; of the great, turreted manor house, the grounds, the moors beyond; and of Lady Rosamond, her mother-in-law, an agreeable lady who had given a ball in her honor and was now making elaborate and expensive plans for enlarging and modernizing the stables. Lady Rosamond was also going to buy several fine new horses, having learned of Deirdre's fondness for riding out over the moors.

But Deirdre's letter, far from reassuring Megan, had left her with a nameless uneasiness. Why should Allen Sutcliffe, married two months, have departed for London immediately after the ball? He had gone on business, so Deirdre had written, but what sort of business, and why had he not taken his bride?

Megan tried to push away her misgivings, telling herself that although Allen might have been influenced by the Drummond fortune, he could not fail to care for Deirdre. What man could be unmoved by the girl's vivid beauty, her charm, her wit and vitality? At any rate, Megan told herself, it was Terence who was getting engaged now, and his future should be her most pressing concern at the moment.

"What do you suppose Elizabeth Hartley is like?" she asked Clay.

"I know no more than you do. She is Senator Hartley's daughter. The family is one of the oldest in Maryland." He smiled wryly. "Terence has always been practical. He's always set his goals far ahead and then worked to reach them. This girl plays some important part in his plans, you can bet on that. Good Lord, you don't think he's serious about going into politics? The senator would be of help to him there, no doubt—"

"Oh, Clay. You make the boy sound so—calculating."

"Practical, that's all," Clay said. "Terence has never in his life acted on impulse— He's not like—"

Clay broke off abruptly, then turned his face to the carriage window. Megan knew what he had been about to say, knew the grief he was feeling at this moment. Brant had been impulsive, hot-blooded, hard to handle. And Clay had, perhaps, loved him all the more because of those qualities.

She reached out and took Clay's hand, pressing it to her cheek. For a moment, he sat unmoving. She brushed his hand with her lips, and then he caught her to him, his arms holding her tightly. "Megan—my love—you're all any man could ask for—"

The carriage turned into the depot, and they moved apart, but Clay did not get out even after the coachman had brought the horses to a halt. He was no longer thinking of Brant. He was remembering what Richard Whitaker had said that night back in December about the resemblance between himself and his nephew, Luke, remembering Samantha's startled look, her swift explanation that Luke was the image of his grandfather, Vance Drummond. But Clay, who had not forgotten that night so many years ago in the summerhouse at Montrose, knew that it was possible that there was another explanation for the resemblance between himself and Samantha's son.

Clay rose hastily, swung down from the carriage, and helped Megan down. He would not think about that possibility, he told himself. It would be madness to search for an answer that, if he found it, might threaten Megan's happiness and his own. She had, he suspected, guessed the truth about his attraction to Kirsten. But he had never slept with Kirsten, and perhaps she had guessed that, too.

Samantha was different, for she had been a part of his life long before he had met Megan. The fortunes of the two branches of the Drummond family were closely intertwined and always would be. Too many people could be hurt if he found the answer to the riddle of Luke's paternity: Megan, Reed, and Luke. And he, himself, could lose all that was important to him. It was better not to question when the answers could tear the family apart.

In June 1889, as Reed was preparing for a trip to New Orleans to attend a meeting for the organization of the United Confederate Veterans, he was surprised by Samantha's wish to go along. "I'm delighted, of course," he told her, and he meant it. "But it'll be hot down there— You've always said that you couldn't stand the heat."

"It will be no hotter than Natchez," she said, but she gave him a flirtatious little smile, so that her words sounded teasing rather than petulant. "Don't you want me to go with you? Perhaps you gentlemen plan to do more than form an organization that will unite all the smaller Confederate veterans' societies. Those Creole belles down there . . ."

"Don't be foolish," he said, putting his arm around her waist. "It's only that much of my time will be taken up with attending meetings. What will you find to do?"

She laughed lightly. "Violet Shepley says she'd heard of a new millinery shop on Royal Street. The lady who runs it has just come over from France, and she has all the newest Paris fashions. I would so like one of those Directoire hats of straw to go with my rose-colored silk. Ostrich plumes over the front and perhaps a small bow inside the brim . . ."

Reed held up a hand, but he was laughing, too. "Spare me,

my sweet," he said. "Come along, and you shall have your bonnet—two bonnets if you wish."

He thought how long it had been since they had laughed together, how long since she had flirted with him and teased him, since she had expressed a desire to go anywhere with him.

"I don't wish to be extravagant," she said demurely. "You want to buy new cattle for Montrose, to put all those extra acres under cultivation."

His arm tightened around her waist. "True enough," he said. "But—" He smiled down at her. "I hardly think a couple of new bonnets will prove an obstacle to my plans for Montrose. And when a woman is as beautiful as you are, she has a right to pretty frippery." He was beginning to feel a kind of anticipation he had not experienced in years. "And I won't be spending all my time at the convention," he went on. "We'll be able to go on drives around the city. We'll go to a few of the restaurants and perhaps the theater."

Samantha looked away, veiling her eyes quickly with her long lashes. "I don't want you to take time from the meetings," she said. "I know how important they are to you. And they should be. You have every right to be proud to be among the founders of this new organization."

"I've always been proud of the service I was able to give to the South. Sometimes I feel—" He had been about to say that he had often felt that the cavalry charge at the Tallahatchie River, where he had been cited for gallantry in saving the life of his commanding officer, had been the high point of his life. But he realized that Samantha might take this the wrong way, and so he stopped himself in time. He could not help remembering, though, the brief flash of fear, then the wave of reckless excitement, the sense of being a part of something so important that fear had no meaning. The glint of the sunlight on his sword and the surging force of the horse under him. He had been twenty, and he had felt a sense of his own power. Nothing could defeat him. He was invincible. . . .

"Do you think that the governor of Georgia will be elected to lead this new organization?"

Samantha's question startled him, bringing him back to the present. "John Gordon's a fine man," he told her. "He commanded an infantry division at Gettysburg, and at Appomattox he made the last charge—he was wounded eight times, and he—"

Samantha listened with feigned attention as Reed went on praising Gordon's achievements. "I'll give him my vote," Reed finished.

"Indeed, you should," she agreed, but her thoughts were racing along on an entirely different course. She would have to make arrangements quickly. Madame Perrault's millinery shop. Of course. If all that Violet had whispered to her about the place was true, it would be perfect. What luck! What fabulous luck that the convention was to be held in New Orleans this month.

By midafternoon, the sunlight was glaring down over the city so that the shops along Royal Street cast purple shadows and the delicate ironwork of the balconies shimmered before Samantha's eyes. The heat from the banquette burned through the thin soles of her slippers, but she was indifferent to the discomfort. She looked about her, then darted into Madame Perrault's shop. But she smiled at her own caution, for even if she were seen by anyone who knew her, it was all quite respectable. Madame Perrault did an excellent business with her millinery. Her other service was less well known.

A few moments later, madame was leading Samantha to one of the small booths at the rear, then through a doorway and up a flight of steps.

"Samantha." Richard Whitaker caught her in his arms and covered her mouth with his. This was their third meeting since the night of the ball at Azalea Hill. Twice she had met him, as if by chance, in a tearoom in Natchez, but she had refused to meet him there a third time. Too many people knew her, and she dreaded the possibility of a scandal. Now, in this secluded room, with the drapes drawn against the heat, she knew that there could be no turning back. And yet she hesitated, putting the palms of her gloved hands against his chest.

"Samantha," he said softly. "Don't pull away from me, darling. Ever since that first time we danced together, you knew it would come to this, didn't you?"

She did not answer him in words but with her lips, her

tongue, her whole body arching up. He stripped off his clothes, then helped her with the buttons and fastenings of her own. And when, at last, they were locked together on the wide, deep velvet couch, she needed no arousal; her hands moved over the hard muscles of his powerful shoulders.

He was not gentle with her. She did not want him to be.

It was twilight when she stood before the mirror, her body relaxed, deliciously tired. She put on her hat, tilting it carefully over her forehead.

Richard came up behind her and put his big hands around her waist. Then his fingers moved upward, to cup her breasts, and she felt the first stirrings of renewed desire. But she said firmly, "No, we mustn't. I have to leave."

"When will I see you again?"

"I don't know—I'm not sure—"

He turned her around to face him. "Samantha, I want more than this. A few hours. I want to fall asleep beside you and have you wake up in my arms."

"Don't you suppose I want that, too? But it can't be that way, not for us."

"There must be a way." She was startled by the harsh urgency in his voice. This was a man who was used to getting what he wanted, whatever the cost, a shrewd, tough-minded man who would not be frustrated in business dealings or in his personal life, either.

"That night at the ball, you told me you like to go to Saratoga for the summer. The season up there will begin in a few weeks. Join me and we'll spend the summer together."

"I haven't been there for two summers now," she said. "My husband is putting every extra dollar into Montrose. He has plans—"

"The devil with his plans. Come to Saratoga. I'll reserve a private cottage, the finest they have. Two cottages if you want to keep up appearances. At the Grand Union Hotel—"

"And how will I explain to my husband where the money is coming from?" Her lips curved in a mocking little smile. "Shall I say, 'Reed, dear, Mr. Whitaker has offered to—'"

His big heavy hands gripped her upper arms. "Don't tease me," he said, his eyes holding hers. "Not now. Not ever.

Samantha, I have more money than any man can spend in a lifetime. I want you to share it—I want you to be a part of my life."

"But I'm married. You knew that when you met me."

"You could get a divorce."

She shrank from the thought. True, in this year of 1889, divorce was no longer unheard of even among ladies from good families. But there was still an aura of scandal, of shame, and there were those houses in which a divorced woman would not be received.

But Richard Whitaker had a great deal to offer her. He was a virile, exciting lover, and he was wealthy enough to keep her in luxury for the rest of her life. She thought of yearly trips to Europe, of a house in New York, on Fifth Avenue, perhaps, and a summer place in Saratoga, or perhaps Newport.

She would have to move slowly, carefully, however, for although Richard Whitaker desired her, she had no illusions about him. He was no impulsive, love-smitten schoolboy, but a man who had been married before, who had known many women. He was not about to propose marriage after a few hours' pleasure, and she was not prepared to divorce Reed to become any man's mistress.

For one brief moment, she felt a welling sadness. Oh, if only it had not been for the war, that senseless, terrible war. The war had taken Clay from her, had driven her to marry his brother. Her eyes filled with tears. If she could have married Clay, the only man she had ever really loved... She ached with the sense of something she had never known, never would know. Tears stung her eyelids.

Richard Whitaker looked down at her. "Oh, my dear, don't cry. We'll find a way to be together this summer, surely."

He thought her tears were for him. His arms went around her, and now he was holding her gently against him. He tried to stroke her hair but only succeeded in knocking her hat to one side. His vanity, his assumption that she was crying at the prospect of not seeing him again, irritated her, but only for a moment.

It was useless to brood over the past. The years moved swiftly, and she had to make the most of them, to take what she could get. And Richard Whitaker was no small prize. But she would have to have a firm promise of marriage before she would consider divorcing Reed. And to win such a promise, she would need time.

"Say you will come to Saratoga," he was urging.

"I'll come," she told him. She did not know how she could arrange it, but she would manage somehow.

She felt his arms tighten, felt his breath, warm on her cheek. "We'll have the whole summer together, just the two of us," he said.

Chapter Twenty-six

DEIRDRE HAD left Yorkshire at dawn, had taken the train to Leeds, and had changed there for the London train. During the journey, she was tense, uneasy about the reception she might get when she arrived at the Sutcliffes' townhouse in Mayfair. Perhaps she should have taken her mother-in-law's advice and waited patiently for another visit from Allen, but patience had never been Deirdre's strong point.

"Allen spent less than two weeks with me here," she had reminded Lady Rosamond. "Then he was off to London on business. What sort of business?"

"Really, my dear, I'm sure that on his next visit, he will explain. In the meantime, you must learn to think of the Grange as your home."

But Deirdre knew that she would never come to think of this great crumbling gray stone house as her home. It was so alien after the years in Natchez; the Yorkshire landscape was bleak, the winds, even now in early spring, damp and raw. But she could have accepted these alien surroundings if Allen had remained here with her. Instead, he had stayed only long enough so that his mother might give a ball to introduce her to the neighboring gentry. Then he had left for London.

He had returned for a few days last month, and even now, Deirdre shivered, thinking of that brief interlude, of the way that Allen had come to her bed, to take her with the same cold, impersonal violence that had marked the consummation of her marriage that night on the *Callista*. Again, he had left her feeling used, unsatisfied, bewildered.

That part of their marriage had been a failure so far, and perhaps it always would be. All the same, she would not give up, not so soon. And she certainly would not return home to Natchez to admit that she had made a mistake. She had her father's pride, her mother's stubborn determination. She would make Allen fall in love with her. She would take her rightful place with him in London, where she would become a part of the world she had dreamed of back at Azalea Hill.

Thank heaven she was not pregnant yet. There would be plenty of time for that, but in the meantime, she would become part of London society; she would give wonderful parties and be invited to others. She would be presented at Court. . . .

One day, in some vague, distant future, she would naturally have a child, the son she knew that Allen wanted, to inherit the title, to carry on the Sutcliffe line. Perhaps two sons. Handsome, cherubic little boys who would be given over to the care of a nanny and a nursery maid. But now she wanted to enjoy herself, to go to the theater, to dance, to entertain in her own London home.

The train had begun to slacken its speed, and then it roared into Euston Station. Eula, who had accompanied her on the trip, gathered up a few of the smaller pieces of luggage: a hat box, her jewel case. She got off the train, feeling overwhelmed for a moment, lost in the huge station with its high, vaulted Doric arches, its hurrying crowds.

But she had little difficulty in finding a porter and then a cab. She gave the cabby the address of the Sutcliffes' townhouse.

It was early evening, and her spirits began to rise again when she peered out the window at the crowds: the beautifully dressed ladies in their carriages, the glittering windows of the shops. Everything would be different now, she told herself.

When she and Allen were living together, really living together day after day, she would find out how to please him. Surely she must have failed him in some way through her lack of experience.

Perhaps, if she had not eloped, her mother would have had a talk with her before the wedding, would have told her all she should know about pleasing a husband. As it was, she had come back from New Orleans to Azalea Hill with Allen, already a wife, married two weeks, and she had allowed her mother to believe that any such advice would have been unnecessary.

Now, as the cab moved through the blue spring twilight, she found herself wondering, as she had so many times since her marriage, if she loved Allen, really loved him. Or had she been dazzled by his title, his background, his manners? Even so, she found him attractive as a man, handsome in a lean, fine-boned way, with the hard muscles of a man who was accustomed to riding and hunting. She felt a stirring of excitement, thinking of his body. If only he would be patient with her, would show her affection, tenderness, she would be everything he wanted in a wife.

The cab had left the crowded streets near the station, and now they were moving along quiet, clean streets, past squares lined with tall, narrow houses. Eula, staring out of the cab window, her brown eyes round with excitement, said, "Never did think to see London, Miss Deirdre. It's a fine place, isn't it?"

"Yes, indeed," Deirdre agreed, "and you'll be seeing far more of it once we're settled. We'll go shopping in Regent Street and Bond Street. I want to see everything— The Tower and Buckingham Palace and— Oh, just everything. And when I'm presented at Court—" Deirdre felt a shiver of excitement at the thought. "Imagine, Eula— I'll wear a gown with a long train and the Sutcliffe diamonds and—"

"Why shouldn't you, Miss Deirdre? And you'll be the prettiest lady there, and I'll help you get dressed up so fine—"

It was a comfort having Eula here, Deirdre thought; it helped to steady her, to give her confidence. All the same, she felt a slight stirring of uneasiness when the cab drew up at last before the four-story townhouse.

Allen wasn't expecting her, for each time she had asked him in one of her letters to allow her to join him, he had replied with a short, formal note that had given her no answer to her request.

Maybe he had a mistress here in London. The thought was disturbing, but she told herself that she was Allen's wife. The mistress, if there was one, would have to be gotten out of the picture; how, she was not sure, but such problems were not unheard of.

And besides, she thought, alighting from the cab, she had no knowledge that any such woman existed at all.

Deirdre and Eula were admitted to the house by a startled butler. "I am Lady Sutcliffe," Deirdre said. "Kindly have my luggage brought inside."

"Oh, my lady—we were not expecting—his lordship said nothing to me—he is not at home—"

Deirdre ignored the man's confusion. "Come along, Eula," she said as she entered the hall. Gloomy and old-fashioned, she thought, glancing about quickly, but there would be time to change all that. She would replace the hangings of faded-red Genoa velvet with others. And those suits of armor and the huge carved oak settle would have to go. She would enjoy shopping for new fabrics, new furniture. Money was not a problem, for her dowry would take care of any expenses she might incur.

"My lady—I was not informed of your coming."

This time it was Allen's valet, Simkins, who was plainly thrown off balance by her unexpected arrival; he had come out of one of the rooms off the shadowed hallway, and he stood staring at her with barely concealed disapproval. She had never liked the man. Although he was outwardly polite, she had always sensed a kind of sly, knowing look in his eyes when he addressed her.

"Please have the housekeeper prepare a room for me," she said.

"There is no housekeeper, my lady. Only the parlor maid, Bessie—"

"Then have her get the room ready," Deirdre said. "My maid and I have been traveling since early morning. We'll want dinner. I assume there is a cook." Deirdre's voice had an edge to it now. Yes, there was something about Simkins that irritated her.

"Naturally, we have a cook, but since the master dines at

home so rarely, I'm afraid Mrs. Appleby is not prepared to serve a suitable dinner."

Deirdre glanced at the gold chatelaine watch she wore on a chain about her neck. "It is nearly six o'clock. I will expect dinner to be served by eight. The meal need not be elaborate. I will also require a room for my maid adjoining my own." Deirdre spoke with a calm authority.

Two hours later, she sat down to dinner in the large, high-ceilinged dining room, a somewhat depressing setting, with its dark crimson wallpaper and its massive black walnut furniture. The meal was not particularly appetizing, either, she thought, but she was hungry, and she ate the cold roast lamb, asparagus, and biscuits, making a mental note to have a talk with Allen's cook tomorrow. Before she could become a successful London hostess, many changes would have to be made here.

She would decorate the drawing room in pale green, or perhaps amber, with silk drapes and delicate rosewood furniture. There she would entertain the wives of Allen's friends over tea. And she would give a ball, a splendid ball, and perhaps the Prince of Wales might come. . . .

Neither Simkins nor the butler were able to tell her when Allen might return, and Deirdre, too restless to go to bed, went instead into the library.

"Begging your pardon, my lady," the butler said, "but there's no telling when his lordship will return. And since you've had a long journey—"

"You may retire as soon as you like," Deirdre interrupted crisply. "I won't be needing anything more this evening."

But when she was alone in the library, she felt the beginning of weariness. It had been a long journey down from Yorkshire, and perhaps she should have sought her room, but she was determined to wait up for Allen. She would have to make him understand why she had disregarded his wishes and had come to join him here in London.

She took down one book, then another, from the shelves that went from floor to ceiling on three sides of the library, but she found herself unable to concentrate. At last, she found a volume of the poetry of Alfred Lord Tennyson. She settled herself in a deep, brown-velvet armchair. But she found it difficult to concentrate, for from time to time, she heard carriage wheels and the clopping of hoofs in the square outside. Each time, the carriage moved on.

By midnight, her eyelids were beginning to close, and she let the heavy book slip from her hands as she fell into a restless, uneasy half sleep. She did not know how much time had passed when she was jerked back to consciousness by the sound of voices and a man's footsteps in the hall. She got to her feet and moved to the library door, but she had only opened it a little way when her hand froze on the knob.

"That's five shillings, please, sir—and I got to have it first— Aunt Annie—she always tells us to—"

The voice was cockney, high-pitched, thin, and frightened. Not a woman's voice. Deirdre felt her insides tighten. A child's voice.

"You'll have your five shillings, and five more afterward— if you do exactly as I say," Allen said softly. His tone was gentle, soothing.

"Five more?" The child's voice faltered. "Wot do I 'ave to do for that?"

"Do you want the money or not?"

"Yes, sir—but I— Ye ain't goin' to—to 'urt me real bad, are ye?"

The little girl—she could have been no more than eight or nine, a small, thin, shabby creature, grimy and barefooted— looked up at Allen, her dark-blue eyes wide with fear. Even in the faint light of the hall, Deirdre could see that the child was a beauty, with blonde ringlets and small, dainty features.

"Come along," Allen urged. "In here." He opened the door to the parlor opposite the library. But the child held back, her bare, muddy feet planted firmly on the black and white tile floor of the hall.

"Be a good girl now," Allen said, his voice coaxing, but there was no mistaking the growing urgency in his manner. "We don't have all night, my little love—"

"Allen!"

He turned as Deirdre came out into the hall. The child shrank back against the wall.

"What the devil are you—" Allen began, glaring at Deirdre, but sickened though she was, she stood her ground.

The little girl seemed to understand, with gutter shrewdness, that the situation had somehow changed. She stared up at Deirdre, then glanced quickly toward the front door.

"Get out," Allen told the child harshly. "Go at once."

Torn between fear and necessity, she shook her head. "Please, sir—I want my money first— Aunt Annie won't let me in unless I bring money—"

Allen thrust a handful of coins into the child's outstretched palm. She put the edge of one of the coins into her mouth, bit it, nodded with obvious relief. Then, like a small hunted animal, she turned and fled, leaving the front door half open behind her.

"Deirdre, listen. I know how you must feel, but if you could try to understand—"

Deirdre shook her head. She longed to flee out into the fog, as the child had fled, but she could not move, could not think clearly.

"I never wanted you to know," Allen said, his face grayish. "If you'd obeyed me, if you'd stayed in Yorkshire, as I wanted you to, you—"

"I'd never have found out that I was married to a—a—" She did not even know the word for her husband's aberration. "You are vile, evil—"

"Don't say anything you'll be sorry for," he warned, having recovered himself. "What do you know of men and their—their needs? London is full of houses where children like that one are trained from the time they can speak to please men. They are better off than those who work in the factories, the mines—"

"If you think you can—can justify yourself—"

"There's no need. You are my wife. You will learn to accept me as I am. Don't look so horrified. Once you've given me a son to carry on the Sutcliffe line, I won't trouble you again."

She did not wait to hear any more but turned and moved to the stairs. The floor felt unsteady under her feet, and waves of sickness swept through her. Eula, who had been asleep in the small dressing room that adjoined Deirdre's room, was awake now and at Deirdre's side. Deirdre clung to her and allowed herself to be helped to the bed.

"Lock the door," she whispered.

Eula obeyed swiftly, then came back to Deirdre. "Let me help you into bed, Miss Deirdre— Let me—"

"No— It's almost morning. As soon as it is light, we're leaving here."

"We going back to the Grange?"

Deirdre shook her head, and Eula had to lean close to hear her words. "We—we're going home. . . ."

"Thank God for Eula," Megan told Clay on the morning after Deirdre's return to Azalea Hill. "I dread to think how Deirdre would have survived the trip home without her."

Clay and Megan were together in Megan's boudoir, the July sun streaming through the tall windows. Clay stared out at the garden, then turned to face his wife. "But what's wrong with Deirdre? She's so changed. What did Sutcliffe do to her?"

"I— Clay—"

"She's told you, hasn't she?"

Megan nodded. "Yes, she has, but—"

Clay took Megan's arm and drew her down on the small wicker sofa near the window. "She's my daughter, too," he said. "I have a right to know, don't I?"

"Of course, but—

"Then tell me."

Megan could not resist her husband's demand, and she told him in a few brief painful sentences, trying to present the facts as temperately as possible; but even so, Clay's face grew hard with anger. "He dared—I'll make him sorry he ever came near Deirdre. I have business connections in England. I'll see to it that Lord Allen Sutcliffe is ruined."

"Oh, no! Deirdre's suffered enough. If she is to have a decent future, the matter must be handled quietly and with discretion. A divorce, yes, but with as little scandal as possible."

"Damn it, Megan, when I think of that—that— One thing I have to know. Did they ever, he and Deirdre—is she carrying his child?"

Megan shook her head. "He—the marriage was consummated, but Deirdre's not pregnant."

"I suppose we should be thankful for that," Clay said, and Megan could see that he was trying to control his anger, to look ahead. "I'll send one of my lawyers to London—he'll do what has to be done."

"But what grounds can there be if the real ones are kept secret?"

"A clever lawyer can always find the right grounds if the fee's high enough," Clay said. "And Sutcliffe had better do as he's told if he wants to hold on to even a small part of Deirdre's dowry. Leave all that to me." He looked at Megan, his eyes troubled. "You'll have to help Deirdre to get over the shock of this filthy business."

Although Megan was comforted by Clay's unquestioning confidence in her ability to help Deirdre, she was uncertain as to how she should go about it, and as the days passed, she became more disturbed by her daughter's behavior. Deirdre was in a kind of numb daze. She refused to leave her room, and Eula waited on her, carrying trays upstairs and bringing them back to the kitchen, barely touched. She brushed Deirdre's long, blue-black hair and helped her to dress. But although she was neat and clean, thanks to Eula's ministrations, she looked dreadful, her skin stretched tightly across the bones of her face, her amber eyes remote, shadowed.

A fear began to grow within Megan's mind, for she could not reach her daughter, and Clay could not bring himself to discuss Deirdre's experiences with the girl.

"She don't hardly get no sleep at all, Miz Drummond," Eula told Megan. "And in the daytime, she makes me keep the drapes drawn in her room."

Megan tried, gently, to coax Deirdre into joining her on small shopping trips into town, but the girl refused; she would not even go walking in the garden. When Megan suggested a visit to Lianne's house, Deirdre shook her head, then turned her face away.

Megan went alone, and after dinner, she drew Mark aside to ask his advice; his reputation was firmly established, and he had as many patients as he could care for. Megan forced herself to confide in him, telling herself that, as a doctor, he must be familiar with all sorts of aberrations, that Allen's sickness, as she thought of it, could not be unknown to him. "I'm afraid for Deirdre," she said after describing her daughter's brief marriage. "It's as if she blames herself for what happened. But Allen Sutcliffe was—what he was—long before they met. Oh, Mark, what can we do to help her?"

"I'm not sure," Mark said slowly. "There was a case of a girl—she lived a short distance from here. She—her mother was an invalid, and the girl was—violated by her own father. He killed himself, and the girl—"

"What happened to the girl?"

"She's kept to her house. She sees no one except the servants. She has not left that house for—it must be ten years now. Her mother is dead now, too, and I hate to think of what would happen to her if the servants were to desert the place. There are institutions for such cases, of course— Perhaps, if it becomes necessary, Deirdre—"

"Oh, Mark, no! I don't want to hear about such places. You know so much. Surely you can help Deirdre."

"I can give her a tonic for her appetite, a sedative to help her to sleep, but that's not the answer. Megan, you must see to it that Deirdre starts going out again, seeing people. There'll be gossip, no doubt, and some questions asked. But if she can get through the first few months, it will pass. She is a Drummond, after all. She has you and Clay to stand by her, and as for Lianne and myself, I don't need to tell you there's nothing we won't do to make it easier."

"It's so kind of you, Mark, but I don't see how—"

"Look here," he said, "why shouldn't she come to Montrose for dinner, to meet Abigail and Major Taggart—or shall we call him Mr. Taggart now?"

Megan looked at her brother-in-law in complete bewilderment. "Abigail and her husband? But what—when—"

"Reed hasn't told you yet? His mother and Preston Taggart will be passing through Natchez in a couple of weeks. He has some sort of business connections in New Orleans—coffee importing, I believe it is, and Reed's mother insisted on coming along so that she might visit Reed. He's her son, after all, and Clay and Lianne are her stepchildren—"

"Reed was never on good terms with the major," Megan said.

"The war's been over a long time," Mark reminded her. "At any rate, there's to be a small family dinner, and Samantha has told Lianne that you and Clay will naturally be invited, and Deirdre, too."

"I don't think she will be willing to go to Montrose—"

"Megan, you must get her to go out of the house, and soon.

I don't care what means of persuasion you use, but you must convince her to start leading a normal life again. And a small family gathering will offer the perfect opportunity."

"Deirdre, you haven't even begun to dress, and we must leave in an hour."

It was mid morning two weeks after Megan's visit to Lianne and Mark, and she had come up to Deirdre's bedroom to find the girl stretched on her bed in a clean but crumpled wrapper, her hair loose around her face. At Megan's words, she turned her face away. "I've already told you—I'm not coming to Montrose. Please, mother, leave me alone."

She spoke in a flat, dull voice, and Megan felt a growing sense of desperation. All her tenderness, her gentle coaxing, had accomplished nothing. She closed her eyes for a moment and tried to draw on all her resources, her garnered wisdom.

Then her eyes narrowed, and she put her hands on her hips in a gesture she had not used since her first days as a housemaid back in Ireland. "Oh, can't you?" she demanded. "Stay here, then, locked away, and know that it's shame you're bringing on your own family."

"I shamed us all when I married Allen. From the first night I went to his bed— I'm sick, unclean. Allen—"

"To hell with Allen! He's back in England, but you're here. And it's what you're doing now that's a disgrace to the Drummond name. It'll be your name again once the divorce is settled. And you'll be the first Drummond to bring dishonor to that name."

Deirdre raised herself, her eyes startled. But at least Megan had her full attention now. "Oh, I'm not saying they were all saints. But none of them let themselves be broken. No, not even your uncle, Reed. We thought for a while that the war had broken him, but now, with Montrose making money again, he's got his pride back. And your father—"

"I know Papa's a fighter. Luke told me about how brave he was in the war. How he had his horse shot from under him and went on fighting until he and a handful of his men were captured—"

"It's not that I'm thinking of," Megan said. "The Drummonds have always been fighting men since the Battle of Culloden back in Scotland— It's what he did afterward."

"I guess he never told Luke about that. I know that Luke never told me."

"Your father spoke to me about it, though—the prison camp on Johnson's Island." Megan sat down on the side of the bed, and drawing on half-forgotten memories, she told Deirdre of Clay's terrible experiences in the Yankee prison camp. "Plenty of men there on Johnson's Island lost their courage. They gave up, and they died. But your father wouldn't let himself be broken. When his men were mistreated, he complained to the commandant and made a bitter enemy of one of those Yankee guards. Twice your father tried to escape and twice he was brought back and beaten and put into solitary confinement—"

"No!" Deirdre cried out in protest at what she was hearing, and for a moment, Megan hesitated, fearing that perhaps she had gone too far, had shocked her daughter too deeply. But at least she was listening and feeling pity for someone besides herself.

"He managed to escape from the island at last by hiding in a boat under a load of dead prisoners who were being taken ashore for burial. He'd been shot himself and tossed aboard the boat for dead. But he got away with the bullet still in him. . . ." Megan did not realize that her voice was shaking, that her eyes had filled with tears, until Deirdre reached out and touched her hand.

"Mother—please don't—don't think of it. I know how much you love him—how much you've always loved him."

"I want to think about it, to remember it. I'm proud of him. I want to be proud of you, too. But how can I? How can your father, when you're hiding yourself in here. You were headstrong and foolish, and you made a mistake. A bad mistake, I won't deny that. But you're leaving your father and me to face the gossip, the questions. You've let yourself be broken—"

"No! That's not true!"

"Then prove it. Stand up, Deirdre. That's right. Up on your feet. Now."

Deirdre obeyed, one hand resting on the bedpost. She was shaky, she had lost weight, and it was a cruel demand that Megan was making on her, but it had to be done.

"Eula will lay out your clothes." Megan went to the closet

and opened it, her eyes moving quickly over Deirdre's costly wardrobe. "Here, this should be suitable." Megan took out a dress of mauve silk with a close-fitting, lace-trimmed bodice and a small bustle.

"Wear this," she said, tossing the gown over a chair. "And be ready within an hour."

Chapter Twenty-seven

IN THE dining room at Montrose, when the family was seated for dinner, Megan looked anxiously across the table at Deirdre, who had taken her place between Mark and Lianne. Deirdre was composed but shockingly pale, with dark smudges under her eyes. The mauve gown, which had been so becoming when Opal had made it only a year ago, now was slightly loose across Deirdre's breasts, and above the low-cut neckline, her collarbones stood out sharply. But it was plain to Megan that her daughter was doing her best to present a calm appearance to the others, that she was even making an effort to finish her soup, the thick turtle soup laced with wine that was one of Rachel's specialties.

Abigail and Preston Taggart—he still relished the title of major—were cordial to Deirdre. Megan, however, suspected that Samantha had managed to tell them both about Deirdre's impending divorce. Thank heavens that Samantha knew none of the details preceding Deirdre's departure from England. And she never would, thought Megan, forcing herself to look away from Deirdre, to let her gaze rest on Abigail instead.

Although more than twenty years had passed since the last time that Megan had seen Clay's stepmother, and although Abigail had grown stouter, she was still an impressive-looking woman, handsomely dressed in a gown of plum-colored corded silk trimmed with broad bands of purple velvet; her diamond and amethyst brooch was expensive, as befitted the wife of a highly successful Boston businessman.

Preston Taggart had put on weight, too, but his face was alert, his gestures forceful, as he leaned across the table to tell Clay about the project that had caused him to take this trip away from his native Boston. "When Abigail and I leave here, we're going to New Orleans, where my company has a branch. We import coffee from Central America. Abigail will spend more time with friends at Lake Pontchartrain while I go on to Guatemala, alone."

"That's sensible," Clay said. "From what I've heard, the climate in Guatemala is far from healthy, and the accommodations are—"

"They're not fit for a lady," Taggart said. "Nothing but swamps that begin at the Caribbean and extend inland for many miles. I'll have to cross the swamps and go on up into the mountains. I've been buying coffee from many of the planters up there, you see, and now I'm thinking of buying up several of those plantations myself. More profitable that way. The problem is the transportation down there."

Rachel, with the assistance of a housemaid, was taking away the soup plates and serving the next course, but although Clay's plate was soon filled with slices of succulent pink ham, rice, beans, and okra, he showed no interest in the food; instead, he was listening intently.

"There are dozens of plantations far from any railroad," Taggart was saying. "The coffee has to be carried by donkey cart to the nearest line. A slow, costly business, but what can you expect? Those Latins are an ignorant lot, backward—don't know a thing about machinery and don't want to learn. And their government! Kick out one tin-pot dictator and put in another, and none of them worth the powder to blow them to hell—excuse me, ladies. What's needed down there is a first-class railway system."

Clay smiled slightly. So Taggart's visit to Montrose was not entirely a social one. "You ought to think about getting in there with a railroad, Clay," Taggart went on. "You'd have a chance to get in on the banana trade, too."

Megan's heart sank as she saw the familiar glow in her husband's eyes: excitement, ambition, the need to expand his holdings. She tried to catch the details, but she could only hear a word here and there, for Samantha and Abigail were chatting about the summer fashions, the latest sensational novels, and other topics suitable for ladies. Megan heard Taggart speaking of places with unfamiliar names: Puerto Barrios, Guatemala City, San José, Champerico, and Ocos. She thought of dangerous swamps, malaria, yellow fever.

"I beg your pardon, Samantha," Megan said reluctantly. "I'm afraid I did not hear—"

"I was only asking if you'd read Marie Corelli's new novel, *Thelma*. It's even more exciting than *A Romance of Two Worlds*. At least I think so."

"I haven't read either of them," Megan admitted.

"Oh, haven't you? But then, I suppose, with all that's been happening at Azalea Hill, you have had little interest in— Yes, I quite understand. But, Deirdre, when you were in England, did you, perhaps, have the chance to meet Miss Corelli?"

"I spent most of my time up in Yorkshire," Deirdre said, her voice tense.

"Did you, indeed. I should have thought that London would have proved more exciting."

"I did a good deal of riding—out on the moors—"

"Deirdre's always been fond of riding; you know that," Lianne intervened smoothly. "And she is an excellent horse-woman." Megan shot Lianne a grateful look. Damn Samantha for trying to pry, to discover what had gone wrong between Deirdre and Allen.

"I hope you will take up riding again now you're home," Mark said. "Outdoor exercise is as beneficial for young women as for men, and riding is most invigorating." He gave Deirdre a warm smile. "In fact, I am prescribing a brisk canter every morning." Mark turned to Reed. "I understand you have some excellent new horses in your stables."

"We do, thanks to Michael O'Donnell. That young man has an eye for good horse flesh. I sent him up to Kentucky and Virginia a few months ago, and he brought back several fine animals. You must try one, Deirdre, since you and your parents will be staying the night—I'll have a horse saddled and waiting for you first thing tomorrow. You don't want to ride in the heat of noonday."

"I haven't brought a habit, Uncle Reed."

"My dear child," Lianne said, "there must be half a dozen riding habits packed away up in the attic."

"And I'll send word to Michael to have one of the stable hands bring the horse up here." Reed's gray eyes were compassionate as they rested on Deirdre, for there was no doubt that he, too, saw the change in his niece since her return from England.

Rachel was serving dessert and coffee, with the maid helping her. The old quadroon woman put down her magnificent eight-layer Charlotte Polonaise, with its filling of custard, almonds, and citron.

"I'd like to try one of your new horses," Deirdre said quietly.

"We'll go up to the attic after dinner, and I'll find something suitable," Lianne offered. "Not in the latest fashion, perhaps, but that doesn't matter. I wonder if my blue velvet is in good enough condition—or Jessica's black broadcloth."

"I had so hoped to see dear Jessica," Abigail broke in. "And her husband. Why I've never met him, and I should have thought that they would have come from—where is that school of theirs?"

"Near Birmingham," Clay said. "And now they have a college for black students." He did not add that he had given substantial contributions to the venture and was on the board of trustees. "There are classes in agriculture and mechanics for young men and a normal school to train the girls to become teachers."

"Indeed!" Abigail shook her head. "Blacks—in college. I never thought I'd see the day— Jessica was always a bit of a bluestocking, wasn't she? Ah well, at least I've had the chance to meet your husband, Lianne. And to meet you too, Deirdre. Not under the happiest circumstances, I fear. Your Aunt Samantha tells me you were scarcely married for six months when you left your husband." Abigail sighed. "In my day, a woman who married had to accept whatever fortune dealt her—to bear her lot with fortitude and resignation. But today everything is so different—"

"And a damn good thing, too—your pardon, ladies," said

Preston Taggart. "These foreign fortune hunters coming over here to trade their titles for the dowries of wealthy American girls. Clay, I hope you'll make Deirdre's husband pay back at least a part of your daughter's dowry. If he hasn't squandered it all."

"My lawyers are doing what is necessary," Clay replied curtly.

Deirdre put down her fork with a sharp, clinking sound, her cake scarcely touched. For a moment, she looked as if she might faint, but then she rallied swiftly, raised her head, and gave Taggart a direct look. "I find that my freedom is worth whatever it may have cost," she told him. "I made a mistake when I married Allen Sutcliffe—but I would have made a worse one had I remained with him as his wife."

Deirdre rose. "Aunt Lianne, if you would accompany me upstairs to the attic now, perhaps we can find a riding habit." She even managed a tight smile, and Megan felt warm with pride. Clay's eyes met Megan's, and she knew that her husband shared that pride in their daughter.

"Ah'll put aside an extra piece of mah cake in case you ladies want a bit more when you're finished lookin' in the attic," Rachel said softly. "An' Ah'll have the habit aired and brushed lak it wuz brand-new, Miz Deirdre."

In later years, when she looked back on that summer, Deirdre always believed that the sickness inside her, the shock and revulsion of her marriage, had begun to heal during that first early-morning ride at Montrose. Lianne's blue-velvet habit was out of fashion, but it fit nicely, and Lianne had even managed to find a high-crowned hat to match. She wore Jessica's riding boots, for her feet were narrow and high arched, like Jessica's, and she carried a riding crop with a silver handle that had belonged to Grandfather Drummond.

Although Rachel had tried to get Deirdre to eat a light breakfast from a tray brought to her room, she had been too impatient to linger in the house; besides, she wanted to be out of the house before the others were up and about. Yesterday's dinner party had been a severe strain on her nerves, and she knew that only her talk with her mother had given her the courage to carry it off.

Uncle Mark had been right, too, she decided, for her brisk

canter along the roads between the fields of cotton and beyond, through the orchard and down as far as the swamp, had revitalized her, had raised her spirits more than she would have believed possible. She found herself remembering the bleak, wind-swept gray moors, the fog and the chill rains of winter there. But now she was home, and at daybreak the air had a soft, seductive fragrance. She spurred the powerful gray stallion and breathed deeply, glorying in the mingled scents of grass, wisteria, and jasmine, of the river that wound beneath the bluffs, of the cypress swamp.

She had not ridden for months, and gradually she began to tire; reluctantly, she turned the stallion in the direction of the stables, and when she approached the long, low, brick structure, she slowed her pace. She was passing a small, whitewashed cottage—the old overseer's cottage—when she smelled the delicious aroma of freshly brewed coffee.

As she drew abreast of the cottage, a young man came out and stood looking up at her. She recognized Michael O'Donnell, no longer the thin, shabby boy she had first met back in New York City but a man, his shoulders broad and muscular, his tawny hair bleached by the sun. He regarded her steadily. "Why it's Miss Deirdre—beg pardon, I mean Lady Sutcliffe—"

"Just Deirdre," she said. And somewhat to her surprise, she found herself remembering that they were cousins, after all, if only by marriage.

"Deirdre, it is. A fine Irish name, too—one of the loveliest to my way of thinking."

If there had been anything flirtatious in his manner or in the look he gave her, she would surely have fled, but his tone was straightforward, even respectful. "Your grandmother's name, wasn't it?"

"My grandmother?" Deirdre thought of the delicate Charleston belle in one of the portraits in the upper hallway of Montrose. Papa's mother.

"Deirdre Rafferty," Michael said. "My cousin, Belle, sometimes spoke of her. She died in the black years after the great famine, she and all her children, except for your mother—and your mother's brother, Terence—him that was killed fighting with the Fenians—but then, no doubt you know all that and are proud of him, as you should be."

Deirdre felt herself going hot with shame, for on those rare occasions when her mother had spoken of the Raffertys, Deirdre had refused to listen, had told herself that she was a Drummond, that those Irish peasants back in County Cork had nothing to do with her. Now she said quietly, "My brother is named Terence."

Michael nodded. "But this is too fine a day to be talking of the past and its sorrows or to be thinking of them, either— would you be having a cup of coffee with me? And some of Rachel's biscuits?"

"I don't think—" Deirdre began, and Michael spoke quickly, respectfully.

"I'll bring the coffee and biscuits out here—" He gave a long, ear-splitting whistle. A moment later, a black boy came hurrying from the direction of a lean-to beside the stables.

Michael lifted Deirdre from the horse's back and swung her down to the ground. *Dear God,* he thought, *the girl's far too slim—and her face—like she'd been living with the devil himself.*

He felt her go rigid at his touch, and he released her the moment her feet touched the ground, then turned and ordered the black stable hand to walk her horse about and then give him a good rubdown.

They had coffee, seated on a wide, flat rock beside Michael's cottage, and then he took her into the stables to show her the new horses. "Look at this little filly now," he said. They stopped before a clean, freshly whitewashed stall where a filly with a shiny, blue-black coat pawed the ground and tossed her head. "She needs training, of course, before she's a fit mount of a lady. She's got plenty of spirit, but—"

"Is that a fault—to have spirit?"

"Now that depends," Michael said quietly. "Spirit is well enough, and a fine bloodline, too, but she needs discipline. And I'm the man to teach her. Miss Deirdre, I can train this filly for you in no time. And when you come out here again, she'll be fit for you to ride. You will be coming out to Montrose again soon, won't you?" He spoke casually, but there was something in his eyes that made her wary.

"I don't know. I hadn't planned to."

"Ah, but that would be a pity," he said. "You're a fine rider. I watched you from my cottage window as you were coming down the road. This filly's a lady's mount, and your aunt—Mr. Reed's wife—will be going off to Saratoga in a few days. You don't want this poor beast to suffer from lack of exercise."

He smiled, and Deirdre could not help smiling back.

"I'll think about it," she said.

His smile deepened, giving warmth to the hard, rugged features. "Good enough. I'll start training her today."

Chapter Twenty-eight

"SO YOU see, dear, since Violet and I will be staying at a boarding house instead of the Grand Union Hotel, and since I haven't bought a single new dress to take along, it will cost so little."

Samantha looked up at Reed, her brown eyes guileless. Her trunk, a huge, iron-bound affair with a curved top, stood near the bedroom door, already packed. It would take two of the strongest stable hands to get the trunk downstairs and loaded on to the carriage.

"A boardinghouse," Reed said. "Oh, but surely, Samantha—you'll be miserable in a place like that after spending all those summers at the Grand Union Hotel. I shouldn't think Violet would care for the arrangement, either."

"We'll both feel safer up North," Samantha said. "After that dreadful yellow fever epidemic last year, I simply shudder at the thought of spending my summer here at Montrose. Think of it—more than four hundred people died and—"

"Most of them in Jacksonville, Florida," Reed reminded her.

"Not all," Samantha said. "It killed Jeff Shepley. Really, I should think you'd understand that even if I were not afraid of the fever, dear Violet needs a change of scene—that dreadful little crackerbox of a house she lives in now. It breaks my heart to see her there and to remember that her people and mine used to be neighbors, and—"

"You are going to Saratoga for Violet's sake," Reed said quietly. "That's thoughtful of you."

"Why, I—I won't pretend I'm not anxious to get away— I've already explained—"

"Yes, my dear, you have."

"Of course, if you refuse to let me go, I suppose I—"

"Do my wishes carry such weight with you, Samantha? Have you ever cared about what I wanted or needed from you?"

He spoke softly, almost as if he were talking to himself. Looking at him, Samantha felt a stirring of guilt, of regret. Reed was younger than Clay, but he looked older at this moment; his hair, once blond, was now dusted over with gray, and his face was drawn, with permanent lines between his eyes and around his mouth. Suppose she had not married him; suppose he had married a girl who loved him, as she had loved Clay?

Impatient with herself, she pushed these disturbing reflections from her mind. Richard Whitaker would be meeting her in Saratoga, where he had already rented one of the most expensive cottages adjoining the Grand Union Hotel. Her mind moved swiftly. She would have to arrange to have her mail from home forwarded to her from one of those modest boardinghouses on the side streets off Saratoga's Broadway, the main thoroughfare. And it was fortunate that Reed could not see the contents of her trunk, for it held an imposing array of fashionable new clothes, suitable for the social round at Saratoga. Her older dresses she had passed along to Violet, who had, no doubt, made them over for herself.

What a shame that she would have to take Violet Shepley along this season. The woman was becoming a positive nuisance. But it would be out of the question for her to arrive alone, and it would be easy enough to have Violet moved into one of the smaller rooms in the hotel itself after the first few days. And really, Violet should be grateful, for without Samantha's generosity, she would have to spend the summer in her dismal little house here in Natchez.

* * *

Although Violet had complained about having to walk to Congress Spring Park instead of riding in a carriage, Samantha had brushed aside her objections. Violet tottered along, her feet crammed into shoes that were a size too small. Both Samantha and Violet carried small cups in which to drink the water dipped up from the spring, water that was said to be beneficial for a wide variety of complaints, from dyspepsia to dropsy. They walked on the elm-shaded sidewalk while the procession of landaus, phaetons, and broughams rolled by, carrying expensively dressed ladies and their escorts to the spring. Violet nudged Samantha as a large open carriage drove passed, carrying one of the most famous of the resort madams, a stout, tightly corseted woman in black corded silk, surrounded by her girls in their brilliantly colored finery. "Shocking," Violet said. "The way those creatures flaunt themselves in broad daylight, one would think—"

Samantha was not listening, for a fine landau drew up beside them at that moment, and a man's voice said, "Why, it's Mrs. Drummond."

Samantha looked up at Richard Whitaker, who had signaled for his coachman to stop. "Mr. Whitaker!"

"I hoped you would remember me," he said, and a few moments later, Samantha and Violet were seated opposite him as the landau rolled on toward the spring.

"They do say that it is healthier to walk to the spring," Samantha said, but she settled back comfortably in the soft leather seat. Then, remembering her social duties, she introduced Violet, who smiled at Richard and batted her lashes. Really, Samantha thought, ever since she had finished her mourning period after Jeff's death, Violet had been giving herself the airs of a young belle. She must have been rinsing her hair with some sort of camomile concoction, too, Samantha thought, for it had gone from its faded ginger color to a startling shade of gold.

"How fortunate to have met this way, sir," Violet was saying. "Why my poor feet— Truly, I don't believe I could have walked all the way to the spring. I declare, I was getting ready to turn back when along you came like a shining knight— Oh, yes, indeed, Mr. Whitaker, that's what you are."

Samantha fixed her eyes on the passing crowd, but Richard kept up the charade, pretending that he had seen Samantha only once before, at the ball at Azalea Hill, and he was careful to divide his attention equally between Samantha and Violet. And Violet, instead of keeping herself in the background, was flirting—yes, flirting with Richard.

At the pavilion in the park, Violet allowed Richard to fill her cup, and she squealed with girlish distaste as she took a small sip of the water. "It really does taste dreadful—but I suppose it is good for one's health."

"No doubt," Richard agreed. Samantha touched her lips to her cup and looked at him over the rim. The warmth in his eyes restored her spirits.

"The waters are said to stimulate the appetite—indeed, that is why we are here. Ever since my poor, dear husband passed away, I have scarcely been able to touch my food, and my friends feared I would go into a decline. That is why Samantha insisted that I come here."

After expressing his condolences, Richard said, "My dear lady, the climate of Saratoga will do wonders for you, I'm sure. And perhaps you will permit me to escort you—and Mrs. Drummond—to dinner at the Grand Union's dining room this evening."

Samantha fully expected Violet to play her part, to refuse the invitation, as she always had during other seasons here. Instead, Violet said, "How kind—how very kind, Mr. Whitaker. But perhaps your wife—"

"I lost my wife some years ago," he said.

While Violet commiserated over the loss, Samantha felt her hands clench so tightly that a small seam popped open in one of her rose-colored gloves.

"And then, afterward, we might drive out to the park to listen to the band concert. I'm told that Victor Herbert will be performing this evening—a most talented musician—plays the violincello—"

"Oh, that would be—" Violet began, but Samantha had had enough.

"We'll be pleased to dine with you, Mr. Whitaker, but you must excuse Violet from attending the concert. Her recent loss—she has no plans for going about to such diversions this season."

"Really, Samantha," Violet said when they were back in the parlor of their ornately furnished cottage, "I don't think you had any right to tell Mr. Whitaker that I would not attend the concert. I've always been fond of music; you know that. And it's been a year since poor, dear Jeff—"

"Oh, for goodness' sake," Samantha snapped. "Mr. Whitaker was only being polite. He and I—" She broke off abruptly.

"Do go on," Violet said. "You met the gentleman only once, at a ball at Azalea Hill; that's what you said. It isn't as if you two were—close friends—"

There was a glint of malice in Violet's eyes, but Samantha, who had become accustomed to using the other woman for her own purposes, ignored the implied challenge.

"You are forgetting yourself," she said. "Must I remind you that you are here as my guest?"

"You've reminded me of that often enough over the years. But I'm not a fool, Samantha. I've been your chaperone, too. I've made it possible for you to travel about without Reed, in perfect respectability. To—enjoy your little pleasures."

"Be careful," Samantha warned.

"I might say the same to you. Mr. Whitaker and I are both unattached, while you have a husband waiting for you back at Montrose."

It took all of Samantha's self-control to keep from shaking Violet until her teeth rattled. "Do you suppose—do you really suppose that Richard—Mr. Whitaker was being anything more than polite when he asked you to join us?"

"Don't excite yourself, Samantha," Violet said sweetly. "You are so prone to migraines— How soon are you planning to have your first headache this time? I'd only like to know so that I can pack and move into one of those rooms in the hotel—"

"You can pack up and move into the hotel any time you like. I'll ring for one of the maids to help you." She waited, sure that Violet would back down, would humble herself.

Instead, Violet looked at Samantha steadily. "Tell me, Samantha, honey—I'd like to know. When you're with one of those others, do you ever close your eyes and try to pretend that he is Clay Drummond?"

Then, turning on her heel, Violet went into her bedroom and began to pack.

* * *

"You mean, she's left the hotel—left Saratoga?"

"That's what the desk clerk told me," Samantha said.

She had made the discovery only a few hours before when she had questioned the desk clerk and had been told that Violet had not checked into the main building of the hotel, that she had, instead, informed the desk clerk that she was leaving, and when he had asked for a forwarding address, she had said that she was returning home to Natchez. Later, during dinner, in the imposing dining room, Samantha had avoided answering Richard Whitaker's casual question about Violet's absence with a brief, noncommittal reply and had enjoyed the lavish meal. Later, they had listened to the concert, and now they were back in Samantha's cottage.

"Mrs. Shepley has not yet returned," he said. "Isn't it rather late for her to be out alone?"

"Violet's gone back to Natchez," Samantha said. "We had a—a little tiff. She's always been flighty. I had no idea she would leave—"

"It's just as well," Richard said with obvious relief. "Lord knows, I tried to keep up the pretense with her that you and I had met casually here, but it would have been a strain to go on play-acting. I want you all to myself, Samantha—all to myself—" His arms went around her, and she felt his hard muscles pressing against her. Her breathing quickened, and she rested her head against his chest, but she could not wholly dismiss her uneasiness over Violet's unexpected departure. Violet had always been a notorious gossip, and even now, when Jeff's death had left her in straitened circumstances, she still managed to entertain a wide circle of friends, ladies from the oldest families in Natchez. Many a reputation had been torn to shreds over platters of Violet's thin tea sandwiches and lemonade.

Perhaps, Samantha thought guiltily, she should not have taken Violet's subservience so much for granted; after all, they had both come from the same background. Their families' plantations had stretched side by side along the river before the war. But Samantha had fallen into the habit of treating Violet as a hired companion, and now she could only guess at the bitterness and resentment that Violet had stored up against her over the years.

"Samantha—my dear—" Richard's voice, soft but urgent,

came to her, and she felt his arms tighten around her, felt the pressure of his thighs through the skirts of her gown. "You're not sorry you came to Saratoga, are you? I'm almost ashamed to say it, but ever since that afternoon in New Orleans, I've scarcely been able to keep my mind on my business—on anything—except being with you like this again. I guess that sounds foolish—a man my age—but you—you're like no woman I've ever known."

The passion and the sincerity in his voice stirred Samantha, and she felt a glow of satisfaction that this man, so wealthy, so masterful, had fallen in love with her. "Your age," she repeated, her voice warm, tender. "Why Richard, you are a man in the prime of life. You're strong and exciting."

Reassured, flattered by her words and the look that accompanied them, he dismissed all thought of anything except this woman, with her soft, creamy skin, her beautiful breasts, half bared by the bodice of her wine-colored gown, the scent of her dark-brown hair. . . . His hands moved quickly as he unbuttoned her bodice and pushed aside her lace-and-ribbon-trimmed camisole, as he found her nipples with his eager, questing mouth. But even that was not enough for either of them, not now.

The wine-colored silk gown made a soft, rustling sound as it slid down, falling about her feet, and she was pressing herself against him harder, her hands holding him, caressing him. Then they were stretched out on the thick, soft carpet there in the cottage parlor. She made a moaning sound deep in her throat.

Samantha, too, had forgotten everything but the white-hot need that grew and grew inside her. . . .

Seth Hunter had come home to his plantation after a day in Natchez, and now he and his wife, Winona, were seated on the upper gallery. They had finished an ample dinner, and Seth was drinking bourbon and water, while Winona sipped at her iced tea. "Didn't you tell me that Violet Shepley was going to spend the season in Saratoga with Samantha Drummond?" he asked, for Winona had just finished telling him that she had been visiting, that afternoon, with Violet.

"She returned only a few days ago," Winona said.

"I'd have thought she'd have been thankful to stay away for the summer. Hotter'n the hinges of hell down here."

"She had to leave," Winona said primly. "As a respectable woman, she had no choice. None at all."

"What's that supposed to mean?"

"I don't know if I should speak of it, even to you. It's perfectly shocking—"

Seth gave a short bark of laughter. His wife was going to tell him; he knew that much from long experience. It was only a matter of letting her tell the story in her own way. He took another drink of bourbon and water.

"Did Samantha Drummond come back, too?" he asked.

"Samantha! I should think not!" She put a plump hand on her husband's arm. "Oh, no, Samantha's still in Saratoga, and she'll be staying there as long as her gentleman friend is paying the bills."

"Gentleman friend? You're not saying that Samantha's up there with some man?" He laughed. "Not that it'd surprise me— Always did have a restless look about her. Like a she-cat clawing at the kitchen door—looking for a tom—"

"Seth—don't be vulgar," Winona said. But she did not contradict him.

"Reed's been too easygoing with her; that's the trouble," Seth said, draining his glass. "Letting her go gallivanting off every summer. All the same, you sure Violet isn't making up the story? Might be she's jealous of Samantha—"

"Jealous? Oh, no. It's the other way 'round. Samantha was pea green with jealousy because Mr. Whitaker—that rich Yankee who bought up all that timberland from Clay Drummond— was taken with Violet, and Samantha couldn't put up with that. And Violet told me—" Winona leaned closer and lowered her voice. "It hasn't been the first time that Samantha's jumped the fence, either. All these summers, she's been carrying on like a—a Jezebel—"

"Took Violet a long time to catch on to what was happening," Seth observed dryly.

"Violet is a respectable woman— Naturally, when Samantha said she had a migraine headache and had to be alone for a night, Violet believed her."

Seth stared down into his empty glass. "I'll have another one of these," he said. "Tell Uriah to bring one out here for me, will you?"

"And I want another lemonade," Winona said. "My throat's

parched—this heat—" She got up and went inside with a rustling of skirts. Seth continued to stare into his glass. Samantha Drummond was raising hell up North, spreading her legs for some rich Yankee, was she? Seth licked his lips. Probably a damn fine pair of legs, too. One hell of a good-looking woman, Samantha Drummond was.

Any other man, he'd have felt sorry for, but Reed— He was a damn fool, giving his wife so much freedom. And he was a weakling, too. Never knew where he stood on anything. Take that night when they'd killed that black bastard down by the swamp at Montrose. Reed had tried to stop them. Tried to keep them from flogging the hide off the Yankee schoolteacher, too. And after that, Reed Drummond had kept a distance between himself and his former friends. He'd never come to another meeting of the Knights of the White Camellia.

Those Drummonds. Oh, they'd fought for the Confederacy, but afterward . . . Clay had joined forces with any Yankee who could help him and had made a fortune. He'd let his sister, his own sister, marry that Yankee schoolteacher, had even given huge donations to a college for blacks. Seth leaned forward and spat over the railing of the upper gallery.

Those Drummonds thought they were something special. Seth could think of a lot of men who'd get a good laugh when they heard how Samantha Drummond was making a fool out of her husband.

In the last week of August, Luke Drummond had come from Texas to Natchez, to Azalea Hill, to pay a visit to Megan and Deirdre before he left for Central America.

"You'll be careful, won't you, Luke?" Megan said, for she had always loved him as she had her own children. "Preston Taggart says that Guatemala isn't safe. There are swamps and the threat of revolutions. Why Clay wants to build a railroad down there is more than I can see."

"You know that Uncle Clay's never happy unless he's planning a new railroad," Luke answered with an affectionate smile. He put his arm around Megan and gave her a hug, and she looked up at him, realizing that he was nearly as tall as Clay, with the same wide shoulders and massive chest as her husband. He had the same eyes, too: dark blue under straight, heavy black brows. "Don't you worry about me, Aunt Megan," he said. "I know how to take care of myself.

"You're excited about the trip, aren't you?" Deirdre asked. "And the new railroad. Just like Papa."

"I can't deny it," Luke said, his voice serious. "And I'm proud that Uncle Clay has so much confidence in my judgement. He wants my personal report, along with those of his surveyors, about the best route for a railroad between Puerto Barrios and the coffee plantations in the mountains. I never thought I'd get a chance like this—it's what I've always wanted. And to think Uncle Clay trusts me to take on the job—"

"You deserve his trust," Deirdre said. "All the same, I'll be worrying about you down there—"

"I don't want you to worry," Luke said. He grinned at her. "You'll get wrinkles in your pretty face."

It was a pretty face, again, Megan thought with satisfaction; for during these past weeks, Deirdre had gone over to Montrose many times to ride the filly, Dark Star, that Michael had trained for her and Reed had given her as a gift. On a few occasions, when Michael had been able to take time from his work, he had accompanied her on her early-morning rides along the bluffs, and she had returned home with a keen appetite and a warm, rosy color in her cheeks.

"Your Uncle Clay is still down in New Orleans," Megan reminded Luke. "Maybe he won't be able to raise enough extra capital to start the project. Maybe Oliver Winthrop won't want to go into partnership with him on such a risky venture."

"Uncle Clay'll talk Winthrop around," Luke said. "Think of the profit to be made. Why once the railroad's built and the trains running, I'll bet Uncle Clay and Oliver Winthrop will both buy up some of those coffee plantations— Oh, not to live down there—as investments. I wouldn't mind having a coffee plantation of my own down there someday."

"And then you can marry one of those Spanish Creole girls," Deirdre teased. "I'm told they're beautiful—"

Deirdre stopped speaking as Ludamae came hurrying into the parlor. "Miz Megan, beg pahdon, but Mistuh Jim Rafferty's here, and he say he wanted t' see Mistuh Clay, an' when Ah tol' him Mistuh Clay's still down there in New Orleans, he say he's got t' see you, an'—"

A moment later, Jim Rafferty came shouldering his way into the room, his weather-beaten face set in grim lines. Megan ran to him. "What's wrong— Aunt Kathleen—"

"Yer aunt's fine. It's—" Jim hesitated, his eyes resting on Luke, and it was to Luke he spoke.

"I'm that sorry t' be bringin' the news, boy, but yer Pa's been hurt bad. Real bad."

"My father— What's happened? Where is he?"

"Miss Velma Kimball's place down on Silver Street. One of my teamsters was havin' a drink downstairs. He saw the whole thing. They got the man that did it—"

"Did what? What has happened?" Megan asked.

"Nobody's got the whole thing straight yet, but the way I heard it, this feller—he owns a few run-down acres of dirt farm up river—he was in Miss Velma's place talkin' to a friend. He said somethin' about—about yer mother, Luke. And your pa, he went kind of crazy. Not that he didn't have the right— He hit the man, and the man pulled a knife. Yer pa's cut up bad and Miss Velma, she had yer pa carried to—to one of the rooms upstairs. And then she sent for Doctor Sinclair— The doctor did his best, but he said—well—it's only a matter of time."

"I'll go to Reed," Megan said.

"You can't go into Miss Velma's place," Luke protested, for even in his present state of shock, he had not forgotten the proprieties. Miss Velma's "girls" took their customers upstairs to those rooms on the second floor.

"Your Uncle Clay would want me to go in his place," Megan said firmly. "Come along, Luke. Hurry."

"Is there anything I can—" Deirdre began.

"Yes, dear, there is. Go to the telegraph office and wire your father at the Winthrops' home in New Orleans. Say he's to come at once. Then send a wire to your Aunt Samantha. I'm not sure where she is staying, but—" Megan tried to calm her whirling thoughts. "Mrs. Shepley should know," she told Deirdre.

Miss Velma Kimball, a stout woman with dyed jet-black hair, was plainly startled to see Mrs. Clay Drummond in her place. Although the two women knew each other by sight, they had never exchanged so much as a word, for respectable married ladies did not recognize the existence of Miss Velma's kind. Now such distinctions did not seem important, and Megan, accompanied by Luke, followed Miss Velma upstairs to a small, stuffy, overfurnished room.

"I'm sorry, Mrs. Drummond," Doctor Sinclair said. "I've done all I can for your husband's brother, but the injuries are too extensive— I've given him laudanum to ease the pain."

Then Megan and Luke went to the bed, and Megan sat down in a chair on one side while Luke remained standing. She saw the pinched white indentations around Reed's nostrils, the unfocused look in his gray eyes, their pupils shrunken to pinpoints, and she knew that the doctor had been right. Filled with helpless pity, she wished desperately that Clay might get here before Reed died and knew that he would not.

Reed fought for breath, his lips dry and cracked. He made a sound in his throat and raised his head, and a thin trickle of blood issued from between his lips. Megan wiped it away with her handkerchief.

"Samantha," Reed said hoarsely.

"We've sent for her," Megan told him, hoping that her words might give him a little comfort.

"Not her fault— Whatever she did— Not her fault."

"Pa, please don't try to talk." Luke put his hand over Reed's.

Reed turned to look at him. "Not your fault, either, Luke. I tried—not to hate you—"

Hate Luke? Megan was bewildered. She had always known that Reed had never been really close to his son, and his coldness had often puzzled her, for surely Luke was a son to be proud of.

"You weren't to blame—" Reed's eyes were fixed on Luke with a terrible intensity. "But I never could forget—never—" Reed was seized with a paroxysm of coughing, and the blood came spurting from his mouth.

"Be still," Doctor Sinclair said, hurrying to the bedside. "You must be still now."

But Reed went on. "Clay and Samantha. It was always— Clay and Samantha. Opal—she knew the truth—she came to me—day after Noah died—and she told me about— Never could stand the sight of you after that, boy—look more like your father every day—"

Megan looked across the bed at Luke. He had gone nearly as white as Reed.

It was true, Megan thought, feeling a sickness in the pit of her stomach. Luke looked like Clay. She had noticed the resemblance before, of course, but somehow she had never thought . . . But Opal had known. Opal had still been living at Montrose when Clay had returned from the war, when Clay, Reed, and Samantha had been there together.

Megan told herself that she must not give way to her own emotions, not yet. Reed Drummond was dying, and although they had never been really close, Reed had treated her with courtesy, even kindness, from the moment that she had become Clay's wife.

"Reed—don't say anymore," she said softly. "Sleep, now and—"

"Shouldn't have married Samantha— But I thought—we all thought that—Clay wasn't coming back from that—Yankee prison camp. And I—I wanted Samantha so much—"

Luke had taken his hand from Reed's, had moved away from the bed, and now he stood in the shadows, staring down at the man he had always believed to be his father.

I have to talk to Luke, Megan thought. *Later, when it's over, I have to talk to him. He's so young. I'll have to try to find the right words.*

Reed tried to raise himself up, choking on his own blood. Doctor Sinclair supported him, but there was little else that the doctor could do. Megan bowed her head and began to repeat the prayers for the dying. But even as she whispered the familiar words, she felt her strength draining out of her. Clay and Samantha. Luke was the son of Clay and Samantha.

Then she heard the death rattle, saw Reed fall back against the pillow. Somehow she was able to close his eyes, to draw the sheet over his face. From somewhere, she heard the doctor's voice speaking quietly, respectfully.

"—and you may be sure, Mrs. Drummond, that nothing the—deceased has said in this room will ever go any farther. Please assure his—the young man—that I—will say nothing."

Megan nodded and looked around for Luke, but he was gone. He was not in the hall or in the saloon downstairs. It was Jim Rafferty who drove Megan home to Azalea Hill to wait for Clay's return.

Chapter Twenty-nine

✍

"AH'LL HELP yuh off with yo' dress, Miz Samantha," Rachel said. "Then Ah'll loosen yo' stays, an' yuh kin lay down on the bed an' rest."

Samantha stood in silence while Rachel took off her black silk dress and her small black bonnet with its long veil. She was shivering in spite of the heavy, humid August heat, and the perspiration made her camisole cling to her body. Rachel worked quickly, deftly, unhooking fastenings, undoing buttons.

"Yuh want fo' me t' send fo' Miz Lianne or Miz Jessica?" Rachel asked.

Samantha shook her head.

"Ah kin get some cologne fo' yo' forehead," the quadroon woman said.

"No," Samantha told her impatiently. She wanted to be alone here in the master bedroom at Montrose, the room she had shared with Reed as infrequently as possible during their marriage. She wanted no one here, for she needed to remain hidden from prying eyes, from familiar faces that accused her of—of what?

"Please go downstairs," she ordered Rachel. "You must have a great many matters to attend to with all these guests."

"Yes'm," Rachel said, and left the room, closing the door quietly behind her.

How much did the elderly quadroon know? How much did all those others know, or guess? Samantha felt her insides quivering, and she sat down on the side of the bed, weak, lightheaded with fear.

All those years, she had lived in dread of the opinions of her neighbors, and now she was facing the scandal that she had tried so long to avoid. Oh, if only everyone would leave Montrose, all those guests who had come to attend Reed's funeral—so many of them down there in the dining room: Clay and Megan, of course, and Deirdre; Terence, and Elizabeth Hartley, his bride-to-be, and Elizabeth's parents, Senator Ambrose Hartley and his wife; Lianne and Mark Burnett and their three daughters; and, surprisingly, Tom and Jessica, who had not set foot on Montrose land since that terrible night so many years ago when Tom had nearly been killed by the Knights of the White Camellia; Abigail, her face puffy, her eyes swollen, leaning heavily on her husband's arm; and neighbors from Natchez and from plantations up and down the river.

Violet Shepley was here, and Samantha had not been surprised when Violet had given her a cold stare and had not spoken a word to her. But those others, Winona Hunter and her husband, Seth—why they had been barely civil. And the Surgets and Dunbars and Vallières, people she had known all her life, all looked at her as if she were on trial for some unspeakable crime.

When General John B. Gordon, who had been elected leader of the United Confederate Veterans, had given the funeral oration and had spoken in moving words of Reed's gallantry in battle, his devotion to the cause, his part in organizing the veterans' group only a few months before, women had begun to weep, and many of the men had been visibly moved.

Samantha had tried to keep her poise, but the air in the Drummond burial ground, heavy with the mingled odors of jasmine, honeysuckle, and roses, had been cloying, and she had felt a growing weakness. Clay had supported her, his hand beneath her elbow, but it was a formality. He had stared straight ahead, his eyes fixed on the grave that had been dug the night before to receive Reed's coffin.

Did Clay know, too? Oh, but he must. Everyone in Natchez must know, for Reed's killer, Charlie Glover, a backwoods farmer, had known, had spoken in a saloon, of Samantha Drummond's infidelities. Glover had been a member of the Knights of the White Camellia. If he had known, the story must have spread like a brushfire. Reed Drummond had died defending the honor of his faithless wife—

Violet had talked. Damn the woman; she had not lost a moment in spreading her account of Samantha's activities in Saratoga. And perhaps not only the liaison with Richard Whitaker but those other summer affairs. Samantha, standing beside Clay, listening to General Gordon's eulogy, had gone weak with dread.

Then Clay had left her side to speak over the grave of his half brother, as was expected. And Samantha had been forced to stand alone. Did Clay hate her, or did he feel only contempt for her? The thick leaves of the live oaks, the gray moss that trailed from the branches, were motionless in the heat.

When Clay had finished speaking, she had tried to move forward to the grave side, but her legs were weak. She saw that all eyes were turned to her and heard the beginning of a murmur from the crowd. She could not face them for another moment; she could not. . . . And then Mark Burnett was beside her, his arm around her, leading her back to the house, where he ordered Rachel to take care of her, to get her to bed.

The burial was over now, and the guests were taking refreshments in the dining room. Some family members would stay overnight; others would begin the journey homeward this evening. But Samantha could not bring herself to go downstairs. Let Rachel and the other servants take care of the menial chores. Let Clay and Megan act as host and hostess; it did not matter, for she did not want to face the accusing eyes of the guests.

"But I'm not to blame," she told herself, lying on the bed, one arm across her face. She had not wanted Reed to die. It had not been her fault that he had been in Velma Kimball's place when that horrible, drunken Charlie Glover had been spreading those ugly stories about her.

No one blamed Reed, not now. Even though he had aroused the hostility of some of his neighbors after his defection from the Knights of the White Camellia, all that would be forgotten. All the neighbors would remember was that a Drummond, a loyal Confederate, had died like a gentleman defending his wife's honor. But already they must be asking one another how much truth there had been in Charlie Glover's gossip. How could she ever face them again?

A faithless wife. Reed Drummond's widow, who had deceived him with another man.

Samantha sat up abruptly. Reed Drummond's widow. But that meant—that meant that she was free. She could not go right back to Saratoga, of course. She would have to remain here for a while, at least until Reed's affairs were settled. But then Richard Whitaker would be waiting.

She would have to play the grief-stricken widow for a time, and perhaps if she was convincing enough, there would be those who would question the truth of the accusations against her. Violet Shepley was, of course, the one who had started the rumors, and everyone in Natchez knew that Violet had always been a gossip.

Samantha's self-assurance began to rise again. Once she was married to Richard Whitaker, once she had his fortune behind her, Montrose would be a showplace, even finer than it had been before the war. As Mrs. Richard Whitaker, no one would dare to ostracize her. She would give balls in this house, splendid entertainments, and everyone would be eager for invitations. She saw herself coming down the long, curving stairway in a wine-red ball gown with Richard at her side. . . .

Tom and Jessica sat outside on the veranda. They had left their son, Evan, talking with Mark Burnett. Evan, whose ambition it was to become a doctor, was, no doubt, discussing his future plans with Mark.

Jessica had longed for half a dozen children, but she had never ceased to be grateful for the one son she had been able to bear, a fine boy, serious, idealistic, studious, like his father.

She took Tom's hand. "I was not sure that you would be willing to come to Montrose ever again," she said quietly.

"Reed was your brother—your half brother. It was your duty to come, and I could not let you make the trip without me," Tom said. "Besides, it's time that Evan got to know the rest of his family. Mark, Lianne, and their daughters. And Deirdre and Terence."

"But what about Luke? Where is he? Surely he should be here at his father's funeral."

"Wasn't he working down in Louisiana? Or was it Texas? Perhaps there was a delay in his receiving word about Reed's death. No doubt he'll be arriving soon."

Jessica nodded. Then she said slowly, "Clay has asked us to stay the night. But I think we should start for home as soon as Evan's finished his talk with Mark."

"There's no need," Tom said. "And I'm sure you could use a night's rest here before we leave. It's a long way back to Alabama."

"I came to Reed's funeral," Jessica said stiffly. "It was my duty. But I don't want to spend even one night under this roof. I—I went down to the cypress swamp—to see Noah's grave."

"Oh, my dear—"

"I remembered that night—and what those men did to you—"

"I think maybe it's time we both forgot that," Tom said. "You know, my dear, I never believed that Reed planned for— I remember hearing him trying to persuade Jeff Shepley and the others to burn the schoolhouse but to do nothing more."

"Perhaps that is true," Jessica said. "I've tried to forgive him." Forgive Reed, yes, she thought. But she would never forget, never. Each time that she held Tom close in the darkness, her fingers touched the hard, raised ridges that still marked his body. Each time that Tom made love to her, she would remember. . . .

In the dining room, Violet Shepley sat with the other guests, eating her second helping of Rachel's apricot nut cake. Samantha had not come downstairs after the funeral, Violet thought, and no wonder. The shameless creature. It was Samantha's fault that Reed Drummond was dead, and everyone here surely knew it.

A small doubt stirred in the back of Violet's mind. Samantha had played the trollop; she had betrayed her marriage vows. *But if I had not spoken of what I knew—*

Violet pushed the unwelcome thought aside quickly. She had only told Winona, and who would have imagined that

Winona would have spread the story? After all, hadn't Violet sworn her to secrecy?

"Megan, where is Luke?" Lianne asked.

Clay stood beside Megan, still shaken by Reed's death and baffled by Luke's absence.

"Luke—" Clay began. "I really don't—"

"Luke has gone to Central America. To Guatemala," Megan said. Clay saw the rigid set of her shoulders, the tension in her whole body. "He's with the surveyors for Clay's new railroad. And Preston Taggart says that the country is so primitive. No means of communication in whole sections. Nothing but swamps and mountains. Naturally, we sent a telegram to— Puerto Barrios, on the Caribbean coast, but it may be days, even weeks before Luke receives word of his—of Reed's death."

Clay's eyes narrowed as he looked at Megan. He was startled and uneasy. What had possessed Megan to tell such a cool lie?

"Then you are planning to build a railroad in Guatemala," Lianne said to Clay.

"What? Oh, yes. That is, I haven't made a definite decision. The reports of the surveyors and—"

"And Luke's report," Megan finished for him. "You know, he's had a great deal of experience working for Clay on the Natchez–Fort Worth Line and supervising the building of a trunk line in Texas." Then, deftly changing the subject, she said, "Evan's a fine-looking boy, isn't he? Tom says that he's set on becoming a doctor, like Mark. We'll be having two doctors in the family one of these days."

Clay stood in silence as Lianne and Megan talked of young Evan, of other family members. He paid little attention to their conversation, however. Why had Megan lied about Luke's whereabouts? And where was Luke? Clay knew only that Luke had come to Natchez to say good-by to Megan before leaving for Guatemala, but he and the surveyors had not been due to set sail from New Orleans for another two weeks at least.

Clay studied his wife's face, his bewilderment growing. Certainly, it had not been an easy time for Megan, being with Reed during his last hours, watching him die down there at Velma Kimball's place. Megan had taken over with quiet efficiency: she had sent for the minister, had arranged with Rachel for the reception of the guests, had welcomed General John

Gordon to Montrose. She had stood between Samantha and a
hostile community.

But last night, in the guest bedroom upstairs, when Clay
had tried to embrace his wife, to comfort her, she had drawn
away. She had shown, for the first time in their marriage, a
physical revulsion toward him. Even when he had told her
gently that he would not make love to her, that he only wanted
to hold her, when he had needed the solace of her embrace,
she had stiffened and turned away. She had slept on the far
side of the wide bed, carefully avoiding the slightest contact
with him.

Clay was badly shaken, first by Reed's death, then by the
gossip about Samantha's activities up in Saratoga. He needed
to feel close to Megan, but she had treated him with polite
coolness.

A few hours later, when most of the guests had departed,
Clay found a few moments to speak with Terence in the library.
Terence, hard working, reliable, a son to be proud of.

"That's a fine girl you're going to marry," Clay said. Elizabeth, a tall, patrician blonde, would be staying the night with
her parents.

"I hope she doesn't find Montrose too great a change from
her home in Maryland," Clay went on. "Our climate takes
some getting used to."

"Montrose? But father, I thought I'd made it clear that we
won't be staying here. As soon as I have my law degree, I
plan to go into practice in Baltimore with Senator Hartley's
old law firm. Then, after a few years, I'm going into politics.
We've spoken about all that—"

"You spoke of it," Clay said. "I never agreed. You will
take your place in the legal department of one of my companies.
The Natchez–Fort Worth Line, perhaps, or one of my steel
mills. Take your choice. But one day we'll be working together.
You'll help me to run all my enterprises. This notion about
politics—"

Terence stiffened. How like Megan he looked, with his
tawny hair and hazel eyes.

"It's not a notion, father. A political career has always been
my ambition."

"Then you'll have to change your plans. Terence, listen. If Brant had lived, I don't suppose it would have mattered, your wanting to go into politics. But now—I need you. Everything I've built up, all of it, will be yours. Forget about a political career." Clay put a hand on Terence's shoulder. "Why, boy, senators are a dime a dozen. I've bought their support whenever I've needed it. I've had them eating out of my hand."

"I know that," Terence said, his smooth, young face hardening as if it had been carved in granite. "That's one of the reasons I want to become a senator. Because this country is changing. We need political leaders whose votes are not for sale."

"Don't talk like a damned fool. What's wrong with spreading money around where it will do the most good? Why shouldn't I buy the legislation that fills my needs?"

"Your needs! What about the needs of the people—what about the—people who work for you?"

"My railroads, my cotton mills and steel mills and mines, my lumber companies—I've done more to contribute to the prosperity of the South than all those politicians with their fancy speeches and their—"

"Their favorable legislation?" Terence's voice was harsh with contempt and anger. "What kind of legislation is it that permits ten-year-old children to work in cotton mills for twelve cents a day? That allows the leasing of convicts to work in the mines and the lumber camps?"

"What the devil do you know about convict labor? If that's the sort of thing they teach up in that Yankee college—"

"I've read the reports," Terence said. "The Report of the United States Commissioner of Labor says that—"

"Don't you start lecturing me," Clay interrupted, but Terence went on, his voice earnest, his body taut with the anger he was trying to control.

"It says that the penetentiaries of the South are no better than rolling cages built to follow the railroads—or stockades hidden away in the swamps, in the turpentine flats—with no government supervision. The convicts are subjected to more brutal treatment than any slave at Montrose ever received. I'm sure of that, and I—"

"That's enough," Clay said. "You'd have done better to be

expelled from college, to come home and work with your hands like Brant. Even when he was in college, he didn't keep his head buried in books— He didn't—"

"I know that Brant was your favorite," Terence said. "It's not my fault that he died while I'm still alive—"

"Damn it, I never meant—"

"I can't be like Brant," Terence went on. "And I can't be like you. I have to do what is right for me— I have to—"

"Clay! Terence! Stop this at once!" Megan had come into the library, her entrance unnoticed until now. She stepped between her husband and her son. "This has been a dreadful time for all of us. It certainly is not the time to discuss Terence's plans for the future."

She put a hand on her son's arm. "Elizabeth is beginning to wonder where you've disappeared to. Why don't you take her for a stroll in the garden?"

Terence hesitated, then nodded. "I'll do that," he said. He brushed his mother's cheek with his lips. "You'd best get some rest," he said. "You've had so much to do these past few days."

He started for the door, then turned. "I'm—sorry, father," he said. "It's only that I—"

"You're a Drummond," Clay said. The anger had drained from him now. "I can remember a night, the first night I brought your mother to Montrose. To a ball. I spoke of my ambitions, and your Uncle Reed did not understand—he—"

It hurt to speak of Reed, for the pain was still too harsh, too raw.

After Terence had left the library, Clay turned to Megan. "You do have a way of managing. I'm glad you came in when you did." He put his arm around her and drew her against him, but her body remained rigid in his embrace.

"Even if Terence doesn't plan to live here in Natchez after he marries, I want to know that he will, at least, return for a visit now and then." Her voice was bleak, her eyes distant. "I've lost one son," she said. "I couldn't let you drive the other away for good."

He flinched at her words and wondered if, after all this time, she blamed him for Brant's death. "Megan, sit down, and we'll talk," he said. "I need to talk to you."

"I have no time," she said. "Since Samantha has shut herself in her room, it's up to me to arrange for the comfort of the guests. Some will have to stay the night, and I must make sure that Rachel has prepared their rooms."

She slipped from his grasp, and moving swiftly, she left the library.

It was nearly midnight when Clay came upstairs to bed and found Megan, in her nightdress and robe, sitting motionless in a chair. Her face was pale, her mouth set.

"I've been out walking," he said. "Down on the bluffs. Megan, I have to know what's happened to you. You've been acting so strangely. Not like yourself at all."

"Have I?"

"You told Lianne that Luke's in Guatemala. A deliberate lie."

"Clay, I'm exhausted. I want to go to bed now, and I think you should, too—"

He took a few long strides toward her, then closed his hands on her shoulders. "Why did you lie?"

Her eyes narrowed, hot with anger. "Don't speak to me of lies! Our marriage, our whole life together, has been built on a lie."

"Megan—"

"Take your hands off me. Luke's gone—and I don't know where. He was with me at Velma Kimball's place—when Reed was dying. Then he—he was gone."

"Gone? Gone where?" His fingers tightened on her shoulders. "Maybe you don't know where he is, but you know why he left. You do, don't you?"

"Yes, I do." Her voice was unsteady, but her eyes never left his. "Luke's young and sensitive. He went away because he couldn't face you, or his mother, knowing—what he does."

"If you mean the gossip about Samantha—and Whitaker—"

"That's ugly enough, God knows. It isn't easy for a young man to face the fact that his own mother is— But he might have been able to deny that piece of gossip—to tell himself that it wasn't true."

"Then what—"

"Reed was still conscious when we arrived at Miss Velma's place. And the laudanum that the doctor had given him to ease the pain loosened his tongue, too." She took a long breath, fighting for control. "Luke loved you, Clay. And he respected you, looked up to you. How could he have come to Montrose today? How can he ever face you again, knowing the truth?"

Now Clay's hands fell away from her.

"It is true, then," he said dully.

"You knew."

"I wasn't sure. I thought—but I wasn't sure."

"You never questioned Samantha?"

He shook his head. "I didn't want to know."

"Perhaps you are telling me the truth; it doesn't seem important now."

"Megan, listen to me—"

"Now you do know. Luke is your son. Yours. And Samantha's."

Chapter Thirty

"RICHARD, I can't possibly marry you, not so soon. It hasn't even been a year since Reed died."

"I know it's customary to wait at least a year," Richard Whitaker said. "But I'm not a boy. And I have no intention of letting any more time slip by before I make you my wife. We've waited long enough."

Samantha, who was seated beside him in his buggy, looked up at him, her dark eyes troubled, a little uneasy. It was spring now in the lush Delta country, and the signs of the luxuriant season were all around them. He had stopped the buggy on one of the sunken trails outside Natchez. Here the soft earth had worn away so that the sides of the road rose at least ten feet, hiding the buggy and its occupants from view. The air was damp and rich with the smell of wild grape and wisteria and of the Cherokee roses that grew above them on the walls of earth that enclosed the buggy.

It was not even a year since Reed had died, yet here she was, Samantha thought, alone with her lover, talking of marriage. Her feelings were confused, eagerness warring against uncertainty. She had not been in love with Reed; but she was, nevertheless, deeply concerned with public opinion.

"Try to understand," she pleaded, her voice soft, persuasive. "You're a man. People never judge a man's conduct as they do a woman's. You know that. Besides, you're a Yankee. You don't come from here; you don't have a family or friends here. I've been living at Montrose all this time, ever since Reed died. I've been able to face down the gossip, though even now there are ladies who turn away from me when I go into town, who pretend not to see me. Why only the other day I passed Miss Amy Drummond on Federal Street, and she—"

"Oh, for— Look here, Samantha. I know the conventions as well as you do. But there's no need for us to let them rule our lives. I've made my money, and now I'm going to use it to get what I want. And I want you. I want to marry you, and I won't wait any longer."

Samantha drew back slightly, but she had been stirred by the intensity in his voice, the hunger in his eyes. He reached out and caught her in his arms, crushing her against him, and she felt her resolution beginning to waver. There was a hunger in her, too, so fierce and urgent that she longed to yield to him now, to let him lift her down out of the buggy and to lie with him among last year's damp fallen leaves. To feel his big, hard hands on her flesh, the weight of his body on hers.

She did not give way to her impulse, however. Instead, she turned her face away from his searching lips and said shakily, "I suppose I might—I might marry you this fall. The year of mourning will be over and—"

"You'll marry me now," he said.

"But don't you see? After we're married and living at Montrose together, we will have to associate with our neighbors. I've planned it all out. We'll give a ball—the biggest ball they've seen down here since before the war. And we'll invite everyone. We'll—"

Now it was Richard who drew back. "Montrose? What the devil are you talking about? After we're married, we'll be living up North, in Grand Rapids."

"Oh, but how can I— Why Montrose has been my home since Reed and I were married. And I was born and raised only a few miles up river from here."

He gave her a long, hard look. "My home's in Michigan.

The headquarters for my business is there. And that's where I'm taking you, Samantha."

"I can't imagine living up North."

"Can't you? No matter, you'll get used to it."

She recognized the steely determination in his voice, the strength of will that was a part of him. He loved her—she did not question that—and he wanted her. But only on his terms. And it came to her, with overwhelming certainty, that here was a man she could not control or manipulate, as she had done with Reed.

"It will take some adjustment, I know," he said. "But you can be sure I'll do everything in my power to see to it that you are not lonely. You'll be accepted by the best families in Grand Rapids; you can count on that. And you'll have a fancy ball—a dozen if you like—in my house up there."

He smiled at her with the complacency of a man who was certain of victory. "I couldn't stay down here much longer if I wanted to," he said. "I've a great deal of business to attend to back home. So we'll be married by the end of the week. A civil ceremony, or if it'll make you feel better, we'll have your family's clergyman perform the marriage."

"My family—how can I make them understand—"

"If you mean Clay Drummond and that charming wife of his, I doubt they'd attend the ceremony no matter how long we waited."

"I'm not sure—"

"I am," he said. "Clay's no fool. He knows by now how Reed died and why. And he's managed to fill in the rest. Yes, I know, the man who killed Reed is locked away in the state penitentiary. And I've heard that Clay used his influence to get the local newspapers to say nothing about the circumstances that led up to the killing. All the same, I doubt he'll care to come to our wedding and give us his blessing." He shrugged slightly. "Too bad. I like Clay Drummond."

Samantha remained silent, for she felt curiously powerless before the determination of this man. "So that's settled," Richard said. "Shall I make the arrangements for the ceremony?"

"Yes, Richard," she heard herself saying. "Perhaps that would be best."

* * *

On the morning of her wedding day, Samantha rose early and watched the sky change from purple to rose and gold outside her bedroom window. She was glad that it was morning, for she had slept fitfully, and now, although it would be a few hours before Richard was to come to drive her into Natchez for the small, private ceremony, she knew that it would be useless to remain in bed with her own thoughts for company.

She rang for Rachel, who came upstairs and helped her dress. Her packing had been completed the day before, and her trunks were piled neatly at the foot of the stairs. In the downstairs sitting room, she drank the coffee that Rachel brought her.

She looked at the furnishings, worn and a little shabby but familiar. She did not want to leave Montrose, to make her home in a cold, alien Northern city, where she would be a stranger. She set down her coffee cup, rose, and went out into the hall, casting an uneasy glance at her trunks, the reminders of her imminent departure.

Her lips curved in a smile of self-mockery as she left the house and went out onto the veranda and down the front steps. All those years she had nagged and bedeviled Reed, insisting that she was bored with Montrose, that she needed a change of scene, that the Natchez summers were unbearable for her. Now, as she looked out over the lawn with its live oaks, its poplars, and its cherry laurels, the leaves gilded by early-morning sunlight, she felt a sadness, a sense of loss.

Last night, on impulse, she had asked Rachel to accompany her to Grand Rapids, to work as her housekeeper in her new home. But the old woman had refused. "Mah Opal, an' mah granddaughtahs—dey all heah, in Natchez. Guess Ah'll stay on at Montrose long as Mistuh Clay wants me to."

"But you won't be needed, Rachel. You'll have no one to keep house for. And Mister Clay may decide to sell the place to strangers. Why should he keep it when he has his own home at Azalea Hill? When Terence and his bride have settled down in Baltimore?"

"Sell Montrose?" Rachel's worn features had become set in a rigid mask. "Mistuh Clay, he ain' neveh goin' t' sell dis place—neveh!" She had spoken respectfully but with absolute certainty. Samantha had not pressed the point, for she had been preoccupied with too many more important matters.

And these matters still troubled her now as she walked along the brick path to the back of the house and down into the terraced gardens. She would be going up North, leaving this land that was a part of her blood and bone. She would have to mingle with Yankee women, strangers, who would never be able to share her memories of the war and its aftermath.

Yet what was the alternative? Ever since the war, there were houses in and around Natchez and up river where lonely women lived on their memories. Widows, some of them, and others who were spinsters. True, Clay would never let Montrose fall to ruins, as had so many of those other plantation houses, but she would be a widow living on the charity of her brother-in-law.

No, that would be impossible. As the wife of Richard Whitaker, she would have unlimited money to spend and a passionate husband who knew how to satisfy her. She would never love him, not as she had loved Clay. But she was excited by her husband-to-be and well aware of the powerful physical bond between them. And perhaps equally important to her was his iron will, his determination that he must be master, that he must shape his wife to his own needs and desires. Richard would make the decisions; he would be generous, thoughtful, but his word would be final. She would never be able to cajole him into doing anything against his better judgment, and, she realized, perhaps she would never want to.

"Samantha."

She stopped and drew her breath in sharply as she saw Clay coming toward her around a curve in the brick path.

"I knew you would come to see me before I—before Richard and I—"

All at once, she lifted her skirts and ran to him, as she had run to him so many times along this same path during the far-off days of their courtship. He had gotten word of her coming marriage, perhaps through one of the servants here—it didn't matter how—and he had come to her. She stopped beside him and looked up at him, and all at once the years fell away, and she was here alone with Clay—her Clay.

"I was down at the overseer's cottage having a talk with Michael O'Donnell. He wants to try a new strain of fig tree, and we discussed that. And the cotton crop, of course. Michael says it should be the best we've had in years."

"You came here to speak with Michael O'Donnell?"

"Why yes."

"Then you don't know—about Richard and me—"

"I know," Clay said. "Rachel told Opal, and Opal mentioned it to Megan."

"But you came here to talk to Michael about the crops."

"He'll still be in charge here at Montrose," Clay said. "I wanted to know what his plans were. He's always full of plans, and most of them have worked well. He's talking about putting in orange trees next year."

"Then you aren't going to sell Montrose? Rachel was sure you wouldn't, but I thought that perhaps now, with Terence and Elizabeth married and living in Baltimore, you'd have no reason to hold on."

"Rachel's a wise old woman," Clay said. "No, I have no plans to sell the place even though I have no son to take over here."

Samantha hesitated. "Luke," she began, and then there was a brief, awkward silence between them.

"Yes, there is Luke. I was going to write you about him. But perhaps it's as well we met here this morning."

"Luke's not— He's all right, isn't he?"

"He's well enough," Clay assured her. He took her arm, and they walked together down the slope in the direction of the old summerhouse. The first pale-green leaves of the wisteria were growing over the top and sides, hiding the latticed wood. "I'd like to go inside for a moment," she said.

"As you please." Together they entered the damp, shadowy stillness of the summerhouse. "Luke's out in the back country. He drives a team for Jim Rafferty—goes to places where the railroad doesn't run. Swamp settlements, small dirt farms. He carries farm tools, seed, pots and pans and calico for the women."

"Luke, working as a—a common teamster—a backwoods peddler! Oh, Clay, you must do something for him. You must—"

"Maybe what he's doing is best for him right now," Clay said. "It's hard work, driving those back roads, some of them no more than rough trails. It'll give him time to think, though, to make peace with himself. To accept the truth about himself. And about us."

"Megan said he'd gone to—Guatemala, wasn't it? With a railroad surveying expedition."

"She lied to save the family any further scandal."

"You and Megan both know," Samantha said slowly. Once the thought would have given her satisfaction, but now she felt only a faint regret. "How long have you known?"

"I guessed at the truth some time ago. That night at Azalea Hill when Richard Whitaker remarked on how strongly Luke resembled me—I suppose I knew then. But I didn't want to believe it because of Megan—" His mouth turned down at one corner. "It was Megan who told me that it was true."

"Megan told you?"

"She and Luke went to Reed when he was dying in one of the bedrooms at Velma Kimball's place. The doctor had given him laudanum, and his mind was wandering. He talked a good deal."

"And now? Are you and Megan— I mean, has she forgiven you?" In spite of herself, Samantha felt a stirring of hope. Megan was a proud woman. If she had turned away from Clay, if she never forgave him, maybe—maybe . . . .

"Megan has always hated deception. But my relationship with my wife is no concern of yours. That's between the two of us." Samantha flinched as if he had slammed a door in her face. "I only wanted you to know that your son—"

"Our son."

Clay nodded. "Our son is all right. Luke's a survivor. He should be—he comes by it naturally." Then his voice turned cold. "I tried to see him last time he was in Natchez-under for a few hours taking on new supplies. But he wouldn't see me. I guess I can't blame him."

"I can," Samantha said. "He has no right to judge us. He doesn't know—" She fought back the sadness that threatened to overwhelm her. "If only he could be made to understand that we were not to blame."

"Oh, but we were. Reed was your husband. My brother. He trusted me. And he worshiped you."

But Reed was dead, Samantha thought desperately. He was beyond being hurt now. While she and Clay— She moved closer, wanting him to take her in his arms, to hold her and comfort her. "Clay— Oh, my love, if it had not been for the war—if I had not been sure that you had died up North, I never would have looked at Reed, never."

"Samantha, for God sake, have you no shame?"

"I only married him because I thought he reminded me of you—a little— But he was nothing like you. You're the only man I've ever—"

"Stop it!" His voice was harsh. "There's no going back, not for any of us. Whitaker must know that, too. He's taking you away from here, to start a new life, and that's as it should be." He put his hands on her shoulders and looked down into her face. "It can be a good life for you, if you're willing to work at it. And you'd better. Because Whitaker's not the kind of man you can twist around your little finger. He—"

"Clay, don't." She fought back the tears. "Doesn't it matter to you at all that I'm going to marry another man? That you and I will probably never see each other again?"

He hesitated. "It matters," he said quietly. "You were the first girl I ever loved. That miniature you gave me when I rode off to war—I carried it with me for months. But it was lost somewhere in the mud on Johnson's Island." He was looking past her now, and she felt him slipping away.

"I'd be lying if I said that it doesn't matter, your marrying Whitaker and leaving Natchez."

"But if you feel that way—"

"Megan is my wife. Even if she never forgives me, she is a part of me. She understands me as you never could. She—"

He stopped and turned his head at the sound of carriage wheels down on the road that ran along the bluffs.

"That's probably Whitaker," he said. He hesitated, then took her hand and raised it to his lips. "You'd better go to him now."

Chapter Thirty-one

SAMANTHA'S ELOPEMENT with Richard Whitaker gave the ladies of Natchez a new subject for gossip. "Less than a year after her poor husband's death," Miss Amy said in shocked tones to the ladies of her sewing circle.

"Violet Shepley was right," Winona Hunter told her husband. "This proves it. Why Samantha and that Yankee must have been carrying on for years—long before poor Reed Drummond—"

Deirdre was only vaguely aware of the gossip, for she was spending much of her time at Montrose this spring. Her vitality had returned, and her senses were more alive than they had ever been. Nearly every morning she came out to Montrose to ride, and today was no exception. The sleek black filly cantered easily along one of the roads that ran between two cotton fields.

Looking out over the fields, she found herself smiling with satisfaction. Soon, she thought, they would be growing white with the soft, lightly packed bolls. Michael had told her that he was expecting the best crop he had had since he had come to work as manager at Montrose. He had spoken to her often over these past months about the land and the crops, the newly planted fruit trees, the new strains of cattle, and to her surprise, she had come to share his pleasure in each improvement.

"I'll always been thankful t' yer father fer givin' me this chance," he told her. "I guess city life's fine for some—Gavin's doin' well up there in New York. Important politician, he is. But me—I'd have gone t' the bad if I'd stayed there. Gavin saw that, 'n yer father was willin' t' help."

Was that why Michael was so kind to her, Deirdre wondered? Out of gratitude to her father? Or was there something more? She had seen the way Michael's eyes had rested on her during the past few months when she had stopped at his cottage for coffee after an early ride. The look had made her uneasy, for it had stirred half-buried fears.

She reined in her horse, and then, moved by an impulse she did not quite understand, she dismounted and drew the sweet, soft air deep into her lungs. To think that once she had imagined that all she wanted was to live in London, to be a part of the society there, to be presented at Court. London— and a tall, narrow house on a square. . . .

As if to exorcise the memory, she stooped down and picked up a handful of the dark soil, crumbled it between her fingers, and inhaled its elemental odor. Then she moved into the deep shadows of an ancient, towering oak. The dew that had spangled the grass an hour before had dried now, and she removed her small, high-crowned black riding hat, laid it aside, and flung herself down on the ground. The veils of Spanish moss shaded her face from the sun.

The moist heat began to envelop her, and she opened the first two buttons of her closely fitting bodice. Her eyes half closed, and she watched the stirring of the moss, the patterns of the leaves overhead. She did not know how long she lay there when she caught the sound of hoofs. A moment later, she raised her head to see Michael O'Donnell getting down from his big gray stallion and hurrying over to her. "Deirdre— are ye all right? I saw yer horse and I thought— Ye've not had a fall, have ye?"

She smiled up at him, the pleasant languor still enveloping her, and she spoke softly, half teasingly. "Now, Michael

O'Donnell, you should know I'm a good rider. And as for Dark Star, you trained her yourself."

But his face was serious. "Even a good rider takes a tumble sometimes, and when I saw ye lyin' there so still, it frightened me, that it did."

She was both pleased and disturbed by the concern in his voice. She knew that she ought to get up, but the softness of the spring morning, the warmth of the sun, the heavy smell of the earth, had woven a spell. Then Michael was dropping down beside her, resting his broad back against the trunk of the oak.

"Nothin's better than the feeling of the earth under ye," he said softly. "And the smell of growin' things. May I share it with ye?"

"Why I—I should be getting back to Azalea Hill."

"Not yet, Deirdre," he said, and his voice, soft and caressing, made her go tense and wary.

"No, but really, I should—"

He put a hand lightly on her shoulder. "What's wrong?" he asked. He moved closer, bending over her to look into her face. "Deirdre, what are ye afraid of?"

She struggled to find the words to explain her feelings. "Michael—these past months—the way you've looked at me sometime— You're so good—you're clean and decent. And you've been so kind to me."

"What is it ye're tryin' t' say?"

She spoke slowly, not able to meet his eyes. "When I came home from England, I thought that my life was over. I was frozen, unable to feel anything. Then that day when Uncle Reed and Aunt Samantha had the dinner for the Taggarts, when I came down to the stables and you were there—"

"I remember," he said softly.

"You made me start to feel alive again. You reached out to me and made me feel— You helped me more than I can say."

He remained silent, his eyes fixed on her face, listening intently. "That's why I have to make you understand—about me—about what happened to me back there in England."

"There's nothin' t' explain," he said. "All that's over an' done with."

"But you have to know."

"Be still, love," he said, and his words, his tone, the way his strong, blunt fingers curved around her shoulder, made her realize that he already cared for her far more than he should.

"There's nothin' ye have t' tell me, nothin' that needs t' be explained." Michael moved closer, and then he was cradling her in his arms. "Deirdre, love."

Her body stiffened instinctively. "Michael, no!"

She shut her eyes, trying to blot out the memories of Allen Sutcliffe: his brutal invasion of her body; the pain he had inflicted on her and the shame; the revulsion that still lay coiled deep in her mind.

Michael held her gently. "Was I wrong, then? Is it that ye feel nothin' for me?" Then she felt his muscles harden. "Or is it that ye're still pinin' after that husband of yours?"

"Allen Sutcliffe was never my husband. Not really. And now I'm legally free. Papa's lawyers have sent word from England. I'm not Allen's wife any longer in the eyes of the law. But I still feel—"

"Tell me," Michael insisted.

"Allen was—he was sick in his mind. And his sickness has left its mark on me. I feel—contaminated—so that I don't think I'll ever be able to—to give myself to any man again. I have nothing to give, you see. Nothing."

"I'll not believe that," Michael said firmly. "Whatever was wrong with yer—with Lord Sutcliffe—whatever he did t' ye, surely ye must know that not all men are like him."

"You don't understand," she began, but Michael went on, his voice urgent, relentless.

"Deirdre, listen t' me. Ye're alive, and ye're young, and there's a strength in ye. I felt that, even the first time I saw ye, after ye'd come back from England. Bone thin, ye were, and yer eyes with that haunted look. But even then, I knew that in time ye'd be well again."

Deirdre tried to draw away, but his fingers tightened around her shoulder.

"Michael, let me go, please—"

"Not like this. Not so ye can run away and hide yerself. Ye say ye're free of the Englishman—that ye're not bound any longer by yer marriage vows."

"We were not married in the church," Deirdre told him. "And papa's lawyers have arranged a civil divorce. Oh, Allen was more than willing, since the settlement permitted him to keep a large share of my dowry."

"Then that's settled. And it's time ye were putting it all behind ye. Time t' come back t' yerself again—strong and proud. And not afraid of anything. I love ye, Deirdre. And ye have some feeling for me. Ye have, I know it."

"Yes, I do, but—it's no use. Michael, a man like you needs a woman who can give all of herself, freely. A woman to bear your children and—"

"Ye're the only woman I'll ever need," he said, and she heard in his words a promise, a pledge.

She felt hope stirring within her. Was it possible that Michael knew her better than she knew herself? He drew her into his arms, and she made herself lie still against him, but her body remained taut, her limbs stiff. Slowly, carefully, he began to remove the hairpins from her intricate chignon. He drew her hair down around her face and shoulders, then buried his lips in the thick, soft, blue-black waves.

"Michael, wait. I'm not sure—suppose I'm not able to—to—"

"I'll not force ye t' do anything against yer will. I'll wait until ye're ready," he told her. He unbuttoned her bodice, slowly, carefully, baring the soft flesh of her shoulders, the creamy curves of her breasts, where they swelled above the top of her ribboned camisole. His lips traced the curves lightly.

The long veils of gray moss that hung from the branches of the oak tree made a soft curtain around them, shutting out the rest of the world. Slowly, tenderly, his fingers began to stroke, to explore. Gradually, she felt herself begin to relax, and she moved closer to him of her own free will.

He stripped off the rest of her clothing, then his own, and then he stretched out beside her, holding her against him. He kissed her breasts, his tongue circling each nipple. She felt her nerves tingling, felt the sensation spreading from her breasts to every part of her body.

"Hold me, love," he said softly. Her arms reached out for him, and she embraced him, timidly at first, then with growing eagerness. "Oh—I didn't know—"

He laughed gently. "Ye still don't. But ye will, Deirdre, my love. Ye will. . . ."

They lay facing each other, and she stroked his shoulders, feeling the heavy muscles. Her hands slid downward. When she caressed the small of his back, she heard his swift intake of breath. His arms tightened around her, and she felt the driving urgency that possessed him.

He turned her on her back, whispering words of endearment. Then he was poised above her, his powerful body over hers. He stroked the soft curve of her belly, the length of her thighs, and then he was parting her legs, his touch sure and knowing.

She cried out softly, but she made no move to stop him, to put an end to this intimate caress. She wanted it to go on and on. . . .

Then he raised himself and moved to her slowly, carefully. "Oh, Michael—"

He stopped, and she sensed that he was forcing himself to remain immobile, to give her time to become accustomed to the joining of their bodies.

Now her hands were holding him, her fingers pressing into his shoulders. "Oh, yes—Michael—yes—"

Her legs encircled him, and her hips arched upward. Her pleasure was mounting, deepening, enveloping her whole body in a web of light and warmth. She felt the spasm that shook his body, and then she was caught up in the shattering power of her own sensations. Even when it happened, the upheaval of the senses, when she had reached fulfillment, they remained locked together. And she knew that he had brought her out of the darkness, had healed her and made her strong again.

Chapter Thirty-two

ON A warm afternoon in early September, Megan stood with Opal in Deirdre's bedroom. Deirdre turned around slowly so that the skirt of her sky-blue taffeta wedding gown made a soft, rustling sound.

"Perhaps a white tulle overskirt," Megan suggested. "And for your hair—"

"Not a veil, mother." Deirdre's face was shadowed for a moment, and Megan wondered whether her daughter would ever be able to put the memories of her first marriage behind her completely. Perhaps, one day, with Michael's love, she would forget the whole miserable episode.

"A kind of a flower headdress, maybe," Opal suggested. "Blue silk flowers an' green leaves."

"Oh, yes," Megan agreed. "I believe—yes—there's an illustration in one of the new fashion journals from New York. It's downstairs in the library. I'll get it."

"Now, Miz Megan," said Eula, who had just come into the room. "Don' go runnin' yuh legs off. Let me go get it."

"Thank you, Eula, but I know exactly where to find it. You'd better stay here and help your mother."

Megan moved swiftly, with the light, graceful steps of a young girl. She hurried down the stairs and along the hallway. There was only a week left before Deirdre's wedding and still so much to do. Thank goodness that one of Opal's daughters was now working with her in the shop and that she had hired two additional assistants. And Eula, who had remained at Azalea Hill as Deirdre's personal maid, would lend a hand, too.

Deirdre's gown was nearly finished, but Megan's needed at least one more fitting. Then she would have to supervise the arrangement of the flowers: an arch of white lilies for the parlor, where the ceremony would take place; hanging garlands of white blossoms in the hallway; vases of lilies and gardenias banked against the walls of the ballroom. The orchestra would be arriving from New Orleans, and she would have to discuss with them the selections they had chosen. The ballroom floor would have to be waxed to satin smoothness and the chandeliers polished until they glittered like diamonds.

Rachel was coming from Montrose to help out; later, she would return to Montrose to keep house for the bridal couple, for Clay was giving Montrose to Deirdre and Michael. "Not really a wedding present," he had said. "Young Michael wouldn't agree to that. He insists that he wants to pay for it out of the profits from each year's crops."

"Oh, but surely we don't need such payment," Megan had protested.

"Michael O'Donnell has his pride, and I respect him for it. I don't believe he'd accept Montrose on any other terms."

Now Megan stopped as the library doors opened, and a moment later, Clay came out, accompanied by Preston Taggart. She had not known that Taggart was coming to Azalea Hill today, had not heard him arrive; but then she had been occupied upstairs, and now she came forward with a gracious smile.

"Major Taggart—is Abigail here with you?"

He shook his head. "She'll be arriving for the wedding, but right now she's still back in Boston," he explained. "This is a business visit. Clay and I have been going over the reports of his surveyors." Seeing Megan's bewildered look, he added, "The surveyors got back from Guatemala last week. Didn't Clay tell you?"

"I've been so busy with the preparations for Deirdre's wedding," she said. She could not tell Preston Taggart, or anyone else, how few conversations she had had with Clay during these past months. Indeed, ever since the day of Reed's funeral over a year ago, she and Clay had kept up a careful façade before others, even Deirdre.

Taggart smiled. "I quite understand," he said. Then, turning to Clay, he went on. "Ah, the ladies—nothing sets them up like the prospect of a wedding. Abigail's getting herself fitted out in such a fine dress, anyone'd think she was the bride."

After Preston Taggart had left the house, Clay started back into the library. Megan followed him. "I won't disturb you," she said. "I only want to find a sketch—I think I saw it in *Harper's Bazar*. It's a flower headdress to match Deirdre's gown."

"Come in, then," Clay said, holding the door for her. "I'll be in here for several hours, going over the surveyors' reports."

"I thought that you and Preston Taggart had already studied the reports."

"We have. But I'm not entirely satisfied."

"They are unfavorable, then?"

"The terrain down there presents a challenge, to say the least. Mountains and swamps. And the political situation is far from stable." He stopped abruptly. Then he said, "I'm sorry. You came down here for a ladies' magazine, you said."

But she made no move to find it; instead, she stood facing Clay. "You've put down tracks through swampland before. When you started the Natchez–Fort Worth Line, you—"

"I'm not saying I won't go into this project, only that I want to give the reports a lot more thought and study. A railroad linking the coffee plantations in the mountains with one of the seaports could make a fortune for me, and for Taggart, if he wants to put money into it. But I haven't made a decision." He went on, half to himself. "I need to be there, to get a look at the area for myself, before I start building a new railroad. I need to get the feel of the country. And a notion of the political climate, too."

She stared at him, and in spite of the warmth of the afternoon, she felt a chill. For the first time since she had quarreled with him after Reed's funeral, she forgot about Samantha, forgot about everything except that Clay was her husband, that he might be preparing to leave her for weeks—perhaps longer.

"Clay, surely you don't mean that you're going to Guatemala yourself." She would not be alone, not really. Deirdre would visit her often, and she could go to visit Jessica or Lianne. But all at once she knew that she needed Clay. "You can't go away again."

His blue eyes were distant. "I should have thought you'd be relieved to have me out of the house."

She did not blame him for his words, for the irony in his tone. How much warmth had she shown him during this past year?

He had been hurt and angry when she had asked him to move out of their bedroom to one across the hall, but she had remained adamant, and at last he had agreed. Since then, she remembered, there had been a few nights when he had stopped outside her bedroom door as she had been about to enter, when he had embraced her and tried to kiss her. Although she had not fought him off and had known how easily he could overcome her, she had used other weapons. She had remained rigid and unyielding in his arms. During the past few months, he had no longer made any more such attempts.

"I'll be here for the wedding; don't worry about that," he said. "But after Michael and Deirdre have taken over Montrose, perhaps I'll go down to Guatemala."

"How long would you have to stay?"

He shrugged. "I have no idea. If you're worried about gossip, you can tell our friends—"

"I don't care about gossip or what our friends think. That's not important. I only want—"

"What do you want? You don't want a husband. You've made that plain enough."

"And do you blame me for—"

"It's not a question of blame. It's only that I kept hoping, after all our years together, you might find it in you to try to understand, to forgive."

"If it had not been Samantha, maybe I could have accepted—" Even now, her hurt pride rose up. "What contempt she must have had for me all these years—and for Reed. Tell me, Clay, who is more to be laughed at, the wife who suspects nothing or the husband, like Reed, who knows and lives with the knowledge of his humiliation? And then there's Luke, of course—"

"Megan, that's enough."

"Luke worshiped you. He respected you, as he could not respect his—the man he believed to be his father. What's to become of Luke? We don't even know where he is now."

"I know where he is."

"You never told me."

"I met Jim Rafferty only a few days ago. He told me that Luke's down in Natchez-under."

Megan felt a measure of relief. "He's back? Luke's come home? Oh, Clay, he must come to Deirdre's wedding."

"He won't come." Clay's unhappiness was plain to see, and Megan could not repress a feeling of pity. "Jim thought Luke would be wanting to come, once he'd heard that Deirdre was to be married. But Luke said he wasn't coming. Jim didn't know what to make of it."

"How long will Luke be in Natchez-under?"

"Only long enough to receive a new shipment of farm tools from New Orleans. Then he'll be setting out for the back country again."

"Oh, but Clay, that's not right for him. He could be doing so much more."

"You think I don't know that? Luke cares about railroad building. It means as much to him as it did to Brant."

Megan flinched at the mention of Brant's name, but she pressed her lips together, fighting down the aching memory of her loss.

"Forgive me, Megan," Clay said. "I should not have said that. I should not have reminded you—"

They stood facing each other, and for a moment she felt the familiar closeness between them. Clay shared her grief for the son they had lost. She was sure that if she took a few steps toward him, he would have caught her in his arms, held her against him. But she remained frozen, unable to make the first advances.

"Deirdre and Opal are waiting," she said quickly. She went to the heavy, carved oak side table and riffled through a pile of journals until she found the one she wanted. When she turned back to Clay, he was already seated at his desk, studying the

surveyors' reports. He did not raise his head to watch her leave
the library.

Deirdre's wedding day dawned, clear and sunny. Abigail,
who had arrived a few days before, had told Megan that the
weather was already chill and gray up in Boston, but down
here in Natchez, the air still held the softness of summer.

The garden beneath Megan's boudoir windows was bright
with flowers even though so many had been cut and carried
into the house. Megan would have to supervise the arrangement
of the garlands, the placing of the flower-covered arch. She
would have to speak with Rachel and her own cook about the
refreshments and discuss with the musicians the selections to
be played. Perhaps if a few of the musicians were seated behind
the potted palms in the hallway, to play for the guests as they
arrived . . . Later, the members of the orchestra would take their
places in the gallery of the ballroom, to play waltzes and quad-
rilles for the dancers. Polkas, too, and perhaps a reel.

Lianne's pretty daughters had arrived the night before, their
carriage barely large enough to accommodate Mark and Lianne,
and three girls, and the long boxes that held their gowns.

"Heaven help the young men who have to provide wardrobes
for these three someday," Mark had said, but he could not
conceal his pride.

Tom and Jessica had come, too, with young Evan. And
Belle and Gavin O'Donnell, the groom's nearest kin, had traveled down from New York with their whole brood in tow.
Thank goodness that Azalea Hill was large enough to accommodate all these visiting relatives. Had she remembered to tell
the coachman last night to make an early start for the depot,
to pick up those Drummonds who would be arriving from
Charleston?

"Miz Megan, Opal Carpenter's here with yuh dress," Ludamae announced. She had already helped Megan into a neat
gray-silk morning dress, but later, when the preparations
for the wedding had been completed, Megan would change
into the far more elegant costume that Opal had brought.

"A fine day fo' a wedding," Opal said with a wide smile.
"An' wait 'til yuh see the dress I made yuh. Why yuh'll be so
grand, the guests won't know who t' look at first, the bride or
her mama!"

Megan smiled when she opened the box. The dress was all that Opal had promised and more, with its taffeta skirt that shaded from amber to cream. Velvet leaves of pale gold, bronze, and warm russet, which had been chosen to compliment Megan's eyes and her tawny blond hair, were sewn across the bodice and among the folds of the train.

"Opal! It's the most beautiful dress you've ever made for me!"

Opal smiled with satisfaction. "Thank yuh, Miz Megan. But I don' guess I did too bad on them other dresses, the ones I made when yuh wuz on yuh honeymoon in New Orleans. Yuh 'member? Yuh come t' the shop where I wuz workin' then. An' Mistuh Clay, he wuz with yuh. An' me so scared he might be mad with me fo' leavin' Montrose like that—without a word t' nobody— But he didn't spoil things fo' me— He praised mah work. An' yuh were holdin' his arm, lookin' so beautiful—"

"That was a long time ago, Opal."

"Yuh jus' as beautiful as yuh wuz then, ma'am."

When Opal had left the room, hurrying to bring Deirdre her bridal gown, Megan remained standing still, heedless of the many things that required her attention. She could not shake off the memories brought back so vividly by Opal's words.

Her honeymoon with Clay in New Orleans. She had not expected Clay to take her on a honeymoon, for he had still been furious with her, believing that she had played a conscious part in Aunt Kathleen's scheme to force him into marriage.

Now she remembered the morning after her wedding. The Drummond family, seated around the dining-room table at Montrose. Samantha, taunting her, pretending sympathy, saying how mean Clay was to leave his new bride behind while he went off to New Orleans alone.

It had been Samantha who had driven her to blurting out that desperate, foolish lie: that Clay was going to take her along. How frightened she had been waiting for him to deny her words, to shame her in front of his family.

But he hadn't. He had backed her up, had turned her lie into truth. He had taken her with him. When she had needed him, he had been there to support her.

As he had been so many times: the night of Brant's birth, in the boxcar in the middle of a swamp, with the rain, driven by the fierce Gulf wind, pelting against the walls; together, she and Clay had shared the joy of Brant's birth; together they had faced the agony of his death.

He had not always been there, of course, for he was a man driven by ambition, hungry for wealth and power, but a man with a sense of justice, too. She thought of the night when he had ridden out to Montrose to challenge his friends and neighbors, the men he had fought beside during the war, even his own brother, to save the life of a Yankee schoolteacher.

But there were other memories, bitter ones. Clay's infatuation with Kirsten and his passion for Samantha. Forget that now. This was Deirdre's wedding day, she told herself. A time for rejoicing.

And it was such a perfect day, with the sunlight flooding the room, shining on polished bamboo furniture, glittering on the Waterford goblet, which still stood in its familiar spot on the small table near the windows. Moving slowly, she went to the table and put her hand on the goblet; then she ran her finger around the rim. She looked down, seeing the chip in the base, the crack that ran halfway up the stem. But somehow, over the years, the goblet had remained, it had held together. It had endured.

But it is damaged, Megan.

Lady Anne had said that, half amused by the young girl's intensity and a little impatient, too.

Lady Anne, the landlord's wife, in the manor house, back in Kilcurran, in County Cork.

It is still beautiful, my lady. Please, may I keep it?

Megan heard her own voice, timid but stubborn, too. Asking for the first beautiful object she had ever wanted to own. Knowing, with instinctive wisdom, that a thing need not be perfect, that it could be flawed but still beautiful.

Like her marriage, she thought, her lips parting, her breath catching in her throat.

Love had gone into the making of her marriage to Clay along with the anger, the deception. Loss, pain, grief, had all helped to mold the shape of her marriage, to make it what it was today. But there had been beauty, too, and strength and loyalty. And now? What remained for her now?

The one quality left to every born survivor, she thought. Hope. A promise for the future.

She turned, hearing a knock at the door, and went to admit Jessica. Her sister-in-law's face, plain, lined but strong, gave her reassurance.

"Megan, forgive me for intruding, but Ludamae says that the gardener has finished bringing in the flowers. And the musicians have just arrived from New Orleans. I've told your cook to give them a good breakfast. And Cousin Lorna and Cousin Hazel have arrived from Charleston. I took the liberty of offering them the guest room in the other wing. Cousin Hazel insists she wants to go down to the kitchen to see that her own herb tea is brewed exactly as she likes it. Will you be coming down soon?" She gave Megan a searching look. "Is something wrong? Are you feeling ill?"

Megan could not answer at once, and Jessica, her blue eyes warm with concern, put a hand on Megan's arm. "What has happened? You look so—"

"Jessica, can you handle the rest of the preparations for the wedding? If Lianne is willing to help you, can you manage without me?"

"Why I suppose— Without you? On Deirdre's wedding day?"

"Can you do it?"

"Certainly I can. And Lianne will help me. But where are you going?"

Megan thought quickly. "The large carriage must be at the depot to pick up the rest of the guests. I'll take the buggy. I can drive that myself. Please tell Ludamae to get one of the stable hands to bring the buggy around to the back of the house." There was no time to linger, to answer anyone's questions about her departure.

"I'll be down as soon as I've put on my hat," Megan added.

"And what about Deirdre? And Clay? What am I to tell them if they ask—"

But Megan did not answer, and, Jessica, after one more look at her set face, went to carry out her orders.

Chapter Thirty-three

MEGAN DROVE the small buggy down the length of Silver Street and thought that the once-bawdy old thoroughfare had a forlorn look. There were fewer saloons; many of the gambling houses had closed their doors forever. Probably, she thought, the sporting houses were also gradually going out of business. For the railroad, Clay's railroad, had displaced the river boats, even as Reed had once predicted it would. No longer did the crews of those boats come ashore seeking liquor and cards and fancy women. Now, in the September sunlight, the district whose name had once been a byword for illicit pleasure was drab and deserted.

Megan drove her buggy into the alley that ran between Uncle Jim's warehouses and the cottage where he and Aunt Kathleen had once lived. Now they had moved to a larger, more comfortable house up on the bluffs. But her uncle's teamsters still hung around the stable doors, and leaning over the side of the buggy, she called to one of them.

The man stared in surprise for a moment, then came over to the buggy to find out what Mrs. Clay Drummond might be looking for down here.

"Can you tell me where I might find Luke Drummond?"

"Luke? His wagon's over there. He loaded it early this morning. Them farmin' tools finally got here. He'll be startin' out on his route in a few hours, ma'am."

"Where is he now?"

"Jim Rafferty's lettin' him stay over there, across the way." He jerked his head in the direction of the gray, weather-beaten cottage. "Nice young fella, Luke is. Quiet-like. Never could figure out why a fella like him—born and raised up at Montrose—would want t'—" He broke off at a sharp look from Megan.

"Please see that my horse is watered," she said. The man nodded, then helped her down out of the buggy. She lifted her skirts and avoided the scummy greenish puddles in the alley, then hurried up the steps to the cottage door. It opened at her touch, and she entered. For a moment, she was assailed by memories, and she saw herself as a young girl arriving from Ireland.

The cottage was far shabbier now, in a miserable state of disrepair, the walls dingy and water stained. And this was where Luke stayed when he came back from one of his trips into the back country.

She called his name, and a moment later the door to what had been Aunt Kathleen's parlor swung open.

Luke stood staring at her in confusion while he finished buttoning his coarse, faded denim shirt and stuffed it into his heavy pants. He looked thinner than she remembered, but his blue eyes were Clay's eyes, under straight, dark brows.

"Aunt Megan! Is anything wrong? Has something happened up at Azalea Hill?"

She shook her head. "I must speak to you," she said.

He hesitated, then swung open the parlor door and stood aside so that she could enter.

"I found out only yesterday that you were back in Natchez," she said. He bundled up a blanket and sheet and tossed them down beside the battered sofa that must have served as his bed. She seated herself and motioned to him to sit down beside her. "This is Deirdre's wedding day. She and Michael are to be married at five o'clock. You have a decent suit around here somewhere, I hope."

"In my trunk—Jim Rafferty lets me store my things here. But I can't come to Deirdre's wedding."

"Luke, you must. You grew up with Deirdre. The whole family is there at Azalea Hill."

"All the more reason for me to stay away."

"But you must not feel that way. Aunt Jessica and Aunt Lianne are there, and your cousins. And Terence and his wife. And think of Deirdre. She knows nothing about the reasons why you've been avoiding Azalea Hill. But she is bound to hear that you were in Natchez on her wedding day, and if you don't come, it will hurt her deeply."

"Then Deirdre doesn't know about— No, of course not. And I don't want her to know, ever. She's always looked up to her father. I hope she never has to find out what kind of a man he really is."

"And what kind of a man is Clay Drummond?" Megan challenged him, her amber eyes steady. "Are you so sure you know the answer?"

"Aunt Megan, how can you, of all people, ask me that?"

"I *am* asking you."

"All right, then. Clay Drummond is a hypocrite and a liar. He—"

"Go on."

"I don't want to hurt you any more than you've already been hurt." Megan was touched by his concern, his affection. But she persisted, reminding herself that her reason for coming here, for seeking Luke out, was far more important than her desire to have him attend Deirdre's wedding.

"Tell me," she said. "All of it."

"All right, then. He seduced my mother. He made her betray my—Reed Drummond."

"It wasn't quite like that," Megan told him. "If you hadn't run away that day when Reed died, if you had stayed on, I would have explained—"

"Explained? There was nothing to explain. I'm not a child."

"Then stop thinking like one," Megan said. She did not want to hurt Luke, but she knew that she must do whatever was necessary to get through to him.

"My husband and your mother were going to be married. Did you know that?"

"I'd heard talk, but I—"

"Then the war came. Clay and Reed went off to fight for the Confederacy. Clay was taken prisoner and shipped up North to a terrible place, a prison camp called Johnson's Island." She went on, her voice controlled in spite of the tumult of her emotions. She told Luke all that Clay had told her on that night in the office over her uncle's warehouse. She described Clay's imprisonment, his escape, the mistaken report of his death after he had found refuge working on a railroad.

"Your mother would never have married Reed if she had thought that Clay was still alive. But she was young—younger than you are now—and I suppose she didn't want to risk being left a spinster, as so many Southern girls were after the war." As she spoke, Megan felt an understanding of Samantha.

"I didn't know," Luke said slowly. "But even so—" His face hardened. "She did marry Reed Drummond. And he loved her. Even when he was dying, he still loved her." His voice was bitter. "Maybe it would have been better if my—father had really died on Johnson's Island. If he'd never lived to come home and—"

"Don't say that, not ever." How hard the young could be, Megan thought, how self-righteous and unforgiving.

"He did come home, though," Luke went on, "and he saw my mother again, and he took her, as he's always taken everything he wanted. And when he was finished with her, he married you. He never even acknowledged me as his son."

"It was years before he knew the truth," Megan said, instinctively springing to Clay's defense. "Your mother never told him. She was afraid of scandal, always. It was only when Richard Whitaker remarked on the resemblance between you and your father that night at Azalea Hill—and even then Clay could not be sure. He—"

"You're making excuses for him. You're loyal to him because—because I guess that's the way you are, Aunt Megan. You can forgive him anything."

Megan thought of her coldness toward Clay this past year. Luke knew nothing of that. But she had overcome her anger, so that now she could accept Clay as he was.

But Luke was so young. He saw those around him as good or evil, with no shadings in between. Time and maturity would change him, of course; but she knew that she must take action now, for she could not allow him to leave Natchez feeling as he did.

"You haven't yet agreed to come to Deirdre's wedding," she reminded him.

"I can't."

"You're thinking only of your own feelings. What about the family? At Reed's funeral, I said you'd already left for Guatemala with the surveyors. They've returned with their report now—"

"Was it favorable? Is—he going ahead with the railroad?"

"Does it matter to you?"

"No—why should it? But I guess I see what you mean about the family. I don't want you or Deirdre to face the questions of your friends. It would look strange if they learned that I was in Natchez and hadn't come to the wedding. I'll clear out right now. And after I make this trip for Jim Rafferty, I'll leave Natchez for good."

Megan stifled a cry of protest, for this was not what she wanted at all. But she knew that if she opposed Luke directly, he would only become more firmly set in his plan.

"Where will you go?" she asked quietly.

"An experienced teamster can pick up work any place," he said. "California, maybe, or Oregon. Don't worry, Aunt Megan. I won't keep turning up here in Natchez to cause talk or to remind you of—everything you want to forget. You won't have to see me again, to remember who I am."

"You're my nephew, you—"

"I'm Clay Drummond's bastard."

"Oh, but Luke—"

"It's all right," he said. "If I leave Natchez, there'll be no risk of my bringing shame on the family."

"And what about your future? Terence cares nothing about the railroads, but you do—you're like your father that way. He's been talking about going down to Guatemala himself because he doesn't have a son to send in his place. But it's a young man's job, Luke. Can't you—"

"I don't want to work on a railroad ever again. I don't want to be reminded of my—father."

"So you will run away. And you will keep on running."

"That's unfair. I'm not—"

"The devil you're not. Oh, you can give yourself all sorts of fancy reasons for what you plan to do. You can tell yourself that you're leaving for my sake or Deirdre's or because of your righteous anger at your father. I can't blame you for being angry, but you don't hate him, not even now. You don't hate Clay Drummond any more than I do. Why do you think I came down here to find you?"

Luke turned away, but Megan went on speaking, the words spilling forth in a torrent. "It's because I love him. And so do you."

"I don't—not now—"

"You do. You always have. You've not forgotten all those afternoons when you came from Montrose to Azalea Hill when you were a child. How you'd sit with your eyes like saucers, drinking in every word of his stories about the work he was doing, about his plans for the next job and the next after that. Asking him to tell you, over and over again, how he got the contract to build that first spur. How he laid the tracks for the Natchez–Fort Worth Line. You looked up to him then; you idealized him. He was a hero to you."

"I was a child—"

"That's right. And a child needs heroes. Larger than life, without any human weaknesses or failings." Megan reached out, and her small, strong fingers closed around Luke's hand. "But you're a man now, and that is not an easy thing to be."

"I don't understand what you expect of me."

"I think you do, Luke."

Chapter Thirty-four

"WHERE HAS she gone? Surely she must have told you," Clay said impatiently. He and Jessica were standing in the upstairs hall. Although a number of guests had come within the past few days, others would be arriving soon, and they would have to be received.

"She told me nothing," Jessica replied patiently. "I've already explained all that, Clay—"

"You've explained nothing! You've only told me—"

"I went to Megan's room early this morning. She looked—"

"How? How did she look? Upset?"

"No, not upset only—far away— She asked whether Lianne and I could take over the rest of the preparations for the wedding. I was startled, of course, but I said that we could manage. And then she ordered the buggy—"

"And you let her drive off? You didn't say a word about it to me? You simply allowed her to—"

"My dear, she did not ask my permission," Jessica observed

dryly. "Perhaps her Aunt Kathleen was taken ill, or her uncle—"

Jessica could understand Clay's irritation over Megan's abrupt departure, but she sensed that he was troubled by something else, something far more serious. There was a look of uneasiness about him, or was it fear? But fear of what? What was wrong between Clay and Megan?

Jessica realized now that she had felt a sense of wrongness between her brother and her sister-in-law ever since she had arrived here at Azalea Hill, a strained politeness where there had always been warmth and affection.

Had Clay and Megan quarreled over Deirdre's choice of a second husband? No, that was most unlikely, for Clay had often spoken with sincere admiration of Michael O'Donnell's achievements in managing Montrose.

"The price of cotton's likely to be down a bit this year, but even so, the Montrose crop will bring in a decent profit," Clay had told Tom yesterday. "And Michael's had the good sense to diversify—not like some of our local planters who can think of nothing except cotton. He's put in fruit trees; he's bought some excellent cattle for breeding. And he knows how to handle the sharecroppers, too."

And a little later, he had told Jessica and Tom that he was turning Montrose over to Michael and Deirdre, adding, with an air of satisfaction, that Michael had refused to take the plantation as an outright gift, that he had insisted that he would compensate Clay out of each year's profits. "Deirdre's found herself a man this time," Clay had said.

Why, then, Jessica asked herself, was Clay so tense, and why had Megan gone off a few hours before Deirdre's wedding? It was no ordinary, last-minute errand, for if it had been, there were plenty of servants at Azalea Hill to do Megan's bidding.

"If she's not back by the time the guests start arriving, what am I going to say to them?" Clay demanded.

"Lianne and I will help you receive them," Jessica said soothingly. "I've already arranged to have four of the musicians seated downstairs in the hall behind the potted palms. They will play softly, light, sentimental airs. I declare, the reception hall downstairs looks like a garden. Those flowers—"

"To hell with the flowers and the musicians. Jess, if Megan's gone—"

"Gone? Clay, you're not making sense." Jessica looked up at him in dismay. What on earth could have happened to cause her tough-minded, arrogant brother to behave this way? Clay had always been a tower of strength for the rest of them. Nothing had broken him, not war or his months in the Yankee prison camp. Not the dark days of Reconstruction when so many of their neighbors had given up, had gone under. Why her own beloved Tom would not be alive today if Clay had not gone to rescue him when the Knights of the White Camellia had raided the schoolhouse at Montrose.

She reached out and took his hand. "It will be all right, Clay," she said, forcing a smile. "My heavens, it's usually the bride who needs to be reassured right before the wedding, not her father."

But Clay did not return her smile. His fingers closed around her hand. "I love Megan," he said. "And I need her."

"Why of course you do." Gently, she freed herself from his grasp. "You must go and change now," she said. "And so must I." He made no move, and she gave him a little push. "Go on now," she said. "You want to be a credit to Deirdre, don't you?"

Opal arranged the delicate wreath of pale-blue silk flowers and tiny seed pearls, threading the ribbons through Deirdre's shining, high-piled hair. "There now," she said with satisfaction. "That's jus' like the sketch yuh mama showed me, Miz Deirdre."

"Where is my mother?" Deirdre asked. "I haven't seen her yet today, and it's nearly time for the ceremony."

"She'll be heah, don' yuh worry," Opal said. "Theah's a plenty t' do, gettin' this big house ready fo' d' weddin'."

"Even so, I'd have thought—" Deirdre began, but then the bedroom door opened and Terence's wife, Elizabeth, who was to be her matron of honor, came in. Elizabeth's cool blonde beauty would be the perfect contrast for Deirdre, with her blue-black hair and tawny amber eyes.

It would be a lovely wedding, Deirdre told herself, her face radiant as she thought of Michael. If only her mother would arrive soon. Where had she gone, today of all days?

* * *

As the first long blue shadows of twilight began to fall, the drive leading up to the doorway of Azalea Hill was crowded with a line of carriages. Clay stood inside, outwardly self-possessed, his face set, unreadable. Jessica and Lianne covered the awkwardness of Megan's absence by saying a few friendly words to each of the new arrivals. So far, the guests had been too polite to ask questions about the absence of their hostess.

It was Kathleen Rafferty, resplendent in maroon silk, heavily encrusted with passementerie braiding, who demanded, "Where's my niece? Where's Megan?"

Because Kathleen had grown slightly deaf over the years, her voice was louder than she realized, and Jessica saw that several of the other guests, who were standing nearby, had turned and stared. No doubt they were asking one another why Megan had not yet appeared.

Clay flushed slightly. Jessica knew that for some reason he had never been particularly warm toward Megan's aunt, although he and Jim Rafferty got along well.

"Now, Kathleen," Jim said, "surely ye know all there is t' do before a weddin'. Why when our Belle got herself married t' Gavin, ye were runnin' around 'til the last minute. And when Belle's girls get married, I've not doubt ye'll be up there in New York managin' the whole show or tryin' to."

Clay said to Jim, "I thought perhaps you might have— Did Megan go over to see you any time today?"

"Megan? Now what would the mother of the bride be doin' out callin' on her relations on her daughter's weddin' day?" Jim's broad, ruddy face showed surprise. "Are ye sayin' ye don't know where Megan is?"

Clay did not reply, and Jessica said quickly, "Your granddaughters are so pretty, Mrs. Rafferty. And so vivacious. You must be proud of them."

"That I am," Kathleen said. "And of my son-in-law, too. Why Gavin O'Donnell's a real important man up there in Tammany Hall now, and I shouldn't wonder if—" She broke off, looking up in the direction of the stairway. "Ah, there's Megan now. An' young Luke with her. Jim, didn't y' tell me that Luke wasn't plannin' t' be here?"

Jim led his wife off, and the next guests, Oliver and Angelique Winthrop, moved up, but Clay was not looking at either of them.

Megan was coming down the stairway, escorted by Luke. The gaslight was soft on her carefully arranged hair; it turned the taffeta of her gown from pale cream to amber with each step she took. As they reached the bottom of the stairway, Megan put a hand on Luke's arm, and they came forward together, across the reception hall. Clay stood unmoving.

"Mr. and Mrs. Winthrop," Jessica said. "How good it is to see you both again—and on such a happy occasion."

Megan came to stand beside Clay, still holding Luke's arm. "There was a mix-up about my dress," Megan said smoothly. "But it arrived at last, and I do believe that Opal has outdone herself. Angelique—Oliver—welcome to Azalea Hill. You remember our nephew, Luke?" She smiled up at Luke and took her place between him and Clay.

Although the ballroom at Azalea Hill had been known as a showplace since the completion of the house, Megan thought that it had never looked finer. The rainbow colors from the diamond-paned dormer windows glowed in the light of the chandeliers, making patterns on the polished floor, where the dancers moved to the strains of a waltz. The air was sweet with the mingled odors of the flowers banked along the walls, the garlands that adorned the railing of the gallery overhead, where the musicians were seated.

Deirdre and Michael had danced together for the first time as husband and wife, and Miss Amy, who had wept through the ceremony, still dabbed at her eyes with a dainty lace handkerchief. Then Luke had danced with Deirdre, while Michael had led Aunt Kathleen through the measures of a lively polka.

Megan smiled a little wistfully as she looked over at Deirdre and Michael, who would soon be leaving for Montrose; for she was remembering her own first visit there. How nervous she had been, afraid of facing Clay's formidable family, uneasy about what they might think of her. And later, when Jessica had taken her upstairs, she had dared to dream that one day she might become mistress of the plantation.

Now she never would be—but Deirdre would, and Megan realized, with surprise, that for her that would be enough. More than enough. Deirdre had put her childish snobbery behind her; she was a woman now, and a survivor, too. Her marriage to Michael would be a good one and, Megan hoped, a fruitful one. She longed to see another generation playing on the wide, smooth lawns of Montrose, exploring the gardens and the bluffs.

Those children would not bear the Drummond name, but that was not important, for they would be Clay's grandchildren and hers.

"Megan."

She turned to see Clay standing beside her.

"Dance with me," he said.

He held out his arms, and she moved into them. For the fraction of a minute, she was tense, and then she felt herself responding to his arm around her waist, his hand holding hers. They moved across the polished floor and she was stirred by his closeness.

"You might have told me where you were going," he said.

"I wasn't sure I'd be able to get Luke to come back here with me," she said. "I didn't want you to be disappointed if he had refused."

"Disappointed? Luke's a man, He's free to live as he pleases."

"Don't pretend, Clay. Not with me. You need him to help you. You said yourself that it was important to have one of the family go down to Guatemala, to report back on the possibilities of building a railroad there. Terence has chosen another path. But Luke—"

"I'll never be able to acknowledge him before the world. You know that."

"Is that so important?" she asked. "I said that you needed him. He needs you, too. He always has."

The waltz came to a close, and shortly afterward, Rachel announced supper. The guests moved into the dining room where a lavish buffet table had been set up. Angelique came to Megan's side to compliment her on her gown. Belle told her what a beautiful bride Deirdre was. Abigail, regal in silver-gray velvet, questioned her about Deirdre's plans for a wedding trip.

"They may take a trip later on, but now Michael still has work to do at Montrose. And Deirdre is happy to be with him. They are so much in love," Megan said.

"And Clay is turning over Montrose to Michael and Deirdre?"

"Does that trouble you?" Megan asked. "It was your home, I know."

"Boston's my home now," Clay's stepmother said. "I can't imagine living anywhere else. But what about Luke? It does seem to me that as Reed's son he should have some say in the disposition of Montrose."

This is how it must be, Megan thought. In the eyes of the world, Luke must always be thought of as Reed's son. And she and Clay must be a part of the deception. She weighed the alternatives and mentally accepted the burden.

"Luke is not a planter," she told Abigail. "He's always cared about the railroads."

"Like Clay," Abigail said. "But Reed—he never wanted anything more than to live at Montrose. And he'd be there still, alive and well, if it hadn't been for Samantha. That woman—"

"We must forget the past," Megan said quietly.

But Abigail was determined to have her say. "And when I heard that Samantha had married that Mr. Whitaker before the year of mourning was out. Shameful, I call it."

"Samantha has done what she thought best."

"She's always done what was best—for herself. I must say, it's mighty charitable of you, Megan, not to speak an unkind word against her." Abigail smiled. "But then you can afford to be charitable. You have Clay, after all."

"Yes," said Megan, savoring the words. "I have Clay."

"And I do believe you're as much in love with him today as you were the first time he brought you to Montrose." She looked over at Clay, who was standing a short distance away, engaged in a discussion with Preston Taggart and Luke. Abigail put a heavy arm around Megan. "They're talking business; I'm sure of it. We'll have to put a stop to that."

"I'm not saying it'll be easy," Taggart said, as Megan and Abigail drew nearer. "The terrain is an engineer's challenge, and during the rainy season, the workers will have hell's own time. But I'm convinced that it can be done. It's a young man's job, Luke, my boy. A young man who knows as much about railroads as you do."

"But what kind of work crews will we be able to get down there?" Luke was asking. "The Indians won't be much use from what I've heard. The Chinese might do it, though—"

Abigail laughed. "Men!" she said to Megan with a shake of her head. "Even at a wedding they think of nothing but business."

"I have the reports in the library," Clay was saying to Luke. "If you'd care to have a look at them—"

"Of course he would," Preston Taggart said.

"Just a minute," Abigail said. "This is a wedding reception, not a board meeting. After supper, I want to dance again."

"And nothing will give me greater pleasure than to dance with you, my love," her husband said gallantly. "We'll only be a few minutes. I promise." He turned back to Luke. "Clay believes we'll have a problem with the swamp that lies between the seacoast, on the Caribbean side, and the mountains, where the coffee plantations are. And I'm not saying we won't. But once we're clear of the swamps—

"Once we're clear of the swamps, we'll still be faced with blasting our way through the mountains or putting up bridges across the mountain passes. Back in Colorado—" Clay said.

"But there are new machines now for hauling the equipment up the slopes," Luke said. "We could—" he broke off. "You could—" he amended.

"Come on," Taggart said. "Let's go into the library and show Luke what we're talking about."

Deirdre had changed to her traveling dress and had thrown her bouquet. It was caught by one of Belle's pretty daughters, who giggled and then gave Evan Langford a long, meaningful look from under her lashes. Evan blushed, but he did not appear to be displeased.

Megan had to go and knock on the library door. She knocked again more loudly, and when Clay came to answer, she said, "You daughter's getting ready to go to Montrose with her husband." She could not repress a smile. "It would be nice if you could take the time to kiss her good-by."

"I'm coming," Clay said.

He embraced Deirdre and shook Michael's hand. The guests clustered around, calling their good wishes.

But when Clay, Luke, and Preston Taggart would have returned to the library, it was Abigail who intervened.

"Even if you're getting too old to want to dance more than

once," Abigail said, "Luke isn't. Am I right, young man?"

"Dance? Why I—I haven't finished studying the surveyors' reports," Luke said.

"We can go over them tomorrow," Clay said, "if you'll stay here overnight."

Megan tensed, waiting for Luke's reply.

"I've promised Jim Rafferty that I'd take out his shipment," Luke said slowly.

"I'll speak to Uncle Jim," Megan said. "I'm sure he can get another driver."

Luke looked at her, then at Clay. "I'd like to stay and look over the reports again in the morning," he said.

It was nearly dawn when the reception ended, and Azalea Hill grew quiet. Megan sat in her boudoir wearing a nightdress, her hair brushed loose about her face and shoulders. She was not tired. Her body tingled with a feeling of a new awakening. The lamplight gleamed softly on the Waterford goblet, and seeing it, she smiled.

At last, hearing Clay's footsteps in the hallway, she rose, went to the door, and opened it. "Megan," he said. She held out her hand to him, and he followed her inside.

He stood looking down at her, his face shadowed by the soft, flickering gaslight. "It's been a long day for you, Megan. Go to bed now."

She felt a swift uneasiness, for his tone, although kind, was distant. She remembered, with a pang, that she had turned him out of their bedroom, that she had never once responded when he had tried to make love to her after that. Her husband was a proud man and stubborn. Had she waited too long before reaching out to him?

Only a few hours ago, when he had danced with her, she had thought she felt a closeness between them; but now, in the silent house, with the guests gone and the music ended, she began to be afraid.

Perhaps Luke's return had brought to Clay the memory of Samantha, of the passion Clay had shared with his first love. She dared not ask him, but she put a hand on his arm.

"I thought that you and Luke might stay up until dawn talking over the plans for the new railroad," she said with forced lightness.

"No need for that," he said, "since Luke will be staying here for the next few days." He hesitated, and she became aware of the tension in him. "I hope it won't be too difficult for you, having Luke here at Azalea Hill."

"I brought him here," she reminded him.

"Yes, you did. A warmhearted gesture, but impulsive."

"It was more than that. Surely you must know—"

"I know that you did it for me. You arranged it so that Luke would be drawn into the new railroad project. And I'm grateful for that."

Grateful? But it was not gratitude she wanted.

"Clay, you don't understand—"

But he went on speaking quietly, his blue eyes fixed on hers. "Think of the future. Luke will be coming back to Natchez, to Azalea Hill. He'll be a part of our lives from now on. A constant reminder that—"

"He's your son, yours," she said fiercely. "He looks so like you, and he is like you in so many ways— He—"

"He's Samantha's son, too."

Why must he speak of Samantha? For one brief moment, Megan was gripped by the old memories, the doubts and insecurities. Then Clay reached out and drew her against him.

"I have to know if you'll be able to accept Luke's presence here. Whether you can live with the memory that Samantha and I were lovers. Can you, Megan?"

She knew that this was no casual question, and she was silent while she reached down into the depths of her being, searching for the strength that had sustained her over the years.

"I can," she said softly. "Because I must. Because there's nothing for me without you. You're part of me."

Her arms went around him. "Oh, Megan," he said. "When you disappeared this afternoon, when I didn't know where you were, I—" She sensed how difficult it was, how difficult it had always been for him to show his feelings. "I need you, too. I always have."

"But Samantha—" She could say the name now without more than a faint stir of remembered pain.

Clay held her away, but his hand cupped her chin, turning her face up to his. "I can't tell you that I never really loved Samantha. Or even that I'll ever forget her completely. But she was a part of another world. The world of Montrose and the time before the war. You and I—we've made our own world—our own home—here at Azalea Hill."

Now he drew Megan close again, and she felt the warmth, the strength of him. "We can't change the past, but there's now. And tomorrow."

Now and tomorrow. His words filled her with peace and joy. For she knew that what he was offering was all she would ever want. This hour, and all the hours they would share, down through the years.